ALIEN ART:

IT WAS MANKIND'S NEWEST WORLD—BUT IT WAS THE ONLY ONE CHARLIE HAD. . . .

. . . and maybe, just maybe, he could save it with his art, if these stranges creatures called humans could see what he was trying to tell them—and if they would hold off on killing him long enough to look. . . .

and a second complete novel;

ARCTURUS LANDING:

Humanity had been given an ultimatum: develop a faster-than-light stardrive by the deadline the arbiters of the Galactic Federation had set, or be denied membership in the interstellar community for all time. But no one suspected that the Federation was working to make sure they failed—and so were some humans.

ALIEN ART
ARCTURUS LANDING

GORDON R. DICKSON

SF
ace books
A Division of Charter Communications Inc.
A GROSSET & DUNLAP COMPANY
51 Madison Avenue
New York, New York 10010

This Ace printing: June 1981
Published simultaneously in Canada

2 4 6 8 0 9 7 5 3 1
Manufactured in the United States of America

To my mother, Maude Dickson

1.

The annunciator on the hotel room door chimed.

"Who's there?" asked Lige.

There was no answer. Lige did not move. He had been buying native art too long on these backward, newly settled worlds to open his hotel room door without knowing who wanted in. Also, he was pushing eighty now; and he was willing to miss an occasional deal rather than take risks.

"Who's there?" he repeated. "Speak into the annunciator —the black circle on the door."

"Mister," said a voice from the door, "I'm Cary Longan. I wrote you about some carvings a friend of mind did. . . ."

It was the right name. Lige put a twenty-second hold on the hotel security button by his phone and pressed it down. In twenty seconds he could find out enough to decide whether to flick it back up or let it sound.

"Open," he told the door. It slid aside and let in a typical New Worlds backwoodsman. The dress varied, as usual from planet to planet, but the smell was always similar. Wood-smoke, sweat, assorted native odors. This woodie was young, young and stringy.

"Mister, I'm Cary Longan," the woodie said, as the door

slid shut behind him. "I was to remind you your full name was Lige Bros Waters, you said in the letter."

Lige reached out and flicked the security button off hold. "Come on in," he said. "Have a seat."

Cary Longan looked uneasily about the hotel room. It was a room that had cost Lige less than half an interworld unit a day. Its carpeting was woven of native fibers, the walls were coated with a single color, and there was no such thing as a float chair in sight. The furniture sat heavily on thick legs, and was built of wood and fabric.

But the woodsman glanced about as if in a palace. He had recently shaved and carefully washed. But under the bony jawline, his thin neck was shadowed with uncleansed grime. In his leather and woolen clothes he looked half-starved and feral, a smoke- and dirt-stained whipcord of a man imprisoned by unfamiliar barriers to land and sky. In his hands he carried a homemade wooden box about ten inches on a side.

"That's all right," Lige said. "Come on, sit down. I pay for the room—people who come to see me can do anything I invite them to, here."

Cary came forward. He perched on the seat edge of a heavy, fabric armchair facing the bed on which Lige was sitting and passed the box into Lige's hands. Its weight was surprising. Lige almost dropped it. "They're in there," Cary said.

"The carvings your friend made?" Lige fumbled with the box, discovered that the top slid aside, and opened it. Within were a number of reddish-brown rocks, very heavy for their size. Lige took them out one by one and lined them up—there were six of them—on the bedspread.

He picked them up and turned them over, examining each again. He looked at Cary.

"What is this? A joke?" he said.

Cary was leaning forward from the waist, painfully tense in his waiting. But when Lige spoke, the tension dissolved in puzzlement.

"Mister?"

"These—" Lige jabbed a forefinger toward them. "These are carvings?"

"Sure, mister," said Cary. "The ones I wrote you about. Charlie made them."

"He did?" Lige stared hard at Cary, but Cary still looked only puzzled. "Did you see him carve them?"

"Some," said Cary. "Some he did when I wasn't there."

"Carvings of what?"

"Of . . . ?"

"When you carve something," Lige said, patiently, "you make a shape like something you're looking at, something you know. These carvings are made to look like certain particular things, aren't they?"

"Things? Oh, sure, mister." Cary lit up. He reached out and easily picked up the closest of the rocks, holding it lightly between thumb and middle finger. Lige had needed to cup it in his hand to lift it comfortably. "See, this here's a fool hen sitting on its nesting hole."

"And this. . . ." He put down the first rock and picked up the one next to it. "That's a bitch swamp rat ready to have little ones . . . and this's a poison thorn bush mudded up for winter. This is a—well, it's a sort of a house Charlie lives in, himself. . . ."

He went on through the row, identifying each one. Lige stared at him a moment, then picked up the rock Cary had put down last and turned it over in his hands, looking at it from all angles. Cary waited, patiently but tensely; but when Lige exchanged the rock in his hand for one of the others, Cary got up suddenly and paced softly over to the room's one window, to stand looking out.

Lige put down the last piece of rock he had picked up and glanced over at the back of this man who had brought it, and the others, to him. Cary still stood, looking out. Beyond him Lige could see, through the transparent glass, a view of the park across the street, where voting booths were being set up, and beyond, the downtown buildings in Arcadia's Capital City. In every direction were the walls and tops of eternally new-looking, poured-concrete structures with glass pane windows. Except for the primitive nonvideo windows, it looked hardly different than any city on any other planet, except for those on the oldest and richest worlds. Bright scrolls of advertising signs filled the spaces among and above the buildings with color.

A HAPPY NEW MORTGAGE TO ARCADIA——THE FUTURE IN ONE GRAND STEP: EHEU AND KILLEY, CONTRACTORS/BANK-ERS, said one of the signs. JOIN THE RANKS OF INDUSTRIAL WORLDS: VOTE TO REMORTGAGE ARCADIA, cried another. TRADE THE WILDERNESS FOR PARKING LOTS, shouted a third.

Lige sighed inwardly. The promise of the signs was no less than would be delivered——although few of the native Arcadians would realize the full meaning of that delivery. All these new colonial worlds were alike——ready to sell their souls to industrialize in the hopes that they would become like Earth itself, or Alpha Centauri Four. Actually, the best they would ever achieve would be a cheap imitation of the richness of those older planets with their unbeatable head start. And the price would be deadly. If the man by the window could manage to stay alive until he was the age of Lige, he would live to see this Arcadia of his with the greater part of its natural resources plundered or destroyed, its atmosphere polluted, its native vegetation and wildlife killed off—all as the price of becoming, at best, a third-class industrial world.

For a moment the finger of temptation touched Lige. He was getting old, and he had never made that lucky find, that rare discovery those in his line of work always dreamed of stumbling upon, someday. It might be there was some truth to what the woodie said. It might be that the million-in-one chance was fact; that somewhere up-country, and soon to be lost forever on a world determined to go industrial, was a talent such as the field of art had not seen before—a talent that could make its own name, and Lige's as well, if Lige could discover it. But to hope for it was a foolish gamble. . . . Lige made up his mind. He spoke.

"Mister Longan."

Cary turned swiftly.

"Mister. . . ." His voice slowed at the expression on the other man's face. "Something not right?"

"I'm sorry," Lige said. "I can't buy these things."

Cary stared.

"But they're carvings," he said, "and you buy carvings, mister! The ad said so. Your letter said so—your letter I got right here. . . ."

He began to fumble inside his leather jacket.

"Sorry, no," said Lige. "Never mind the letter. I know what I said. But I don't just buy anything that's been carved. I buy art. Do you understand?"

Cary stopped searching under his jacket and let his hand fall helplessly to his side.

"Art. . . ." he echoed.

"That's right. And these aren't art," Lige said. "I'm

sorry. But if anyone told you they were, he was playing a trick on you, or your friend—what's his name? Charlie. . . ."

"Charlie. Well, that's what I call him. But, mister—"

"There's no art here," said Lige, firmly. "I buy art pieces to sell them to other people. Other people wouldn't buy these . . . pieces of yours and Charlie's. Maybe you can see them as representations of something; but I can't and my buyers wouldn't. They'd see them just as rocks—rocks that had been carved, maybe, but not into anything recognizable."

"Mister, I told you what they were—each one."

"I'm sorry. Maybe it's because I don't know the originals they were carved to look like—the fool hen, or whatever," said Lige. "But neither would the people who buy from me. Try to understand, Mister Longan. For me to buy it, your friend would have to make a carving of something I could recognize as a carving."

Cary's face lit.

"Like a man?" he said. "How about a carving like a man?"

"Yes," said Lige. "That's a very good example. Now, if Charlie had carved something in the shape of a man—"

"He did! He carved me, mister, long gun and all. Full size. It even looks like me. You'll buy that?"

Lige sighed, aloud this time.

"Well," he said. "I'll look at it. Bring it in."

Cary looked anxious.

"Can't hardly do that. It's pretty heavy, being full size. Maybe you'd come look at it. It's just a couple hours' fly inland."

Lige shook his head with a touch of relief.

"I'm sorry," he said. He got to his feet and started putting the stones back into their box. "I'm leaving this afternoon for a couple of stops on the other habitated world in this solar system of yours."

The look on the woodsman's face made him add, rashly:

"I'll be back in ten days to pick up handicraft on your Voting Day from the people coming in. If you could have it here then, I could look at it."

"How much?" The words trembled on Cary's lips. "What price might you pay for something like that?"

"Impossible to tell." Lige hefted the heavy box and passed it into Cary's uneager grasp. He spoke briskly. "It could be anything. Two cents, or two thousand interworld units. We buy outright or sell for you on consignment, expenses plus a forty percent commission. Now, I've got to get at my packing—"

"One thing, mister," said Cary, resisting the slight pressure with which Lige urged him and his box toward the door, "I had to borrow money for an outfit to bring these here carvings to you. I was counting on selling them to have money for . . . I mean, I got to pay back, and it takes money besides to hire an airboat to fly back in and fly out with that big carving. If you could lend me just a little cash. . . ."

"Sorry," said Lige. He spoke over Cary's shoulder to the hotel room door. "*Open.* Forgive me, Mister Longan. I really have to pack. I can't lend you anything. It's not my money; it's the money of the company backing me. I have to account for it. Now, if you don't mind. . . ."

Cary let himself be pushed out. The door closed in his face. Numbly he went down in the elevator and past the people in the street-level register area. It was not until he found himself on the sidewalk outside that his mind began to work again. He went down the street to look for a public phone booth.

When he found one, he searched in his pocket for a smudged list of numbers and dialed the first one.

"Harry?" he said, when the party answered. "Cary Longan here, Harry. Listen, I need an airboat to fly upcountry and back, just one day. Going to make two thousand big units, Harry. Only thing is—"

"Hold it. Wait a minute," said the voice at the other end. "Are you talking about credit? Because if you are, Longan, forget it. You get a boat for cash—that's it."

"But listen, Harry—"

The phone went dead as the connection was broken from the other end of the line.

Cary dialed the second number.

Fifteen minutes later, his wide shoulders bent with defeat, Cary abandoned the phone booth. Still carrying the box, he walked on, aimlessly. After a while it began to register on him that he was out of the hotel area and into a section of small shops carrying farm goods and equally small bars—in the back section of the City. He passed one bar as the door opened and a man in a neatly pressed, slightly stained, white suit lurched out.

Cary cat-stepped lightly aside to avoid being blundered into and went on. A few steps later, however, his pace slowed. He stopped and went back to the bar entrance. For a moment he hesitated there, shifting the box from one arm to the other. Then, he went in.

Within, it was dimly lit, dark after the day-bright street. There was a bar all down one side with a long row of dispensers behind it, lit from below. The rest of the room was full of tables: slick, darkly gleaming tables. Cary, who had hesitated a second just inside the door, breathed out a little in relief and went forward to find a gap between empty seats, halfway down the bar.

The bartender, a heavy man, came along the other side of the bar to meet him.

"You aren't too high-priced here, mister?" Cary asked.

"No, we're not too high-priced, cousin," said the bartender, sourly, looking at him. "You found what you're looking for, unless you want to buy some packages of booze and take them back out in the scrub."

"What I was hoping for—" Cary put the box carefully on the bar, "was a length of weed."

"No weed. We don't like the customers spitting green all over the floor in here. You got money?" The bartender's voice sharpened.

"Money? Sure, mister," said Cary. "I just felt like a chew, is all. Give me a double—your cheapest booze and a beer."

The bartender turned away to fill the order. When he brought the glass and shot glass back, he thumped them on the bar in front of Cary, who had been fingering cautiously through a pouch he held in one hand.

"Fifteen cents, interworld—that's two dollars, local. Right, mister?" He fished out a single bill and dropped it on the bar. "I give you a five."

"Script!" said the bartender disgustedly, looking at it. But he picked it up, turned to feed it into the slot below the dispenser from which he had drawn the booze, then turned back to slide three one-dollar script bills at Cary. Cary picked them up cautiously and tucked them away before tossing down the booze and beginning to nurse the beer.

"Mister. . . ." he began, but the bartender was already off down the bar serving another customer.

Cary drank, and ordered again. And drank and ordered some more. The jagged, painful edge of hurt inside him at not selling Charlie's small carvings began to be blunted. A warm fog seemed to fill the room.

"Again, mister," he said to the bartender.

As the other brought the drinks back, Cary patted the box before him on the bar. "You see this, mister? Guess what's in there. Carvings, that's what. Want to see one—"

"Forget it, cousin," said the bartender, taking the five Cary dropped on the bar before him. "You showed them to me twice already."

He turned and spoke down the bar. "Rocks. Carved, he says, by some damn animal—one of those swamp otters, upcountry. That's all I got to do, is look at rocks!" He turned away, shoved the bill into the slot below the dispenser, and started off down the bar.

The warm fog cleared, suddenly.

"Mister," said Cary. The bartender went on. *"Mister!"*

The second time he said it, his voice was loud enough to quiet the hum of other voices in the now clearly seen bar.

"What's the matter with you?" the bartender said, turning and coming back up the bar to him. "We don't like shouting in here—"

His voice broke off in a gasp. His heavy body was jerked suddenly, halfway across the bar by one thin, hard hand clutching his jacket. Another thin, hard hand materialized only inches before his face, holding a dark brown, six-inch thorn.

"My change," whispered Cary. "You were going to cheat me, mister."

"Don't—don't scratch me with that!" The bartender yammered slightly, his jaw unhinged by fear of the poison thorn. "I got your change. I just forgot, that's all—that's all."

His hand came forward and dropped three one-dollar script bills on the bar. Cary let him go, gathered in the bills with his free hand, and backed to the door. All at once he was alone, outside on the sidewalk.

He looked about him, surprised. Night had fallen while he had been inside; but the artificial lighting made the street as bright as ever. No one was in sight.

He pinned the thorn back under the collar on his jacket and let out his tightly held breath with a sigh, relaxing. With a surge, the amount he had drunk took hold of him again. The fog did not move back in; but the whole street and its facing buildings seemed to take a sudden wild sweep halfway around him, then steadied again.

"Yeaaaahooo!" he yelled suddenly, tossing the box in the air and catching it.

Clutching his box, he reeled off down the street into a blur of gleaming concrete and more brilliantly gleaming signs.

2.

A jar, as if he had been dropped from some small height onto a hard surface, jolted Cary back to life. For a moment he felt nothing; and then a wave of nausea and a splitting headache took possession of him. He struggled to open sticky eyelids and looked up to see what seemed to be two men and a young woman. They were standing over him in a building that seemed to be a warehouse piled with trail goods.

"All right, men. Thank you," the woman was saying, crisply, in a voice he knew. "It's a Prayer Day, so I can't tip you. But come back here tomorrow after four in the afternoon and I'll give you thirty percent off on anything you'd like from the stock you see around you."

One of the men grunted.

"Took," he said. "We should've known, Jass."

"I beg your pardon!" The female voice sharpened. "Orvalo Outfitters has been in business twenty-three years and I'm an honest, religious city woman. If I say you'll get thirty percent off, that means an actual thirty percent off. Go check the lowest price from the other outfitters on what you'd fancy, then come back here and tell me. I'll give you thirty percent off that. You're being paid in dollars, pards, for a penny-rate job. It didn't take you five minutes to carry him here for me!"

"What if we don't have the spare cash to buy——" one of the men began, grumblingly.

"Then sell the discount to someone that has!" she snapped. "Do I have to think for you as well as reward you? Any more objections?"

Muttering, the two went out.

"Mattie," muttered Cary, mostly to himself, "you know you're going to make money, even at thirty per——"

Panic suddenly hit him. He jerked himself up in a sitting position, for the second completely forgetting the nausea and the headache, and stared about.

"My box!"

Then he saw it, on the floor within arm's length. With a gasp of relief he gathered it in and hitched himself backwards, so that he could sit, half-reclining against a pile of knapsack frames. Pain and sickness returned. He closed his eyes against them.

"That's right!" said Mattie's voice. Painfully he opened his eyes to see her standing over him. "You were holding it there under a truck-loading dock where you'd passed out. And the carvings are still in it! I can guess what that means. You couldn't even wait to see that buyer before getting drunk."

"Mattie. . . ." He rolled his head in negation against the hard edges of the frames that supported it.

"Don't tell *me*!" she snapped.

He shook his head weakly again, staring up at her. She was a tall, dark-haired girl of about his own age, with brown eyes in a tight-lipped, severe but almost beautiful face. She seemed to waver like an out-of-focus image to Cary's bloodshot eyes, as she stood above him, in a plain and rather stiff white suit-dress, white gloves, and holding a book bound in silver cloth. *Sermons for the Day* read the title on the cover of the book, in fiery red letters that gave the illusion of flaming and flickering as he watched.

"Mattie, how can I tell you if you don't let me talk?"

"Just answer me one thing!" she said, fiercely. "You saw the art dealer? Yes? No?"

"Yes!" he said. "That's what I'm trying to tell you. . . ." The room swam about him suddenly, and the headache was like an ax blade between his eyes. "Mattie . . . I got to have a drink."

She snorted. "From me? Not likely!"

He managed to fight back the discomfort enough to speak.

"I saw him, I tell you. I stopped by here first, too. Go look in the delivery bin below the wall slot of your office. I slid my guns and gear in there to keep safe, early this morning."

She breathed through her nose at him.

"If you're lying again. . . ." She whirled about, and he heard her heels tapping away through the warehouse and up the three steps onto the glazed, different-sounding floor of the outer office. The heel sounds ceased. Then they began again, coming back toward him. She appeared back over him, carrying the not-inconsiderable weight of his backpack, rifle, and handgun, which she threw down beside him with a crash.

"All right!" she said. "So you came by here. And you saw him. Why've you still got the carvings, then? He wouldn't buy after all, was that it?"

"Mattie, listen . . . I need a drink real bad."

"You're not getting one from me," she said. "Even if I wanted to, it's a Prayer Day. I won't handle liquor on a

Prayer Day. You talk—or I'll call the marshal's office to
have you kicked out of town."

"No, Mattie. Listen. . . ." Cary licked parched lips with
a dried rag of a tongue. "He took them . . . on consignment. He didn't have any place to carry them. He's coming
back in ten days to pick them up."

"On consignment!" she cried. "That means you won't get
paid and I won't get my money for maybe two months!"

"Not that long, Mattie—"

"I don't care! Two months is too long!" Her face was furious. "I need that money *now*, Cary. The New Worlds
mortgage is going to be voted on in ten days. In a month,
the factories and projects this world will get from remortgaging itself will already be building—"

"If there's enough people who vote to renew the
mortgage—" began Cary.

"There will be!" she flashed. "Do you think a few woodies like yourself can stop the march of progress?"

"Aw, Mattie."

"Don't aw-Mattie me! Do you think a world like Arcadia is finished up, just because it's paid back the original
mortgage its colonists signed, just to get them here and give
them the bare essentials of survival?"

"But it's *our* world now, Mattie," Cary protested.

"Our world! Our mudhole! Look around you—" She
threw out an arm furiously, pointing here and there about
the room. "Do you think this is civilization? Earth had this
much of things back in the nineteenth century, when stars
were just little things going twinkle, twinkle in the sky—"

She broke off, suddenly.

"Oh, what's the use of talking to you?" she said, wearily.
"You *like* a wilderness world. Well, I don't. And I want my
money. When the new mortgage goes through, the money

from it will finance an industrial expansion on this world
like no one here's ever imagined. And I'm going to buy
shares in the new industries with every cent I can raise. By
the time you get shot to death, or die of some fever out
there in the muskeg swamps, I'll be well on my way to
being rich, with a decent roof over my head, and some decent appliances to make life livable, and my own private
aircar. It's the first real chance for me or anyone else on
this world since it was first settled, ninety years ago—but
you don't understand that."

"I understand, Mattie," he said.

"No, you don't!" she said. "You don't understand anything but booze and that crazy swamp otter—"

"He saved my life!"

"I know!" she blazed at him. "You've told me. He saved
your life. He carves rocks. What's that got to do with me,
and how I've worked and slaved and sweated and held a
job days while I tried to run this place nights and keep the
business going? I've scrimped and saved and cut corners,
and worked two shifts to get that money I lent you to bring
those carvings down here and sell them! That script you
drank up last night was *my* script! And I want it back!"

Guiltily, he fumbled inside his jacket and came out with
his money pouch. She snatched it out of his grasp before he
could open it and tore it open herself. She held it upside
down; only a few local coins fell out.

"Well, I'll take your gear and guns for part of it!" She
kicked savagely at his property on the floor beside him.
"And I'll get a judgment against you for the rest and have
you bound out to the City labor force, with your wages
coming to me. There'll be ditches you can dig and errands
you can run, if nothing else—"

"Mattie, listen!" Desperately, he broke in on her. "You

didn't let me tell you. The statue—he'll pay cash for that!"

She stared down at him with his pouch still held out in the air upside down. A single, crumpled script dollar floated down from it, ignored.

"What statue?" she demanded.

"You know—the statue of me Charlie made," he said. "I told you about it."

"Statue of you. . . ." Memory suddenly lighted her face. "That's right. You said he carved you, standing and holding a gun. The art dealer wants *that!*"

"It's like a man, that's the thing," Cary said. "It's recognizable. He'll pay cash, all right. Interworld units. . . ." He delayed a second, drawing the suspense out. "Two thousand."

"Two thousand!" The arm holding his empty pouch fell limply to her side. "That's more than the stock here and all I've been able to save, put together. . . ."

Her face tightened. She turned fiercely on him.

"You're lying!" she said. "You're lying again. Two thousand interworld units for a piece of rock chewed by a swamp otter! No one'd pay that!"

"No, Mattie. Truth!" he said. "You can call the hotel and find the record of my coming in to see him. He's gone off-world by now. Left yesterday afternoon, but you can check with the hotel. He'll be back in ten days—they'll have a place saved for him then, likely. Ask them. How'd I know that unless I'm telling the truth? He told me just when he was coming back and where, so I could have the statue down here for him."

She glared at him for a moment; but he faced her unflinchingly.

"Come on!" she said.

She turned and stalked off toward the office section. He

scrambled painfully to his feet and lurched after her, feeling his head throb with each footfall.

He followed her into the outer office, which was unchanged from the way it had looked when her father had been alive. It was a wide room, divided front from back by a counter running across the room except for a swinging gate at one end. She passed through this gate and he followed her—into the area holding two desks, the suspension files, and the office equipment.

"That's why I decided to have a few drinks to celebrate," he said. "That's why—"

"Be quiet," she said, sitting down at one of the desks. She punched buttons on the desk phone for the number of Capital City's best hotel. In a moment she was speaking to the reservations and information computer there. After a moment she punched off the phone and swung about in her chair to face him.

"See?" he said. "It was the truth, all of it. Mattie, I just got to have a drink—"

"What about this two thousand, now?" she interrupted him. "You have to deliver the statue down here to get it?" Her mouth tightened. "I suppose you want me to outfit and supply you again, so you can go upcountry and bring it down?"

"Well, you see, that's the thing. I can't just go up and bring it down overland. Not enough time. Also, it's too heavy. That's the thing, now. I got to fly up and fly back out with it."

"*Fly!*" She was on her feet. "Rent an airboat both ways? With *my* money?"

"Don't yell," he said, feebly. "Please don't yell, Mattie. My head—"

"Who cares about your head? Outfit you again—that's

bad enough. Fly in one way—that's unthinkable enough. But fly up and cargo-fly back—it'd take most of the ready cash I've got!"

"Two thousand," he said, softly.

"Two thousand—two thousand—" she mimicked. But her eyes, focused on the wall, had grown thoughtful. She spoke more to herself than to him. "Fly up. Maybe. But down. . . ."

Her eyes came sharply back to focus on him.

"What's it weigh, Cary?"

"The statue?" He frowned, thinking. "Never really figured its weight . . . four, five hundred kilos, maybe."

"Four, five hundred kilograms. . . ." she muttered to herself. "Thousand, eleven hundred pounds, local, at five dollars' script the pound-mile. No, no . . . it'd break me. But fly up . . . eleven hundred pounds."

She broke off suddenly and looked at him again.

"We'll fly up and bring it down overland," she said. "There's time and I can outfit us from the stock here, so that won't take cash. What'll we need?"

"Mattie!" He stared at her. "Not overland. It can't be done. You don't know!"

"I know one thing," she said grimly. "It's coming down here overland or not at all. That's all I'm gambling on top of what I've lent you already. Not a penny more—not even for two thousand units."

She took a step back toward the desk and reached out toward the phone buttons.

"Take it," she said. "Or I'm calling the marshal's office right now and the statue'll never get here. I mean it, Cary!"

He stared at her miserably, his head splitting, his stomach floating queasily, and his thoughts floundering like stock deer caught in the mud.

"I don't know, Mattie," he muttered. "Maybe a man could. . . ."

"It's settled, then," she said. "I'll help you."

He stared at her.

"You?"

"Why not? You'll need help. I've been upcountry before. You know that."

"But, Mattie, even if I can do it, it'll be a terrible—"

"I don't care." Her face was stiff. "I'm not letting you out of my sight, this time, until you've got that two thousand in your hand. —And that's another thing. I get half of it. Half of whatever you get, now or later. We'll sign a paper on it. You understand?"

Cary wobbled his head numbly.

"What can a man say, Mattie?"

"Nothing. Because I'm right, as always. All right, we'll draw up that paper right now and pick out equipment. What'll we need?"

"Need." He forced the mired machinery of his mind to work. "Well, axes, of course. Block and tackle. And rope, plenty of it and strong enough to lift the statue—"

"Wait!" Sharply, she broke in on him. "Don't say another word about it. I forgot. The papers and the equipment'll have to wait. It's Prayer Day."

Cary frowned.

"We're going to need every day we got in ten days," he said.

"Can't be helped. I can't do business on a Prayer Day. It's not right and I won't do it. We'll wait for tomorrow— one minute after midnight."

"If you say so. . . ." He let out a weary breath and leaned against one of the tall file cabinets. "Mattie, though —seeing we're going to be pards in this, how about just one drink for me? I need it bad. You don't have to give it to me with your own hands. Just tell me where you keep your trade booze—"

"I'll help no one to liquor on a Prayer Day." She hesitated, however, looking at him a little less harshly for the first time. "I'll make you some coffee. Come on."

He followed her through a door into the back office, which she had set up as living quarters, converting it into a large, one-room apartment, with a cooking unit in one corner. Next to it was the accountant's desk stacked high with file cards from the disbursement company in town for which she worked a five-day week, regular hours.

"Sit down," she said.

Cary collapsed gratefully into a wide-armed inflatable chair and let his aching head loll against the yielding backrest. He closed his eyes as she went over to the cooking unit. In a minute or two, the mouth-watering odor of real coffee from the variform bean ranches down tropics-way made him open his eyes again. He opened his eyes, feeling humble. She could just as well have been close about it and given him synthetic. By her own lights, in her own way, she was a good woman.

She brought him a good quarter-liter mug.

"Many thanks," he said sincerely, taking it. The good smell was overpowering from the cup. He put it to his lips and sipped at it. Over the rim of the cup he caught sight of her watching him with a strange and unusual expression on her face.

"Cary," she said, as he lowered his cup, "how old are you?"

"Twenty-one," he answered.

"I'm nineteen," she said. "You know, if we'd been born back on one of the rich old worlds, you and I both'd be still in school with years of learning to go yet before we were off on our own."

He laughed, the noiseless laugh of a woodsman.

"You might be in school," he said. "Not me." And he drank again, gratefully, from the coffee cup.

Her face tightened up again.

"Meanwhile," she said dryly, sitting down and picking up her silver book which she had laid aside to make the coffee, "as long as you're sitting there drinking my coffee, I might as well be reading my sermons. I'll read out loud so it'll be to your benefit too."

Hastily, he put the coffee cup down on a side table.

"Mattie," he said, starting to get up. "Come to think of it, maybe I ought—"

"To what?" she cut in. Her eyes were dangerous.

"Nothing. Nothing, Mattie. . . ." He sank back into the chair and picked up the coffee to sip at it again. "Mighty fine and nice, this real coffee."

"It ought to be, at what it costs." She opened her book. Cary leaned back as she lowered her head over the open pages, closing his eyes and filling his nostrils with the rich smell of the hot coffee, trying to fill his mind with being back in the upcountry.

"Sermon Eighty-three," read Mattie, in a clear, penetrating voice, "by Alman Michaels, on The Law of All Things Made Right. *'Never doubt that there is a law that governs all things in the universe. Never doubt that law governs you. Never doubt that by that law all things in the universe are sifted, including yourself; that by it the flower is separated from the weed, the industrious from the unindustrious; and by that law the grain is saved while the chaff is thrown aside.*

" *'Moreover, entertain no doubts in what direction that*

chaff is cast. For Hell always reigneth—another universe of torment eternal, to which shall go all who falter, who founder, who fail or flee. They shall be delivered into that which is far worse than that from which they shrank, into unending punishment. . . .'"

3.

The airboat droned its heavy way inland, its rotors chewing through the upper air. Stretched out on the piled gear and equipment they were taking with them, Cary dozed in catnaps, waking momentarily to a reflexive alertness, then sinking back into a doze again. His hangover had almost worn off.

They had lifted above the neatly ordered, morning-white concrete shapes of Capital City shortly after dawn, having gotten everything ready in the hours between midnight and five A.M. Almost immediately they were above the farm country to the east and north of the City with its black earth and dusky green variform oaks and maples. They had flown above these colors and the morning brightness of rivers winding down to the coast for nearly twenty minutes. Now the farmlands were giving way to patches of forest even more dusky than the trees of the farm belt, for here among the variform plants of Earth, the first few native varieties were to be seen.

Up front, seated next to the airboat driver, Mattie kept up a running, argumentative conversation. Snatches of this came to Cary's ears in his moments of wakefulness.

". . . your prices are outrageous, anyway!" That was Mattie.

"What else?" That was the driver. "You use complex equipment, it costs. Shoes are cheap. Riding cattle not much more. Hovertruck starts to cost—not just turbine fuel. Parts and upkeep. Naturally, airboats need more parts, and we can only make those by hand in machine shops. . . ."

"Ten months after the new mortgage gets voted in, pard, your 'boats'll be made by automated machinery, at a dime a dozen."

"Sure. But by the time they're that cheap, I'll be driving plasma craft on intercontinental hops and you'll want to hire one of those for whatever, and it'll cost you ten times what this boat does."

"By that time," Mattie's voice was sharp, "I'll be making fifty times what I do now; and I'll be able to afford it. I'm buying into more than one private subsidiary factory. When production starts in the big government general factories built with the mortgage credit, the companies I've invested in will get the subcontracts. I plan to be rich."

"Better than factory shares, then," said the driver. "You ought to put your money in timber and water rights. That's what I'm going to do. There's millions of board feet of lumber just waiting to be mowed. Throw in a few big dams and you've got hydroelectric power and cleared land for highways and industry. Hell, there's going to be men getting rich from garbage dumps alone, upcountry, if they got the sense to stake them out in the right spots. But raw materials and power are the sure bets."

"Maybe for fifteen years from now," said Mattie. "But I want my money while I'm young enough to enjoy it. . . ."

Vaguely troubled by the talk—just why he could not say —Cary dozed off again.

When he opened his eyes the next time, the forest belt was past and they were above rolling foothills covered with a tweed-like coat of cattle grass in which stalks of green, dull red and dark, dead brown, were intermingled. Occasionally a clump of scraggly native bire trees, their twisted low, un- gainly shapes with fur-like tufts of green along their naked- seeming black limbs, broke the grassland scene.

". . . everybody but the cousins," the pilot was saying up front. "The farm hicks and the woodies like your friend back there."

"Don't be so sure some of them won't be investing in the building from the new mortgage too," retorted Mattie's voice.

"Come on, Mattie! What've they got to invest? The farm- ers, something maybe. Upcountry, they've got nothing. They probably won't even come in to vote—and we almost won't need them if the farmers turn out. Farms and cities can put together sixty percent of the population. We only need two-thirds voting to remortgage."

"If we don't need them, why all the free food and booze signs going up for the day before voting?" demanded Mat- tie. Back with the gear, Cary's ears pricked up. He had not noticed those signs when he was in town—too occupied with the art dealer and drinking. But if they could get the statue in at all, no reason they couldn't get it in a day early. . . .

He dozed off again, dreaming of free food and drink.

A jolt of the airboat as it dropped suddenly in an air pocket brought him awake again. Up front, for once, there was silence. Mattie and the driver were taking a rest from their talking. Cary looked out the small window beside the pile of gear on which he rested.

Below them now was the low ridge-mountain country, ragged, sloping, and cut by swift-running shallow rivers. He put his face next to the window and tried to see ahead as far as he could. He caught sight of the dull brown wall of cliff rising sharply three thousand feet to the plateau area on which was the highland swamp where Charlie and his kind lived. Lucky, thought Cary fleetingly, it was high summer. Winter would make it easier on the plateau itself, skidding the statue out over the ice. But down the cliffs in winter, with ice-toothed winds cutting into them, and sudden blizzards of smothering snow. . . .

"You never did tell me what you're after, up there." The sound of the driver's voice broke into the silence and Cary's thoughts abruptly.

"That's our business!" said Mattie.

"Just wondering. Your friend could be going fur hunting on those swamp otters; but you aren't in that line of work."

"He's not a trapper."

"Looks like one."

"He was once. Now he's made friends with the swamp otters. He protects them."

"Protects them?" There was a little pause. "You're buying me one, Mattie."

"Believe what you want, pard."

"But what's the percentage in *protecting* them? You can sell hides, how can you sell pro—". The driver's voice changed tone suddenly. "There isn't some kind of gemstone deposit up there, these otters can get at?"

"If there was," Mattie's voice was tart, "you'd be flying us back."

There was another pause.

"Sure. I guess so. Can't figure that otter business, though. . . ."

Cary dozed off briefly and woke again as the airboat tilted to climb to the plateau altitude. Cary raised himself on one elbow and looked out.

Just ahead now, the nearly vertical cliffs rising to the plateau were like bastions of dark granite. Here and there upon them a poison thorn bush clung, its white summer flowers looking speckled by the near-invisible dark clumps of thorns surrounding them. Nothing else grew on the cliffs.

The airboat mounted on the updrafts along the cliff face, flying alongside the cliff and rising as it went. After some fifteen minutes, it lifted above the edge of the plateau and Cary saw once more the black and gray-green tableland of the swamp where Charlie's people lived, and the bare earth stretched beyond interspersed with poison thorn, snake trees, native cactus, and clumps of bire, temp, sourbark, and upland vine.

". . . where do you want me to set down?" the driver was asking. Mattie's head turned and her face looked back at Cary.

"Where, Cary?"

Cary got himself up from the pile of gear and crouched forward under the low roof of the airboat until he was able to look between the two heads there and ahead through the windshield.

"See that clump of bire, about ten o'clock over there?" Cary pointed. "The one with open water nearly all around it?"

"I got it," said the driver.

"Take a line on that, mister. About eight, maybe nine klicks straight on, you'll come over some dry ground, a sort of spit coming out from the land beyond. We'll be setting down about there. I'll tell you just exactly when we get there."

"Eight-plus kilometers. Right," said the driver, starting his short-run log from zero. He flew on. Cary watched the log as its numbers slowly mounted toward eight point zero. Just before it reached that number, he spoke again to the pilot.

"You see it up there now, mister? You can tell where the ground starts because of the swamp grass being darker there."

"Right," said the pilot again. "I see it."

"We'll want to set down where you see a sort of star-shaped earth patch. There's a log hutch there with a vine roof that's gone black from being out in the sun. That's mine. You go down there."

"Right."

The airboat slanted earthward. A few minutes later it came to rest in the clearing Cary had described. They started unloading.

"Sure you don't want to make a pick-up date?" the driver asked, before taking off.

"No," said Mattie. "We told you we wouldn't need you."

"Right. Shut the door. Luck," said the driver.

They shut the door and the airboat waddled forward some forty feet before becoming airborne. It droned off to the southwest, leaving them standing between the dark earth and the dark blue sky with its swiftly drifting white clouds. A cool wind blew about them, although the sun was warm.

"Real pretty country, isn't it?" Cary said.

Mattie glanced about her, at the flat landscape with its dingy swamp grass leaning this way and that in thick patterns under the varying pressures of the wind, its black water, and its few dark clumps of taller vegetation. Rustles, squeaks, and whistles sounded from the swamp, with an occasional deeper sound something between a boom and a pop. Seeing she was not going to answer, Cary walked over toward the swamp side of the clearing, put his hands on either side of his mouth, and gave a long, fluting whistle. He waited, then whistled again. Then once more.

No answer came back from the swamp. He turned and walked back to the center of the clearing.

"What's that?" Mattie looked sharply at him. "Are you calling this Charlie otter of yours?"

"Not calling. Just passing the word I'm here." Cary revolved slowly about, head up, sniffing the air. "Something off here. I need to ask Charlie about that."

"You can *talk* to him?"

"Some," he said briefly, almost curtly.

He turned abruptly on his heel and started off into the swamp grass.

"On second thought, I'll look about a bit," he said. "You set the gear up."

Before Mattie could argue, the tall grass closed around him. He walked easily through it, for it was nowhere so thick or matted here as it was where it grew directly out of the water. After a moment he emerged into open ground again, where a little strip of swamp shoreline showed.

He crossed the clearing, closely examining the dry, blackish earth of it as he passed, and went on into the grass on the far side, following the pattern of the shoreline. It was not until the fifth small clearing he encountered that he found something interesting—a stick-like piece of hard, half-round black earth about two inches long and half an inch thick. He picked it up, nodded to himself and, still holding it, returned to the clearing where he had left Mattie.

She had sorted their gear and slung one of the self-supporting hammocks—not inside the cabin, but outside, in the middle of the clearing.

"I looked in that hutch of yours," she greeted Cary. "It's a mess. I'm not going to clean it up for you, and I'm not going to sleep in it either. I slung my hammock out here. It'll just be for tonight. Tomorrow we'll start moving the statue to town."

He turned without answering her, walked over to the door of the hutch, and opened it. He looked inside.

"Sure," he said softly. He came back to the pile of gear, took his rifle and ammo belt, and thumbed a smoke cartridge into it. He held the rifle up in one hand casually and fired it skyward. The white plume of smoke mounted toward the clouds.

"What're you doing?" demanded Mattie.

"I'll give him until the morn," Cary said.

"Him? Who're you talking about?"

"The mister that messed up my hutch," Cary answered. He laid down the rifle and held out his other hand to her to show the piece of earth he had picked up. "Mud from a boot cleat. He's swamp-wise enough to take off his boots in the water and come ashore in mocs. But he hung his boots at his belt and some of the mud in one of the cleats dried and fell out."

"You mean there's another woodsman around here?" Mattie asked.

"Unless he's left already," said Cary. "I'll sling out here and ask him to clean up in there for me tomorrow."

"Where's the statue?" asked Mattie. "I want to see it." He looked at her.

"Close," he said. "Put your boots on. It's wet all the way."

She complied, pulling on the heavy wading overboots and rolling their elastic tops up her legs as high as they would go. Cary led her off into the swamp. After a twenty-minute slog through the ankle- to thigh-deep water and the matted marsh grass—not so tall, here in the water, but much more thickly grown together—they emerged onto something like a small island overgrown with the marsh grass.

"Why did this Charlie put it way out here?" demanded Mattie. She was panting. Cary looked at her. She was not used to the marsh boots. She had been trying to lift each foot directly from the sucking mud at each step, instead of breaking the heel loose first to cut down the suction.

"He didn't put it," said Cary, pushing through a stand of marsh grass ahead of her toward the crown of the island. "It came up here. Swamp mud pushes rocks up every spring when it thaws. Most're not this big, though."

As he spoke, he broke through into a small clearing; and there, surrounded and hidden by the grass, was the statue.

It stood leaning at a slight angle above the black earth in which its lower end was still sunk. It was a narrow finger of a rock now—whatever its original shape had been—and as tall as Cary. Like the earth which had given it up, the statue was black—but it was a different color black than the soil. The black of the rock was like the black of Earth obsidian, in that when the sun caught its surface at a certain angle, the surface there looked gray. Somehow, standing as it did in the high-altitude sunlight, the marsh grass leaning to the wind behind and all around it, the statue seemed a natural part of its surroundings in spite of its carved shape.

Mattie stared at it.

"Not much of a statue," she said after a moment. "Hardly make out it's a man with a gun, let alone you. . . ." She hesitated, still staring at it. "No, there's something about it like you, after all. But I don't know what."

"You like it?" Cary asked.

She shivered slightly.

"I don't know," she said, in a lower voice. "It scares me, a little."

"Nothing to be scared about," said Cary.

"I don't mean scared, like . . . scared," she said. "I mean . . . it just makes me feel as if we shouldn't move it from here, maybe."

"We can move it any place we want," Cary said. "It's a statue of me, Mattie."

She pulled her eyes from the statue and looked about the ring of tall, surrounding swamp grass.

"How are we going to get it through the swamp?"

Cary smiled.

"You were the one so sure we could shift it down to the town," he said. "Don't you know?"

Mattie turned on him.

"I don't know the upcountry like you do!" she said. "Of course, I was counting on you to figure out how to move it!" She lowered her voice. "I suppose we'll have to build a raft or something and float it through the swamp to the edge of the plateau."

"No trees up here make logs that'll float," said Cary. "Also, too many spots too shallow for floating a raft through."

"All right," said Mattie. "You tell me, then. You must've had some idea when you said we might be able to bring it down overland."

Cary nodded.

"Sledge," he said.

"Sledge?" she echoed.

Cary nodded.

"Right," he said. "Couple of good, round-bottom runners with turned-up ski noses, slats across them. Dried grass mats on the slats to swell up around the statue and keep it from rolling off. The statue'll be under water most of the time—that takes half the load off. Smooth runners'll slide through the muck of the bottom nice and easy without getting suction-caught."

He turned abruptly.

"Better get back to the gear and at it. Take all afternoon to make."

They returned to the clearing where Cary's hutch sat. On the way in, Cary gathered a huge armful of the land-growing swamp grass; and once they were back he demonstrated to Mattie how to take fist-thick bunches of the long grass and plait these together to make mats.

". . . doesn't matter much if the mat holds together pretty loose for now," he wound up. "Once the stalks get wet and start swelling they'll hold together just as if they grew so. You go ahead. I'll go chop logs for the runners."

He took an ax and some rope and went off into the grass. Shortly, Mattie heard the sound of chopping, and in a little while he came back into the clearing, dragging two roped-together chewbark logs about ten feet long. As Mattie, plaiting the grass mats, watched, he went about making his runners.

He cut a deep V-shaped notch with the ax about a hand's length back from the end of one of the logs. Then, turning the log on its side, he split it in half from the notch back to the other end, leaving a length of half-log with a full thickness of head on it. Rapidly, using the ax, he barked this, exposing the smooth wood underneath. Then, turning the barked half-log upside down, he took the ax high on the handle near its head and proceeded to use it almost like a jackknife, to whittle the head-thickness into a curved angle.

When he turned this back over on its rounded underside, he had what was very plainly a runner with upcurving front end for the sledge he had described. Turning to the other log, he duplicated the procedure. Then he went into the hutch for a moment and returned with a long pair of obviously hand-split boards. He cut these into lengths and nailed them crosswise on the two runners.

"There she be," he said, putting the ax aside. He looked over at Mattie. "How're you coming with those mats?"

Mattie blinked and looked down at her hands.

"I've almost finished the second one," she said.

"We're going to need about eight," Cary said. "I better give you a hand." He looked up at the sun, which was now down close to the western surface of the plateau, the land beyond the swamp. "We'll be ending up by firelight as it is—"

He broke off suddenly and looked back toward the swamp.

"Mattie," he said. "Stay put where you are."

In three long, quiet strides he reached the pile of gear and picked up his rifle. Tucking it under one arm, barrel pointing down, he turned to face the stand of grass into which he had walked earlier to find the small piece of dried mud from a boot cleat. He stood balanced, legs a little spread, facing in that direction, but tense as some wild animal on the alert.

Mattie gazed at him startled, her hands gone still on the ropes of dried swamp grass. There was nothing visible to call forth such a reaction in him.

"Cary—" she began.

"Hush," he said.

She looked from him to the grass and saw nothing. Then, without a rustle, there was suddenly another woodsman standing just inside the clearing at the edge of the grass. He was a bigger man than Cary, heavy-bodied, with long legs and a short gun holstered at his hip. He carried his rifle in the crook of his elbow, barrel waist-high. For a moment he seemed so like Cary in dress and attitude that he looked related.

"Mister," he said to Cary.

"Afternoon, mister," Cary answered. "Drink and eat a bite?"

"Thanks kindly, no. I ate some already."

"Sad to hear it, mister," said Cary. "You saw my smoke?"

The other shook his head.

"Must have been looking otherways," he said.

"The airboat?" Cary said.

The other only looked at him.

"Well, I tell you something, mister," said Cary softly, after a moment. "These swamp otters here aren't for trapping."

The other woodsman gazed back and cradled his rifle a little more closely.

"Free country," he said.

Cary shook his head slightly.

"No, mister," he said. "Not this place."

"Cary—" It was Mattie suddenly speaking.

"Shut, Mattie," he said, without raising his voice but

without taking his eyes off the other man. "You hear me, mister?"

The woodsman gazed at him for a long second without movement or change of expression.

"Mister," he said at last, "you must think you a real Cary Longan."

"Happens I am," said Cary. "That's me, mister."

The larger woodsman continued to gaze at him steadily, this time for several seconds.

"Heard you was placed elsewhere. If it's you, then—" he said at last.

"Heard wrong," said Cary. He did not move, only stood waiting.

Slowly, almost without his seeming to have anything intentional to do with it, the rifle in the other's hand slipped out of the crook of his elbow and on down until its butt rested on the ground and he held it by one hand at the muzzle end of the barrel.

"Guess I did, mister," he said. "I'll be moving on then."

"We'll be moving on likewise, in the morn," said Cary. "Makes no difference. I'll be back."

"Sure," said the other. "Makes no difference."

He looked for the first time from Cary to Mattie and nodded his head at her.

"I'll say you both good night," he said.

"Mister," said Cary.

The eyes of the other came back to him.

"My hutch back there," Cary said, jerking his head at it. "Might be you'd take a look at it sometime before you pack up and leave for good."

The other looked at the hutch and back at Cary.

"Sure. I'll do that, mister," he said.

Abruptly, he was gone. Cary walked back to the pile of
gear without a word and laid the rifle back down. But he
picked up his gunbelt with the short gun in it and strapped
it around his narrow waist. Looking up from doing this, he
caught the eyes of Mattie upon him.

"Sorry about saying you shut, Mattie," he said, mildly.
"I didn't just have the time to talk with you then."

She looked at him a second or two longer, and then
without a word went back to her mat-making. He came
over, sat down cross-legged on the ground on the other side
of the pile of pulled, dry grass stems, and began plaiting.

They worked industriously until the light began to dim.
Then Cary built a fire while Mattie cooked supper on the
wick-stove they had brought along. After supper, by the
light of the fire, they took up the making of mats again.
Sometime during the evening, with the darkness like a wall
all around them, the stars overhead, and the fire burning
warmly in front of them, she spoke, unexpectedly:

"When's that Charlie otter going to show up?"

"Don't know he will for sure," answered Cary, looking
up at her from his plaiting. "Hope so, though."

"I'd like to see him," she said. After a moment she
added, "You know what it is in that statue that makes it
look like you? It's because it stands the way you stand,
sometimes—like you stood when you were talking to that
other woodsman today."

"Why, how'd that make it look like me?" he asked.

She glanced up and her eyes met his.

"Everyone stands a little different," she said. "Your
way's like nobody else's, and I recognized it in the statue
—that's all."

He nodded, a little wonderingly.

"I guess that's true," he said. "Everyone's different."

They finished their mats and turned in. At first light of dawn they woke and made breakfast. They were just about to sit down with their plates when a sharp, prolonged whistle made them turn about.

Mattie took a sudden, reflexive step backwards.

Less than fifteen feet away, just out of the swamp water onto the shore, sat a sleekly black-furred creature about four feet long in the body and looking as if it weighed as much as a man. It had a long, sinuous neck and head that was otter-like in every way, except for the glint of long, flat, sharp-edged teeth between the black lips.

4.

"It's Charlie all right," said Cary. He whistled.

Charlie gave a chorus of whistles in return and came up the slope from the water to them, moving suddenly and very swiftly. He did not hump himself along like an Earth otter, but instead undulated up the slope on his short legs, with a snake-like motion. Still whistling, he stopped for a moment before Cary, pointed his head for a second at Mattie, then circled the sledge, moving his head over the items of gear already on it, as if checking each one of them out.

Cary whistled, and Charlie paused to lift his long neck to look at him. Cary patted himself on the chest, pointed out over the swamp, whistled again, and stepped over to squat down and pat the sledge. He was whistling steadily meanwhile—short sharp notes in several different tones. He moved his hand in a circle over the gear, stood up, and moved to the front of the sledge and pulled on one of the drag ropes attached to it, so that the sledge moved forward slightly. Then, dropping the rope, he went over to Mattie, put his arm around her shoulders, and rubbed his cheek against hers.

Mattie gasped and tried to pull away, but his arm held her immobile.

"Sorry, Mattie," Cary said, "act like you like it. This is the way they rub heads with each other."

"You shave from now on, if you're going to try something like that!" snapped Mattie—but her voice quavered on the last words.

He let her go.

"Sorry, like I say," he said. "I was just trying to explain to him about the sledge and all."

"And me—what was that supposed to mean? I suppose you told him I was your mate or some such thing!"

Cary smiled slightly.

"Well no, Mattie," he said. "I just told him you were female and left it at that. Don't go worrying about what he understands. He's bright enough, but I can't really talk to him much more than in sign language."

"You seemed to be doing all right," she said.

He shook his head.

"We're too much different, us and his people," Cary said. "He says he understands about the statue and the sledge, but I don't really guess he does. Anyway, he'll find out when we get to the island."

He turned back to the fire and squatted, picking up his plate.

"Come on," he said. "We better finish up here and get going."

They ate and finished loading the rest of their gear on the sledge. Then, with each one of them on a drag rope, they pulled the heavy sledge down into the swamp water. It followed tautly at the end of their lines and nosed down out of sight below the surface.

But as it touched the mud, the change in the effort required to drag it was immediate and startling. It glided at the end of the drag ropes, somewhere back there, a foot or so under the black face of the swamp water. Mattie could pull it easily alone. In fact, there was less effort to the pulling than there was to the walking itself.

"Remember what I told you," Cary said, sloshing alongside her and watching. "Break your heel loose first, then sort of lever your foot up, toe last, as you swing your weight forward on your other leg. Get the rhythm of it, sort of. It's like walking on snowshoes, only different. I mean, you got to get in the pattern of it."

Mattie tried, but it was still a struggle.

"I'll take the sledge to start with," Cary said, taking the rope from her. "You just concentrate on the walking."

"I can pull and walk too," said Mattie, grabbing for the rope but missing.

"Sure. And you'll get lots of chance to," said Cary, striding ahead effortlessly with the sledge following and Charlie swimming with just his nose out of water, smoothly alongside. Mattie floundered in their wake.

When they got to the island, Mattie took a rope determinedly, and this time Cary did not stop her. Together they pulled the sledge to the clearing where the statue waited.

Charlie had gone quickly on ahead of them. When they emerged into the clearing, he was up on his back legs, his front paws pressed against the stone shape of the statue, and his restless head searching over the stone surface before him. From time to time he whistled softly; and once his lips drew back, exposing the full four-inch lengths of yellow chisel teeth with which he made some small alteration in the shape on which he pressed those front paws.

Cary pulled the sledge up with one end against the lower part of the statue. It now seemed to lean threateningly above the gear piled on top of the grass mats covering the

sled to a depth of at least a foot above the slats. He un-
loaded the gear, then dug down under the rear ends of the
runners so that the back of the sledge settled and the back
slat lay flat on the earth. Then he tied a rope around the
upper part of the statue and ran it forward, around the
front slat of the sledge and back, so that he stood beside the
statue with the end of the rope in his hands.

"Mattie," he said, "stand on the front slat there. Help
hold the sledge down." He whistled at Charlie; and as Mattie stepped up on the front slat, Charlie came with a bound
to rest on the upcurving front end of one of the runners.

Cary took a couple of turns of the rope around his wrists
and began to pull.

His heels dug deep into the dirt with his effort. For a moment it did not seem as if the statue was going to move at
all. Then, slowly at first, then quickly, it toppled forward
onto the sledge, sending out a spray of moisture from the
newly dampened grass mats as it sank into them.

The statue lay embedded in the straw mats, almost hidden from sight among them, fairly in the center of the
sledge. That part of it which had been underground, however, projected beyond the back of the sledge.

Cary rummaged among the gear and came up with what
looked like a loop of thick wire between two small wooden
handles. He unlooped the wire to give himself a length of
perhaps two-thirds of a meter stretched between the handles, and with this began sawing off the extra rock at the
statue's feet.

The abrasive wire cut smoothly through the rock. Charlie hopped off the sledge and ran back to sit, giving an occasional, almost whimpering whistle as he watched Cary
work. When the end of rock finally fell off onto the ground,

Charlie's head dipped over it and he examined the smoothly cut surface closely, before turning to examine the other cut face on the base of the statue.

Cary watched the swamp otter for a second as he recoiled the abrasive wire.

"Give me a hand getting this gear loaded back," he said to Mattie, turning away. Together, they got the gear back on and roped down.

"Take a drag rope now, if you'll be so kind," he said to her when this was done. Together, they leaned on their ropes. The sledge resisted for a moment, then moved grudgingly forward. They struggled with it at the limits of their strength until it entered the grass. With the crushed stalks under its runners, it moved a little more easily; and with the help of the slope, they got it down and into the swamp water, the top of the pile of gear barely showing through the surface of the water behind them.

"All right now, Mattie, stand clear," Cary said, "and I'll turn her."

Mattie let go of her drag rope and stood back. Cary moved in close to the invisible front of the sledge, took hold of both ropes, and tugged sideways, stepping back as the front of the sledge slued around.

Charlie, who had followed them from the clearing into the water, suddenly swam to the pile of gear on top of the sledge and climbed up on it. He extended his head toward Cary and gave a long, low, fluting whistle that was almost a wail.

Cary let go of the ropes.

"Now we have it," he said. He waded over to stand beside the sledge, looking at Charlie. Their heads were almost on a level and only a few inches apart.

Cary whistled, and drew a circle with his hand, ending up with an outstretched arm pointing toward the edge of the plateau. Charlie went into a fluttering succession of small whistles in a large range of tones. Cary shrugged and, turning, went back to the front of the sledge and picked up a rope. Charlie whistled shrilly behind him.

Cary turned and whistled once. Charlie repeated the shrill whistle twice. Cary turned to Mattie.

"He's got it straight now," Cary said. "He says he's going with us."

Mattie stared.

"You aren't going to let him?"

"Rightly," said Cary, slowly, "I don't see how I could stop him."

"But he doesn't understand what he's getting into!"

"Sure doesn't," said Cary. "He thinks we're taking the statue to someplace where there's a lot of people like me who'll like it. It's the one big thing he did. He wants to be there to see them liking it."

"Can't you—" Mattie looked at the swamp otter. "Isn't there some way to explain to him it's not like that?"

"Tried," said Cary. "I told you his people and us are too different. How'm I going to explain money, and art buyers, and other worlds like this to him? I can't even make him understand what it's like off the plateau, properly."

"Then make him stay, for his own good."

Cary shook his head.

"Can't do that," he said. "Wouldn't be right."

"But can't you understand!" Mattie's voice was fierce. "He may not make it!"

"Likely, he won't," said Cary. His eyes met hers for a moment.

"Then you've got to stop him, don't you?" demanded Mattie. She watched him incredulously. "It's better for him to live, even if he doesn't understand why, isn't it?"

"Not surely," Cary said. He frowned, and stood thinking. About them the cool, high-altitude wind whistled faintly in the marsh grass and ruffled the surface of the dark water in which they stood. Charlie himself was motionless as a statue on top of the gear, seeming almost to float on the water. There were no clouds in the dark blue sky this day; and all about there were no light colors to be seen, only blue and black and brown and gray.

"If you're fond of him," said Mattie, in a lower voice, "you won't want him to kill himself for something he doesn't understand." He stood as if he had not heard her.

"No," he said, rousing himself at last. "But he's got a right, like anyone else. Come on."

He whistled at Charlie, who plunged off the top of the gear back into the water. Cary went back to take up a drag rope. Mattie picked up a rope herself and fell into step automatically beside him, looking up at his face. But her help was hardly needed. Even loaded, the sledge slid as easily through the bottom muck once it was started as if through a thick layer of grease.

Suddenly, the sled surged forward and their ropes went slack. Looking back, they saw Charlie's muzzle and a glint of yellow teeth at the edge of the sledge. He had taken some of the ropes binding down the gear firmly in his jaws and was swimming forward strongly, pushing the sledge as he went.

"Look out," said Mattie tartly, "or he'll run us down. Why don't you get four more of them to push and you and I could ride to the edge of the plateau?"

Cary looked over at her and found her expression a good deal more gentle than her voice had indicated.

"The rest don't care for Charlie. Or me," he said.

"They don't?" she said.

"That's right."

"But you protect them from the trappers!"

"They don't believe I do so much," said Cary. "I've tried to tell them, but they don't believe me. They don't believe Charlie, either. See, they all make shapes with their gnawing on things. Their food's swamp clams; and their teeth keep on growing all their lives, so they've got to keep gnawing on things to keep them the proper length. But Charlie's the only one who got mixed up in making shapes with one of us people. They're kind of down on him because of it."

Mattie looked back at the powerfully swimming otter.

"You'd think they'd be proud," she said.

"Nothing to be proud of, way they see it," Cary said. "Any more than with us." He met her eyes for a moment. "Everybody human thinks I'm crazy to have doings with otters. The other otters think Charlie's crazy to have doings with me. Not much difference either way."

They splashed on through the swamp, stopping at noon on a small grass-covered island to eat.

"Will we make the edge of the plateau by dark?" Mattie asked.

"Ought to," said Cary. "Weather's good, and we've only got about another four-five klicks to go."

But after lunch they ran into a succession of shallow areas in the swamp that were too large to go around. It took all three of them, heaving together, to get the sled across a couple of long, dry islands that barred their path.

"Should be deep enough water from here on," said Cary,

after they had crossed the second of these. He looked up at the sun, now nearly halfway down the western sector of the sky. "Still ought to make it by sundown."

They went on; and the wide, grass-tufted lagoons through which they had passed most of the day gradually gave way to what was almost a channel of thigh-deep water between walls of water-growing swamp grass some twenty meters apart. The close horizon of the plateau edge could already be seen, a reddish-brown ridge lifting above the tops of the grass and the water ahead.

They reached a point where the channel narrowed to less than twenty meters in width. As they passed through this neck of water, there was an abrupt chorus of shrill whistles, and swamp otters appeared from the grass on both sides of them.

Charlie, who had been pushing at the back of the sledge with Mattie pushing beside him, leaped suddenly up on top of the gear and whistled back at his own kind.

"Cary!" called Mattie.

There was a note of panic in her voice. Cary turned his head, still leaning against the drag rope on which he was pulling.

"It's all right, Mattie," he called back. "Don't figure they'll hurt us."

Mattie hastily abandoned the rear of the sledge and came splashing hurriedly up to join him.

"What is it? What're they here for?" she demanded.

"Charlie—and me," he answered, still slogging forward. "I told you they didn't think too much of him. Or me."

Mattie put her hands over her ears.

"I can't think!" she shouted to him above the whistling. "Look at them. Look at him!"

From the grass on each side of the channel otters were making little dashes out at the sledge, then stopping and turning back into the stalks. Their long necks were outstretched and curved. Their lips were wrinkled back to expose their teeth, and they clashed them together, whistling and hissing at Charlie.

Charlie himself, on top of the gear, was transformed. His neck was also curved and outstretched; his lips were drawn back. He also gnashed his teeth, marching back and forth on the gear of the sledge as he did so, whistling and hissing first at the otters on his left, then at those on his right. As with some of the otters along the grass fronts, a yellowish foam was beginning to cling to his teeth and lips. His eyes were bloodshot, and a sharp, acid-musky odor began to drift forward from him to Cary and Mattie on the following breeze.

Then suddenly, inexplicably, he stopped pacing and whistling and sat down on the gear. His jaws closed; his lips covered his teeth once more. He sat, staring back at the other otters, unmoving and silent.

Gradually, the whistling of the otters dwindled in numbers and volume. Their dashes at the sledge became less frequent and ceased. As the channel began to widen out, they gradually began to fall behind until the sledge was moving steadily away from them; and they sat silent in the water behind it.

Charlie lifted his head on its long neck and sent a long, fluting whistle back at them. They moved about in the water uneasily, but none of them answered.

After a while, Charlie repeated his whistle. Again there was movement among the dwindling figures behind him, but no answer.

Once more he signaled before the other otters were lost to sight in the glare of the westering sun on the water behind the sledge; and this last time as well no answer came back.

They trudged on toward the edge of the plateau. Then Charlie slipped off the gear and swam around behind the sledge to put his teeth in the ropes and push.

They moved on. The sun was just touching its lower edge to the western horizon of the plateau land when they tugged the sledge finally up onto dry earth again. It was not the black earth of the swamp but iron-rust-colored soil, studded with gravel and small boulders. Two hundred meters beyond them the ground disappeared where it sloped steeply away to the rock edge of the plateau cliffs.

"Start setting up camp, will you, Mattie?" Cary asked. "I'll go take a sight down the cliff while there's still some light to see by."

He went on across the two hundred meters of rock-strewn ground until his boots scuffed on bare rock, and he looked down at the steep slope leading to the cliff edge. Turning sideways, step by step, he went carefully down that slope in the dim light to where a wall of rock dropped off. He looked over.

It was hard to see in the gathering dusk, but the cliff proper fell away in a series of vertical drops to various shelves and pockets, in what amounted to perhaps a sixty-degree slope overall. His eye picked out a series of such shelves below him on which it would be possible to start lowering the statue. But less than fifty meters below him, all details were lost in the gathering darkness.

"Have to check it again tomorrow morn," he said to himself. "Don't want to get stuck on some ledge with no way out but back up."

He returned to the shore of the swamp. Mattie already had most of the camp gear off the sledge and the wick-stove going. Cary himself built a fire; and as the new flames licked upwards, brightening their immediate vicinity but throwing the rest of the landscape into further darkness, he sat back, squatting on his heels, and looked over at Mattie.

She was moving about the business of cooking with automatic motions like a sleepwalker. He straightened to his feet and walked over to her, taking the spoon she held from her hand.

"My night with the grub," he said. "Lay yourself down a bit until supper's done."

He pushed her gently back to the pile of gear and made her sit there with her back supported by the unrolled sleeping bags. Then he went back to the wick-stove and the dried meat and rice she had already in one of the pots, covered with water, swelling and cooking. When he glanced over at her a few minutes later, he saw her still in a sitting position but deeply asleep.

He stirred the meat and rice mixture and looked across the fire to where Charlie lay, head upright on his long black neck, eyes fixed on Cary himself.

"So," said Cary. He whistled softly, and Charlie whistled back.

"All right then," said Cary. Quietly, so as not to wake Mattie, he began to sing across the fire to the swamp otter. Charlie responded with a series of accompanying low whistles and warbles that was almost like crooning.

The two of them were enclosed in the light of the fire, together, the otter with his head high upright and whistling, the man squatting on his heels by the low stove and singing. . . .

"Bonnie Charlie's noo awa'
Safely o'er the friendly main.
Mony a heart will break in twa,
Gin he n'er comes back again. . . ."

5.

The next day dawned with a gray overcast that extended solidly from one horizon to the other, torn only occasionally by the wind to show a ragged patch of the dark blue above. Sporadic bursts of sunlight from such rents found the camp from time to time.

As soon as the light was good enough to make out details, as far as the eye could ordinarily see in daylight, Cary was once more on top of the cliffs proper, sighting out a route downward from ledge to ledge toward the seamed and rugged country at the foot of the cliffs. This time Mattie and Charlie were with him.

"See there, Mattie," said Cary, pointing down the cliff face. "What we want is a route down with easy drops or slopes from ledge to ledge. Not more than eight-ten meters between ledges, for easy handling."

"Well, there's lots of that," said Mattie, gazing downward. "It doesn't look too hard."

"No, doesn't look hard," said Cary. "Harder'n it looks though—you'll see when we get down a ways. Also, there's two things to watch for. We don't want to get trapped with no ledge close enough below to reach, because coming back up's not easy and with what we got to move, maybe not possible. Also, we want to come out at the bottom by that river down yonder."

He pointed toward what looked, from this height, like a glinting thread, below and off to their right. The thread began in a patch-sized pool at the foot of the cliff, a pool fed by a waterfall that sprang directly from the rock of the cliff face, about a third of the way up from its base.

"The river?" said Mattie. "Why?"

"From here on we got to carry or float that statue," said Cary. "There's variform oak and scrub woods down there such as make a raft that'll float." He looked up at the sky, frowning. "Just hope the weather holds. Rain going down's not good. Slick rock's bad rock to travel. Come on."

He turned and led the way back to the camp. While Mattie had slept the night before, after rousing briefly to eat dinner, Cary had been at work upon the statue and the sledge. He had cut the sledge runners with an ax into rough boards. Then he had bundled the statue in the grass mats and lashed a fence of boards about it on top of the mats, so that the boards would act as fenders on the statue's descent down the cliff face.

With the boards around it now, the statue made a roughly cylindrical bundle that could be rolled along the ground, somewhat clumsily. Using the two axes they had along as pry bars, Cary and Mattie together rolled the statue with only minor difficulty up the slope to the high point from which it fell off sharply to the cliff face. Then, tying an anchor rope around one of the large boulders embedded in the earth at the crown of the slope, Cary assembled sheaves and blocks of the block-and-tackle units among their gear. With these stayed to the anchor line and with Charlie and Mattie, each at an end of the bundle to keep it from sluing around, end on, to the cliff edge below, they cautiously let gravity roll the tethered statue down to the edge.

A half-meter short of the cliff edge, Cary stopped the statue. Leaving it anchored there, he went back for the rest of their gear.

When this was all piled at the cliff edge also, Mattie put on a climbing belt. With another rope snapped to the belt ring, she let herself be lowered by Cary—leaning back and fending herself off from the cliff with her feet as she went down—to the fairly wide ledge of rock six meters below. She unsnapped herself from the line and used it as a guide rope to hold the gear away from the cliff as Cary sent it down on a partnered line, load by load.

When the gear was down, Cary strapped a climbing belt around Charlie's waist, whistling softly and reassuringly to the swamp otter as he worked. Charlie made no audible answer, but the smooth black velvet of his furred throat throbbed with unvoiced whistles; and when Cary first swung him off his webbed feet into the air above the cliff edge, the otter's body and limbs were rigid.

He made no attempt to fend himself off from the cliff on the way down. But Mattie held him clear with the guide rope, as she had protected the loads of gear being sent down. Once on the ledge below, and free of the belt, Charlie burst into a chorus of whistles directed up at Cary.

Cary whistled back shortly and sharply. Charlie's whistling ceased.

"All right, Mattie," Cary called down to her. "Charlie'll help you. Keep that guideline tight so's it doesn't bang the rock."

He anchored the statue by two new lines running from each end of it to the boulder on the crest of the rise behind

him. Then, handling the block-and-tackle line himself, he
let the bundled statue roll slowly off the edge of the cliff.

"Hold clear, Mattie!" he shouted to her, invisible on the
ledge below. He leaned back hard against the block-and-
tackle line, letting the statue lower and pause, lower and
pause, as he checked it against the end anchor lines and
took a fresh grip on the block-and-tackle rope.

After what seemed like a long time, there was a call
from Mattie below.

"Almost down! Easy. . . ."

The weight on the block and tackle suddenly ceased, and
the line went slack in his hands. Cary straightened up,
wiped his forehead with the thumb edge of his hand, and
glanced at the sky. It looked hardly changed, but the rents
were fewer and farther apart in its cloud cover now.

"Be right down with the ropes and tackle!" he shouted to
Mattie. "Make one big bundle of the gear. From now on
we got to move some faster."

When he had untied his anchor lines, gathered his block
and tackle, and rappelled himself down to join the others,
Cary found Mattie had bundled the gear as he had said.

"Fair wrapped," he said, approvingly, looking at the
bundle. He stepped over to the rim of the ledge and looked
at the one below. "About half again as far down, this time.
Hook up, Mattie, and I'll start you down."

This second drop went faster: first because the gear went
down in a single bundle, secondly because both Mattie and
Charlie now knew what they were to do. On the drops that
followed as the day brightened toward noon, they became
more practiced. By the time the sun, visible only as a bright
area among the clouds, was in its noon position overhead,
they had covered more than half the distance to the foot of
the cliff. They sat down to a quick, cold meal, the rock

slope down which they had come since morning leaning back awesomely above them.

"Pretty good," said Mattie, looking over the rim of the ledge on which they sat. "Looks like the drops are all longer from here. I can see . . . twelve, thirteen . . . fourteen or fifteen more, that's all. Then we'll be able to roll it down that slope at the foot of the edge of that pond where the river starts."

"Sure," said Cary. "But it's going to rain."

She looked up at the now unbroken overcast of the sky.

"You can't be sure," she said. "Clouds are a little darker, that's all."

"Going to rain," said Cary, with finality. He finished eating, peeled off the surface film of his layered plate, and threw the film aside. He put the plate back into the food pack, clean side in.

Mattie gulped the last few bites of bread and dried meat and followed his example. Ten minutes later they were lowering the statue to the ledge below.

But as they went for the ledge below that, there was a cold touch upon the side of Cary's cheek, through his three-day stubble of beard. He said nothing; but when the statue was down safely on the lower ledge, he loosed his anchor lines quickly and rappelled down to join Mattie and Charlie as swiftly as he could.

"Get set to camp," he told Mattie, as his feet touched the barely sloping rock on the ledge.

"Camp?" She stared at him, then held out her hand, palm up. "Just because of a few sprinkles?"

"There'll be more," said Cary. "That rock you're standing on gets mighty slippery, just like it was oiled, after it gets wet enough."

She confronted him.

"But even then," she said, "it's a long way from being wet. We could get down two or three more ledges before a little water like this gets them wet enough to bother. And maybe by that time the rain will have quit."

"Not going to quit," said Cary. "Anyway, look down. Next three, four ledges all got a good slope to their flat—or they're too narrow. No place to camp overnight. Here, the ledge is nice and wide and almost level. Got room for a fire, even."

She opened her mouth.

"No use arguing, Mattie," he said. "You aren't going no place by yourself, without Charlie and me to help you."

She closed her mouth abruptly and turned away to gather up the ropes Cary had let down from the ledge above before coming down himself. Cary turned to search the ledge for small pieces of rock with which to chock the statue bundle against accidentally rolling toward the edge of the drop, three meters away.

As soon as the statue was secure, he set to work to rig a rain shelter flush with the cliff face behind them at one side, so that a patch of the ledge rock would stay dry underfoot. Out beyond the rain shelter he built a fire in the center of the ledge, using pressed fire bricks from among their gear, for the ledge was bare even of moss.

By the time the fire was going well, the first tentative drops of moisture from the cloud-laden sky had become a steady drizzle. This continued steadily throughout the afternoon while they sat idle under the shelter. Charlie lay without moving, his long neck lowered, his head on his right forepaw, staring out and down through the rain at the country below. Cary sat leaning back against some of the piled gear, his eyes closed, half-dozing. From time to time he was roused by the restless sounds of Mattie.

"Might as well settle back, Mattie," he said after a while. "There'll be plenty to do when the time comes for doing."

"At least," her voice came back, sharply, "we could have a breeze around here. There isn't a breath of air stirring."

Cary opened his eyes to see what was disturbing her before he realized it was Charlie's smell. He himself had gotten so used to it that he took it for granted. It was not the acid-musky odor that had come from Charlie earlier when the other swamp otters had roused his anger. This was a fainter, generally fishy stink that was mainly from Charlie's breath. It was not normally too noticeable in the open air; but here under the rain shelter, at close quarters with no air moving, there was no way not to notice it.

"No way Charlie can help it, smelling the way he does," said Cary. "Want to change places with me, Mattie—"

He broke off, catching sight of a silver speck in the far sky below the heavy-bellied clouds, moving steadily to the east.

"What good would that—" Mattie broke off her answer. Glancing over, he saw she had followed his direction of sight and was also watching the silver speck.

"Surveyor craft," she said. "The mortgage people must have it out here mapping."

They watched it out of sight, until it vanished into the overhanging cloud layer itself.

"Cary," said Mattie. He turned and saw her watching him. "Cary, what're you going to do after the new mortgage's voted in?"

He shrugged.

"They'll not be changing times this far upcountry, anyhow," he said. "Not for a while, yet."

"In just a few years. It's all going to be developed, all this—" She gestured at the plateau above and the cliff and the country below. "There'll be roads and cities up here."

"Maybe," said Cary softly. He looked into the fire, burning brightly in spite of the drizzle of drops falling into it. "Be a real fight first, anyway."

"A fight?" Mattie's words pounced on his. "Why a fight? Who'll be fighting?"

"Upcountry people." He looked from the fire to her and found her face tense. "They got guns. They'll fight." He picked up one of the axes and with the metal head prodded the burning brick pieces in the fire together, so that the flame leaped up even more brilliantly. "Won't have no choice, city people and those mortgage misters wanting to change the world all around."

"Violence?" said Mattie. "Violence won't work. If the woodies don't want progress, the only way they can stop it is to turn out down at the city and vote against it. But why should they want to stop progress, anyway? It means a better world for them too."

He shook his head.

"No," he said. "Us people upcountry can't change. Got to die—like the land got to die. Like Arcadia's going to sicken and die from this progress of yours if it comes."

"Die? What're you talking about—die?" The tone of her voice roused Charlie from his gazing and the black head raised on the long neck to look at her. "This world's going to be improved with the mortgage money—not killed."

Cary closed his eyes and relaxed back against the gear.

"Mattie," he said, "don't you ever get tired of arguing?"

"I'm not arguing!" he heard her beyond his closed eyelids. "I'm just trying to talk a little sense, and all I get from you is—there's going to be a fight, the upcountry people're going to die, the land's going to die. You can't kill land."

"Mattie," he answered softly, speaking into the darkness

of his eyelids, "now you know what it is you're doing. You know what I'm talking about; but you want me to say it isn't so, so's you can feel better about it. But what good's my saying, when things're going to happen just the same?"

"I tell you, you can't kill a world! A world's not like a man—or an animal!"

"Sure you can kill a world, Mattie," he said. "All you got to do is level so many mountains, change so many rivers, bring in too many variform trees and such to choke out the native-born stuff like the briar and the thorn bush. All you got to do is plow enough fields, fly enough boats, build enough cities—and you've killed it dead."

"You!" Her voice raged at him. "You talk as if we started here, on Arcadia! It isn't a hundred years since the first people came here to settle. You talk as if we belonged here!"

"Don't take a man more'n a lifetime to belong in the place where he's born," said Cary.

"All right—but then I belong here too! The city people belong just as much on Arcadia as you upcountry woodies."

Eyes still closed, Cary rolled his head from side to side against the gear supporting it from behind.

"Guess you don't though, Mattie," he said. "City people don't belong anywhere—except in any city, on any world, because they're all the same, one city just like another, here on Arcadia. And no reason to think they're different on any other world. Move your city people to some other city, some other planet; it makes no difference."

"That's not true!"

He did not answer. After a while with some sniffs and snorts and some small rustlings around, she also was silent.

When night fell, the fire made its usual curtain of darkness around them, so that they seemed not so much perched on a ledge as enclosed in a roofless room walled in rock and black air. They ate a hot meal this time.

"What about Charlie?" Mattie asked.

Cary glanced at the swamp otter, who lay still, head down, watching them.

"Anywhere there's running water," Cary said, "there's shellfish and waterplant roots like up in the swamp there. And we're going to be following running water, most of the ways. When we're where there's food for him, he'll be able to eat. Otherwise, he's going to have to do without. Can't eat our food."

Sunrise the next morning showed a dark blue sky streaked with high, filmy cirro-stratus clouds. The rock of their ledge was dry outside the rain shelter, and the air was dry and cool.

"Three days of good weather coming anyhow," said Cary, squinting under his palm at the bright sky. "Make the most of it."

They ate a quick breakfast and started the rest of their descent toward the foot of the cliff. Shortly before noon they let the statue bundle down at last on the pebbled slope falling away toward the edge of the waterfall pool. Charlie stayed with Cary and Mattie, impatiently waiting while they rolled the statue down to the edge of the pool. The moment it came to rest by some water grass like that in the plateau swamp, but much taller and thicker-stemmed, the otter plunged into the pool and disappeared.

"He won't go far," said Cary, looking after the otter. "Guess he got pretty dry coming down all that rock. I'll start cutting float logs for the raft. Mattie, you better throw up a camp though. Don't suppose we'll be ready to move on before morn."

He took an ax and strode off through the water grass. A few minutes later Mattie, already busy untying the camping equipment from the gear bundle, heard the distant, steady sound of chopping.

By midafternoon, Cary had cut, rough-trimmed, and dragged to the poolside campsite enough variform oak logs some six to eight inches in diameter to make a raft about three by nine meters in area. He proceeded to tie these logs together with the thin, but extremely strong monomolecular wire he had brought along in the gear. He double-tied each log to the next at both ends, and then laced in and out among the logs and each end with one long strand, which he tightened before tying with a cinch-lever.

Under the pull of the cinch-lever, the fine wire bit into the wood of the logs until it was nearly invisible.

"Look at Charlie," said Mattie.

Cary looked up from completing his last wire tie. Charlie had reappeared at the campsite some time since and had been busy bringing shellfish out of the pool in his mouth. These were bivalves, almost clam-like except for the fact that they were thick enough in the middle to be almost round. Cary had noticed this out of the corner of his eye; but now Mattie's words directed his attention to the fact that, seated in the shallow water at the pool's edge, Charlie was using his forepaws to carefully pat bottom mud from a pile before him around each bivalve, then putting the resultant mudball aside on the shore.

"Charlie, that's not going to work," Cary said. He got to his feet.

Charlie looked up at the sound of his name and watched as Cary came toward him. Cary squatted down beside the otter and whistled intricately, patting the nearest mudball with his hand, pointing to the cliff down which they had just come and out over the surface of the pond.

"What won't work?" It was Mattie, who had come up behind the man.

Cary got to his feet.

"It's the way they store food for the winter, up in the swamp," Cary said. "He thinks he's going to store food that way for the rest of the trip, in case we're someplace like last night where there's no running water. I can't make him understand."

"Understand what?"

"Up on the plateau, when they do it, it's already turning to cold," Cary said. "The mudballs don't only dry, they freeze. But down here they aren't going to freeze. Those shellfish'll spoil in two days inside mud. But I can't get the notion rightly into him. Well. . . ." Cary turned back toward the raft. "He'll just have to find out for himself."

Left with his shellfish and mudballs, Charlie nosed among them and even picked up some of the mudballs in his raccoon-like paws to handle them puzzledly. Then he abandoned them and went off into the swamp grass. Cary could hear the otter rustling about invisibly in there.

"Now," said Cary to Mattie, recoiling what was left of his monomolecular wire, "we'll lever this into the water to see how she floats—"

A sudden, blindingly bright thread of brilliance reached down from the sky above them into the swamp grass briefly, then disappeared. Charlie whistled piercingly and they heard him thrashing around. Then no more sound, as an amplified voice boomed above them:

"Look out, down there! There's an animal as big as a bear in that swamp grass right beside you. I got it before it could spring, but maybe it's still alive. Careful! Don't move —I'll be right down and finish it off!"

6.

Suddenly, many things were happening at once. Cary headed toward the place in the grass from which Charlie's whistle had come. As he went, the fat, teardrop shape of a one-man surveyor craft dropped to earth by the new-made raft, its brilliant white paint and green lettering looking garish against the muted dark tones of the land and vegetation. A slightly overweight, black-haired man in white shirt and blue shorts stepped out.

"Hey!" he called, as Cary brushed by him. "Don't go in there. Maybe it's not dead yet—"

"Better not be dead," said Cary, plunging into the grass. He found Charlie, lying on his side in a little nest of crushed grass. The fur high on one shoulder was still smoking. Charlie lay still, eyes wide open and staring, but when Cary put one hand under a foreleg, the throb of a beating heart pulsed lightly through the rib cage under his palm.

Gently, he picked up the limp, black body and carried it back out to the pile of gear. He laid Charlie down by the gear and jerked a medical kit from the pile. A thick shadow fell across him, and across Charlie.

"What's the matter with you?" The voice of the man from the surveyor craft hammered at him. "I just saved your life,

65

that's all, and here you go monkeying with that beast as if
—" The voice tone changed as if the man were speaking
off in a new direction. "What's the matter with him, anyway? It's big as a wolf. Look at those teeth. What's he
doing?"

Cary was running a small pair of power surgical clippers
over the burned area to get rid of the hair.

"It's all right, Mattie," he said, putting the clippers aside.
"Far as the burn goes, anyway. Just slid along his side. But
the shock's got him. If he just doesn't go and die from
that—"

"What're you people doing up here, anyway? You don't
act very grateful, either of you. What is it, some sort of pet?
How was I to know? You there—" the voice was aimed
back at Cary again, where he knelt over Charlie. "You
know that's one of the native wild species? I've got every
right to shoot it. I said, *you*! Stand up and answer me when
I talk to you. I'm an interplanetary Senior Survey Officer in
the firm of Eheu and Killey—that's a multiworld outfit,
woodsman! I'd like to know what you're doing here and
what you're doing protecting a wild predator. I think you
better show me your identification—"

Still holding a surgical knife in his hand, Cary got to his
feet and turned as swiftly as the sun blinks behind a fast-
moving cloud. But the Survey Officer was four paces from
him, and Mattie was only a step from the man. Before Cary
could cover the distance, Mattie was between them, her
back to Cary, facing the surveyor.

"*Show you his identification?*" she exploded. "Let's see
your identification, looper! I mean that! Think you've got a
couple of ignorant woodies here you can bully around, do
you? Let me tell you something—I'm Matilda Mary Or-

valo, Orvalo Outfitters of Arcadia City. A citywoman, a native, and a taxpayer. Show me *your* papers!"

"Now look—" the surveyor stared at her, stiff-faced, jaw out-thrust. "I'm a Survey Officer—"

"You!" The word seemed to curdle in Mattie's mouth. "You're a tinker-toy! You're a hired hand for a couple of mortgage contractors who're guests on this world. Guests! And you're not even that. Show *you* his identification? The man you're talking to was born here. He's a citizen, looper. You're nothing! Where's your passport—where's your permit to take native game? Who gave you permission to carry an energy weapon?"

"Nobody said—" the surveyor chewed air furiously.

"That's tough!" said Mattie. "You know why, looper? Because that man here and me, we don't need papers. We were born here. But *you* do. You need a license to breathe —because it's not your air. It's *ours*—understand that? It's *our* air, *our* land, *our* animals, wild or tame. Those two bosses of yours—Eheu and Killey, men so far up in their company they probably never laid eyes on someone like you—they know that, even if you don't. They aren't going to be too happy with an employee who's gone around killing native animals and threatening native citizens, just a couple of weeks before those citizens are due to vote on a five-billion-unit planetary mortgage offered by Eheu and Killey. So you get back in that craft and get your passport and your alien work permit and show them to me, unless you want to leave your flitter here and go back to Arcadia City overland with us in a citizen's arrest!"

Slab-cheeked, pale, and a little wild-eyed, the surveyor backed from her, stumbling, until he came up against the side of his craft.

Without turning, he reached back in through the open doorway, fumbling around.

"And one more thing—" said Mattie. The surveyor froze with his arm in the doorway. She pointed at Cary. "You see that man? You see that short gun at his hip? Well, he can blow your head off with that before you could even get that energy rifle of yours out of that craft. So don't try anything!"

"I wasn't—I wasn't going to—"

"Get those papers, then. Get on with it!"

The surveyor turned about and rummaged hastily inside the doorway. There were the sounds of small objects falling to the metal floor of the craft; then he turned back, holding a small gray booklet and a yellow folder. He brought them to Mattie.

She took them, opened each, and read them through silently and deliberately. Then she handed them back to him.

"Now get out!" she said. "This time we're letting you get away with it. But just keep it in mind from now on. You wanted to know what we're doing here?" She pointed at the wrapped bundle that was the statue. "It just happens we're bringing a very important work of art down to Arcadia City. A statue that's got to be there by the day of the voting —a statue so valuable we wouldn't risk an airboat crashing with it, so we're bringing it down overland. And we're the two *you* wanted to check up on! Go on—get going!"

Carrying passport and permit, he turned back to his craft. As he began to climb in through its doorway, the sound of Mattie's voice brought him to an abrupt halt once more, his back to them.

"And just remember this!" snapped Mattie. "Think of the kind of trouble I could make for you if I went to Eheu and Killey—to the very men themselves—and told them how you tried to interfere with our bringing that statue in, and the kind of reaction the voters of Arcadia might have if they heard about it!"

She stopped. He stood there for a second or more, his back to them, waiting, then plunged on inside his craft.

The door slammed behind him and the craft jerked up into the air.

"Well, Mattie!" said Cary, looking admiringly at her.

She snorted, evidently still too wound up for compliments.

Suddenly above them the amplified voice blatted down, and looking up, they saw the survey craft hovering some two hundred meters overhead.

"YOU THINK YOU CAN MAKE TROUBLE FOR ME?" it roared, in the surveyor's voice. "WAIT'LL YOU SEE WHAT TROUBLE I CAN MAKE FOR YOU. A FIRM LIKE EHEU AND KILLEY DOESN'T LIKE HICK NATIVES GETTING IN THEIR WAY. YOU WAIT AND SEE!"

Abruptly, the craft went into motion, scooting away into the southwest, in the direction of the coast and Arcadia City, lifting in altitude as it went. Mattie looked after it, the fierceness of her expression slowly changing to a frown.

"I talk too much," she muttered, after a second.

"Wouldn't say that," Cary grinned at her. Her frown remained, though, and he stepped over to touch her lightly and briefly on the shoulder, so that she turned her head from the sky to look at him. "Nothing to worry about. Mister like that's going around asking to be hung all the time. Sooner or later someone's going to take him up on it."

Mattie nodded slowly and relaxed. She even smiled at him, a little.

"I suppose you're right," she said. Her head came up

suddenly and she turned about. "How's Charlie—"

"Leave him be," said Cary, catching her arm as she
started toward the otter. Charlie still lay, eyes wide open
but unseeing, motionless on his side on the ground where
Cary had put him down. A lattice bandage covered the
long rectangular area of the shoulder wound from the energy rifle. "It's not the burn. It's shock. Nothing we can do
for him now but let him come out of it or not. Up to him."

"Up to him? *Shock?*" She turned on Cary.

"Not regular shock—don't know what else to call it
though," Cary said. "His people go that way when thii gs
get too much for them. You know how it's been—him getting hooted out of the swamp by his own relatives, then
coming down that mountain. Now, out of nowhere, he gets
shot like that, with no way to see it coming, no way to
dodge, no way of knowing what it was for. So, he's gone
like this. He'll come out of it or he'll die, one of the two.
But nothing we can do about it."

Mattie stared at the unmoving black form.

"How do you know he'll come out of it?" she asked, in a
surprisingly hushed voice.

"Seen his people like this before. Seen him this way once
before, too, after he saved my life. I told you that."

Mattie turned to look up at him.

"No, you didn't," she said. "You never said anything
about his being like this."

"Didn't I? Maybe not, then," said Cary. "I told you how
come he saved me? How I was sick with blood poisoning
but running my trapline anyway?"

She nodded.

"And I caught an otter in one of my traps—dead she
was by that time," Cary said. "And the whole tribe

swarmed me when I folded up, trying to get the body out of the trap. It was Charlie's mate."

"You told me that," Mattie said. "You said the others wanted to kill you, but he made them keep you alive so that he could try to find out why you wanted to kill them, so maybe they could stop the killing."

"Sure," said Cary. "It was after the others promised not to kill me, he passed out like this." He shook his head slowly, remembering. "You know, Mattie, for a long time I thought it was his mate being killed that made him fold up, but he held off long enough to save my life first. But that wasn't right. I got to know his people some better, then I understood."

"It wasn't his mate?"

"Oh, sure it was that too," said Cary. "But what I mean is, that was just part of it. Truth is, they don't have any real control over passing out like this. Part of what did it to him then was losing his mate—they only match up once a life-time, you know—but the other part was me. You saw how the others don't have much use for him. The only reason they gave in to him about me was because it was his mate I'd killed. So, all of a sudden there he was, not only with his mate dead, but with a sick, two-legged trapper to care for and all the responsibility to the rest of the tribe for keeping me alive."

Cary laughed suddenly, one of his rare, soundless laughs.

"You know—it was me, sick as I was, who tried to take care of him? Instead of him, me? Until he came to; and I really folded up, of course."

"Did you really know he'd saved your life then?" Mattie asked. She was looking at him penetratingly.

"Why sure," said Cary. "Maybe I couldn't whistle-talk

with them then—I can't really now, for that matter. But I was pretty well conscious through the whole thing. When a gang of black demons with teeth as long as your middle finger start dancing all around you and taking nips, and another black demon jumps up on your chest and whistles at the rest until they all back off, after a big hullabaloo—you get the idea. True. Fact is, when I first passed out and came to for a bit to see him lying there like he is now, I thought his people'd come back and killed him for backing me up."

"You keep saying you can't hardly talk to him," Mattie said. "Seems to me you understand him pretty well."

"Well, that's right enough," said Cary. "But it's not so much from talk, or sign language, or anything. You just get to know a person after a while, and you pick up a lot of stuff about him without him having to tell you."

He stopped talking and gazed at Charlie for a moment.

"Nothing to do but wait," he said. "Morn'll bring us the answer, one way or other. Meanwhile, you and I can get that raft floated and loaded right and everything ready for downriver."

They woke next morning to a warm and cloudless day and the white, dead ashes of the campfire. Beyond the fire, where Charlie had lain, the ground was empty. Cary climbed out of his sleeping hammock and saw Mattie, still in hers, her eyes on him.

"Nothing to do with me, if that's what you're thinking," Cary said. "I didn't get up in the night and put him somewheres else. He's come to on his own and gone off a bit, that's all."

In fact, before breakfast was fairly started, the waters of the pool parted to reveal the head of Charlie, carrying in another bivalve shellfish in his mouth. He climbed out of the water with it, sat down by his mudpile, and started covering the mollusk with the mud.

Cary whistled to him.

"Let's look at that shoulder, Charlie," he said

Charlie finished mudballing his shellfish and came up to Cary.

"Good enough," said Cary, examining the wound. He patted the bandage back in place. "No inflammation, hardly. Never tell how a native animal's going to take doctoring. Right; we'll load what's left and travel."

They finished breakfast, got the rest of their gear aboard, including Charlie's mudballed shellfish, and floated the raft, which they had loaded with the statue and dragged into the shallow water at the pool's edge the night before. The raft rode evenly; the statue, still in its wrappings of rope and ax-trimmed boards, lay a little to the rear to counterbalance the weight of the pile of gear up front.

"On our way," said Cary.

They poled across the pond, then had to get off and half-drag, half-push the raft through the shallow water where the pool spilled out to begin the stream. Once past this, the raft floated well again, with Cary and Mattie aboard. Charlie swam alongside for perhaps the first half-mile or so downstream, then climbed aboard and lay in the sun, occasionally examining the bandage on his shoulder with his nose and delicate touchings with his teeth.

"You think there's something wrong with that bandage?" asked Mattie, watching the otter, the tenth or eleventh time he did this.

Cary shook his head.

"Just itching him probably," Cary said. "I'll look at it again at noon, or after."

By noon, the character of the mountain stream they were following had changed markedly. From a slow, meandering thread of water in spots hardly deep enough to float a raft, it had increased in average depth to nearly a meter and had widened to perhaps thirty meters. It was now taking a more direct route down the slope of the mountainside. The current was fast and the water mounded up as it passed over submerged boulders, or broke into swollen collars of foam and turbulence around large, half-submerged boulders.

Mattie stood at the back, holding a steering oar made of two ax-trimmed boards wired to a long pole fastened between a pair of upright pegs in the end of the center log. Cary rode up front with his pole to fend them off from the black, gray, and darkly reddish-brown boulders rearing like granite trolls out of the swiftly swirling water. Charlie, although he seemed tempted to get into the water less than a meter from him, lay on the deck by the statue, nosing its boards and ropes from time to time.

The river widened further and increased its pace. The roar of its waters was like a wall around them now, and the spray thrown up from the water-assaulted boulders at times hid the clumps of briar and variform oak on the rocky shores. A faint sound began to worry Cary, demanding his attention, and after a second, he realized it was Mattie shouting to him from the back end of the raft.

He turned his head.

"What?" he called.

"Can't we slow down a bit?" her voice came to him, thin and thready amid the steady water sounds, which did not seem that loud, but which muted everything else. "I can hardly steer it!"

He frowned and shook his head at her.

"River's higher'n I figured!" he shouted back. "Water get's

even faster the next three klicks or so. Tie yourself to something, so you don't slip off—and stick with that oar!"

She nodded, saving her breath apparently; and he turned back to his poling. Just in time, for a reddish boulder the size of ten statues was looming before them, all but dead in the path of the raft.

As he had predicted, the waters increased their speed. The raft was not into real rapids, even now, but it leaped and plunged among the boulders like an ox unbroken to saddle or harness. Once again, Cary got the small, irritating feeling that Mattie was calling to him; but he could not turn around now, with boulders appearing in front of him in every direction. Then the raft's front end was lifted over a drowned boulder from which Cary had not been able to pole them clear. It pitched up at an angle—

And a scream brought Cary whirling about.

Behind him, dwindling in the distance, the statue, half of its boards and matting knocked away, sat in the river, propped half-upright against the boulder. Mattie clung to the statue, and he heard her scream again. Bits of ax-hewn board and matting were strewing themselves along the stream below the statue. The black head of Charlie bobbed in the water by the boulder.

The raft grated on another boulder and lurched sideways. Cary spun back to look ahead of him and got his pole out just in time to fend them off from a square chunk of black rock like a closed door in the way. His eyes ranged ahead. Just a hundred meters farther on the river bent to the right, and the inner side of the curve, behind a fence of riverbed boulders, had a patch of calm and open water touching on an open bank.

Cary reached out with the pole and thrust hard, trying to swing the raft in toward the open patch.

For a moment there was no reaction. Then, caught by a spinning current, the raft began to revolve, end for end. Once more Cary heaved desperately on his pole—and the raft, by now level with the upper rocks of the fence of boulders, tried to go through sideways between two of them. It slammed hard against the lower of the two boulders, and rode at last into the slower, open water.

Cary poled the raft to the bank. The current pushed strongly against it, holding it halfway up the small slope of the level earth beyond.

He snatched up a length of rope that was anchored in a cleat nailed to the center log. He jumped ashore carrying the rope and found a briar tree up on the level ground to tie the raft to. Then, finally, he could take time to look back upriver.

There was nothing to see. Mattie was back up around the bend of the watercourse and out of sight. Cary leaped down to the raft and rummaged through the gear, coming up with ax, rope, light line, and a block and tackle. Ax in hand, and with the other items tied to his belt or hooked onto his clothing, he began to lope back upstream along the bank.

Bushes impeded his passage. Several times he was forced to go down the bank and wade in the shallow water at the river's edge to get by clumps of trees or vines. But finally he saw Mattie up ahead, still clinging to the half-submerged statue in the middle of the tumbling river, with the black otter head of Charlie holding station in the waters just downstream of her.

He reached the shore opposite her, leaned against the trunk of a taup tree for a moment to get his breath, and then tried to call her.

But plainly she could not hear him over the noise of the river. She continued to stare downstream. He whistled, and Charlie's head turned toward the shore. A second later the head was parting the water strongly, swimming toward him. Within a couple of minutes, Charlie hauled himself, dripping, up onto the bank.

Looking out at Mattie again, Cary saw that she, too, was now looking shoreward. Evidently she had watched Charlie's swim to shore. Cary waved to her. She did not let go of the statue in order to wave back; but she nodded her head violently, and he could see her lips moving. But it was impossible to hear whatever she was saying.

Cary made one end of the light line fast to the rope and fitted the rope into the block and tackle. He held out the other end to Charlie, who took it in his mouth. Cary pointed to Mattie, clinging to the statue with the foam-flecked water plucking at her legs.

"Okay, Charlie," Cary said.

The swamp otter turned and went smoothly once more into the river current. He seemed to move almost without effort at right angles to the rushing current, but Cary noted that the black head pointed, not straight across the river, but at an angle upriver as it progressed.

Charlie reached the statue and Mattie grudgingly loosened the grip of her right arm around the carved rock to take the end of the line from Charlie's mouth. With both arms still around the statue, she stared at Cary, ashore. He made pulling motions with his arms, as if hauling in something on a long tether.

Her head went up and down, nodding. She began slowly drawing the light line in to her, letting the pulled-in part trail behind her in the water. The head of the rope to which

Cary had attached the line lifted from the bank and began to curve its way against the current through the water to her.

It reached her at last. She looked at Cary. He made the motions of tying off the rope around the narrow part of the statue that was its waist. She struggled to obey, once los- ing her grip on the statue and sliding halfway down into the water before she climbed back up to finish the job. When she was done, she nodded vigorously to Cary.

Cary anchored the block and tackle to the trunk of a heavy variform oak and used the tackle to pull the rope taut. He locked the sheaves of the block and tackle. Then, holding the now-tight rope stretching between tree and statue, he inched slowly into the river.

For the first third of the distance, he kept his feet under him with the help of the rope. Then he stepped down into a place where the water was waist deep, and his legs went from under him. For a moment, he felt that the current would pull him from the rope in spite of anything he could do. Then fury boiled up in him. He pulled himself back above the rope like a man chinning himself on a bar. Sud- denly he felt assistance, something pushing his legs back and down against the pressure of the water.

It was Charlie, swimming strongly and pressing against Cary's lower body. Cary got his legs on the riverbed once more and went back to working his way out to the statue. After a while he reached it and looked up to see Mattie, wet hair hanging around her face, looking down at him.

"You all right, Mattie?" he shouted.

She nodded.

"Easy, then," he said. "All you got to do is get down into the water behind me and keep hold of the rope with your hands outside my hands. We'll go back together."

She nodded. Her face was as white as if there were no blood left in her; but she let herself down into the water behind him and reached around him with her right arm to take hold of the rope beyond him.

With the river pressing her weight against him, Cary's feet started to leave the bottom again. Pressure from Charlie's black body held them there. All three together, fighting the river as they inched with great effort toward the shore.

When they got into shallow enough water so that Cary and Mattie could hold their feet down by themselves, Charlie abandoned them. He swam into the bank, pulled himself up its small slope onto level ground, and abruptly lay still, neck outstretched.

Minutes later, Cary and Mattie blundered up the bank and also collapsed. Cary lay only a few seconds, however, before rousing himself to move over and inspect Charlie.

"Bandage gone," he said, looking over at Mattie, who lay exhausted on the ground, watching him. "He's wore out too, of course; but that's all. Didn't do himself any real hurt on top of what he had, seems to me."

He got creakily to his feet.

"I'll go see about moving the raft up here," he said, and went off down along the shoreline. However, not a hundred meters from where he had left Mattie and Charlie, his legs began to tremble, and his knees folded up under him like frozen lengths of rope thawed by a campfire.

Kneeling, slumped on the ground, he looked at his legs.

"Well," he said to them, "you could have let me down earlier, and you didn't. I'm beholding to you for that."

7.

There was no hope of getting back on the river that day. Cary had to spend several hours working the raft back up along the shoreline against the current, anchoring it to one tree, and then hauling it by block and tackle up to a new anchor point where it could be tied off and the whole procedure repeated. For the last hour or so, Mattie came and worked with him. But Charlie lay where he had stopped after climbing out of the water, and he had not moved by the time they finally brought the raft up level with the statue and anchored it to the bank under the taut rope curving out to the tooth-carved stone.

There were still a couple of hours of daylight left. Cary fitted a new bandage on Charlie and then set about hauling the statue in to shore. Under the pull of the rope the statue toppled slowly sideways and vanished under the surface of the river. Charlie came to his feet. He ran down the slope, plunged into the water, and headed out to where the rope vanished into the swirling current. But less than a third of the way out he slowed, turned, and swam slowly back to shore. He climbed the bank, his head held low and wagging on his long neck as if he was shaking it to himself over the

situation. He dropped down at full length on the ground
once more, to lie with his throat throbbing with unvoiced
whistles, watching Cary at work.

The statue was more stubborn an object to move than
even the raft. Four times it got caught on boulders underwater on the way to shore; and four times Cary had to
wade out and lever it free, fighting current, pole, and statue
all at once. But just before sunset it was finally dragged to
the river's edge, and Cary levered it aboard the raft,
grounded in the bankside shallows.

It was dark before their meal was over. The food and the
sudden end to the need to keep himself moving and working operated on Cary like the effects of some heavy seda-
tive. He sat propped against a pile of gear, legs stretched
out, eyelids heavy, barely able to keep awake enough to
finish the second cup of strong coffee in his hand.

His body felt limp and useless as an unraveled string.
Clouds had moved in with the sunset. There was no light
overhead and no moon on the river, which roared by unseen except for the small patch of shallows where the raft
with the statue upon it lay touched by illumination from
their campfire. The flickering light and shadow upon the
statue seemed to make it move like a live thing, seemed to
give a living expression to its face. Cary found himself, with
Mattie, sitting and staring at it.

"You know, Cary," Mattie said, soberly, "I almost
drowned for the sake of that thing there, today."

Cary nodded heavily and roused himself to answer.

"Two thousand units's a lot of money, Mattie."

She scowled.

"Yes," she said. "But it's more than just the units—ever
since that surveyor early today. That crim looper! I'd bring

that statue in now just to set it up in the public park of Arcadia City, even if your art dealer wasn't paying a script dollar for it!"

Cary opened his eyes more widely and gazed at her.

"Would you, Mattie?" he said.

"You heard what I said!" she retorted, but there was less heat to her voice than the words signaled. She gazed at the statue for a moment without saying anything. "Charlie was worried too, wasn't he?"

She looked over at Cary.

"It was the statue, really, that made him go into the river and help us, wasn't it—and he wasn't actually up to it. Remember how he tried to swim back out to the statue when we started to drag it ashore and he couldn't make it? But before that, he'd helped you save me. Only, it wasn't so much for me he did it, was it? It was so the statue'd get saved?"

Cary nodded slowly.

"I guess he'd have tried to help anyway, Mattie," he said. "Maybe not so hard though." Cary watched her. "Can't blame him, you know, for thinking a lot of that statue. He's put out a lot for it, first to get it made, and now to get it this far. All he wants is to see it someplace where people'll want to come look at it."

"They will too," said Mattie. She was watching the statue in the dancing firelight again. "You know, I didn't really look it over back up in the swamp when you first showed it to me. All it seemed to me then was a stone with just a few little angles to it that made it look like a standing man with a long gun. The light's a lot worse here, but I can see better. I can almost make out the expression on your face—or the statue's face. Because it's you, all right—only, you know, it's something else too. It's you, but then at the same time it's like every woodie I've ever seen come into Orvalo Outfitters. You know what I mean?"

She turned to him.

Cary shook his head above the coffee cup.

"Looks just like me, to me," he said.

"You aren't looking at it the right way," said Mattie. "There's something big about it that's like you, all right— but it's like something more than you at the same time. There's something about it as if it was still standing with its lower end in the earth—like you couldn't ever take it out of the earth. Like it was protecting the earth. . . . You can't see that?"

Cary lifted his head and squinted at the statue through grainy eyes.

"Looks like me saying I own something, all right," he said, after a moment.

"No! *More* than that." She was frowning at him. "More than you, don't you see . . . ? What do you see in it, anyway? Tell me how it looks to you."

Cary took a deep breath and tried hard to focus on the statue in the shifting firelight.

"Well, it's me—just the way I say," he answered. "That's my old long gun I'm holding ready—the one that got lost in the mudhole, not this one here. I got my heavy leathers on, because it's late fall and you can see how the mud's frozen in clumps, like high on my boots. I got my short gun slung forward where I can get at it, but the flap's still down to keep the sleet off it. Same time, I got no gloves on; and you can see how I'm holding my hands back against my jacket front to help keep my fingers from getting too cold and stiff in the wind. There's the knife in my boot top and a light pack on my back. . . ."

Heat burned his right leg suddenly, and he jerked upright out of a half-doze into which his own voice had tricked him, to discover the cup fallen from his hand and coffee spilled on the leg below. Then he was so exhausted his head spun. Out of the spinning he became aware of the face of Mattie only a few inches in front of him. His vision cleared. She was holding the now empty cup and rubbing his damp leg with a corner of a sleeping bag liner.

"But you see even more than I do. . . ." Her eyes glowed strangely at him. There was an odd expression on her face. "No, don't try to talk about it now. You're out on your feet. Here's your bag—slide into it." Clumsily, he obeyed and found himself horizontal on the ground, the sleeping bag warming around him, the firelight making rapid changes of expression on Mattie's face—framed by her darkly hanging hair—and floating above him.

"Sleep. . . ." she said.

"Maybe. . . ." he began. And suddenly he realized he did not know what he had been going to say. Before he could remember, slumber took him.

He came awake, hardly realizing he was doing so, some time later in the night. He rose and propped himself on one elbow to look about the campsite.

Mattie lay sleeping on her side in her bag on the hammock. The fire was down to little trickling flames and glowing coals. Beyond the fire, Charlie lay, head down but eyes open and bright with reflection from the firelight, silently watching Cary. There was a sleeping bag liner to one side of the swamp otter, which looked as if it had been covering him but had been pulled off or shrugged aside. Beyond, the unseen river roared unceasingly, open-throated, but seemingly muted now, because of the familiarity of its voice.

Cary slid out of the bag and got quietly to his feet. As

Charlie's eyes watched him, he stepped over to add fresh wood chunks to the fire.

As the flames licked up on the new fuel, Cary straightened up and stepped further on, to stand by the side of Mattie's hammock, looking down at her face. Her hair had recovered from the straightness of its wetting in the river. It had been brushed back into soft waves and her face was clean. The fingertips of one hand, showing above the edge of the sleeping bag, up by her face, were clean, with no dirt showing under the nails.

Cary turned and held his own hand up to the firelight. It showed darkly there with tan and ingrained soil. The nails were jet black in semicircles under their ends. He ran a hand over his jaw and the wire-stiff bristles of a six-day beard scratched thickly at his palm.

He turned away from Mattie. Charlie's eyes still watched him. Cary went over and squatted by the swamp otter, placing his hand lightly on the black shoulder above the line of white bandage. Under the velvet-soft fur, the shoulder was hot.

Cary got to his feet, went to the gear, and came back with another bandage, which he spread out as he walked until it was like a small, thick blanket about the area of a table napkin. He went on past Charlie down to the edge of the river. He dipped the bandage into the water and held it there until it had been soaked by the cold stream. Then he brought it back and spread it all over the bandaged shoulder.

Charlie lifted his head briefly from the ground to look at it and then laid his head back down again, watching Cary. A small whistle warbled in his throat.

Cary rose and went to the pile of gear again. This time he rummaged out soap, solvent, and a self-sharpening razor. He carried these down and squatted by the water's edge.

Charlie whistled softly behind him.

Cary got to his feet, leaving on the bank the things he had brought, and went back to the otter. Carefully, he picked up Charlie and carried him to the raft, laying him down on its inner edge. Charlie whistled again. Reaching back with his supple neck, he took the wet, unfolded bandage in his teeth, dipped it in the running water between raft and shore, then laid it back up on his shoulder.

"Should've thought of it earlier," Cary said to him, squatting once more by the river edge.

Cary dampened his face with the cold water, dipped one end of the soap in the stream, held it there for a second, and then scrubbed the softened end of the soap into his beard. When it was thickly coated, he took the razor and began to shave while Charlie watched, occasionally giving little whistles like soft questions. Cary did not answer.

When the beard was gone, Cary stripped off his jacket and shirt and began to wash his arms and upper body. He soaped and rubbed his clothes in the running water, with the firelight flickering redly upon him, the river roaring by invisibly, and Charlie watching.

In the morning he was up before Mattie, wearing clothes not yet quite dry that steamed before the fire as he fixed breakfast over the wick-stove. He looked up from this after a bit to see Mattie awake in her hammock, staring hard at him.

"Morn," he said.

"Morning," she answered. She looked at him for a moment longer. Her face changed as if she was about to say something—then changed again. She got out of the hammock without a word and went past him into the bushes, saying over her shoulder, "Breakfast ready? Good. I'll be there in a minute."

Later on, with the food eaten, and as they were finishing their coffee, she spoke to him in a lowered voice.

"Charlie's worse, isn't he?"

"Feverish-like all around that place he was shot," Cary answered. "Don't know how bad that means it's getting. Maybe it's just natural, his heating up like that."

"Don't you know?" she asked. "You must've seen his people when they were hurt, before this."

"Hurt, sure," he said. "Cuts, bites, scrapes, feet frozen —even bullets in them. Never seen one burned, though. Nothing up there on the plateau to burn any of them, 'less he walked into a fire, and he'd know better'n that. He feels better with a wet bandage on it, so I fixed him up."

She nodded slowly.

"He better not move around any, though," she said. "Nothing that's sick or hurt gets better unless it can rest. He won't have to leave the raft today, will he?"

"Guess he will," said Cary. "Not more than an hour downstream we come to Apfur's stock station. Mister there named Aige Apfur's got a store and some harness-broke cattle. We'll need to leave the raft there, hire a couple oxen, and then travois cross-plains to the Strike River. Strike River runs all the way down to the farmlands by Arcadia City. This stream don't."

"What's travois?"

"Travois—that's what they call a drag cart. You'll see." Cary got to his feet. "Not as easy riding as the raft, but it'll carry Charlie and the statue overland to the Strike. We'd best start packing."

The sun was barely into the upper branches of the oaks along the river when the stream broadened out and became tranquil. Just around a further bend they came upon a clearing with a large log building with a porch under a vine roof sitting well back from the river. Alongside the building was a pole corral holding a number of variform cattle— short-bodied, deeper-chested and more nimble-legged than the domestic Earth-native strain from which they had been derived.

There seemed no one in sight when they came around the bend, though a curl of gray smoke was coming out a stone chimney at one end of the building. But by the time Cary had poled the raft into the bank below the building there were five men coming down to meet them.

The one in the lead wore bush pants and a heavy up-country shirt under a leather jacket, a city-processed one with a slick exterior. He was a short, broad, brown-faced man with very white teeth. The other four were pale-skinned men, dressed in white dirt-resistant static shirts and blue shorts with the EK symbol of the mortgage contractors' firm overlaid in gold on the right leg of each pair of shorts. The faint gold glow of a weather shield surrounded each of them.

"Loopers," muttered Mattie.

Cary did not bother to answer. For the fact that the four were interlopers was written as plainly on them as it had been on the surveyor earlier. Those skins and clothes had never originated on Arcadia. As they stepped ashore from the raft, Cary could see to the right and behind the log building a pair of white plastic igloos, also with the Eheu and Killey symbol in gold on their dome roofs.

"Aige," said Cary, as the brown-faced man in local clothes reached the raft first. He nodded at the man.

"Cary. And I don't know the missus—" began Aige Apfur, turning to Mattie. But Mattie broke in sharply.

"Miss. Matilda Mary Orvalo. Orvalo Outfitters, Arcadia City."

"Orvalo Outfitters?" Aige grinned. "That'll be Dave Orvalo—"

"My father," said Mattie, with a snap. "Dead seven years ago."

"Why—regrets." Aige's grin sobered. "And your mother—"

"Dead three years after that. No need for courtesies, Mister Apfur. I'm Orvalo Outfitters now, and we've got some business to do with you."

She looked unfavorably past him at the four loopers who had by now reached the river bank beside him and were examining the statue and Charlie with some amusement.

"Why, glad to," said Aige. "Used to do business with Dave, once upon a time—"

"And you paid for what you got?" said Mattie.

"Paid?" Aige stared. "Why sure, Miss Orvalo. I always did business cash."

"No offense, Mister Apfur," said Mattie, stepping ashore. "It was a weakness of my father's—doing business with people who didn't pay for what they got. I believe in cash myself, just like you; so we'll have no trouble." She turned to Cary, still on the raft. "What'd you say we'd need from Mister Apfur?"

"Travois," said Cary. "Couple of drawing oxen. Leave you the raft here, Aige, for what it's worth."

"For what it's worth, Mister Apfur," said Mattie. "Even a raft's got worth."

"Why, sure," said Aige. "We'll figure that in, of course.

Cary, there's maybe half a dozen travois, all sizes, around back of the house. Whyn't you pick one out and the oxen you want from the corral and load up. I'll take Miss Orvalo up to the house for a cup of coffee. When you're done, we can come back out, see what you picked, and figure our deal."

"Maybe I'd better stay here," said Mattie, looking sourly at the loopers, who had been muttering and laughing among themselves, and showing a tendency to crowd around the statue and Charlie on the raft. "Unless these gentlemen can be trusted not to touch anything."

"You don't need to worry about us, Orv—Miss Orvalo, is it?" a lean, middle-aged looper with receding hair said to her. "We're just getting a kick out of the whole thing. You must be the people sent old Sam Moroy scooting back to the City as if you'd set his pants on fire. It was you, wasn't it? This the statue?"

"It's the statue we're taking overland down to Arcadia City," said Mattie. "Valuable property."

"Why sure—sure. You know workingmen like us don't know a lot about art. Could have been just any old rock for all we could tell. . . ." The other loopers began to grin. "No, no. Cut that out, Team."

The grins vanished from the faces of the other three.

"You've got to forgive us, Miss Orvalo," said the lean looper. "We all know Sam, and it was the funniest thing we ever heard, the way you told him off, and the way he went sailing down to the City to tell his tale about you. I'm Harby Wiles—Jeth Horogh, Noyal Penz, Mace Droy." The other three nodded to Mattie as they were introduced. "Now, we won't touch a thing. We'll come up to Aige's place there, and have a cup of coffee with you; and you can tell us how it really was when you set fire to old Sam's tail that way."

The four men and Mattie went up the sloping bank to the combination store and house that Aige Apfur owned. They mounted the steps, crossed the narrow porch, and disappeared inside. Left alone, Cary walked up the slope, around the house, and examined a row of travois leaning against the log wall.

These were light, long, odd-looking vehicles made of two bire tree trunks with some of the heavy, curved roots still attached. They were stripped of skin and limbs and joined together at the top end to a harness-bearing yoke for two drawing beasts. From that joining, the two tree trunks spread out at a forty-degree angle, with the polished, tough, curved roots resting curve down on the ground. Extending from near the joined tops almost to the roots, the two trunks were joined by board slats to make a flat bed.

Cary picked out the larger of these, a travois nearly five meters from yoke to roots. Getting between it and the log wall, he lifted its yoke end from the wall, swiveled the travois around on its roots, and laid it down flat to examine it. The slats were firm and well nailed, and the bearing yoke was a single S-shaped pad of steamed wood, padded generously with leather underneath. When Cary stood on the roots of both tree trunks, one at a time to test them, they had good spring in them yet.

There was a harness spike-punch, like a wooden-handled ice pick stuck into the log wall by the end of the row of travois. Cary pulled it loose and used the sharp metal point to probe the leather underside of the yoke. The leather was soft and new and was firmly glued to the wood above it over all its connecting surface.

He left the travois where he had laid it and went down to the pole corral. Taking halters from the top pole of one of the sections, he let himself in and set about the business of first choosing, then capturing the variform oxen he had picked for the trip to the Strike River.

Ten minutes later the pair of oxen he had picked were outside the corral and yoked to the travois. He led the beasts down to the raft, trailing the travois with the up-curved roots bumping and sliding over the ground behind them.

He backed the travois up to the edge of the raft where it was grounded at the river's edge, and whistled Charlie from the statue. While the variform oxen stood patiently, he levered the statue around so that it would be headed end up on the travois, and then he put a rope about its head. Latching a block and tackle to the crown point of the bearing yoke between the two beasts, he slowly drew the statue up onto the slats of the travois, locked the block and tackle, and tied the statue in place.

Charlie, making little whistles in his throat, crept off the raft and up onto the travois, until he lay once more on top of the statue.

Cary loaded the rest of the gear onto the travois and tied it securely in position. Then he stood back. The two oxen bore the weight of the joined top end of the supporting trunks upon their bearing yoke with complacency. Cary nodded to himself, led the oxen up between the house and the hotel, and tethered them to a ground stake there.

Mattie and the men were still inside the log building. Cary went in and found them sitting around the store section at the front—a large, open room piled high with gear and food supplies. Mattie and the men were sitting among the stacked blankets with coffee cups in their hands. The smell of something more than sugar in their coffee perfumed the still air.

"All set," said Cary, briefly to Mattie and Aige. "Want to come outside and look it over?"

"Don't rush there!" called the lean looper named Harby Wiles, from his seat on a counter beside a pile of import equipment, four energy rifles, and other gear that obviously belonged to him and his companions. Wiles reached over to a stand beside the counter on which a coffee maker stood, and filled a cup. "Taste some import coffee, friend. Want it royale?"

"Which, mister?" asked Cary.

"With booze in it—booze," said Wiles, reaching into the pile beside him for a large white flask from which he poured a brown stream into the fresh cup of coffee. He poured generously. Cary was conscious of Mattie's eyes on him, but she said nothing. Cary's woods-sensitive nose caught the same smell of liquor coming from her own coffee cup.

"There you are, friend," said Wiles, passing the cup into Cary's hands. "Coffee and import booze such as you never tasted before. Drink happy." He slid off the counter and headed for the front door. "Excuse me, folks. Be right back."

He went out. Cary tasted the liquor-laced coffee. It did not taste as powerful as he had expected, seeing the amount Wiles had poured into the cup. Cary sipped it carefully. There was a long day of travois ahead. Take it down slow and it wouldn't slow him up as much.

"Poor old Sam," one of the other loopers went on. As Cary remembered, it was the one called Mace something, a short young man with a big-boned face. "Never seen him so peeled off. He was bound and determined to get right back to headquarters at your Arcadia City and start blackening your reputations—"

"That reminds me," Mattie interrupted, turning to Aige, "you wouldn't have a radiophone here I could use to call down to the City?"

"Sorry, miss." Aige shook his head, apologizing with a flash of white teeth. "Parts cost too much. Just an airboat in once a month. It's due in tomorrow though. Want me to send a message?"

Mattie shook her head.

"No. Never mind." She turned back to Mace. "Didn't mean to interrupt. Go on."

"Well," said Mace, "I was just telling you all. Sam was bound to spread a story that'd get you into plenty trouble with E and K—you know, the big boys." He winked. "So, just before he took off, he was asking us all what ought to be done about you two—"

A shrill swamp-otter whistle from outside the building sounded through the log walls as if they had been made of woven swamp grass.

8.

Cary dropped his cup, spun about, and made it to the door in three long strides. He jerked the door open and was through it, running along the porch toward the corner behind which he had left the travois, while the reverberations of that single piercing whistle were still making his ears sing.

He leaped off the porch, turned the corner of the building, and confronted the lean looper, Wiles. Wiles was standing over the statue on the travois, a sledgehammer still held upraised in his hands. His shirt was torn open, and one leg of his shorts was torn and flapping. Charlie lay beside the travois, half on his back, his neck outstretched and his eyes closed, his teeth half-grinning between his lips. His body quivered slightly and occasionally, like the body of a sleeping dog. Dark blood welled slowly from the fur on the right side of his head.

At the sight of Cary, Wiles dropped the sledgehammer and snatched up Cary's own long gun, which lay on top of the gear lashed to the travois.

"Hold it!" said Wiles. His face twisted. "Just hold it. That's right. Unhook that gunbelt around you and let it drop. Now back off four steps."

Slowly, Cary obeyed. The belt with his short gun in its holster thudded to the hard dirt at his feet. He backed.

"That damn beast of yours went for me," said Wiles, grinning a little now. He raised his voice. "Hey, Team! Get the woman out here—oh, there you are."

Cary moved his eyes without moving his head. Mattie came around the building, followed by the three other loopers, all now carrying energy rifles. Aige walked with them. They came back and stopped.

Cary looked down at Charlie, lying bleeding and quivering on the ground, then back up to Wiles.

"You're dead, mister," he said.

Wiles laughed.

"No. *You're* dead, woodie," he said. "That is, unless we decide to be generous and let you go, in about a week from now." He looked over at Mace. "Did you explain things to them, Mace?"

"I'd just got as far as Sam asking us for advice about what to do when the animal whistled," Mace said.

"Well, that's good enough." Wiles turned back to Cary. "That's right, Sam asked us for advice. And we told him— go on in and spread his story about, but we'd handle it up here for him, just to make sure."

He smiled.

"You know what I told Sam about you?" he went on. "I said you aren't the first smart local hick to give a company man trouble. Lots of time the Team has trouble with some native or other on an outback world like this. We're used to it. And we like to handle it ourselves without getting the company moneymen involved. The moneymen like it that way too—"

"What do you think's going to happen with your moneymen when they hear about this?" interrupted Mattie fiercely. "With an election coming up and a mortgage worth billions up for vote—"

"But they aren't going to hear about it," Wiles interrupted in his turn. "That's the line you used on old Sam, wasn't it? But there's a simple answer. E and K might worry about this a bit if they heard of it before the voting. But once the mortgage's voted, they're not going to give two hells. Because by that time they'll have the signatures of enough citizens on the dotted line, and it'll be all over, lady. In fact, once they get the mortgage in their pocket, they'll be just as glad we instilled a little respect in you hicks."

"Only," said Mattie, savagely, "they're going to hear about it before the voting, just as soon as we get to town."

"You aren't getting to town," said Wiles. "We'll just stash you away someplace with one of the Team to guard you until the voting's over. Then, if you've been real nice people all the while, maybe we'll even just turn you loose. Of course, we'll skin your beast here, and crack up this statue thing of yours, just to teach you a little lesson—but that's not all that bad, is it? As long as you come out of it alive?"

Cary looked at Aige, standing behind the men with the rifles by the end of the tall row of travois leaning against the log wall.

"Aige," he said.

"That's right—I was forgetting Aige." Wiles looked over at the store owner. "You've got a stake in this too, Aige, you know. You wouldn't want a couple like these two here getting down to Arcadia and stirring up trouble that might somehow get in the way of this world's new mortgage, would you? I'd imagine a man like you is planning to buy into half a dozen of the subsidiary companies that'll be growing up after the mortgage."

Aige grinned and backed up against the log wall beside the first of the racked travois.

"Well, that's a fact," he said. "I've been saving for years here for a chance to make a little money. Sure, I have."

His grin widened. He leaned his shoulders back against the logs. Wiles looked at him a trifle sourly.

"Sure you have," he said. He stood staring at Aige for a minute, during which the storekeeper grinned even more broadly. "All right, what's the joke? And it'd better be funny. We can tuck three people away as easily as two."

"Well, it *is* funny," said Aige. He pointed. "That's Cary Longan."

Wiles glanced at Cary.

"So that's his name," Wiles said. "All right, what about it?"

"Nothing," said Aige. "Just that Cary's got a reputation for keeping his word. Done business with him some years now; and it's true. He always keeps his word."

"What're you babbling about?" snapped Wiles. "What's his word got to do with it?"

"He just gave it. That's what makes it so funny," said Aige. "Here you are making all these plans for what you're going to do with him and Miss Orvalo, and he already told you you're a dead man. Here you are, making plans like mad, and on his word you been dead for three minutes—"

With a sudden movement, Aige jerked the harness spike-punch loose from the log wall beside him and threw it to Cary, ducking back around the corner of the building. Cary caught the tool in midair, threw it in one direction, and dove in the other, rolling head over heels on the ground until his body covered his dropped gunbelt. He came out of his final roll holding his short gun and firing at the three loopers with the energy rifles.

They were already firing back—to where Cary had been a split second before. A bullet from Cary's short gun hit one of them high in the shoulder, so that he seemed to fling his weapon from him. The other two dropped their guns and backed off, hands up.

"Get their rifles, Aige," called Cary, rising to his feet.

He turned toward Wiles. But Mattie was there before him, kneeling beside the man, who was lying on his back, choking out his life with the needle shaft of the harness spike-punch through his throat. Cary turned away and went to squat beside the dark form of Charlie, now no longer quivering. He felt for a heart beat and found it. With a deep sigh, he sat back on his heels and began to explore with gentle fingers the bloody area on the side of Charlie's head, which was now beginning to swell.

He got up to go to the loaded travois and bring back the medical kit. He cleaned the damaged area of blood and began to dress the wound. A shadow fell across it, and he looked up.

It was Mattie.

"He's dead, Cary," Mattie said.

Cary glanced over at Wiles, who now lay still, the punch still in his throat. Cary nodded, and turned back to his work on Charlie.

"He's dead." It was Mattie's voice again, making him look up. Her face stared down at him from only inches away. "Cary, *it's wrong to kill!*"

He stared at her. Then he spoke to her, meaning to sound no different than ever; but his voice changed somehow in his throat and came out with a tone he had never used to her before.

"Mattie," he said, "get out of my light."

All the color went out of her face. She straightened up

and stepped back from him. He bent his head once more over Charlie and went back to the business of bandaging. After he had finished this, he lifted Charlie gently back onto a bed made of two sleeping bags lashed on top of the statue on the travois. It was as he was doing this that Charlie's eyes opened, and the swamp otter stirred.

"All right?" asked Cary. He whistled at Charlie.

Charlie whistled back, at first weakly, and then more strongly. The notes of his last whistles were demanding.

Cary nodded and got to his feet. He turned and looked, but he was alone with the dead body of Wiles. He walked around the front of the building and in through the door on the porch.

The three remaining loopers were not to be seen, but he found Aige by the counter where they had all been grouped earlier. Aige was standing over Mattie, who sat with a coffee cup held in both hands, hunched over it as if it was the only source of heat in an icy world.

"Cary." Aige acknowledged Cary's presence as he came up. "I locked those three up in a storeroom. Miss Orvalo here's some upset."

"Mattie," said Cary softly to her. "Charlie's all right, he says. He doesn't want to waste time. He wants to get going."

She paid no attention to him. She spoke above the coffee cup in a low voice, not to either of them, to no one.

"It was for money I wanted to bring the statue down to the city," she said. "And now a man's dead. Because I wanted money."

Aige looked at Cary. Cary bent over her.

"Mattie!" he said, more loudly.

She did not move for a second. Then she straightened up

slowly, as if her attention had just been caught. She set the cup carefully aside.

"What is it?" she said.

"We've got to be moving on," Cary said.

"Yes," she said, and looked at Aige. "What do we owe you, Mister Apfur?"

"Hundred and forty script," Aige answered. "You don't have to pay now, though. I can put it on the books and the next time Cary's by—"

"Never wait to collect what's owed you, Mister Apfur." Stiffly, she got to her feet and reached into one of the inside pockets of her jacket, bringing out a fold of script. "A hundred and forty, you said?"

"Be back in a minute," said Aige, ducking around her. "While you're counting out there. . . ."

He went out the door to the porch without finishing his sentence. Mattie carefully counted out a hundred and forty dollars in script and laid them on the counter. She turned toward the door.

"Wait," said Cary.

She stopped and stood waiting without asking why. After a few minutes, Aige came back in and held the door open for them.

"I'll see you off," he said. "I suppose you're heading for the Strike, Cary? Ought to make it by sunset with no trouble. Those are prime oxen. If you don't—it's near a full moon. Couple hours travel after moonrise'll see you on the bank of the Strike for sure—"

"Mister Apfur," Mattie interrupted him as they moved off the porch, out of the shadow of its roof into the sunlight, and turned left. "You'll notify the Arcadia City authorities about this?"

"Guess so," said Aige to her. "Ordinarily, we don't say anything—there's no City law up here anyway. But since these loopers belong to the mortgage company, I'd probably better. I'll hand the other three over to the airboat pilot when he comes in tomorrow, along with a report on the whole thing, explaining how they started it. You don't need to worry about how the story'll be told."

"That wasn't my worry, Mister Apfur," said Mattie.

They turned the corner. The travois was there waiting for them, and Charlie lifted his head from the sleeping bags. The body of Wiles had disappeared.

"Well, good luck," said Aige, as Cary took hold of the halter rope of the off ox and began to lead the pair with the travois behind them up the slope behind the store building. "Just turn those cattle loose when you reach the Strike and they'll find their way back to me here in a day or so."

"Right," said Cary, moving off without looking around. "Thanks for all, Aige."

"Welcome!" Aige called after them. They mounted the slope and went down the other side into rolling landscape of thigh-high grass, ranging in color from light brown through gray to black. There were only a few isolated trees to be seen between them and the now cloudless horizon.

They began their crossing of the plains area, moving along together without talking. As the sun rose toward noon, this silence between them became a part of the day, with its sun, its continual small varying breezes that left the footsteps of their passage in the bending grasstops, and an occasional working snort from one of the oxen. At first Charlie also was silent, riding the travois. But after a while he began to talk to himself in small, musical whistlings. Looking back once, Cary saw the swamp otter stretched out on his sleeping bags with his head near the head of the statue as if he was holding a conversation with the dark, tooth-chiseled stone.

To reach the dark, broad waters of the Strike River, it took them the rest of a day's silent journeying, with the native winged orthopters rising from the sea of grass before them and settling to one side or another with small insect sounds. In fact, the early-rising moon was well above the horizon and the sun had been down better than an hour when they at last halted on the river bank in a grove of oak and bire.

The nearly full moon had made travel possible, but it did not throw enough light for proper raft-building. They made camp and turned in early. Cary was up before the first dawn paleness had begun to appear in the sky. Once again he washed and scraped his beard, while coffee water came to a boil on the wick-stove. In her sleeping bag and hammock Mattie still slept; and Charlie too was asleep. He drank coffee and went off into the tree grove with an ax.

By the time the sun was clear of the horizon, he had the logs cut, pulled to the clearing, and ready to tie. Glancing over at Mattie, he saw her eyes open, watching him; but she was still in her sleeping bag.

By the time he had finished tying the raft together with wire, the day was beginning to warm as the sun beat more directly down on them. Mattie, Cary saw, was up now; but she had still made no move to start breakfast. Cary went over and started it himself. By the time the pressed brick of meat and vegetables had softened in the cooking water and turned into a stew, the biscuits and coffee also were ready. Mattie still had not come over to the stove. Cary filled her plate and carried it to her.

"Thanks," she said in a low voice, not looking up as she took plate and eating tools from him.

He stood over her as she took the plate into her lap— sitting cross-legged on the ground at the foot of her hammock—and began to eat.

"Don't want to rush you, Mattie," he said, "but we've no time to burn. Soon's we eat, we better get loaded and started downriver."

At that, she did raise her head. Her face was drawn and her eyes looked bleakly into his.

"I'm not going anywhere today," she said. "It's a Prayer Day."

He stared at her.

"Prayer Day?"

"Haven't you kept count?" she said. "This is the seventh day since we started; and it was a Prayer Day the day I found you and brought you back to my premises. I couldn't start then because it was a Prayer Day; and I'm not going to go on now, on a Prayer Day."

He shook his head, as if to shake her words into some pattern of common sense.

"Mattie—"

"I'm not going to talk about it," she said.

She set down the plate, got to her feet, and walked over to the pile of gear. She rummaged in her personals bag and came out holding the familiar white volume with the writhing, fire-red letters. Opening it, she sat down and began to read, there by the gear, ignoring her breakfast which still sat beside the hammock. Cary studied her for a long moment and then turned away.

He went back and ate his own breakfast, then methodically set about striking camp. He packed up his own hammock and the rest of the gear except Mattie's hammock, bag, and the still untouched plate of stew. Then he dug some deep stake holes at the river's edge, planted anchor posts in them, and block-and-tackled the raft to the edge of the water.

He levered it into the shallows at the edge of the bank and began loading it. Still, Mattie had not stirred. She sat, still reading.

Charlie looked curiously from her to Cary as Cary went on about loading the statue and the gear aboard the raft. After a while he whistled curiously at Cary.

Cary whistled back shortly and shook his head. Charlie queried him again, but this time Cary only shook his head. Then Charlie turned and made his own way to the raft, lying down on it beside the head of the statue. The sun by now was several hours up from the horizon, and there was nothing left to pack but Mattie's gear.

Cary walked over to her.

"Mattie," he said. "Charlie and I both got a stake in getting that statue into town on time."

She put a finger in her book to mark her place, closed it, and looked up.

"Charlie and you?" she said. "I know what stake you've got in getting it to town. You're looking forward to mixing in with all that hoorah and celebrating when the mortgage is signed, with your pockets full of money to throw around. But don't tell me Charlie knows who that statue's going to, or what it's worth to you and me to get it there by a certain time."

He looked down at her for a long second.

"Charlie may not know who," he said, "but he knows the statue's going someplace where it'll maybe finally be appreciated. And he knows there's some hurry to get it there. As for what it's worth—what it's worth to me is seeing Charlie knowing somebody understands what he's done, before he dies. Comes to the money being that important, you get aboard the raft now and you can have my share. Sure, I like cash when I'm in town, like anyone else; but I don't got to have it or die, like you City people. Out here, money don't do nothing for anyone. Long as I got my gear, my weapons, and some ammunition, there's not a thing more I need in the upcountry."

She kept her eyes on her book.

"This is a day of rest," she said. "Not a day for the taking or making of profit—which is what I'd be doing if I had anything to do with moving that statue further toward the City today."

He shook his head.

"We got to go," he said. "And we're going, Mattie."

"I'm not," she said, calmly.

"I can't leave you alone out here," he answered. "Have to take you whether you want to go on or not, Mattie."

"You signed a contract with me," she said, clearly and still calmly. "You can't sell that statue to the art dealer if I say no. Put me on that raft by force, and you'll hear 'no' from me for now and ever—if you carry the statue and Charlie to Arcadia City times over."

She stopped speaking. He stood, looking down at her, saying nothing.

"Go if you want," she said. "I won't try to stop you. But I'm staying here."

She opened her book and went back to her reading. For a second more he watched her. Then he turned and went to his own gear. He brought his own long gun back, laid it beside her, and went to the raft.

Charlie whistled. Cary answered. He untied the shore line, stepped aboard the raft, and picked up a pole. He pushed strongly with the end of the pole against the bank, and the front of the raft swung out into the stream until the current caught it and pulled it slowly from shore.

In a minute, it was floating downriver over a bottom too deep for the pole to work against. Cary pulled the pole inboard, laid it down, and went back to take the rudder oar. Steering the raft into the central current, he looked back up toward the campsite, now steadily falling behind them.

Mattie still sat where he had left her, reading. The brilliant white cover of the book caught the sunlight and seemed to burn in her hands as she held it. She had not changed position, and she did not move as he watched. But as the raft moved away from her, she dwindled steadily in size until she was so small that her seated figure could be covered by the tip of his uplifted little finger. Then the raft swam around a bend in the river, and she was lost to sight.

9.

As the black limbs and the dark green leaves of the trees moved between the raft and the view of Mattie, Charlie whistled sharply. The otter was up on all fours, standing by the statue with neck outstretched toward Cary. As Cary looked at him, Charlie whistled again and looked back toward the river bend questioningly.

Cary shook his head and turned his gaze once more to the water before the raft, settling the shaft of the steering oar under his arm.

Charlie whistled a third time.

"No!" snapped Cary aloud. He shook his head, two sharp, distinct moves from one side to the other. "She wants it like that!"

Charlie stopped whistling. The effort of standing was beginning to show on him. His legs bowed and gave under him so that he sank to the raft. Still he held his head up for a long moment on his slim neck, looking at Cary.

Cary stared stone-eyed as a statue himself at the water ahead.

Charlie's neck bent. His head dropped to the logs beneath it. He whistled once more, almost as if to himself, a low, long-drawn-out whistle that faded into silence at last.

With Cary at the oar, they drifted on downriver in silence.

Cary whistled, abruptly and fiercely, and Charlie's head came up. Cary had shoved the steering oar to one side, and the raft was now drifting slowly at an angle back toward the land. As soon as it grounded close to the right-hand bank, Cary jumped overboard with a rope, hauled the raft as close to the bank as it could be pulled in the gravel shallows, and ran ashore.

He tied the rope hastily to the twisted trunk of a bire tree, and turning, headed through a clump of bushes at a steady lope back upstream alongside the river. He ran lightly and easily, without heavy breathing, but with his mouth in a thin line and his eyes fixed ahead. Twice he was forced to head inland from the river, but always he turned back to the bank at the first opportunity. And it was only a few moments before he came out through the trees where he had cut logs for the raft that morning, and found Mattie still sitting as he had left her, the book in her hands.

He stopped running and walked up to her. She did not look at him as he approached. Her eyes were still on the pages of the book before her. He came up and stood over her.

"Mattie," he said.

She did not answer. Her attention was all on the pages before her. He reached down to take the book from her, and his fingers touched her hands. They were chill to the touch.

His expression changed. He bent and looked into her down-tilted face. It was as white as the face of a woman in shock.

"Mattie—" he said. Gently, he put his fingers under her chin and forced her face up to look at him.

"What're you doing here?" she whispered.

"Guess I can't leave you, Mattie," he said, and let her go, straightening up to look at her almost grimly. "Never thought there was nobody I couldn't leave, nothing I couldn't do. But I can't go on and leave you here. Guess you've done that for me. So we'll stick with you, if you won't move, Charlie and I."

"You're wrong," Mattie said, barely above the level of the whisper in which she had answered first. "This time, you're wrong. You ought to go on. Leave me."

"Like this?" Cary's straight, dark brows came together in a line across his face. "Leaving you with the long gun and a day's walk back to Aige's is one thing. This here's something else. You planning to sit here and die, Mattie?"

There was a sick feeling in him that came out in his voice, and she heard it.

"I don't suicide! You think that of me?" she flared for a second; and then the coldness took the life out of her voice again. "You don't understand."

"What don't I understand?"

"The universe is not mocked," she said, not looking at him, rocking herself a little. "There is a physics of life, and what is taken must be counterbalanced by what is given—"

"Mattie!" The hardness of his voice stopped her voice and her body movement, all at once. "What you talking about?"

"You killed a man," she said. "I was the cause of it, but you were the instrument. A man was killed for the sake of worldly gain." She looked up at him. "It's wrong to kill, Cary. To kill puts you in debt to the natural law of the universe. It makes you vulnerable. You killed him and the law of averages is against you now. I was the cause. If something happens to me, that helps to balance the forces. Otherwise the physics of the universe stays tilted against you. You killed—"

"Mattie!"

The sudden explosion of his voice stopped her, but only briefly.

"You don't understand," she said, dully.

"It's you who don't understand," he answered. "You think you got some reason to pay out for me? There's nothing you owe, Mattie. Me neither. Mister takes a weapon to me, I take one to him—it was him started it, not me."

"But you killed him. There's man dead back there—"

"I killed him because Charlie was laying there like he was dead. I thought he was," Cary said. "Thought the looper'd killed him."

"Even if he had," said Mattie. "It's not the same thing. That looper was a man—"

"Charlie's a man!"

A black, hot tide washed over him for a second, so that he could not see. When he had his sight back, he saw Mattie sitting frozen, staring up at him. The fury in him had finally stopped her mouth.

"You listen to me," he said, barely above a whisper, and the jagged words tore his throat raw, getting out. "Charlie's a man. You know who's not a man? That looper's not a man. None of them's men. No mister on this planet, not Aige, not me—none of us, men—to Charlie's people. And that's what counts."

She leaned back a little from him. He bent down over her.

"You know what we are?" he said, low-voiced. "We're animals. Aliens. We're alien animals come out of someplace else where we had a right to be, to here where we got no right. And you know what we do, now we're here? We poison the earth and kill off the vine and the char. We bring in our own plants that got no right here, neither, and we plant them to drive out the plants that belong here. And you know what else we do? We cut, and we burn, and we build; and finally, we go and kill men and women—real men and women with a right here, because it's their world—in order to skin them and sell their hides to be shipped off the planet to other animals like us who don't even know where those hides came from."

He stopped to draw breath, and the air seemed burned like flame against his raw, tight throat.

"I told you, Mattie," he said. "I told you Charlie's people hadn't any use for me. I told you they didn't think it was any great thing, my keeping the trappers off them. And I guess you thought that was real strange of them. Strange? Strange they don't feel grateful and thankful an alien animal like me don't come around killing their brothers and sisters and wives and children no more? Grateful one like me stops another from killing them? That's some real great kindness and favor, is it then?"

He broke off.

"But Charlie, he's even more than the men the rest of his people are," he said. "Because Charlie can see an alien like me hidden in a dirty chunk of stone and carve that stone until it's art—until that alien's there for all to see. You and I can't do that; but he can."

He turned and strode off blindly. It was only when bire branches whipped him in the face that he realized what he was doing. Then, with a great sweep, the fury left him, and his mind cleared. Suddenly he felt washed clean, empty, and hollow inside. It was not like him, talking so much. He turned around. Mattie was still seated, staring wordlessly after him with a white face. He went back to her. Taking her hand, he pulled her to her feet.

"Sorry, Mattie," he said, more quietly. "Sorry. It's not you—it's a thousand misters like those loopers, over the past six years. Listen—if you're right and the universe makes all even, it don't matter then what shape of body there is about a person. If I'd done nothing back there, it'd be Charlie dead now, and that looper living. Happen it's the looper that's dead and Charlie's still alive. We didn't start what happened, none of us—Charlie, you, or me. It was the loopers figured to kill Charlie and smash his statue from the first, before we even showed up at Aige's. If it's a universe knows what happens, then it's a universe knows that it had to be Charlie or the looper. And the one which lived had the best right to be living."

She shook her head, her face still white, but said nothing.

"Makes no matter now, anyway," Cary said. "Raft's at the bank, just below the bend there, and we aren't going further today. You'll walk that far to be with the rest of us, even if it's a Prayer Day, sure?"

"Yes," she said.

"Good. I'll help strike your hammock here and pack up," said Cary, moving to do just that. In a few minutes he had the gear he'd left with her packed and ready to carry. He took it in a bundle over his right shoulder, and with the long gun in his left hand, he led her back down along the river toward the raft.

When they reached the bushes screening the spot just upstream of where the raft had touched the shore, for the first time Cary became conscious of a sound from just ahead where the raft would be. It was a steady, rhythmic thumping and rustling like nothing he had ever heard before. A small noise, but strange. Dropping the gear, he sprinted ahead of Mattie, into the clearing.

Charlie was no longer on the raft. He was ashore, and the trail of crushed grass in the soft earth of the river bank showed how he had gotten there. His eyes were closed, his jaws were lathered in foam and snapped unceasingly, and his body and limbs jerked and twitched with such force that he moved about on the ground. The sharp odor that had accompanied his earlier violent outburst against his own people when they had left the plateau was heavy in the air.

Cary dropped at the otter's side and tried to hold the jerking body still, but it was too strong for him. He felt himself violently shoved aside. Looking up, he saw Mattie, who knelt in his place beside Charlie.

"Convulsions!" Mattie snapped at him. "Don't you know convulsions when you see them?"

She grabbed up an eight-inch length of stick, perhaps two inches in diameter, from the ground nearby and thrust it between Charlie's mindlessly snapping jaws. The swamp otter's chisel teeth went through the wood as if it were a twig. Mattie reached up blindly, pulled Cary's short gun from its holster, and thrust the gun barrel between Charlie's jaws. The gleaming teeth clicked and chewed on the metal, but could not cut it through. She reached in a finger behind the barrel to pull Charlie's long, black tongue clear of his throat.

"Sleeping bags!" she cried. "Liners. Anything to wrap him in, Cary! We've got to get him warm!"

Cary turned and jumped onto the raft. When he came back a moment later with his arms full of bedding gear, Charlie was still convulsing. Dark blood had begun to trickle from his nostrils, staining purple the lather and foam just below the nostrils. Together Mattie and Cary wrapped the twitching body thickly in bedding and held the bedding in place with their arms in a cocoon of warmth about Charlie.

Gradually, his convulsions became less violent. They slowed and became intermittent. Finally, they dwindled to heavy shudders and then stopped entirely. Charlie at last lay still, but his eyes were still closed and he breathed heavily through his blood-encrusted nostrils.

Mattie met Cary's eyes and sat back, letting go of the bedding she and Cary had been holding in place about the swamp otter. Cary let go also. Mattie kneeling, Cary squatting, they looked across Charlie at each other.

"Nothing to do now but wait," said Mattie.

They got to their feet. With the automatic motions of habit, Cary set up the wick-stove and made coffee. They sat drinking coffee and saying little while the sun rose to noon overhead and started to lower toward the western horizon beyond the other side of the river.

Charlie still lay, breathing heavily, his eyes closed, when they checked him for perhaps the dozenth time.

"When did he eat last that you know of?" Mattie asked Cary.

"Pool at the foot of the cliff," said Cary. "Unless he was in the water some of the nights while we were sleeping. But I don't guess he was."

"I guess not," said Mattie. She reached out her hand, first over the area of his bandaged shoulder, and then over the swollen side of Charlie's head where the dead looper had struck him. "Feel."

Cary put out his own hand. Over both damaged areas, he could feel the feverish heat radiated up against his palm.

"I don't suppose it'd make any difference, here or on the raft," said Mattie. She glanced at the sun. "You suppose he'd want to move on?"

"Guess so," said Cary.

Mattie got to her feet.

"Then we'd better travel while the light lasts," she said.

10.

Cary looked at her, and she looked away from him. He nodded and got to his feet.

"Sure," he said. "We'll get packed and moving."

He folded up the wick-stove, while Mattie took on board the raft the gear he had left with her and which she had carried in from the bushes after Cary had dropped it there to run to Charlie. Last of all, they carried Charlie gently on a blanket-wrapped litter out to the raft and laid him on a soft pile of bedding beside the statue. He showed no signs of knowing he was being moved. His eyes were still closed, and his breathing sounded heavily. Cary shoved the raft off from the bank once more into the main current of the broad, dark river.

The day had begun bright, with only a few clouds. But during the morning a haze had moved in, and by the time they were once more on their way, the haze had been replaced by a cloud cover that was almost solid from horizon to horizon. Under these clouds, the day itself seemed dulled, and all its sounds muted. They went down the brown flow of water with hardly a gurgle, as Cary moved the steering oar to avoid a floating deadhead or one of the occasional rocks to break the surface of the stream.

The grasslands they had crossed by oxen and travois were being left behind them now. At first only in patches but then more solidly, the forest area began to close in about both sides of the river. The forest here was barely touched by human influence. Here and there a solitary variform oak could be seen with its stiffly upright trunk and limbs stretched out at right angles to the trunk's vertical line. But all around were bire and temp, sourbark, and bushes of poison thorn. They all wound about with the great green hawsers of midland vine and the heavy dull-purple bunches of the epiphytic char, that was both blossom and fruit at once, clinging with invisible root filaments to the rest of the vegetation on which it parasitically fed.

As the sky darkened overhead with the clouds and the lowering sun, so the forest darkened, closing in around the river on which they traveled. By nearly sunset, shadow and dark color—the black and gray and deep brown of the trees and the dusky purple of the char—surrounded them on every side. The woods were strangely quiet after the insect-filled plains—only an occasional hooting or whistling came from their depths.

"The loopers wouldn't like it here," said Mattie, unexpectedly.

Cary looked about him. It was true. Everyone knew that loopers found Arcadia a drab, dark world compared to whatever they had been accustomed to on other planets where men had settled. Mostly, on Arcadia, people born here figured that the loopers' reaction was just another way of looking down their noses at a new world struggling to pay off its first mortgage. But, watching the surrounding forest now, Cary suddenly understood something of how the loopers must feel.

It must look chill-like to them, he thought, something like this river and forest—chill-like, sad-making, even fearful—a fearful, sorrowful sort of place, with its duns and grays and blacks and heavy purples.

"You're likely right," he said to Mattie.

Just as he spoke, the sun—low on the horizon now, down behind the nearer treetops—broke through the clouds just before setting. Suddenly the forest was flooded by a back-lighting of fiery illumination that sought through the upper branches of the twisted bire and the other trees, making their limbs stand out twisted and black and stark. Not just a fearful, sorrowful place now—but such a place, hell-lighted, it would seem to loopers. But to Cary and Mattie, watching, it was sweet and beautiful.

The land, the trees, the vine, the char, and the river—all of them—were tied together into something to touch you, deep inside, by the last light of the day. It was a hard, dark land, this Arcadia, but there was something strong in it to make you love it, like a song heard far off and going away just as the sun goes down, once you were born to this world and grown up on it.

They ran on through the forested country under a bright moon until midnight, with Cary at the steering oar. At midnight Mattie relieved him. He barely had time to pull a sleeping bag liner over him before he fell into slumber.

He woke to find it nearly day, rolled himself up into a sitting position at the side of the raft, and splashed cold water on his face. Awake, he went back to Mattie.

"Your turn," he said. "I'll take the oar now."

She nodded wearily, gave him the oar, and went forward to drop down on the bedding he had just abandoned, pulling sleeping bags and liners into a mound over her.

Cary settled himself to his steering. Reaching overside with one hand, he brought up a palmful of cold water and drank. The river current was steady now, and they were making good time.

During the next few hours, however, the river widened and slowed. It was now perhaps twice as wide from bank to bank as it had been up in the forest, and occasionally they drifted past a log hutch with a woven vine roof blackened by the sun, perched on the very edge of the water. But there was no sign of life to be seen about any of these buildings.

"Voting," said Cary to himself, looking at the tenth one they had passed since his wakening. "Gone to the City, likely." He glanced at the mound of bedding that was Mattie, but it gave no sign of anyone awake within it. He weighed the idea of tying up the raft to the bank and resting now, against the hope of finding a chance to rest later. But the City was still distant, overland; and with Charlie the way he was . . . sleep later was the word. Himself, he could always make do one way or another.

He steered on into the rising brilliance of morning that was making the river now into a white ribbon of light.

After a while, when the sun stood at about ten o'clock, he steered the raft to the bank and stepped ashore to set up the wick-stove and make some coffee. When it was ready, he filled a cup and carried it onto the raft. Cup in hand, he squatted beside the pile of bedding hiding Mattie and carefully lifted back sleeping bag liners until he uncovered her face.

For a moment he squatted there, cup in hand, looking at her. In the bright midmorning light, her sleeping face was wiped smooth of most of the tightness that it held always

when he had seen her back in the City and oftentimes during waking hours on this trip with the statue. Interestingly,
he found himself remembering what she had said, the day
before they had left, when she had asked him how old he
was. How old had she said she was?

Nineteen. Usually, she looked older. Well, not older, but
some general age between nineteen and middle age. Now
though, sleeping, she looked younger. Cary tried to remember what his younger sister had looked like before she died
of a bad cold. Mira had been—what was it? Twelve. She
had been the last of the family to die. Cary wondered—if
Mira had lived would he have stayed in the City like Mattie?

Probably not. Mira would have turned woman and got
married or got a job or something. Anyway, he had wanted
to go to the upcountry, even then. He had tried to talk his
dad into it. . . . His thoughts came back from their wan-
dering. What was it he had had in mind? Oh, yes—Mira,
when she was young and sleeping. Was that what Mattie
looked like now?

He considered Mattie's slumbering face, thoughtfully, the
cup of coffee growing cool in his hand. No, there was
something there like Mira, but it was different. They were
all different, just the way no two swamp otters were alike.
Charlie was one in a million. Mattie too. Strange where
they came from, different from all the rest. Strange where
they went to. But Mattie was no otter; she was a
woman. . . .

Mattie's eyes slowly opened, then blinked against the light
of the sun. She turned and hid her face in the bag liner beneath her.

"What is it?" she asked, muffledly.

"Brought you some coffee," said Cary. He became aware of the temperature of the cup in his hand. "Better warm it though. Stay put."

He went back to the fire, poured the cold cup back into the pot, swished it around with the warm coffee, and filled the cup again and brought this to Mattie. She was up on one elbow under the covers when he brought the cup of fresh coffee. She smiled when she took it from him.

"Thank you kindly, Cary," she said. She sipped at it. "Tastes good."

He stayed squatting, watching her drink it. She became aware of his gaze on her and looked down at the cup.

"Where are we?" she asked. "What's going to happen today?"

He heard her, but he paid her words almost no attention.

"Mattie. . . ." he began.

Her head lowered further toward the coffee. The line of her mouth grew hard.

"You didn't answer me," she said, sharply, but not looking up. "I said—"

"Hush, Mattie," he said gently. "I've something to talk to you about—"

She sat up suddenly, spilling coffee on the sleeping bag liners. Her face was tight again.

"No!" she said. "I don't want to talk. I've got no time for talk. It's no use talking to me, anyway. Money's all I'm interested in—money's all I'm ever going to be interested in. I learned that the hard way, trying to stay alive, and it's too late to unlearn it now. I'm what I am, and I wouldn't change if I could. So, there's no point my talking to anybody about anything else. Not to you—not to anybody!"

Abruptly, she scrambled to her feet and stood looking around her.

"We're tied up," she said. "Why? Why aren't we moving? You realize we've only got three days to get to the City in time to meet that art buyer of yours?"

Slowly, Cary uncoiled to his own upright height. He looked down at her a little sadly.

"Time to eat a bite, Mattie," he said. "Come ashore and we'll cook something."

11.

They made a late breakfast on the bank over the wick-stove, and then reboarded the raft and put it out into the current again.

"Lock and dam not too far down from here," said Cary to her. "Once past that, it's only a few klicks until we've need to leave the river and begin travel overland to town. Happen we can pick up oxen and a wagon from there on into town."

"How far from here to the City?" Mattie asked.

"Three days, not more," said Cary. "We ought to be there just in time—for voting and for Mister Waters, that's the art buyer."

Mattie nodded.

"Good," she said. She was fussing over Charlie, cleaning him up, in fact.

"Fever's down a little more, it seems," she said. "I wish he'd come to, though. Cary, do they usually stay unconscious this long when they've been hurt?"

Cary shook his head.

"Never seen it," he answered. "I told you, I don't know that much about them. I can talk a little with Charlie, and there was that time in the beginning I lived a while where they have all their hutches—or nests, or mudball dens, whatever you call them. I've helped some when one'd get shot or trapped. But there's little I really know about them any more than the next mister."

"But there ought to be something we can do!"

Cary looked down at his boots and shook his head emptily.

"Wait," he said. "That's all."

A little later they came around a very wide, sweeping curve of the river into what was almost a small lake of its ponded waters. At the far end a dam and buildings of white concrete glittered against the dark land—almost eye-hurting in their reflection of the sunlight. An opened spillway in the right part of the dam beside the lock let dark water through.

Cary angled the raft to a landing on the side of the lake near the lock. A slight figure with a soft brown beard, wearing woodsman clothes and carrying the inevitable long gun, wandered down to the shore of the open grassy area where they landed. He stepped knee deep into the water and helped pull the raft into shore, to tie up.

"Thank you, mister," said Cary to him, when the raft was at last tied and they were all, except Charlie, standing on the bank.

"My pleasure, mister," answered the small woodsman. He was perhaps a few years older than Cary, but already his face had gone into placid, leathery lines from sun and weather. "I'm Mul Oczorny. You'll be Mister Cary Longan and this"—he turned toward Mattie—"Miss Orvalo?"

"The same," Cary said. He looked at the little man curiously. "We know you, mister?"

Mul shook his head.

"Piece of news about you been broadcast out from the

City," Mul said. "Some looper run into you upcountry, said you were bringing down a statue some sooger of a swamp otter made." He nodded to the raft. "That it? I'd mighty like to take a look."

Cary nodded.

"Statue's for looking. That's why Charlie made it," he said. "Charlie's the name of the otter. You see him there."

"Do," agreed Mul. "Thank you kindly."

He stepped down the bank and lightly onto the raft. He approached the statue and leaned over to inspect it. For more than a few seconds he stood, bent above it, examining the stone shape. Then he straightened up and his eyes went to Charlie, lying beside it.

"This sooger's hurt some," he said.

"Looper gave that news you heard, burned him with an energy rifle," said Cary. "Another looper later on hit him with a sledge."

Mul nodded, looking down at Charlie's still form. Then he turned and came back off the raft up onto the bank to face Cary and Mattie once more.

"Loopers," he said, without emphasis. He turned his head politely to one side and spat green. His brown beard in front was tinged with the color of the fresh-cut vine he had been chewing. He looked back at Cary and Mattie. "That's a mighty fine statue he made there. You, isn't it, mister? Like you was in the stone. I never seen anything so fine and real as that. Guess I understand why you want to get it to the City."

"Karl Turnbull home?" asked Cary, looking across the length of the dam at the white concrete buildings on the far side which housed the electric generating plant powered by the dam structure, and the family that owned and operated the plant.

"Him and his boys. All," said Mul, leaning on his rifle and watching Cary.

"Guess I'll walk over and ask him to let us through the lock," said Cary. He glanced at Mattie. "Supposed to be free—passage through that lock. But it's a kindly thing offering to pay him something. You mind paying?"

"If that's what's done, all right," said Mattie.

Cary nodded. He picked up his own rifle and walked away from Mattie and Mul, down to the near end of the dam. He stepped up on it and began to cross it. A catwalk ran the full length of the structure, suspended airily on a pair of stressed concrete girders over the open spillway. Cary strolled on over and up to the door in the largest concrete building on the dam's far side. He knocked.

"Come in," said a voice from within.

Cary laid his hand on the door panel and pushed it open. He stepped into a small room like an office, fitted with a pair of heavy wooden desks and several sets of plyboard files. The back of the room was closed off by a wall-sized sliding panel from the rest of the interior of the building. Behind the farthest of the desks sat a heavy man in his forties with coal-black hair and eyebrows.

"Mister Turnbull," Cary nodded at him. "Likely you don't remember me? I'm Cary Longan, from upcountry."

"Remember you," said Turnbull. He was clad in upcountry pants and woven shirt, but his skin was almost as pale as the skin of someone from Arcadia City. "I know all about you. Heard about you and that outfitter miss and the statue and otter on the broadcast from the City."

"Honored," said Cary. "Then I guess you can figure what I'm here for. We'd take it kindly if you'd open the gates to your lock and lock us down to the lower river below your dam."

Turnbull leaned forward. Both his arms lay on the desk already; and as he hunched over them, the muscles in the big forearms swelled and his fists closed.

"I'll see you all dead, first, Longan!" he said. "You think my great-grandfolks worked their heads off back before emigration so they could bring in enough funds to buy a power station out of the first mortgage here on Arcadia—and for four generations we've built on and saved cash here for the day when the second mortgage'd be signed and people'n industry'd move upcountry—you think we went through that for five generations, and I'm going to help you move that chunk of rock down to the City to bust up all chance for a second mortgage? You must be full of bad weed, woodie!"

Cary did not move. But his voice became quieter and his eyes more alert to watch the office about them.

"You're not making much sense, mister," he said. "We're just taking a statue down to sell it to a looper art buyer from the Old Worlds."

"Statue!" Turnbull jumped to his feet and came around the desk. He was not short. But he was shorter than Cary, so that his bulk made him look abnormally broad, like the lower half of a dutch door. He stamped across the room to the wall beside the door where Cary had come in. There was a scope-screen there, with controls below it. Turnbull punched buttons and the meter-wide screen lit up with a view of the raft across the ponded water behind the dam. They saw the raft, what was on it, and both Mattie and Mul beyond as if from a distance of less than that of the raft's length itself.

"Look at that!" Turnbull grunted. "If it was a real statue, I might believe there was something sensible to it—

not just that crazy upcountry hate you woodies have for anything that looks like decent, high-class civilization. But that's no statue—look at it! A chunk of old rock with a few grooves in it, that's all that is—"

"It's a statue, mister," said Cary softly.

"Don't try telling me that! It's part of this crazy deal all you upcountry people have for this world the way it is. Who cares what a world is to begin with? The point is, it ought to end up civilized, with all the trash weeds and the trash animals and such cleared out and good mutated Earth stock moved in. Good cities. Good, well automated farm-land. Neat hunting preserves. Industry. Some good tourist attractions. God knows that's one hell of a lot to hope for on a dingy, dark, dirty, backwoods planet like this one—but my family's invested five generations in just that. And you expect me to help you wreck the chance?"

He turned around, went back to his desk, and sat down.

"Get that rock and that bundle of logs off my lake," he said.

Cary stood for a second, without answering. The silence stretched out in the office and a little bead of sweat ran down the side of Turnbull's angry face.

"Mister," said Cary, finally, quietly, "what set you so much against us?"

"You buying me one?" snorted Turnbull. "This is a power station. We get all the broadcasts from the City. One of the mortgage company surveyors flew down from up-country nearly a week ago telling how you were bringing that rock in to try and stir up the woodies, and maybe even the farmers against voting in the new mortgage. Told how you jumped him and held guns on him and threatened him. Sure, and the word came how you killed another mortgage company man for just touching the statue, up at Aige Apfur's station. You got nothing to tell me I don't know about you, Longan."

"Just otherways, mister," said Cary slowly. "Doesn't sound to me like you got anything about me or the statue right yet. But I can see there's no use my trying to change your mind. So we won't talk. Just you open up that lock, though—"

Turnbull's hand flicked out and threw a toggle switch on the surface of his desk. Behind him the sliding wall slammed abruptly back into its recess. Revealed behind it were four short young men, each with a rifle at his shoulder aimed at Cary.

"My boys," said Turnbull. "All of them good shots, even if they aren't woodies. You back up slowly now, Longan —back up until you hit the wall and then feel along it to your right for the door button. When you find it, out you go —and no reaching for that short gun at your waist."

Cary looked from the four young men to Turnbull. The family resemblance was plain on all of them. He backed away as Turnbull had said, felt along the wall until his finger touched the smooth, half-round shape of a door button, and pressed it. The door opened behind him, and he backed out.

"Be gone by morning," said Turnbull. "One way or another—I don't care which. But be gone by morning or me and the boys'll open fire on you from the top of the generator building."

The door closed in Cary's face. He stood for a moment, gazing at its blank surface of pressed concrete, like the heavy concrete walls of the building surrounding it. Then he turned and headed back across the catwalk over the dam.

He found Mul and Mattie seated on the bank with the wick-stove and a coffeepot going between them. Mattie offered him a cup as he came up and he took it without a word.

"Likely," said Mul, looking up at him, "he wasn't friendly, that Turnbull mister?"

Mattie looked startledly at the little man and then back at Cary. But Cary was looking at Mul himself.

"Might have told us," Cary said.

"Thought you'd figure. 'Scuse," said Mul, apologetically. "I said you'd been talked about on the video broadcasts. Figured you'd know he knew."

"He knows wrong," said Cary.

"Cary!" Mattie broke in on him. "What is all this?"

He turned to her.

"That looper that shot Charlie—you remember, back at the foot of the cliff," he said. "Seems the same looper believed what you said, Mattie, about the statue being important. He went on into town and said we were hauling in Charlie's statue to make trouble for those wanting the mortgage voted in. Turnbull, over there, said the statue was supposed to stand for leaving Arcadia the way we want it, us in the upcountry. And we're taking it to the City so woodies and farmers'll see it and not vote for the mortgage."

He stopped and drank from his coffee cup.

"Turnbull's not going to open his lock for us," Cary said. "Raft can't be run over the spillway—it'd break to pieces falling that far to the lower level. But Turnbull's got four sons and rifles. Says for us to clear out by morning, one way or another."

Mul looked across at the heavy concrete building with its parapet roof and high, narrow windows.

"No way to go in and change his mind," Mul said. He looked back at Cary. "You say he knows wrong?"

"Taking this statue to the City to sell it to a looper art buyer," said Cary.

Mul gazed at him strangely, holding the coffee cup in his hand as if he had forgotten it was there.

"You saying," said Mul slowly, "there's nothing to it?"

"Of course, something's to it!" Cary's voice came as close to sounding his anger as it ever had in his life. "There's something to it for you, for me, for Charlie, even if not for—" he checked himself, catching Mattie's eye, "Turnbull and misters like him."

"But," said Mul, "you're selling it off Arcadia—"

"That's as will be." Cary looked at the smaller man coldly. "It's somehow a business of yours, mister?"

Mul looked back at him simply. Then he put his cup down carefully on the ground of the bank and began to fumble inside his shirt.

"You're Cary Longan," Mul said. "Heard about you more than some little. This hears different from what I heard. Word said what the broadcasts said—you taking a statue to town. No business of mine—you're right. Happen it's something to do with cash, though. I got me some script here—"

He produced a small leather money pouch at the end of a thong around his neck.

"Put it away!" snapped Mattie.

He turned his head slowly to look at her in astonishment, the pouch still held in his hand.

"Put it away, I said!" cried Mattie again. "Do you hear me?"

"Yes, miss," said Mul. He put the pouch back in his shirt. "No offense meant—"

Mattie whirled and stalked off.

"No offense taken," said Cary gently. "It's us ought to be apologizing to you, Mul. Thank you kindly for what you figured to offer."

Mul shrugged embarrassedly and looked at the ground.

"Only script," he said. He cleared his throat and looked up again. "How you going to get the raft and all down below the dam?"

Cary turned his head to look at the woods sloping steeply off at the right end of the dam.

"There a portage around and down?" Cary asked.

Mul nodded.

"Regular trail," he said. "Not wide enough for a raft though, even you've got some way of carrying it."

"Maybe we'll break the raft up, portage the rest, and build a new one out of the timber below."

"No timber there now." Mul shook his head. "Turnbull and his boys logged it off last year. Oh, there's trees, but not for raft-making." He hesitated. "Maybe I could help a small some?"

Cary looked at him closely.

"If I had another man," Cary said, "we could take the raft apart and portage the logs one at a time, maybe. Can't do it alone."

"Miss Orvalo, she can't help either, sure," said Mul. "Too heavy for a woman. I'd be in favor of giving you a hand with those logs myself, you don't mind."

"Don't mind. Thank you kindly," said Cary. "I hoped you'd say something such." He looked at the sun, which was now approaching the noon zenith. "Guess we might get started right now."

Cary had Mul take him down the trail. It was not bad for a portage trail, a little steep in spots, but wide enough to maneuver the logs down it and free of roots and brush underfoot that could trip up whoever was carrying a load down it.

"How about Charlie?" Cary asked Mattie, when the two men got back up to the raft. "Think he's all right to go down on a litter?"

"I think he's better," Mattie said. They were all standing on the raft looking down at the still, black form of the swamp otter. "He's still unconscious, but I've been giving him water and he's been taking it—look."

She reached over the side of the raft, dipped up a cupful of the fresh water, and stepped over to Charlie. Lifting the long upper lip on the top side of his jaw, she poured the water between his long teeth. It disappeared, and they could see the smooth movement of his throat under the black fur of his neck as the swallowing reflex occurred.

"And he doesn't feel so hot now," said Mattie, moving her hand over Charlie's head and shoulder. "Maybe he just needed rest to start to mend." She looked up at Cary. "If you don't joggle him, carrying him down. . . ."

"We'll go sure careful, miss," said Mul.

They carried Charlie down and left him on the litter under the shade of the single large tree that grew among the brush and new growth on the bank of the foot of the dam. Then they returned, to rope and skid the statue down the slope.

During the rest of the afternoon, Mattie carried the smaller pieces of gear down, load by load, while Cary and Mul unwired the logs of the raft and, one by one, struggled with them down the twisting, sloping portage trail.

With practice, they grew experienced and clever. Stripped to the waist, and their lean bodies dripping with sweat under the leather pads strapped to the shoulder on which they each rested an end of the log they were carrying, they learned each hard spot and how it might be avoided or circumvented. There were points where it was necessary to back up to go around a corner. Turns so steep the man behind was well advised to go to his knees to keep from throwing too much of the log's weight on the man at the front. There were slippery spots where the earth had worn slick, protruding tree roots or bushes that could trip feet not expecting them. And, in the end, there was the need to always be braced for a slip or stumble by the man on the other end of the log that might throw unexpected weight upon his partner.

Still, they got the logs down. At first at a steady rate, and then more slowly, as the climb back up the portage trail became steadily more of a trial for already weary legs.

About sunset, with a little less than half the logs yet to go, Cary's feet went out from under him suddenly on a turn. He had sufficiently alert reflexes still to shout a warning to Mul, who was carrying the rear end of the log, and to throw the front end from him as he fell, so that it should not come down on top of him. But, the next thing he knew, both Mul and Mattie—who should have been down at the foot of the portage trail—were bending over him.

"He's got to have some sleep!" Mattie was saying, furiously. "He didn't rest hardly at all last night and not at all yesterday. . . ."

"All right," said Cary, and he struggled to his feet with their hands helping him. But when he was upright, his knees gave like hinges of oiled leather. Although he objected, they led him down to the foot of the portage.

That was the last he remembered, until he woke to new moonlight and sat up to see the outlines of Mul and Mattie seated before a fire.

"What time is it?" he asked. But his glance at the moon and the night shadows had already told him it must be nearly midnight. "Mul, we've need to get those other logs down here before dawn."

The other two, however, insisted he eat first before going back to work. He started to protest, then realized the sense of it. Gratefully, he filled up on hot coffee and canned stew. When it was eaten, Mul offered him a fresh-cut length of vine.

He started to reach for it, glanced at Mattie, and then shook his head.

"Thanks kindly, no," he said.

"Go ahead," said Mattie, roughly.

"No, I guess not," he said slowly. He ran a hand over his chin and found the stubble stiff upon it. He smiled over at Mattie. "Never could go back, once I made up my mind to something. Guess maybe I won't shave, though. Reason in all things."

He got to his feet and, with Mul, headed back up the portage trail through the black shadows and silver light. With the rest and the meal, he felt like a giant. He was almost lightheaded with the strength he had recaptured.

"Doesn't take much to bring a man back," he said to Mul.

"Bear us a few logs down the hill first," remarked Mul. "Then you tell me that."

Nonetheless, although the little man was right and Cary soon found that he had gained back only part of his normally rested energy and power, he was once more up to the work. It was slow; but as dawn was breaking, they brought down the final log, assembled the logs on the bank of the river below the dam, and set about tying them together.

Mattie had fallen asleep by the fire. They let her rest

while they finished tying the raft, and they did not even disturb her when they went over to the wick-stove to make coffee. But, as the water bubbled in the pot, some ancient instinct seemed to rouse her and she sat up, rubbing her eyes.

"All done?" she asked joyously, seeing the assembled raft by the water's edge. She got to her feet. "Here, let me make you something to eat—"

She broke off, turning toward the shadows where Charlie lay.

"I better tend to Charlie first though," she said. "He hasn't had any water since the middle of the night—"

"Just a minute, Mattie," Mul said.

"What?" she turned to him.

"You don't need to water him none," said Mul. He looked down at his coffee cup for a second and then looked up again at both of them. "I checked up on him just a little while after you fell asleep, Mattie, and while you were down with the log we'd just brought, Cary. I didn't see it'd change nothing to speak of it then, rather'n later, so I just let it go until one of you brought it up. The poor sooger's dead. Been dead since just before sunrise."

12.

"And so we commend him," read Mattie, and paused to turn a page in the white book with the fiery red letters on its cover. She searched a moment for the proper commendation, of which there were several at that point in the service. Cary and Mul stood quietly listening and waiting at the side of the newly dug ground; Mattie herself stood at the foot. At the top were a pair of stakes holding a roughed out piece of plank with a message burned into it—the letters having been traced out in vine sap and gunpowder and then set on fire.

CHARLIE
Do not disturb—Cary Longan

"... We commend him," went on Mattie, having found her place, *"to the universe to which he returns, and from which he will once again return some day, as all things turn and return in time. As the rain to the earth, the water to the stream, the stream to the river, the river to the ocean, and the ocean to the clouds which will fall again in rain, so he to the universe and the universe to him—in that cycle which is without end, unbroken, indestructible, and eternal.*

"*Therefore in this way do we find comfort, that our brother Charlie is in no way gone from us, but for the moment passed behind a veil which our temporal and momentary eyes have not the skill to pierce. He is among us yet in all things, though we see him not. He is with us, as we are and shall be with him, now and forever, undeniably.*"

Mattie closed the book and stopped speaking. They all stood for a second, looking at the mounded earth and the sign; then Mattie turned away and Cary, with Mul, imitated her. They walked slowly back to the raft which was now afloat, tethered to the bank and loaded with all their gear. Cary and Mattie stepped aboard.

"Mul," said Mattie, turning to the smaller man on the bank, "thanks for everything."

"Pleasured myself entirely. No need for thanks," said Mul. He stared earnestly at her. "Likely you've no need for more company, so I'll say my so long here."

Cary turned around.

"You'd care to travel on a ways with us?" he asked.

"Grateful—if not unwelcome."

Cary looked at Mattie.

"Of course, come along!" she said. "What made you think we wouldn't want you after all the help you gave us?"

"Fine statue like that here, you'll not be lacking help," said Mul, stepping onto the raft and jerking loose the tie rope that had held it to the bank. "Thanks kindly though."

They moved out, staying close to the bank until they were well past being level with the spot where the water thundered down from the spillway into the pool at the dam's foot. Then they moved out into midstream of the broadening river where the current now ran more slowly.

"Couple hours we'll be into the farmlands around Beta

Center Grain Elevators," said Cary. "We'll stop off by some likely farm and ask to buy or rent wagon and oxen. Overland then, we ought to be coming into the City by tomorrow morning."

"Will these farmers have phones?" Mattie asked.

"Why, I guess most likely," Cary looked at her. "Bound to be a broadcast unit at Beta Center. Phones'd be cheap to run, with a unit that close."

"They've some little money for such extras too, farmers have," put in Mul.

Mattie nodded. They floated on downriver. Well before noon, they found themselves surrounded on all sides by tilled fields, interspersed with occasional farmhouses, stretching to the horizon in all directions. Occasionally a woman in a yard, a man working in a field, or a child on the river bank, exchanged waves with them.

"There's a possible-looking farm place," said Cary, after a while. He put the steering oar over and shortly they drifted up to a sturdy, dark-wood dock below a farmyard green with variform Earth grass. This was in front of a two-story building of rammed earth blocks patched with narrow, green lowland vines. Beyond the building oxen milled in a corral with a concrete fence.

By the time they had tied the raft to the dock, there were a couple of children down to meet them, a boy about twelve and a girl perhaps half that age. Just behind them came a tall, wide-shouldered woman in her twenties, with a calm face. She was wearing a heavy apron and blacksmithing gloves, which she stripped off to shake hands with Mattie.

"I was shoeing one of the beasts," she said. "Miss Orvalo? I'm Miz Pferden. Saw you coming and phoned my husband back from the neighbor's. Be here directly." She nodded at Cary and Mul. "One of you're Mister Longan I've no doubt. Broadcasts didn't mention any other."

"Mul Oczorny, Miz Pferden," said Mul. "This mister's Cary Longan."

"It's pleasure to have you as our guests," Miz Pferden said. Her glance went down to the raft. "That the statue? Mind if I look up close at it?"

"Go right ahead, Miz Pferden," Mattie said. "Meanwhile, could I use your phone for a call to the city? I'll find out the charges—"

"Pay no attention to the charges," Miz Pferden said. "We're not a poor family. Been on this land three generations. Stand to get rich from it, selling it for expansion building if the new mortgage gets voted in. But there's no lacking here for us, regardless, even if all mortgages went up in smoke. Svart Pferden'll be with you in a moment— excuse me while I look over that statue."

She went on down to the dock and Mattie went up to vanish inside the house. A few minutes later a light wagon drawn by a single trotting ox came around the house and halted in the graveled road part of the farmyard. A bunchy-shouldered, tough-looking, middle-aged man, an inch or so shorter than the farmwife, got down from the wagon and came up to Cary and Mul.

"Svart Pferden," he said, acknowledging their introductions. "That the statue down there? Excuse me, got to take a look at that."

He went down to join his wife on the dock.

Cary started to follow him, but just then he saw Mattie emerging from the house. She came toward him, walking slowly.

"Something, Mattie?" he asked, as she came up. She raised her face to him, frowning and angry.

"Cary, you must know some hop-skip-and-jump airboat outfit that'll lease to anybody for anything?" she said. "I've called every outfit in town I know and they all pretend they haven't got a free boat to rent us to bring the statue in. It's all because of that story the looper spread about the statue being a symbol of not voting for the new mortgage. People I've lived and dealt with most of my life, and they—"

She broke off.

"Anyway, you must know someone with an airboat who'll rent to us, Cary," she said. "Just tell me who, and I'll get him on the phone."

He gazed at her, troubled.

"Mattie," he said, "thought you didn't want to spend for an airboat. That's why we brought it by hand this far."

"I didn't," she retorted. "But I've changed my mind. Besides, from here on in it won't cost much. Even if it did, I'm not so sure I want to put all my money into subsidiary companies from the new mortgage anyway."

"But that's what you said you've been saving for—all the years I've known you," he said. "You haven't changed mind in just these couple weeks, sure?"

"Maybe I have," she said. "If I have, it's my business, isn't it?"

He nodded slowly.

"Your business," he said slowly. "But it makes some difference to me to know why you'd change."

"You know why!" She flashed an angry glance at him. "Charlie. The loopers. Everything. You're right; all that mortgaging and remortgaging is going to end up doing is leave us one more carbon copy of every other quick-built industrial world. When we aren't—we're Arcadians, with water and air and land and people like none of the rest of them, and we ought to stay that way!"

The emotional explosion burned itself out suddenly. She stood looking up at him.

"I take it," Cary said, "you won't be voting for the new mortgage yourself?"

She shook her head. He breathed out unhappily.

"Mattie," he said, "I can't let you spend for an airboat, even if you figure you want to now. Happens I lied some to you, after all, about that art buyer."

Her eyes slowly widened, as she stared at him.

"The art buyer," she said. "He—there isn't any art buyer?"

"There's one, right enough," said Cary slowly. "He'll be there too, waiting for us in the City as I said—if he keeps his word. Likewise, he said he'd buy the statue and told me two thousand interworld units. Only one hitch. It wasn't just all that cut and dried. That much money was the most he said he could pay for something like the statue—and only if it turned out he liked it that much."

He stopped talking. Her eyes were still wide open upon him.

"But he'll pay something?" she said.

Cary slowly shook his head.

"Can't be sure, even of that," he said. "He wouldn't pay anything for the little carvings Charlie made. Didn't want them. That's how come I still had them when you hunted me up next morning."

He stopped again. Still, she stood looking at him. They were like two statues themselves when Mul, Miz Pferden, and Svart Pferden himself, with Svart in the lead, broke the spell that bonded the two of them.

"That," said Svart to Cary, coming up from the dock

with his wife and Mul a little behind, "is something I've lived this life to see, that statue. Don't know art—can't make it out all that good, except that it's clear and plainly a statue of you, Mister Longan—but I look at that, and I can feel the earth."

He held out his blunt-fingered, wide-palmed hand, the fingers half-curved upward, in front of Cary.

"I feel the earth, right there. My earth," he said. "Mul here tells me you need wagon and oxen to cart it to the City. I'd be proud, Mister Longan, to drive it myself. And my wife also." He looked at his wife, who nodded.

"Mister Pferden's oxen," she said, "will pull all day and night and never slack until you set your statue down where in the City you wish it. You won't find better carrying by anyone."

Cary looked from her to her husband.

"We were figuring just to rent . . . or buy," he said.

"Rent or buy? Not from me," said Pferden. "I'll carry that statue to town for the pride of it and nothing else, or I'll thank you to ask elsewhere for cartage."

"Mister Pferden," said his wife, placidly, "is a strong-minded man." She looked at her husband, and for a second he looked back at her in a glance of something almost more solid than affection.

Cary nodded.

"If it's that way," he said, "we'd be proud ourselves to have you do so."

"Then it's settled!" said Pferden, almost fiercely. "Got a heavy wagon with a winch and crane already in it. Lend me a hand, misters, and we'll have it out here and the statue in it before a quarter hour's past. Amathea," he turned to his wife, "maybe you and Miss Orvalo would make us up some lunch to take along."

It was closer to an hour, however, before they were actually on their way down the compacted dirt road leading from the Pferden farm toward Beta Center and the direct route to Arcadia City. By that time a small crowd of other farmers had gathered, and with them three woodsmen who said they had been heading to the City from upcountry for Voting Day. They said little; but when the wagon finally started out, they ended up walking along with it, talking in brief, quiet sentences from time to time with Mul, who rode in the rear of the wagon and told them, bit by bit, of his own experiences with the statue and its three escorts.

All along the road to Beta Center, they passed farms where people had come out to the road to speak to them, and sometimes to come close and peer over the wagon sides at the statue. Only one farm produced a tall, round-faced man with a young-looking body but graying hair, who stood squarely in their road.

"Move, Tom," said Svart Pferden from the wagon seat, without raising his voice as the oxen bore down on this man. "I'll drive over you, otherwise."

"You're everybody's fool, Svart!" shouted the man, shaking a finger at Pferden. "Who sold you a license to take the bread we've worked for out of all our mouths, father to son, since folks first landed here?"

But the oxen came close, and he moved aside. Still, his voice shouted after them.

"I'm not the only one sees sense!" he called. "You'll find that out before you're halfway to the City!"

A few moments later a tall young man, panting heavily, burst out of a field of tall grain and fell into step beside the cart. Pferden looked over at him.

"Your dad's not going to be happy with you, Jay," he said.

"Someday—he will—" said the young man, between pants. "You need to understand, Svart. All his life he figured it to come in his time, the second mortgage, and the family'd always remember that. '*It was in Tom Arrens's time we got rich, they'll say,*' he used to tell us. But it's not really the money, it's the happening in his time he wants. Just, he doesn't see yet this *is* the happening, this statue. Later, someday, he'll see."

"Well," Pferden said, flicking the reins to urge the oxen on, "you ought to know your own dad. Like he said, though, there's others feel like him—and for most of them it'll be the money that matters."

They drove on, passing through Beta Center, where several more woodsmen on their way to the City fell in about the wagon. Large numbers, it seemed, not only of the woodies, but of the farmers themselves, were on their way in for the voting, tomorrow. As the afternoon wore on and the sun went westward over the fields of dun-colored grain, less than a week or so from being harvest-ready, the number of those accompanying the wagon with the statue increased. Easily the greatest number of these were woodies —and even now and again one of them would lounge up to the wagon and speak; and Cary would look down from the wagon seat where he sat with Mattie and Pferden, to see someone he knew personally from the upcountry.

"Hey you, Oren," he said to one lean woodie, "you misters keep coming, you going to crowd out the farmers entirely. Thought you was the one said swamp otters are no use except for hides."

"Guess I was wrong, Cary," said Oren. "You was right; and no upcountry mister'll be raising gun or trap to otters from now on, like you always said we shouldn't. Guess too, if it was really Arcadians voting, none but otters'd be going to the polls here. But as for crowding farmers—we woods folks got a right."

"Whose wagon d'you think's hauling this statue?" growled Pferden.

"Never you mind, mister," said Oren. "It's for everybody on Arcadia, that statue—but it's ourn, first after the otters, remember you that. Because we aren't likely to forget it ourselves, we upcountry misters!"

The sun set, and still the train escorting the wagon increased in numbers. For five or six meters on either side of the road now, the grain was being trampled flat by upcountry boots—something that made Pferden mutter under his breath. Steadily, the oxen pulled the wagon forward at their unvarying pace that was scarcely more than a brisk walk for a man, but which the oxen could keep up for forty-eight hours without pause, given food and water as they went. The rise of the moon, now down to a fingernail clipping, gave little light—but shortly thereafter, they began to see a glow of light on the horizon ahead.

"Alpha Center," said Pferden. "We'll pass through there at midnight, easy—and from then on there'll be highway wide enough for these upcountry trampers to leave the fields alone."

"How far from there to the City?" asked Mattie. It was almost the first word she had said as she sat between Pferden and Cary on the wagon seat. Cary looked at her.

"Make the City by dawn easy, from Alpha Center," said Pferden. He chuckled. "Some of these woodies maybe'll find themselves under lock for the night if they don't behave themselves going through the Center, though. Our Beta Center's not bad, but Alpha's a real little city."

He referred to this again when at last they did come out
on the short stretch of wide-paved cement highway just before the city limits of Alpha Center.

"See there," he said, with a chuckle, pointing ahead.
"Regular line of police hovercars set up across the road and
out into the fields on each side. Word of this mob's gone
ahead. They're going to see we walk nice and polite
through their streets!"

He urged on the oxen and they pulled up until they were
within a dozen meters of the line of police cars barring the
road. There were police standing between and behind the
cars, wearing light heat armor and carrying energy rifles.

"*All right, that's far enough!*" boomed a voice from the
amplifier of the central hovercar.

Pferden cursed, startledly, sharply reining the oxen to a
halt. Around and behind the wagon, the walkers stopped in
chain reaction, like a caterpillar which has run its head up
against an obstacle. The central car hissed up on its jets
and slid forward, revealing another car in place behind it.
It pulled up alongside the wagon, and a helmeted man
looked out the window at Pferden, Cary, and Mattie up on
the wagon seat.

"Turn around and get out of here—you and all the
rest," the man under the helmet said. "The citizens of
Alpha Center aren't letting any upcountry totem through
their streets to break up the mortgage voting in Arcadia
City tomorrow."

His gaze fastened on the tall form of Cary.

"You'll be Longan, I suppose," he said. "Well, listen to
me. I've got two hundred armed and armored men there
with police energy rifles. Take your fake statue and get this
mob out of here or we'll open fire."

13.

"Fifteen minutes?" said Cary calmly. "Sure, mister."

He turned to Pferden.

"Turn the wagon around, Svart," he said.

Pferden blinked at him without moving. Mattie stared, then exploded.

"Turn around! Just like that?" She turned on the helmeted man in the police hovercar. "Who do you think you are, telling us to turn around? The people in Alpha Center don't own the road through their town, or anything like it! The streets belong to all the citizens of Arcadia; and these are citizens on their way in to vote on the new mortgage—or not to vote, according to their consciences—"

"Mattie," said Cary.

She broke off, staring at him.

"Let's go," he said softly, and turned to Pferden once more. "I said, turn her around, Svart."

Pferden was also staring at him. But now, slowly, he picked up the reins and began to turn the wagon around. Mul and the woodsmen around the wagon were already passing back the word of what had been encountered up front.

By the time the wagon was turned around, the crowd of marchers behind it had parted to let it go back the way it had come; and many of the woodsmen were also turned around and ambling away from Alpha Center. A bright light shone suddenly around and beyond the wagon from behind it. The police hovercar had turned its spotlight on the wagon.

"Keep moving," said Cary to Pferden, who grunted angrily under his breath, but obeyed.

"But, Cary. . . ." Mattie began and then stopped at the sight of his face, which was now thin and tight. Ahead of them the crowd of woodies who had followed them were thinning out—they almost seemed to be evaporating into thin air—so that it could be seen that there had been a considerable percentage of farmers among them after all. Then, right in front of the plodding oxen, a woodie put a friendly arm on Jay Arrens and led the young man off into the dark, shoulder-high grain to the side of the road. The other farmers, like the woodies, began to disappear into the grain.

"Five minutes left—then we open fire!" boomed the amplified voice from the police car.

"Sound right eager, don't they?" commented Mul.

"I thought we passed a track going off just about back here, someplace," said Cary. "There it is. Turn the team down that, would you, Mister Pferden?"

Pferden hauled on the reins and the oxen turned off down the road onto a dirt wagon path going away through the grain.

"Now what?" said Pferden, once they were on this new track. There was a crackle of energy weapons, back at the police barricade.

"Don't guess they hit anyone—everybody'd be out of sight by now," said Cary.

"Energy weapons can't hit what they can't see," commented Mul from alongside the wagon. "We'll just round up some of our upcountry misters with their long guns—"

"No," said Cary. "Maybe a couple of weeks ago, I'd have thought of that myself. But this is something different we got here in the wagon, what Charlie did. Using guns wouldn't just work out with it. What we got to do is vote, not shoot, if we want to keep Arcadia natural and sweet without a second mortgage. Mul, why don't you slide off around and pass the word for as many of our misters from upcountry with names everybody knows—them like Pid Gewaters, Haf Miron, and the like—big men. Tell them they can find me and the statue at a farmhouse around here someplace. You guess there'll be some farmhouse that'd put us up, Mister Pferden?"

"There'll be," said Pferden, economically.

"And maybe Mister Pferden will likewise ask around for those farmers that the other farmers all know about?" Cary looked at Pferden, who nodded. "Come morning we'll all get together at the farmhouse and talk this thing over."

"Right," said Mul, and disappeared into the grain.

Pferden drove on until the track ended in a farmyard. He went up to the door, which opened, and he talked to the silhouette of a woman seen against the light inside the house. He came back.

"Missus of the house, Miz Canameer," said Pferden, "says she'd be honored to have you come in. Mister Canameer should be home directly. He was out to join us when we were on the road."

They went in.

Four hours later Mattie was still sleeping in the bedroom to which Miz Canameer had taken her. But Cary, who had also gotten some sleep, was up and facing some half-dozen men, half-farmers, half-woodies, in the farmhouse kitchen.

"Heard you didn't want guns used," said Haf Miron. He was a big, thick-necked woodie with a scar on his chin. "So we all passed the word to the misters. Don't see why, though. No hundred—two hundred—police going to trouble us."

"If it comes to that," said a heavy-bodied farmer, "we don't need no woodies to clear the police out of the way. Enough land people here to do that chore and never notice."

"How many farm people are there?" Cary asked the last speaker.

"Counting those that came in for Voting Day," said the man, "thirty thousand maybe, who could make it to City this morning."

Cary looked over at Haf Miron.

"And the upcountry people," he said. "How many?"

"Fifteen-twenty thousand," said Haf. "Misters been coming in all week."

"That's a lot of people," said Cary. "Enough to vote down the mortgage. You see why we don't want to use guns, no way. If we start shooting, we give those who want to mortgage again a chance to say we scared off their voters, and the voting don't count."

"That statue got to come in though," said Haf Miron. "If the statue stays out of the City, everybody'll figure the mortgage people got us licked."

"We'll get it in," said Cary.

"How?" asked the heavy-bodied farmer.

Cary laughed, his noiseless woodsman's laugh.

"In two hours we'll hitch up Mister Pferden's team and move out," he said. "Just all of you go spread the word to tell the City folk that thirty thousand farmers and fifteen thousand upcountry people are coming in to see Charlie's statue brought to town."

Two hours later Pferden's wagon rumbled back out of the farmyard and onto the wagon track. Mattie, still sleepy-eyed, stared around them in astonishment.

"Where did all the people come from?" she said.

For the track was lined with farmers and woods people alike. As the wagon passed, they fell in behind it. Their numbers grew; and by the time the wagon pulled once more up on the road, it was surrounded by faces for fifteen meters in every direction.

They started once more down the road toward the City. Ahead, as on the wagon track, people stood waiting on either side along the way, peering at the statue as the wagon passed. But when the oxen approached the place where the police barricade had been the night before, there was nothing but open road. They continued on toward the City.

"Cary," said Mattie, "we've done it."

"Not yet, maybe," he said.

She looked at him oddly. But when they approached the edge of the City proper, her face tightened. Standing across the road before them was a line of police double the size they had faced the night before, this time armed with light energy cannon and holding back the sea of farmers and woods people that stood waiting.

"Keep going," said Cary to Pferden.

They drove on until the nose of the left ox was almost touching the jacket of the Captain of Police, who stood in the center of the roadway. The Captain was a narrow-faced man, perhaps a shade paler than normal, but determined.

"We're not letting you by, Longan," he said.

Cary, sitting on the front seat of the wagon, beside Pferden, nodded. He sat silent. The Police Captain waited, and time stretched out.

"Well?" demanded the Captain. "What are you going to do?"

"Nothing," said Cary.

"Nothing?" the Captain stared at him.

"That's right," said Cary. "You're not going to let us pass, so I guess we just have to sit here."

He went back to silence. The Captain stared at him a moment longer, then turned and walked up and down the length of the line of his men, checking weapons. He came back after a while to where the wagon sat. The oxen were patiently standing. Behind the oxen were Pferden, Cary, and Mattie; and behind and surrounding these, the multitude of farmers and woods people, also silently waiting. The Captain looked out over the ocean of standing people, then back at Cary.

"You're still not getting through," he said to Cary.

"Look behind you," said Cary.

The Captain turned, and stiffened. From out of the City behind his double line of armed men, a second crowd of people were forming—City people obviously, but waiting as quietly as the farmers and upcountry people without.

"Count off!" shouted the Police Captain. "By twos!"

"One . . . Two . . . One . . . Two . . ." The count went along the double line as each policeman counted up or down from the man next to him.

"Odd numbers," ordered the Captain. "About-face!"

Every other policeman in the line wheeled about with his weapon. Now half of them faced outward toward the country people and half faced inward toward their own City dwellers.

"Mul," said Cary, in the silence following this maneuver, "would you and some of the boys come help me? Long as we can't take Charlie's statue into the City, maybe we can stand it up here, so the folks can see it."

"Coming," said Mul.

He and everyone else standing nearby was scrambling into the wagon. Tanned hands took hold of the dark stone and heaved, then heaved again. The statue Charlie had carved rose upright in the wagon, tottered a moment, and stood still. Those who had lifted it dropped away over the wagon's sides.

The eyes of those on both sides of the police line went to the statue; and a slow, deep sound, like the sound of wind over a sea, swept across them as each one of them reacted to the sight. There was a surge on both sides of the line of police toward the armed men.

"No!" shouted Cary, standing up on the wagon seat. "No violence. That's not what Charlie carved it for!"

The surge sagged back. Once more the crowd stood still. The line of police stood still. The sun was warming, rising high in the sky.

"What are you trying to do?" whispered the Captain up at Cary.

"I'm waiting—only waiting," Cary answered, sitting down on the wagon seat once more.

The minutes crawled slowly by. Suddenly, down the line of police, there was movement. One of the men there had dropped his energy rifle and broken ranks. He was walking toward the wagon.

"Briggens!" shouted the Captain. "Get back in rank!"

Briggens paid no attention. He moved forward into a crowd of bodies that parted before him and closed after him, shielding him from the handgun the Captain had just drawn. He came forward at last to the very edge of the wagon and stood looking up at the statue. Then, slowly and deliberately, he took off his uniform cap and stripped away the pistol belt he wore.

Once more, sound rumbled through the crowd—but this time it was the word being passed back of what had happened by the wagon; and this time the sound maintained and mounted in volume toward a roar of triumph. Other policemen were breaking ranks, throwing down their weapons and mingling with the crowds on both sides.

"Mister Pferden," said Cary. "Time to move, I guess."

Pferden whistled at his oxen and picked up his reins. The two big beasts began to move forward, and the police melted away before them.

"No!" shouted the Captain. "No, you—"

He aimed his handgun at the wagon, and a moment later the crowd swallowed him up before he could fire. The steady legs of the oxen moved on toward the City. Men had already sprung from the crowd about, into the wagon to hold the statue upright; and upright it entered into the City.

The sun was above the buildings at full noon when the wagon rumbled finally through the streets of Arcadia City to stop across the street from the same hotel in which Lige Bros Waters had greeted Cary, two weeks before. People— city people, farmers, and woodies, particularly the last— filled the street about it and spilled over to choke the park facing the hotel where the voting booths had been set up. As the wagon reached the park, Cary put his hand on Pferden's shoulder.

"Stop here," he said. "Don't let them unload the statue yet."

"Cary!" cried Mattie, as Cary swung himself down from the seat of the wagon. "You're not going for that buyer *now*, are you? You aren't going to try to sell Charlie's statue with what it means now to all these people? What'll stop the mortgage being voted in then?"

Cary's face was grim.

"Asked Mister Waters come back to see. My word, my deal," he said. He turned swiftly and went across the street into the hotel, not looking back. In the lobby he hunted down the list of those in residence, found Waters's name, and pressed the call button.

"Who?" asked a computerized voice.

"Cary Longan," Cary said. "To see Mister Lige Bros Waters."

There was a second's pause.

"Admitted," said the voice. Beside the list, one of the elevator doors slid open. Cary stepped in, rode up, and stepped out to search down a corridor of doors for the one bearing the name Waters. He spoke to the door.

"I know that voice," said the black annunciator circle on the door. "Come in." Cary touched the door, and it opened before him. Inside was the art buyer, looking no different than the last time Cary had seen him.

"That statue," Cary said, as he stepped into the room. "I brought it. But things are some different—"

"So I gather." Lige Waters's voice was old and hard and dry. He waved to the window on the far wall showing a view of the street before the hotel and the park beyond it. "What's it doing out there?"

"Out there?" Cary stepped closer to the screen.

The statue was no longer in the wagon. It had been removed, and taken into a central part of the park among the trees facing the voting booths. It stood upright there, leaning a little to one side, evidently because the cut across the stone of its base had not been level. But to all intents and purposes the carved stone stood vertical enough. A line of people flowed into the park, moving slowly past it, each one pausing a little to examine it before pressure from the line behind forced him to move on. They were woodsmen mostly in the line; but there were farmers as well, and astonishingly, not a few men and women in city clothes, patiently waiting their turn with the rest.

"Let's go down," said Lige. "I want to look at it up close."

They went down, across the street, and into the park. To one side behind the statue and its passing line, stood a little knot of people—Mattie, Mul, Pferden, Haf Miron, and a farmer Cary did not recognize.

"Mattie," Cary said as he and Lige came up, "what's this?"

She swung about to him, stiff-backed.

"I'll tell you what it is!" she said. "You can't sell it without my permission—and I'm not giving it." She glanced at Lige. "Do you hear that, looper? This statue's not for sale."

Lige's face drew in until it was wrinkled and grim, like the face of an old snapping turtle from Earth.

"I've been hearing how you got into this business, Miss—"

"Orvalo."

"—Miss Orvalo," said Lige. "I should tell you. I've got the recording of a verbal contract with this man, that antedates any deal you may have made with him. You can sue him if you want to, but you can't stop any sale to me."

"See you dead first, mister," said Haf Miron, casually from the side. Lige turned his snapping-turtle face, unmoved, to look at the big, scarred woodsman.

"Interworld business is a little bigger than you think, friend," he said. "The company I work for can get a pan-stellar judgment giving them the statue, and if your local courts won't execute it, we'll embargo all your off-world trade. Even, if necessary, get a Union Navy ship in here to make collection."

"We don't care—" Mattie was beginning.

"Hush, Mattie. You too, Haf," said Cary. "My word, my deal. I'll do the talking." He turned to Lige. "Like I started to say back upstairs, mister, things are some different from when I first talked to you about Charlie's statue. Guess maybe we could sell you something other instead. Maybe those little statues of Charlie's I showed you first."

Lige's head turned sharply to him.

"Told you I didn't see anything worth buying in those lumps!" he said. "What makes you think I'd change my mind now?"

Cary gazed quietly at him.

"Back then you didn't sound like you had much interest in talking a deal," Cary said. "Now you do. Guess if you see something worth buying in the statue there now, you'd see its like in the little statues, once you look them over again."

Lige stared back at him, then slowly moved his gaze to the statue.

"All right," Lige said. "Maybe there's something here. Not much—but something. Maybe I'd have seen it for myself, even if I hadn't heard and seen how all your people here are being moved by it. Or maybe I needed to see them looking to go looking myself. I've been in business long enough to know that there's no single person knows all there is to know about art. But that doesn't have to say I was wrong when I didn't see anything the first time I looked at those things you call little statues."

"Doesn't have to say it," said Cary. "But you know now you were, don't you, mister?"

The snapping-turtle face jerked back to Cary. It was a moment before the art dealer spoke.

"And even if I did see something in the small statues now, after all," he went on, "a boxful of small pieces aren't going to make up for losing a life-size work that's got a whole world of people acting as if they just discovered religion. I'd need a lot more small pieces to make up for that —and the word I hear is your native—that swamp otter, or whatever—who carved this is dead."

Cary nodded.

"Charlie's dead," he said. "But all his people carve some. Their teeth keep growing all their lives, so they've got to keep them worn down. So they all work on stones—some better, some worse. I can get you as many of those you want."

Lige glared at him.

"Listen," he said, "do you know—have you any idea how many men there've been with no art in them at all, compared to one great artist?"

"Point isn't how many weren't artists. Point is, more'n one was," said Cary. "That's right, isn't it?"

He pointed to the statue. Lige still glared at him, saying nothing.

"Mister," said Cary, "you better deal with me—because there's no one else for you to deal with. You want to buy those small statues of Charlie's instead of this big one, and for me to go back to the upcountry and get you more of what his people did? Or not?"

The grim and wrinkled face slowly relaxed. Slit-mouthed, he nodded.

"But these carvings by the other swamp otters," he said, "better be worth it!"

"They are," said Cary. "But you could use them even if they weren't, couldn't you, mister?"

Lige's old face went suddenly pale, then flooded with dark surging color.

"Come on! *Cary*." Mattie pulled hastily at Cary's elbow before the art dealer could speak. "You come on with me, right now! You need to shave and clean up. We've got to draw up new articles of partnership, and besides there's things I want to talk to you about. . . ."

Talking unceasingly, she drew Cary away. After a first second of hesitation, he smiled, and let himself be drawn. Lige stared at their retreating backs, at first wordlessly, then finding his voice to yell after them.

"I buy *art*, you young backwoods hick!" Lige shouted. "ART. . . ."

Neither Cary nor Mattie turned their heads, nor slowed their pace. The color fading slowly from his face, Lige turned back to the statue and saw Haf, with the others, watching him.

"And the rest of you," he snarled, "don't fool yourselves. Maybe there's art in that thing there"—he jabbed a finger at the statue—"but it's about the level of a child playing with clay. It's the art of a stone-age savage painting buffalo on the wall of a cave. A spoonful of art to a whole wagon-sized chunk of stone. It's got some accidental form to it and a little lucky deliberate shaping that lets your eye read something into it that may or may not be there at all. Real art's not like that—accidental. Real art's unmistakable—it reaches out and takes hold of you and makes you into something different. I know! And if there was art like *that*, there in that thing, I'd see it."

Haf looked back at the dealer, then swung his woodsman's gaze over to the voting booths, now no longer with lines of people waiting to sign up for the second mortgage. It was not yet noon, and already the booths were standing empty. A second mortgage would have required enough signatures to keep the booths busy all day. Haf looked away from the booths, back to the endless line of people filing past the statue.

"Mister," he said to Lige, "you're blind."

ARCTURUS LANDING

GORDON R. DICKSON

SF
ace books
A Division of Charter Communications Inc.
A GROSSET & DUNLAP COMPANY
51 Madison Avenue
New York, New York 10010

1.

The first unusual thing to happen that day—and maybe it was an accident, and maybe not—was that someone had switched belts with Malcolm Fletcher, where they hung on hooks along the wall of the Company's downtown penthouse lunchroom. Mal put on the strange belt without noticing it and when he stepped off the edge of the rooftop to fly to Warehouse and Supply—some thirty miles away at White Bear—the power pack in the belt gave him one kick into space and quit dead, leaving him falling through thin air toward the rose-colored pavement nineteen stories below.

Luckily, the safety force shield around the building at the lower levels caught him, slowed him down and stopped him before he hit, but it gave Mal the cold shivers to think what might have happened it he hadn't discovered his mistake before stepping off some unshielded building—say, like Laboratory Annex itself—where he had been working these past few months. Five feet eleven inches of sandy-haired young physicist would have been spread out over considerable area.

As it was, he suffered nothing worse than embarrassment. An Archaist, riding by on a white horse and in a full suit of chain mail, stopped and guffawed at the sight of a man in sedate kilt and tunic of scientist green tumbling head over heels on the resilient pavement. And even a few Neo-Taylorites, holding an impromptu prayer-discussion on the corner of the street, tittered appreciatively as Mal, scowling, got up and brushed himself off. They would have done better to keep quiet, for their giggles drew the attention of the Archaist, and he wheeled his horse toward them with ominous ponderousness, causing them to scurry for sanctuary in the Company building, their ornate yellow robes flapping like the gowns of frightened dowagers.

Seeing he had missed them, the Archaist reined up and turned to Mal.

"Down with the Aliens!" he said formally.

"Go drown yourself!" growled Mal, brushing himself off. He was in a bad humor at the thought of what the result might have been had the powerbelt switch remained uncovered, or the building behind him had its shield turned off.

The Archaist's face darkened and he reached for a mace hanging at his saddlebow. Mal put a hand on his own holstered side arm and the Archaist changed his mind. "Not my weapon," he said, reining his horse around. "Some other time, bud."

"Go pick on a Neo," snapped Mal—but the Archaist, riding off down the street, his plume aflaunt from his helmet, professed not to hear him.

After a few seconds of time had allowed him to cool down, Mal found cause to be rather glad of this. He carried the gun because you had to carry something nowadays to protect you from the crackpots. But he had never actually used it on anybody and didn't particularly want to begin now. He had reached for it in a reflex of anger, and that was all. Nor was there anything really surprising about the Archaist's reaction either. A lot of them were a good deal less rough and tough than they professed to be—just as a lot of Neo-Taylorites occasionally slipped from being as sweet and kind as their vows of Non-Violence were supposed to make them. Not but what there weren't plenty of fanatics in either camp. Mal felt he had got off luckily.

He stepped into a supply shop along the way and showed his power pack to the man behind the counter.

"Fused," said the other, prying off the back lid and examining the interior. "What'd you do, take a hammer to it? Nothing left here but scrap. You'll need a new one."

"All right," said Mal.

He paid for a new power pack, socked it in his belt and took off. His route led him over the hotels and downtown office buildings of Greater St. Paul. As he drifted along through the air, some eight hundred feet up, the ill humor engendered by the power-pack failure began to fade. It was a magnificent day, summery but cool, with a few stray clouds and no more, the sort of day that could make a man want to turn his power belt away from the cities and go bird-chasing over the treetops of the few forest areas that still existed on the north part of the continent. Below him the buildings were large, but toylike, somehow unreal. And the bright garments of the other power belt flyers, flitting along below him on the regular commuters' level some two hundred feet underneath, looked like thronging scraps of bright paper eddying in some slow, invisible stream. For half a second, he was tempted to take the day off and either spend it floating around the city or actually shooting north and spending a few hours sightseeing around the lakes and forests.

He shook himself out of the mood. You're thinking like a Neo-Taylorite, he admonished himself sternly. Sit and daydream while the world staggers by. And he grinned wryly.

Whom was he kidding with thoughts of a vacation? Two hours of killing time and he'd be champing at the bit to get back to his lab. The equipment for the final work on his test drive was waiting for him at Warehouse and Supply right now, and on it hinged not only his own dreams, but the seventy-three years' standing Company reward for whomever would be the first to come up with a faster-than-light drive. To say nothing of the hopes of the human race. No time for time off for Malcolm Fletcher.

The young man shook his head, touched the button that snapped a force bubble around him, and clicked the power belt up for speed. The city slid by at an accelerated pace below him, as he altered course slightly to head north and east toward White Bear. Beneath, the large buildings of the business sections gave way to the fantastic plastic architecture of the suburbs; the suburbs thinned out and were replaced by the garden-like tree clumps and rolling parklands of the larger estates: and Mal found himself sharing the air with nothing but clouds and an occational distant, silent flyer.

The peace and beauty of the scene below him struck Mal very forcibly; and almost against his will reminded him of all that Alien technologies had done for the human race since the first experimental star ship, headed for Arcturus with its three generations inside, had been politely intercepted half a light-year out from the solar system and sent home again, shocking the brave young egotist that was the human race with the knowledge that it was actually very small and very weak and its future among the stars very much dependent on the good will of older, wiser neighbors who had walked the same path before it.

For the first ship to be sent outside the limits of the solar system—product of fifty years and the best in human brains and research—had been picked up and carried home, like a lost puppy wandered from its mother's breeding box, by a titanic creation of metal, an unknowable warden of the skies who brought the explorers back and disgorged a delegation of strange beings to inform stunned humans that their time was not yet—that they were under Quarantine and would stay so until their infant science could conquer the problem of a drive unlimited by the speed of light.

Result—resentment. Born into a world aware of Alien culture for nearly a hundred years, educated in schools that taught a wider view of the universe than any human had conceived before, Mal still felt the gnawing anger, the clutching complex of inferiority that had resulted from that strange homecoming. A belief in its own superiority was bred into the very bones of the human race. And wasn't it just that which had driven Mal into the task and work and research that was leading now to the drive solution he thought he had?

And yet . . . the cool limits of his upper mind struggled to fight down the emotional reaction and take a fair view. The facts showed nothing that was not good. One Alien technology had designed the power belt that lofted him now through the high air. Another, from a different race, had taught Earth the building or altering of homes via a simple, easy blown plastic process. To make possible the terraforming of Venus other alien biological technologies had been supplied, and these were still at work to transform that planet. Land, sky and sea throughout the solar system were being tamed and brought to order by the knowledge of far-flung, star-born cultures.

But—and yet—it was all a prison. For it is what the mind considers, rather than the walls which enclose, which incarcerates the spirit. A wide and beautiful prison from Mercury to Pluto in a system touched with Alien skills. But prison still, beyond the point of denial. No wonder the Neo-Taylorite philosophers withdrew into their fragile artistic shells of the intellect. No wonder the Archaists wore antique clothing of leather and cloth and talked of a past golden age when everyone knew that former history had been full of blood and pain and sorrow. No wonder the high executives of the company warred and intrigued with each other.

Prison it was, and prison still.

With an effort, Mal shook these thoughts from his mind. When he thought about such things occasionally, he went in deep—too deep. He was a physicist, not a philosopher; and there was work to be done.

He looked ahead. White Bear was coming in below him—a resort hamlet of brilliant bubble homes around a lake and the large white buildings of Warehouse and Supply. Mal notched back the belt, snapped off the force shield and went down in a slow glide. He landed outside the low, transparent-sided building that housed the offices for this division of the Company, and went inside.

"Hello there, Mal," said a voice, as he stepped into the shipment receiving office. He turned his head to see lounging against the counter a tall, black-haired, knife-thin man whom he recognized as Ron Thayer—a cyberneticist on some project of his own, whose working quarters were down the hall from Mal's, back at Laboratory Annex. They hardly knew each other in spite of this closeness, and Thayer's easy familiarity annoyed Mal.

"Hi," he growled.

"How's the hush-hush project coming?"

"It wouldn't be hush-hush if I could tell you," said Mal. He was turning toward the brown-eyed, blonde, young woman in green coveralls, behind the counter, with the intention of ending the conversation fairly before it was begun, when he noticed the belt around Ron's waist.

"Hey—" he said. "That's my belt you've got on."

"Is it?" said Ron, with nothing more than mild surprise showing on his face. "I knew I'd got somebody else's by mistake at the lunchroom. But I didn't know whose."

Mal stripped off his belt and held it out.

"Trade," he said, a trifle grimly. "And you owe me for a new power pack. Yours was smashed inside."

"Is that a fact?" said Ron, trading. "I'll leave you a new pack back at the lab. Lucky you found out."

"You can say that," said Mal. He looked at Thayer penetratingly, but the thin man's face was bland. Mal turned away, toward the waiting attendants.

"Hi, Lucy," said Mal. "Got that stuff for me on Order J37991?"

Luey bit her lower lip, looking flustered.

"No—" she began.

"*No?*" echoed Mal, staring at her.

"It isn't here," she said. "I don't know just what the trouble is, Mal. But Mr. Caswell told me to cancel it out of Philadelphia. He's waiting to see you about it. You better go in and see him."

With a frown on his forehead, forgetting all about his recent passage with Thayer, Mal went around the counter, pushed through the swinging gate, and went on through a further door. It opened before him politely, into an inner office, where a stocky gray-haired man sitting behind a large desk looked up nervously as he came in.

"What's up, Joe?" asked Mal, coming up to the desk. "Lucy says my order's been canceled."

Joe Caswell got up jerkily and came around his desk.

"Sorry, Mal," he said. "The order was canceled from the Eastern Office; and your Chief's been trying to get you ever since you left Lab Annex. You're to go east and report to Vanderloon, himself."

Mal stared. "I don't get it," he said.

"Don't ask me, Mal." Caswell shrugged.

"But why would the Chairman of the Board want to see me?"

"Mal, look—" began Caswell and hesitated, "why don't you just go east and find out? I've got a flyer waiting for you since it's a long way by belt."

Mal looked closely at the older man.

"What is it, Joe?" he asked. "What's it got to do with you? Why're you so bothered?"

"Far as I know, said Caswell, "nothing, Mal. It's just that when things happen suddenly like that there's usually something happening on the upper levels. And I don't want to get caught between."

Mal laughed.

"All right," he said. "Where's your flyer?"

"Hangar nineteen," said Caswell.

"See you," said Mal, and left. He did not see, as he went out, the Warehouse and Supply manager reach for a private line on his desk phone that had been open all this time.

"He's on the way," said Caswell into the phone.

2.

Scudding east through the sky at a hundred and thirty thousand feet with the torn thunder of his passage lost behind him, Mal puzzled over his summons. It was not merely the fact that the Chairman of the Board, an almost astronomically remote figure, should require a personal interview with such an underling as himself. It was the mode of the requiring.

Alone in the three-place cockpit with nothing but the empty sky to keep him company, he let his mind slide back and forth over the Company (as it was commonly called)—Instellar Trading Company according to the records.

Interstellar was its official present name. Very few people used it. Originally, back around the middle of the twentieth century, it had been the Seaways Export and Import Company, a middleman trading outfit in the days when a good share of the world's commerce was carried over oceans. From then until the present it had had many names. Certainly too many to remember. The important thing was that in a world from which the family unit had almost disappeared, it had remained, staunchly and jealously, a family concern.

This was not to say that the original family still owned all the stock of the Company, or even a majority of it. The Company was too large nowadays to be controlled by any single individual or any group. But the family did own considerable shares, and working in and with the Company had become a family tradition, so that one of them was sure to be either the President of the Board or something close to it.

The family itself was a New York Dutch one; and its beginnings were lost in a maze of old records. The Company's history became important with Walter Ten Drocke, who as a young man saw his opportunity in the export franchise to be awarded by the new Inner Planets government to a single exporter furnishing the troubled asteroids with freight service. By the medium of what amounted to bare-faced bribery, he had secured the franchise and the future rise of the Company had been assured. Within fifty years it had crowded out its competitors in the field of interplanetary trading. And when Alien contact opened up trade with the rest of the Galaxy, the Company had found itself the only concern with the warehouse and equipment to handle the two-way flow of goods.

So the Company had grown, strongly and steadily. Until, in the relatively short period of years since Alien contact had been made, it had come to handle the major part of the solar system's output, where that output was for export, to the myriad of extra-solar system markets. In the exact meaning of the word, it became a monopoly. But in the process it had at the same time become so widespread and basic, so intertwined with the lives of everyone in the solar system, that it had almost lost its character as a business and become an institution, a part of the culture.

This, to be sure, was a situation brought about not merely by Company expansion, but by the influx of—by human standards—luxuries which trade with the outer stars developed.

The resultant rise in the living standard in the end made it unnecessary in a strict sense for anyone to work unless he really wanted to. And then only four or five hours a day, three days a week. The fact that most people wanted to work, and ended by chafing not at the length but the shortness of their hours, was something that came into the public awareness only slowly and belatedly. So it happened that many people found themselves searching for an occupation that would satisfy their need to be engaged in useful activity—and to many of these, the Company offered a solution.

The flyer had been making good time. By the time Mal had come out of these thoughts, he was almost at his destination. He cut power and dropped down to a thousand feet of altitude, to come out through a low-lying bank of clouds and find the estate of Peer Vanderloon lying below him, cupped like some brilliant plastic gem in the palm of a gentle valley. Abruptly his controls went dead, and a mechanical voice sounded over the flyer's speaker.

"Automatics have taken over. You will be landed under remote control. Automatics have taken over, you will be landed under remote control—"

Mal grinned. Evidently Vanderloon was just as leery of Archaist crackpots as any of the other high Company officials. He settled back to wait while the automatics took him down and landed him. As the flyer settled to a stop, he stepped out. A polite guard in Company Police uniform of black and white was waiting for him.

"Malcolm Kenneth Fletcher?" asked the guard.

"Yes," said Mal.

"This way, please."

The guard led him across a soft green lawn and up a moving ramp into the interior of the building, after first relieving him of his side arm. They progressed along moving corridors to a

spacious, large-windowed room something like a library. And
here the guard left him. Mal looked about him somewhat cautiously. The only other occupant of the room was a tiny, red-
headed young woman with gray eyes, wearing a short one-piece
dress of gold and dark blue, who had been perched on the arm of
one of the chairs, looking out through a window aperture; but
who now turned and came toward him.

"Who are you looking for?" she asked. "Dirk? Or Mr.
Vanderloon?"

Mal looked at her in some puzzlement.

"Mr. Vanderloon, I thought . . . " he said.

"Oh, well it's none of my business, then," she replied. She
turned and wandered back toward the window. Somewhat un-
settled and unsure, Mal followed her.

"That is—" he said, "unless I'm supposed to see Mr. Dirk
first?"

She turned and looked up at him. The gray eyes were large
and serious, but with a pinpoint of bright humor in their smoky
depths.

"Not Mr. Dirk," she said. "Dirk Ten Drocke, Vanderloon's
nephew. I'm Margie Stevenson, his personal secretary."

"Oh?" replied Mal, still more or less at a loss. "Then this is
Mr. Ten Drocke's office?"

Margie Stevenson threw back her red head and laughed.

"Does it look like an office?" she asked. "No, this is just the
anteroom for one of Mr. Vanderloon's offices—if you can even
call them offices. Lounging rooms with a desk in them is a better
way of putting it. Dirk, now—Dirk doesn't have an office. All
he has is a personal secretary to keep him from forgetting
things." She looked at Mal searchingly. "Who are you, anyway? Haven't you ever heard of Dirk Ten Drocke?"

Belatedly, recognition of the name came to Mal. He had seen

it not once but a fair number of times in the newsfax. According to what he had seen, Dirk was the lineal descendant of old Walter Ten Drocke. An enormously wealthy young man whose estate was being managed by his Uncle Vanderloon, an Archaist and a general wildhair.

"I didn't know he had a secretary," was all he could think of to say. Hastily, he remembered his manners. "Pardon me. I'm Malcolm Fletcher."

"Fletcher?" she looked at him sharply, as if his name had just now penetrated. "You're the one who's working on the drive?"

"You know about the drive?" he demanded.

"That and other things," she replied, unperturbed.

"Then maybe," said Mal, "you know why Mr. Vanderloon has sent for me."

"I might guess." she said. "But privately."

"I see," Mal answered. He was about to say something more, but just then another door in the room swung open and the tallest, thinnest young man that Mal had ever seen came striding through with his face twisted in angry lines.

"—And that's it!" he shouted over his shoulder, slamming—or rather trying to slam, for it was built so as not to be capable of being closed in that manner—the door behind him. He took a long stride inward to the room, saw the two other people waiting there, and checked himself.

"You here, Margie?" he said, with a note of surprise in his voice.

"Where did you expect me to be?" she demanded a little tartly.

"I thought I left you in Mexico."

"You did leave me in Mexico. In fact I had to fill out an emergency travel voucher to get back here."

"Oh," said Dirk. He looked around the room as if searching

for a change of subject and his eyes lighted on Mal. "Hello?" he said uncertainly.

"This is Malcolm Fletcher, Dirk," said Margie. "He's working on the faster-than-light drive."

Mal jumped. "I—" he began, then hesitated. "That information isn't supposed to be—"

"Have you forgotten?" asked Margie. "Dirk is the Company's largest stockholder."

"Yes," said Mal, "but—" He checked himself just in time. He had been about to say that, stockholder or not, Dirk did not look like the kind of person to be trusted with restricted information. Nor was this an illogical attitude. From the soles of his soft leather boots to the feather in his cap, this youngest son of the Ten Drocke line had clothed his six-foot, ten-inch body completely in seventeenth-century cavalier costume, complete with four-and-a-half-foot sword. He looked like a character actor stretched to the proportions of caricature. Not that the costume did not become him. It did. Dirk was undeniably eye-catching. The soft, hip-length leather boots, the fawn-colored breeches, the wine-red doublet, the scarlet cloak, all fit him to perfection. The only thing was that they were too perfect. Dirk and his costume were too much of a good thing. So that instead of being impressed, Mal was tempted to grin.

"Down with the Aliens!" said Dirk automatically. "So you're the man on the drive. How's it going?"

Mal was torn between the knowledge of the secrecy surrounding his work and the information he had just received concerning Dirk's name and position with regard to the Company.

"Well, of course it's too early to say anything definitely—" he began. But to his relief Dirk took him up without further explanation.

"Fine. Fine. Lick the Aliens on their own ground. . . ."

Margie—''

''Right here,'' said Margie.

''I've got a terrific idea. You know how I can't get any lawyer to take my case against Uncle Peer. Well, we'll hire some private detectives and set them to running down the background of some—hum,'' Dirk broke off, eying Mal. ''Excuse me,'' he said. ''No offense to you, Mr.—er, Fletcher, but I think we'll step outside.''

He drew Margie out.

Mal sat down on one of the chairs to wait. But he had barely seated himself before an annunciator hidden somewhere in the wall told him to come into the interior office from which Dirk had just come out.

Going on into the next room, Mal found himself face to face with a large bland man in late middle age who was rising from a desk to greet him. His appearance was mild and rather harassed; and Mal caught himself for a minute doubting if this was really Vanderloon, President of the Board.

''Ah, Mal,'' said this man—and with the sound of his voice all doubts vanished. Mal had heard him speak not once but several times in recorded messages from the Board to Company branches. ''Glad to meet you at last.''

Taken a little aback by the warmth of the welcome and the familiarity of the greeting, Mal fumbled his way through the social amenities and did not fully recover possession of himself until Vanderloon had them both seated and the conversation brought around to the matter of the drive.

''Now, I don't want any technical details,'' said Peer Vanderloon, sitting back in his chair. ''But how does it look, Mal? Like success?''

''Well—'' said Mal cautiously. ''I don't want to sound too

optimistic; but if I can follow out my present line of work on an out-and-out experimental basis, I've got high hopes of running into a solution.''

"Mmmm . . . hmm," said Vanderloon, pinching his lips together. "That close, eh?"

"Well, I wouldn't exactly describe it as close—" said Mal.

"I see," said Vanderloon. "Now, tell me," he turned to look directly into Mal's face, "is any part of this experimental business you propose liable to be dangerous—to you, or anyone else?"

"Dangerous?"

"Yes," said Vanderloon.

"Why—" stammered Mal, "of course not. Why—it's impossible. I use force fields of very minor strength—not anywhere near enough to do any damage, no matter what."

But you *do* use force fields?" said the older man.

"Well, yes, but—"

"I see. Yes. I see," said Vanderloon, nodding his head as if in agreement with some inner thought. He came back to Mal. "No doubt," he said, "you wondered why I canceled your order for supplies?"

"Yes, I do," answered Mal.

"Well, I'll tell you," said Vanderloon. "I was told to. Tell me, Mal, did you ever hear of a race of Aliens called Sparrians?"

"No," answered Mal blankly. "Should I?"

"I don't believe you should," went on the older man. "The point is—and this is very secret, Mal—they seem to be something on the order of our guardians. We've had one riding herd on us ever since we started research on the possibility of a faster-than-light drive."

"Guardians?" echoed Mal bewildered.

"That's as good a word as any."

"But," said Mal, "I thought the idea was that the Aliens wanted us to develop the drive on our own."

"It was," nodded Vanderloon. "But on several occasions now they've stepped in, with a word of advice—or warning."

"But I don't understand," repeated Mal. "It still doesn't make sense."

Vanderloon shrugged. "I'll let you find out for yourself," he said. "The Sparrian has asked to see you. I don't know what he wants to talk to you about, but this is so similar to other occasions I can't help guessing. And I've told you this so that you'll be at least partially prepared." Mal sat with his head spinning, trying to sort out his thoughts. "Now?" was all he could say.

"If you're ready," said Vanderloon. He stood up. In a daze, Mal followed suit. Looking back over his shoulder to make sure the younger man was following, Vanderloon led the way out through a large dissolving force screen window and across a small, terraced lawn hidden in the mansion's interior, and to the door of an apartment on its far side. Here he halted.

"Inside," Vanderloon said.

Mal hesitated. Then, feeling embarrassed over his obvious qualmishness about the meeting, he put his finger on the latch button of the door, opened it and stepped inside.

He stepped into a deep gloom only barely short of total darkness. The room seemed small and bare of furniture. Little flickers of light seemed to come and go in the darkness, having the effect not so much of lighting up the room as of dazzling the eyeballs for a split second, so that Mal was blinder than before.

"Malcolm Fletcher," said a flat, mechanical voice unexpectedly.

Mal blinked in the gloom, looked about him, and made out a dim heavy shape close to the floor at the far end of the room. He moved toward it.

"For you own safety," it told him, when he was about half a dozen steps still distant, "do not come too close."

Mal stopped. Peering forward, he could still see next to nothing of the Sparrian. It seemed, if anything, to have a sort of large, sluglike shape with something very like feelers or antennae sprouting from one end.

"I understand," said Mal, "you want to talk to me."

"I want," said the Sparrian, "to caution you."

"Caution me?" Mal felt a sudden coldness gathering in his middle.

"Caution you," repeated the other. "Your present line of research has dangerous implications."

"But—how could it be dangerous? It's impossible. Where would the danger come in?"

"I am sorry," said the Sparrian. "I am not permitted to tell you that."

"But the force fields I'm using are too weak—"

"I am sorry."

Mal took a protesting step forward.

"Stay back," warned the voice. "I mut warn you that to approach me too closely is dangerous."

"Why can't you tell me what about the drive'd be dangerous?"

"It is not permitted."

"But—"

"That is all."

"If you won't give me anything but your unsupported word, I'll have to disregard it," said Mal. He found himself becoming furious. There was a smugness, an assumption of authority about this alien that grated on him.

This time there was no answer. The Sparrian seemed to have closed up permanently as far as this particular conversation was concerned. After waiting a long moment more, Mal gave an angry exclamation and turned on his heel. He went out of the door, fuming.

Outside, the terraced lawn was deserted. Mal crossed it and went slowly back through the window and into the office. Vanderloon was waiting for him in a chair.

"What was it?" asked the Chairman of the Board, getting up as Mal entered.

Mal scowled. "This is ridiculous," he aid. "The wildest thing I ever heard from anybody. Dangerous!"

"Then," said the older man, "I was right?"

"Yes," growled Mal. "But he's wrong!" he added swiftly. There's no danger. There's no possible danger—"

"Mal, listen to me," interrupted Vanderloon quietly. "Sit down."

Mal sat down, scowling. Vanderloon seated himself behind the desk.

"This is going to be a blow to you, I know," he said. "But the Federation knows what it's doing and if it says further work along the line you're following would be dangerous, we've got no choice but to scrap it and start fresh."

"But—"

"Now, wait a minute, Mal," said Vanderloon. "Tell me. Did you ever hear of Cary Menton?"

Mal shook his head.

"Brilliant man. Brilliant. A little erratic, which was why he was never named to head the Project. He worked under Tom Pacune. You recognize that name?"

Mal nodded.

"Pacune was the first Chief Scientist on the Project, wasn't he?" he asked.

"That's right," answered Vanderloon. He took a deep breath. "Well, Cary got an idea. Pacune liked it— recommended it to me. I liked it. But before we could set the wheels in motion to begin research on it, that fellow you just talked to, or one almost exactly like him, showed up from nowhere and introduced himself as an adviser from the Federation.''

Mal stared at the older man. Vanderloon went on.

"This Alien—the Sparrian, as he called himself—told me that it was his duty to warn us that the idea Cary had just produced not only would not work, but was dangerous in its implications. Well, I made some kind of answer and officially scrapped the projected research—I was a young man then,'' said Vanderloon, a slightly wistful note in his voice. At any rate, I cooperated officially, but on the side I set Cary to work on the idea after all in a secret laboratory of his own.''

Vanderloon paused and looked at Mal.

"What happened?'' asked Mal.

"The force fields Cary was experimenting with got out of hand,'' answered the Chairman. "Maybe you can imagine it. We came out one day to find the lab building, Cary, and all the men who had been working with him, folded into a neat little lump of condensed matter about twenty feet on a side. They must have died instantly.''

"But the force fields I'd be working with would be far too weak—''

"Now,'' said Vanderloon, "now, Mal, be reasonable. That wasn't the only time I went against the Sparrian's advice. Every time he was right; and I lost more good men than I care to think of. I finally found myself forced to the conclusion that he knew what he was talking about.''

"Look,'' said Mal, "I'll bring my calculations. You can have them checked by any man in the system. It's not a complicated theory, it's just a matter of hitting the right combinations. You'll see—''

"No!" said Vanderloon decisively. "If I've got to make it an order, I'll make it an order. There will be no more work done by you or anybody else on this line of work you've started." He looked across the desk. "Don't be insubordinate, Mal."

Mal stood up. He was almost too full of emotion for words, but he would have tried to speak once more if Vanderloon had not forestalled him.

"Better luck next time, then," said the Chairman of the Board. "And now, I've got some things to do here—" He let the words trail off.

The dismissal was obvious. Looking into the older man's eyes, Mal felt the fury rising inside him to the point where it threatened to break through all his control.

"Good-by," he said. Turning sharply, he strode out of the room, so stunned and at the same time so angry that he walked blindly and automatically, following the luminous arrows that pointed his way back to the flyer awaiting him outside at the landing.

3.

The mansion was enormous, almost a city in itself, so that discreet signs in pale white glowed on the various corners of the motorized halls and rampways, directing those unfamiliar with the establishment to their destination. Mal switched from one moving strip of bright color to another—it seemed—without end.

He went up hallways and down rampways. Also up rampways. The signs were most explicit, or seemed to be; but it struck Mal after he had been traveling for some twenty minutes that it was taking him a lot longer to exit than it had to enter. Puzzled, he watched closely for the sign at the next corner. There it was, a softly gleaming arrow and the legend—TO LANDING FIELD—but it indicated another turn up a long ramp that led in a curve into the upper levels of the house. Mal hesitated, but the gentle glow of the white arrow left him no choice. Once he left the marked route he would be lost in the many acres of the building. He put his foot on the smoothly upward-flowing ramp and let it carry him up and around the corner.

Hardly had he turned the corner, however, when the lights

went out; and he was plunged immediately into total darkness. Out of this a hand reached forth, grabbed his arm and dragged him sideways. Caught unaware, he stumbled several steps to the right, feeling beneath his feet the moving surface of the ramp give way to stationary flooring. Then the lights went on again.

He found himself in an apartment which—by mansion standards—was a small one and unostentatiously furnished. It was evidently high in one of the towers, for two large force screen windows overlooked the landing field. Mal caught a glimpse of his flyer far below and felt a sudden flash of longing for the power belt he had left inside it. Then he recognized the two occupants of the room, and together, power belt and flyer, vanished from his mind.

The two in question were Dirk Ten Drocke and his little secretary, Margie. Dirk's long hand still held Mal's arm. He shook it off and reached instinctively for his gun before remembering that the guard had taken it from him.

"Hold it," said Dirk hastily. "I'd like to talk to you, Fletcher." Mal relaxed slightly, stepping back. He looked at both of them.

"What is this?" he demanded. "How'd I get here anyway? And if it comes to that, just where am I?"

"In the North Tower," answered Margie. "Dirk used to live here when he was a boy and he rigged up a few small gimmicks to plague people. One of them was a gadget to alter the directional signs. He had the controls in here. This was his room."

"You still didn't tell me why I'm here."

"I'll tell you," said Dirk. "You've been had, Fletcher. That uncle of mine has led you around with a ring through your nose."

Mal looked at him narrowly.

"What are you talking about?" he asked.

Dirk stepped over to one of the walls, pressed a button and a panel slid back revealing an assortment of switches, speakers and screens.

"I listened to your conversations," he said. "Both of them." He pressed two buttons and the screens above each lit up, one showing the interior of Vanderloon's office, the other the Alien Mal had seen earlier represented on the screen. It was still so dark he could barely make the Sparrian out.

Mal turned back to Dirk.

"Well?" he said. "What of it? Aside from the fact you've been prying into something that isn't strictly your business?"

"My business? It is my business!" said Dirk. "You're blind like most of the rest of the world. The Aliens are out to take us over; and my uncle's working hand in glove with them."

"Archaist nonsense," snorted Mal.

"Nonsense!" echoed Dirk vehemently. "Do you believe what you heard from my uncle and that?" He pointed to the second screen.

"I'm a scientist," replied Mal a little stiffly. "If the evidence warrants it, I'll believe it."

"I'll give you evidence," said Dirk. "How'd you like to have another talk with that so-called Alien?"

Mal stared at him. "What do you mean?" he asked. Dirk turned to his secretary.

"Take him down, Margie," he said.

"Down where?" demanded Mal. Dirk indicated the Alien's room on the screen.

"There," he said succinctly.

Amused, Mal let himself be led by the hand through another panel in the wall and down the stationary steps of an archaic stairway. The light in this narrow passage was so dim as to be practically nonexistent; but Margie's small fingers in his own led him surely on. He followed her down the stairway, along a narrow winding passage and out through another panel into a hallway. The hallway had a dissolving window opening on the little lawn Mal had crossed previously on his way to the Alien's apartment. With Margie he crossed it again and entered, and found himself once more facing the Sparrian.

"Now what?" he demanded of Margie, lowering his voice in spite of himself to a whisper, for the dim shape at the far end of the dark room was still impressive.

"Now, what do you think?" demanded the Sparrian, suddenly, in its flat mechanical tones. "Turn on the light."

Mal jumped.

"You turn on the light, Margie," directed the voice.

Behind him Mal heard a muted click and the room stood out suddenly in bright illumination. Blinking his eyes against the sudden glare, Mal made out the Sparrian, a green-colored sausage shape with—he had been right—two antennae sprouting from one end.

"Is that you, Ten Drocke?" he asked incredulously. For having once made up his mind that the Sparrian was a living creature, he found giving up the idea was hard.

"It sure is," replied the Sparrian. "Now, do you start to believe me?"

Mal strode over and stretched out his hand to explore the green skin. It was leathery to the touch and cold.

"Give him the knife, Margie."

Mal looked up as Margie pressed the hilt of a small, sharp blade into his hand. Cautiously he slid it edgewise over the skin until a flap fell back, to reveal a maze of metal rods and wires, the interior supports for the so-called Sparrian.

"Good job, huh?" said Dirk, still speaking from the voice-box in the dummy's head.

Mal's lips thinned to a hard line. He straightened up and stepped back, letting the hand holding the knife fall to his side.

Margie produced a little instrument that she ran over the edges of the cut pseudo-skin, flowing them back together once more. Then she took the knife from Mal, and led him again out and back to the tower apartment.

"Satisfied?" inquired Dirk, as the two of them re-entered.

"Not by a lot," said Mal. "What's your angle in all this?"

The tall young man took him feverishly by the arm and led him over to a window.

"Do you see that?" said Dirk, indicating the estate spread out below. "This was waste land before the Federation stopped that ship headed for Arcturus. Skills taken from Alien botanists replaced the top soil. Alien science dreamed up the materials for the buildings. Alien technology constructed them. Money from Alien trade keeps it going. You can't point to one human item in this whole structure. Can anyone look at that and say the solar system still belongs to humanity?"

Mal gently freed his arm from the other's grasp.

"I've heard all this before," he said. "From other Archaists."

"But you don't believe it," said Dirk. "Not even now when I've pointed out how it concerns you yourself!"

"Can't you see what Dirk is saying?" said Margie. "He's pointing out to you that the Company is deliberately killing the faster-than-light drive research."

Mal snapped his head around to stare at her.

"That's crazy," he said. "Why would they do that?"

"Because the Company stands to benefit from things as they are," said Dirk. "And because there's a small group in it, with my uncle at the head, who see their chance to take over—not only the Company, but the whole system, if they can be given a few more years to get themselves dug in. That's the trouble with people nowadays—they don't care any more. My uncle is out to take over. And the Aliens are behind him."

"Why?"

"Because they can't take us over openly without open war. But they could through a puppet leader like my uncle."

Mal snorted noncommittally.

"Doesn't make sense," he said. "When they could blow us to bits before breakfast and never notice the effort."

"Maybe they can't blow us to bits—ever think of that?" said Dirk. "What do we know about them, except that they've got a faster-than-light drive and bigger ships than we have?"

Mal snorted again. But in spite of himself he was stirred. Fantastic as it seemed, Vanderloon had actually lied to him in an attempt to stop work on his drive—his theory—and the theory was Mal's obsession, the one big work-to-be of his life. He wandered away from the other two and stood looking out the window, thinking.

Dirk looked at him, his lean face searching. "Do you want to do something about the situation?" he asked.

"I'll resign and build it myself!" said Mal.

"How?" demanded Dirk. "Even if my uncle would let you get away with it—which he won't—where would you get the money to do it?"

Dirk's speech sobered Mal. The principle of his drive was what might happen if weak force fields were used to align and synchronize the basic wave components of the object to be moved. A simple-sounding job, but not one that was undertaken with what every man has lying around the house. Mal himself had a few thousand saved; but these were about as adequate as the contents of a child's piggy bank. He turned back to Dirk and Margie.

"I don't know," he said heavily. "What sort of idea have you got?"

"It's Dirk's idea," said Margie.

"It all hinges on my gaining control of my Company stock,"

said Dirk. "It's that stock that gives Uncle Peer his authority in
the Company. He doesn't own much in his own right. But he's
been administering the estate since I was fifteen. My age of
discretion was left up to him, and he keeps delaying the time
when he'll have to hand the stock over."

"Well, how are you going to get it?" asked Mal.

"That's the thing. It'll take a court battle to end all court
battles. And that'll take a young fortune in cash, which I haven't
got now. But the point is, there's a way to get it. I grew up in this
house for fifteen years before Uncle Peer moved in. There's a
time-lock safe in one of the ground-floor rooms keyed to the
personal vibrations of all living family members. In it there's ten
million in cash that my father kept on hand for emergencies. If I
can get my hands on that—"

"Why haven't you done it before?" asked Mal.

"It's walled up," said Dirk. "My uncle didn't know it was
there so he had it built over when he added on a new section
about six years back. There's Company Police making regular
rounds of this place. The most you can count on is half an hour's
free time to tear down the wall and open the safe. And one man
can't do it in that length of time. On the other hand, with ten
million, cash, I couldn't just hire the first person I met to help
me."

Mal hesitated. The whole business had a fantastic flavor to it.
Unconsciously, he turned to Margie for confirmation of this
wild tale. She nodded seriously.

"You've got no idea how efficient Vanderloon's spy system
is," she said. She hesitated, as if gathering courage, then went
on. "For instance, I'm supposed to be informing on Dirk."

Mal stared at her in amazement. Then, wrenching his
thoughts back to the matter at hand, he turned back to the tall
man.

"What happens if I help you?" he asked.

"We take the money and hide out somewhere," answered Dirk. "I get my court fight under way—and you go ahead with the drive, financed by me."

"But look here—" Mal said. "They'll be looking for me now—"

"No, they won't," answered Dirk. "The attendant at the landing field's a friend of mind. He won't be reporting that you haven't left yet; and with all the other flitters and flyers out there, nobody'll notice that yours is still on the ground."

Mal sighed. He did not like Dirk's ideas; but they seemed at the moment the only alternative to giving up the drive altogether.

"It's a deal," he said.

4.

The three of them waited in the apartment that had once belonged to Dirk until the sky faded beyond the dissolving windows and sunset gave way to night. As the automatic lighting of the room came on, throwing the space beyond the windows into deeper, purer blackness, so that they seemed walled off and more secluded than before, Dirk gave the signal and they started off, down another of the secret passages such as that by which Margie had led Mal to the Sparrian. It led them by a route too complicated for Mal's sense of direction to follow, down and around until they finally came out on a different lawn.

"There!" whispered Dirk, as the three of them emerged into the night air.

They halted. Across the dimly lit, open space was what appeared to be a small summerhouse attached to a wing of the main building.

"In there," said Dirk.

They flitted like silent-winged owls across the grass, up the few shallow marble steps that led to the summerhouse's dim, cool interior.

196

"Sh!" whispered Dirk, halting them again. Mal, startled, caught himself with one foot in mid-air. He put it down cautiously.

"There goes the guard," said Dirk. "We timed it just right."

There was a whisper of booted feet on pavement, and the shadow of a man carrying a warp rifle looped over his shoulder went past on the screen of one window opening. The sound of footsteps died away.

"Now," said Dirk. From the inside of his doublet he produced a couple of collapsible crowbars and a pocket cutting torch. He fumbled with the latter. There was a snap, a sputter, and the hot blue flame of the torch sprang to life, throwing gigantic shadows on the summerhouse wall.

"Stand back now," said Dirk. He applied the torch to the walls and cut an outline of something the size of a small door. When he had finished, he turned off the torch, unfolded the crowbars, and handed one to Mal.

"I'll take this side," he said. "You take that. Stick your point in where the torch cut, and pry."

Mal obliged. A quick thrust of his arm drove the point of the crowbar into the crack. He heaved. Dirk heaved. Both men grunted and for a moment it looked as if the section of wall were going to resist the best of their efforts. Then there was a straining creak, the section gradually began to tilt outward, tottered for a second half in, and half out, and fell finally with a tremendous crash.

"Blast!" said Dirk. "We should have put something underneath it. That noise'll wake everybody."

"Fine time to think of that," grunted Mal. Margie was annoyedly brushing dust out of her hair. "Well, now that you've got it, open it up."

Dirk was peering at the lock on the "newly-uncovered" door.

"Just a minute," he said. "I've got to remember how you uncover the lock hole. Let's see, you twist the lever and lift this little cover—"

"Who's there?" shouted a voice from outside suddenly.

"Oh," breathed Margie. "The guard!"

"Hurry up," said Mal.

"I can't," said Dirk, "The cover's stuck."

"Let me do it," said Mal.

"Too late—" said Margie. "Here's the guard."

The sound on the resilient pavement outside was now the slap of running feet. They turned and dived for the entrance just in time to collide with the guard as he entered. There was a thud, four grunts, and the guard picked himself up just in time to see three figures vanish into the interior of the mansion.

"Help!" shouted the guard. "Stop!" And having missed his chance at his targets, he discharged a blast of his warp rifle straight up in the air by way of a general alarm.

Mal, Dirk and Margie found themselves racing along moving passageways with the mansion beginning to hum like an aroused beehive about them. Voices called excitedly from rooms as they raced past. Somewhere, some kind of an alarm was going off. Over loud-speakers at various intervals along the corridors, a babble of voices could be heard issuing confused and contradictory orders to the contingent of Company Guards on the premises.

"This way!" yelled Mal.

"No, this way!" cried Dirk.

"No. Wait!" called Margie. "*Stop!*" She grabbed both of them and dragged her heels, forcing a halt.

"Now, look," she said. "We can't just run. We've got to find some place to hide."

"My flyer," said Mal. "We'll take off."

"No, wait," broke in Dirk. "That's no good. We'd never make it. I've got a better idea—my old underground tunnel to outside. You know what I mean, Margie?"

"I've heard you mention it." She thought a minute. "It means we have to go back to your room."

"That's all right," said Dirk. "We're near the delivery ramp." And he led the way, again at a run, around a corner and onto a steep, narrow little ramp that rolled swiftly upward.

As the delivery ramp carried them up to the tower, the sounds of pursuit behind them began to die away. This was an older, little-used section of the mansion; and most of the corridor speakers and other devices had evidently not been installed here. They relaxed, and let the ramp do the work of carrying them along.

"They'll be here in a minute," said Dirk, as by a back way they entered his familiar room. And, indeed, they had barely closed the door and locked it before they heard approaching feet, the thunder of knuckles on the door panel and Guard voices.

"This way," said Dirk. He loped across the room, his long legs covering the distance in five big strides, and punched savagely at the frame of an ornate mirror set in the wall. It slid back and aside, revealing another of the antique stairways. Mal blinked a little at Dirk. The tall man seemed to produce secret passages out of his hat. They hurried through and the panel closed behind them just as a splintering crash from beyond it told them that the apartment door had at last been forced.

"They'll never get us now," aid Dirk. "The wall behind that mirror is three feet thick." They paused a moment to collect themselves and then started off down th stairway.

"Where does this go to?" asked Mal.

"Out of the estate grounds," aid Dirk. "It comes to the surface in open country."

They came abruptly to the end of the stairway and found themselves in a circular tunnel that led off straight and level from where they stood. They continued along it.

"What surprises me," said Mal, as they settled down to a steady walk, "is that you were able to construct all these things without your uncle knowing about them."

"He's gone most of the time," said Dirk. "Besides, no one watches what an Archaist nut does; it's only in business Uncle Peer's smart. In other ways, he's stupid."

"Hah!" said Margie.

Less than ten minutes later they came to three branching passages. Dirk stopped.

"This isn't right!" he said.

"What isn't right?" asked Mal.

Dirk scratched his head for a second without answering.

"I think," said Margie, "he's lost."

"These tunnels," protested Dirk. "I only had one."

"How'd the other's get here, then?" asked Mal.

"I don't know," said Dirk. "I didn't put them there. They're building new passages all the time around here, that's the trouble."

"I thought," put in Margie acidly, "that outside of business your Uncle Peer was stupid."

"I can't understand it," said Dirk.

"Well, if they knew about your tunnel and added to it, they're probably on their way down here. We've got to take one of them," said Mal. "Want to flip a coin?"

"Why not just take the one that goes straight ahead?" demanded Margie.

"Why not?" said Mal. They took it.

But the central passageway, after a short distance, began to wind and dip alarmingly. Moreover, as they went forward, the lights along the way became fewer and dimmer, until at last they were groping their way along in almost complete darkness. Eventually they were forced to join hands and feel their way.

"Wait a minute," said Dirk suddenly, after a few minutes of this confusion. "I've bumped into something." Mal and Margie came up level with him and extended exploratory hands. A thick, soft substance that gave to the touch was barring their path—some sort of hanging drape, it seemed.

"What now?" whispered Margie.

"Just a minute," said Mal. He was fumbling with the curtain where it touched the side wall of the tunnel. After a moment he got a grip on it and pulled the hanging aside. He stared for a second, let out a low whistle of surprise and let the curtain fall back into place, shutting off the weak gleam of light that had come momentarily through the opening.

"Guess what?" he said.

"Don't ask silly questions!" snapped Margie. "Tell us!"

"Well, it looks—mind you, I never saw one myself—but it looks like a Neo-Taylorite temple. There's a lot of them out there in their yellow robes, and some kind of altar. We're behind the altar."

Dirk grunted something uncomplimentary.

"This is no time for philosophical dislikes," said Mal. "We either go through them, or we go back."

"We go back," said Margie decisively.

"That sounds like a good idea," said Mal, "but what if the guards managed to find their way through that mirror? They may be behind us right now."

"That's right," agreed Dirk. "But what else is there to do?"

"On the other hand," said Mal, "Neo-Taylorites are sup- posed to be vowed to hurt no living thing. Let alone other humans."

"Are you suggesting we walk right through them?" demanded Margie.

"I don't see why not," said Mal.

"Good idea," seconded Dirk enthusiastically. There was an audible screech as he drew his rapier from its scabbard, followed by a groan from Margie.

"Look out for that damned thing," growled Mal. "It's sharp."

"Lead on," said Dirk, brushing Mal out of the way and taking the lead himself. They went out through the hanging.

A fat Neo-Taylorite in front of the altar was delivering an address on The Importance of Essential Kindness to Insects. Dirk prodded him impolitely from the rear. The Neo-Taylorite jumped and yelped. The assemblage, listening, gaped and gasped in awe.

"Coming through!" yelled Dirk, waving the rapier.

The yellow-robed group burst into a babble of sound and drew back, like the retreating surf from a beach.

"See," said Dirk, over his shoulder to Margie. "Nothing to it." And he led the way down and into the crowd, which parted before them.

They marched grandly between the shrinking ranks, and were about to congratulate themselves on finding the road to freedom at last, when an ear-splitting roar from a loud-speaker broke on the air.

"*Attention all!*" it boomed. "*Attention all!* Three enemies of the new civilization are attempting to flee the premises. Halt them at any cost."

Having issued its warning, the loud-speaker attempted to repeat itself. However, this time its thunder was drowned out in the chorus of yells that arose as two-thirds of the Neo-Taylorites present broke their ranks, scurrying for all corners of the temple while the remaining twenty or so flung themselves valiantly upon Mal, Dirk and Margie.

Overwhelmed by numbers, and with Dirk's sword wrenched away from him, they were on the point of being swamped when a sudden bellow of rage drowned out all other sounds. Margie, pinioned and helpless, Dirk, with four or five Neo-Taylorites striving to bring his tall body to the ground, and Mal, flailing energetically against what seemed to be an endless round of faces, found their attackers magically plucked off them and tossed violently in all directions.

"Outrageous!" thundered a voice about three feet off the ground. "Disgusting! Utterly reprehensible! My most profound apologies!"

The last attacker went sailing off to land with a thud at the foot of the altar; and the three fugitives found themselves face to face with their deep-voiced rescuer.

He beamed up at them with the tip of his nose and long black whiskers elevated engagingly in the air. The yellow Neo-Taylorite robe, torn to shreds by his exertions, revealed the rest of his squat, furry body, which resembled nothing so much as that of an oversized squirrel, lacking the bushy tail.

"Hypocrites!" he puffed. "Apostates! How can I ever express my regrets, my young friends?"

Mal, Margie and Dirk stared down at him in amazement. Dumfounding as his appearance was, it was nothing compared to the exhibition he had just given of being able to toss full-grown men around like Indian clubs. He looked back at them; and his furry-faced expression changed immediately to one of embarrassment.

"I beg your pardon!" His little black hands, rather like the oversized paws of a raccoon, beat the air in chagrin, as his tone overflowed with contrition. "So impolite of me! Allow me to present myself. I am an Atakit from Jusileminopratipup, one of the planets of—but then, you wouldn't know that. Never mind. Never mind. My home world is not important, really, except—'' the little Atakit began suddenly to swell with rage ''—for the people who live there, my so-called race, the thick-headed, half-witted jugars sar linotrmpsik ve rupstiok gh cha up yii yi plmurke jhuhey—''

The Atakit checked himself suddenly. He had been fairly chittering with rage; but suddenly noticing his three new acquaintances draw back as Dirk's sword, which the Alien had picked up with a view of handing it back, twisted itself into a lover's knot in the grasp of those delicate-looking little hands, he stopped abruptly.

"Oh, I beg your pardon!" he cried. "I *beg* your pardon—" And to the surprise of all three of them, a large tear rolled down his nose and splashed on the floor. "My temper! My cursed temper. When will I ever learn to control the jukelup ta mechi ve—but enough of that, my young friends. Enough that I am a poor, weak sort of person, still but a short way on the long road to perfection. Allow me to introduce myself. I am an Atakit, and my name is Panjarmeeeklotutmrp."

The three stared at each other and at the Alien.

"What?" managed Mal after a second.

"Oh, call me Peep. Call me Peep!" insisted the little Atakit exuberantly: "All humans do. My unfortunate name is impossible for them to pronounce. Excuse me. Excuse my temper. I did not mean to shock your sensibilities by a demonstration of violence, which is, alas, only too easy for one like myself on your light planet where gravity is much less than I am accustomed to. But conceive my astonishment and shame when I saw those whom I fancied sworn to Non-Violence—these Neo-Taylorites—actually attempting physical coercion on other living creatures. I—'' He hung his head. ''Are many of them fatally injured?''

Margie had been examining the bodies.

''No,'' she said, ''but there aren't any conscious, either.''

''Thank the great spirit of Non-Violence that it was no worse,'' said Peep fervently. ''However, you are the sufferers, my young friends, victims of an unprovoked attack—not, dear me, that provocation is ever any excuse for an attack. How can I serve you?''

''Well,'' answered Mal, ''for one thing, you can show us the way out of here.''

''Willingly, willingly,'' the little Atakit bowed to each of them in turn. ''But surely I can do more to make amends. Are none of you fatigued? May I carry you?''

Mal, Dirk and Margie all hastily expressed their complete lack of fatigue and their positive affection for navigating on their own two feet; and Peep, satisfied, led the way toward the farther end of the temple.

5.

The little Atakit chattered incessantly as they went. He told how he happened to be on Earth and in such a place as they had found him. Jusileminopratipup, it seemed, was a heavy gravity world some fifteen thousand light-years from the solar system. It was a planet about the size of Saturn and populated by a rich variety of native species, of which the dominating one was that of the Atakits, Peep's people.

"Alas," sighed Peep, describing them, "the Unenlightened."

It seemed that the Atakits had evolved from a primitive life form which had made up in ferocity for what it lacked in size; and still, after untold ages, the instinct of a hair trigger temper popped out in each new little Atakit shortly after birth. It followed that in spite of a high cultural level, relationships on Jusileminopratipup tended to be on the active side; and it was because of this that Peep had determined to come to Earth.

"I saw, you see," he said, "the basic error of emotion just recently. I conceived of a happy universe, a universe which had Non-Violence as an aim. And I sallied forth to carry the message. Alas, alas—"

"What happened?" asked Mal, fascinated in spite of himself. He had never heard anyone actually say the word *alas* in his life.

"My horrible temper!" said Peep. "Logically, I knew better; but over two hundred years (I translate roughly into terms of your Earth Standard Calendar) of early training were too much for me. I told my belief first to the confrere that shared my tree house with me. He obstinately refused to see the light. Before I knew what I was doing, I had lost my temper, picked him up and beaten him unconscious against the tree trunk. I went out in search of a more reasonable individual and met another friend of mine on the catwalk above a near-by waterfall. I earnestly begged him to consider my discovery. He proved so purblind that I lost control of myself and threw him into the waterfall; it took him some while to make it to shore. And so it continued. After a few short weeks of this I was forced to the decision that I was not yet ready to carry forth the great message and hearing about your Neo-Taylorite movement, I came here to give myself a lesson in humility."

While Peep was talking, they had gone from the far end of the temple into a tunnel like the one that had led to the latter and through this to the surface of the ground in an open field.

"Hmf!" said Dirk in some surprise. "This was where my tunnel was supposed to come out."

"Good!" said Mal enthusiastically. "Then you know your way from here?"

"Of course." Dirk stared at him. "Why?"

"Because," said Mal, "I'm leaving. I don't know how I'll go about completing my work, but there must be better ways than you dream up."

"You're leaving us?" cried Margie.

Mal hesitated. The one thing that was bothering his conscience was the thought of leaving Margie in the spot she was in—although that same conscience was relatively tranquil where Dirk was concerned.

"Can you figure any good reason for staying together?" he asked gruffly.

"Yes, I can," replied Margie promptly. "There's safety in numbers. United we stand, divided we—"

"My young friends," interrupted Peep, "may I enter the conversation?"

They looked at him rather blankly.

"Go ahead," said Mal at last.

"Young friends," said Peep, "reasoning from known facts it seems logical to assume that you are pursued. The thought of such action alarms me; and the thought of such violence as might come to you tugs at my conscience. Consequently, I must insist that you stay in one group so that I may do a better job of protecting you all."

They stared at him.

"Now, look—" Mal was beginning, when Peep stopped him with delicately upraised hand.

"No thanks, my young friend, no thanks," he said. "No thanks are due me. I am merely doing my Non-Violent duty as I see it."

"I wasn't going to thank you," snapped Mal. "Assuming what you say is true—don't you see that we'll stand out like a bright light if we all stay in one group with an Alien as a sort of nursemaid? The thing to do is split up."

Peep sighed, picked up a near-by rock the size of a small grapefruit and thoughtfully crumbled it into tiny chunks as he closed his eyes and considered.

"No," he said at last, opening his eyes again. "I have asked myself whether more violence would result from letting you go than from forcing you to stay with me. And the former is by far the more violent possibility. I must—I must indeed insist that we got together, even if I am forced to carry you against your wills."

A bleak silence descended on the little group standing under the stars in the open field.

"Forgive me, young friends," said Peep humbly.

"Excuse us a minute," said Mal. He drew Dirk and Margie aside into a huddle and they talked it over. The general consensus of opinion seemed to be that they couldn't do anything about it anyway, so they might as well accept Peep's protection.

"I sort of like him, anyway," added Margie unexpectedly. The two men scowled at her.

They went back to Peep and notified him of their agreement.

"Fine, fine!" Peep, who had been sitting on his haunches, bounced to his feet. "This way. I have a modest six-place atmosphere flyer over beyond the trees there; and we can go wherever we decide to go from here in comfort."

The flyer proved to be all that Peep had said. It was a luxury model for tripping around a planet's surface and probably, if pressed, could have made it to the moon, although no one in his right mind would think of trying it with so many good commercial shuttle services available.

They lifted from the ground.

"Where to?" asked Peep. The three humans looked at each other. . . .

"Some place in the north woods," said Mal.

"No," said Dirk. "There's nothing for us in the north woods. On the other hand, I've got a cottage on the Pacific coast below Seattle; we can go there and make up our minds what to do then."

The suggestion had a sound ring to it. At least, none of the

others could think of a better one. Dirk gave Peep the proper
directions and they headed west, arriving at their destination
shortly after midnight.

The cottage turned out to be a low, rambling building perched
on a high cliff in a deserted section of the coast line. A long
porch overhung the cliff itself and looked directly down on the
narrow strip of rocky beach and the pounding breakers. A moon
was riding high in the sky above scattered clouds, and a cool
on-shore wind was blowing. The three humans, who may well
have been considered to have had a hard day, tottered out of the
flyer into beds and collapsed. Peep, who needed little or no
sleep, expressed a desire to go walking along the beach and
meditate on the concept of Essential Goodness. He said good
night to them all after having been talked out of sitting guard in
front of the cottage's front entrance; and trundled off into the
moonlight, humming to himself.

The cottage was little less palatial than the mansion. The
rooms were large and furnished with the most modern of com-
forts. Mal's bedroom had automatic temperature control, automatic air pressure and odor control, so that a flick of the wrist
would perfume the room with anything from the scent of pines
to bananas. His bed was the most luxurious model of Leasing-
Dillon Slumber Force Field. Nevertheless, he slept no more
than four hours of uneasy, tossing slumber with his mind flitting
fantastically from one odd dream to another. At the end of that
time, his tired subconscious gave up and woke him completely.
He lay there in the before-dawn darkness, facing his problem.

What were they going to do?

He got up, clipped his kilt about his waist and stepped across
the room out onto a little porch whose balcony overhung the
ocean. The late night air was cold and salty and sweet. The tide
was in; and little flecks of foam floated up the long distance of

the cliff from the crashing breakers pounding against its base below. The chilliness and the space around him seemed to clear his head; and floating in from somewhere in the night came an idea.

The drive was the answer. The drive was the only answer; and the drive would always be the answer. The problem was to construct the drive. Dirk had let Mal know that he was broke; but surely he must own property like this place, which obviously his uncle did not know about and which could be liquidated for a small fortune, easily enough to build the drive.

Surely Dirk could do this. Surely they could take the funds, buy the equipment and build the drive. Then, with a working model in his hands, he could announce the fact to the solar system and no power of the Company that Vanderloon could control would be enough to prevent so large a piece of news from reaching Alien ears.

And then a new thought struck him suddenly. Peep was an Alien. Peep must know what kind of Alien contact was being kept with the solar system, and how to reach some responsible official of the Federation. Galvanized into action by the implications of this thought, Mal dodged back into his room just long enough to pick up his tunic and went off in a run down the cliff in the direction Peep had taken, slipping into the tunic as he ran.

He ran some distance before his wind began to give out. As he slowed to a panting halt, it occurred to him rather belatedly that Peep's heavy gravity muscles could carry him over the ground much more swiftly and easily than any human's. Consequently, the little Atakit was probably some distance down the coast and it would be a long tramp to catch up with him.

Accordingly, Mal waited long enough to catch his breath; and then continued on at a more sedated pace, turning over his ideas in his head as he went. The more he thought of his plan the more excellent it appeared. Sell property. Buy equipment. Build drive. Get in touch with Aliens through Peep. Turning it over in his head, he saw only one possible objection: the fact that Peep, being a member of the Federation, might be under some rules prohibiting him from helping in such a project. In point of sober fact, Mal was far from beginning to understand the little Alien. Peep did not talk or act like one of the Galactic overlords which the general consensus of human opinion pictured members of the Federation to be.

It was about an hour and a half later, and the rising sun had already flooded sea and shoreline with dawn light before Mal finally caught up with Peep. At first he did not recognize the Atakit. What first appeared to his eyes was a small bedraggled object inching its way up the wooden steps that led from some ancient boat house to the strip of sandy beach below. So unlike Peep did it look that Mal's first conclusion was that it was some small bear or large dog which had been swimming in the ocean. It was only when he came closer that he recognized it as Peep.

The little Atakit was a sorry sight. His fine fur was plastered down with sea water and he was somewhat muddy about the feet.

"Peep!" cried Mal when he was close enough to be heard. "Did you go in swimming?"

Peep sat down at the top of the ladder and began to squeeze handfuls of water out of his fur.

"Inadvertently," he said. "Yes."

"But what happened?" asked Mal.

"We will say no more about it," said Peep. "It is a tender subject."

"Oh," said Mal. "Of course."

"I will merely postulate," Peep went on, "that the life of a non-violent person is a difficult one. A short ways up the beach from here is a sort of quay or jetty sticking out into the water where it was deep. I strolled out on it and found myself a comfortable spot near the end of it where I could sit and meditate. Happening to glance down into the water, however, I was interested to discover a good deal of marine life in the vicinity."

"Oh?" put in Mal, filling a pause in the narrative.

"There was one large fish in particular that seemed to use the rock supports of the jetty as a sort of lurking place in which to waylay other, smaller fish. I became quite absorbed in him as I lay there, feeling a particular surge of empathic feeling which caused me to imagine myself, lying in wait, powerful, silent, single-mindedly alert for prey. I responded, in fact I thrilled to the feeling. At that moment I felt as if that fish was my own kin."

"Uh—I see," said Mal.

"And then—without warning—my lurking brother shot forward—his jaws flashed open, and when they closed again, a smaller fish twitched helplessly in their grasp. I need not detail you my reaction."

"No, of course n—"

"As quick as thought itself, all my love for the predator was wiped away, and in replacement my heart broke for the poor victim. Without a thought, I launched myself into the water, my hands outstretched to rend and tear the murderer. Of course I missed him—"

"You did?"

"And had to walk back along the bottom until I came out on shore, being far too heavy to swim in the impure hydrogen oxide you have so much of around here. But the point is—" wound up

Peep, severely— "that both attitudes were completely honest ones. And the two together form a paradox."

"I suppose it's natural," began Malcolm vaguely. "But you were lucky you didn't drown."

"Drown?" echoed Peep, interrupting his fur-squeezing to look up curiously. "Oh—*drown!* That was hardly likely, my young friend. As you must know, there is oxygen in what you call water. Even your lungs could extract it if they were used to doing so and had the chest muscles to breathe such a medium easily. Doing so does, of course, require a much higher respiratory rate, since there is not all that much oxygen there. So you might say I more or less had to pant a bit to breathe underwater—nonetheless, the exercise was quite practical. But to return to my moral dilemma. To give a problem a name is not to solve it."

He paused, looking severely at Mal.

"Oh?" said Mal, numbly, his head still occupied with the thought of Peep breathing underwater.

"Indeed," said Peep. "And the dichotomy involved is common. I, the individual, abhor the idea of a living creature being the target of a hunter's sport. But let me, the same individual, casually pick up a weapon such as those used on such occasions, and I thrill to the thought of that same creature being *my* target. Yet the second feeling is no more to be conquered than the first. In fact—" added Peep, a trifle wistfully— "I sometimes weasel a little bit by imagining that my quarry on such occasions is another Atakit. There is such a long and glorious history of extermination among ourselves, and justifications for it, that it is hard to feel guilty where one of my own species is concerned. I have the lingering impression that they ought to be able to take care of themselves by this time—if you follow me, young friend."

"Look Peep—" broke in Mal, who had been waiting impatiently for this peroration to come to a close. "You're a Federation citizen, aren't you?"

Peep got to his feet and started back toward the cottage; and Mal fell into step beside him. The little Atakit considered the question as he walked, his head thoughtfully a little on one side.

"I suppose you could say no," he answered at last. "Your word *citizen* doesn't quite fit, but yes, I think you could say so."

"Well, tell me," said Malcolm impatiently. "Is there some kind of Federation representative here on Earth that we could get in touch with?"

"Representative?" echoed Peep.

"You know," said Mal, "a sort of consul."

"Dear me, no," said Peep promptly. "There's no need for anything like that. Since you people can't leave your system, why have someone on duty here? The nearest—er—person of official status would probably be on Arcturus."

Mal's hopes fell.

"How do you get in touch with the authorities if you need to?" he demanded somewhat desperately.

"What for?" asked Peep.

Mal gave up that line of questioning; and brought it back to grounds with which he was more familiar.

"The point is," he said, "I *do* want to get in touch. If we could build a model of my drive and show it to some Federation official, the Quarantine would be lifted, we'd automatically become Federation citizens and the Company couldn't touch us."

"Well, there'll be an interstellar ship by in about ten years that I was thinking of taking when I left," said Peep thoughtfully. "But you seem in somewhat of a hurry. *What* drive?"

Mal blinked. He had forgotten that the Atakit knew nothing of their situation. They had reached the porch of the cottage by the time he finished explaining it, up to and including his plans for building the drive.

"An excellent idea," said Peep without the slightest hesitation, when Mal finished explaining. And referring to the plans he added: "I can see a lot of violence being avoided."

6.

It was two o'clock the following afternoon before Mal thought fit to spring his plans upon the rest of them. By that time they had all risen and eaten what was either breakfast, lunch or dinner, depending on how you looked at it. It was, in fact, just as Margie started feeding the disposable plates into the converter and Dirk shoved back his chair preparatory to getting up from the table that Mal decided to call the meeting to order.

"Come back and sit down," he said to Margie. "We've got something to talk out."

Thoughtfully, Margie disposed of the last of the plates and then returned to the table. They sat facing each other, the four of them, including Peep, who beamed on them all impartially.

"What's the idea?" asked Dirk.

"Plans," said Mal. "I had a talk with Peep last night—"

"Peep!" interrupted Dirk.

"That's right," said Mal. "What's wrong with that?"

"Well—" said Dirk. They were all looking at him and he flushed a little with embarrassment. "After all he's an Alien," he said doggedly.

"I like Peep," Margie said.

This had the expected effect of bringing the attention of both men at once upon her while they explained simultaneously but for differing reasons that *liking* him had nothing to do with it, it was a matter of hard fact, etc. And in the verbal melee that followed the issue was lost and they were finally able to settle down to business.

"What it boils down to, Dirk," said Mal, when this enviable point had been reached, "is that I've been thinking that the drive may be the solution to all our problems."

Dirk nodded. "You may be right at that," he replied.

"I've been concentrating too much, probably, on my own problem. If the Quarantine was lifted, that'd break most of the Company's power here and I shouldn't have much trouble getting a court hearing on my rights."

"Well, do you all want to hear what I've thought of?" asked Mal.

"Go ahead," said Dirk.

The other two nodded and Mal launched into his ideas of the preceding night—or rather, early that same morning. When he had finished, there was silence around the table.

"Well? What do you think?" demanded Malcolm.

"I," said Peep, "must confess to ignorance of your economic system and cannot therefore comment. But—" he beamed at Mal— "I like your spirit."

"Thank you," said Mal.

"Not at all," said Peep.

"I think it sounds fine!" burst in Dirk. "I've got all sorts of junk lying around that's salable—haven't I, Margie?"

"You certainly have," said Margie. "But I'm not sure it's going to do us any good." The seriousness of her tone brought the eyes of the others upon her.

"It's a good idea," she went on. "But I don't think any of you stopped to think of how many plain, ordinary business contacts the Company has. Just how long do you think we could stay hidden if Dirk were involved in commercial transactions where he had to use his own name?''

Her words brought an immediate pall of silence. Margie had, unfortunately, put her finger on the flaw in the plan. Mal frowned at her.

"What else have you got to suggest?" he demanded. She hesitantly.

"Nothing," she said truthfully, "except—" She stopped.

"Go on," prompted Dirk.

"Just a small suggestion," she said. "I've been thinking where we could hide. The best thing, it seems to me, is to be a needle in a haystack."

"And how do you propose to do that?" Mal broke in. The gray eyes she turned on him were troubled and uncertain.

"There's a place on Venus called New Dorado," she said hesitantly.

"That's right," said Dirk, excitedly catching on to her idea. "The place where the pellucite strikes are being made. The new frontier. The—"

"And what's all this got to do with us?" asked Mal.

"New Dorado is growing so fast," said Margie. "The population is supposed to have grown—oh—almost quintupled in the past six years alone. In a place like that it would be awfully hard to find three strangers—let alone the fact that they'll probably be looking for us in the empty areas here on Earth."

"But how about the drive?" demanded Mal. "That part of what I was talking about still holds. Building the drive is our only way of getting the Federation's protection."

"Then what's the use of even trying?" said Dirk. "How could we ever get to Arcturus, even if you did build it?"

"Let me build it and I'll get *us* to Arcturus," said Mal. Suddenly his face lit up with an idea. "Say!" he cried. "How about my building a working model into the flyer—that one of Peep's?''

"Young friend," interrupted the Atakit suddenly. "You forget my flyer is primarily an atomsphere model and would never take you as far as Venus. That is—if you really intend to go to this New Dorado of yours." The look of triumph that accompanied Mal's last suggestion faded from his face.

"That's true," he said thoughtfully.

"But there's no problem in that!" burst out Dirk excitedly. "There isn't a Company millionaire on the east coast that doesn't have a space yacht. And I know them all and where they keep them."

The others exchanged looks.

"Not a bad idea," said Mal calculatingly. "Which one do you suppose would be the easiest to get away with?" Dirk thought for a minute.

"Josh Biggs!" he said at last. "That old son of a gun drops his on his front lawn and lets it lie there until he thinks about it two weeks later. All we have to do is walk up, get in, and take off."

"Doesn't his pilot lock up?" asked Mal.

"Oh, Josh doesn't have a pilot," answered Dirk, "he fancies himself a hot spaceman and does his own piloting."

"Well," said Mal slowly, "it sounds like a good idea." The tension broke around the table and he grinned at the others. "Everybody agree?"

They agreed.

Late that evening they took off. At Mal's direction, Peep took the flyer up and leveled her off in a screaming run across the continent. Inside of two hours they were nosing down toward the eastern edge of the continent. Dirk took over the directions and they dropped, gently as a falling leaf, into the shadows flung by a stately group of conifers, tall and silent in the moonlight.

"Here we are," said Mal, swinging open the flyer door. He looked out on the moon-silvered lawn and back into the shadowy interior of the flyer.

"Margie," he said. "You stay here. And be ready to take off. It we don't make it, we'll come hooting back in one large hurry. Dirk, you and I'll have a shot at getting the space yacht into the air. Peep—?"

In spite of himself the little Atakit's black eyes were dancing with excitement. He blinked once, and the light in them went out.

"I am sorry," he said simply. "There is too much danger of my being aroused to violence. And I've done too much already. I will wait for you both here."

Mal nodded. He beckoned; and Dirk followed him out. The lawn on which they approached the mansion was clipped and thick and soft beneath their feet.

"Now what?" asked Mal in a whisper. "Where does he keep it?"

"Around the other side of the mansion," answered Dirk. "I'll show you the way."

It took them close to fifteen minutes to circumnavigate the tall, sprawling building. They rounded a corner finally and saw it—a long, beautiful torpedo shape bright-glistening in the moonlight. The thick observation windows in the nose gleamed with the dull luster of black obsidian, reflecting the darkness inside. The heavy, circular port stood half ajar on the side facing them.

"This is it?" said Mal, almost in awe, for even his imagination had not been able to conjure up anything as luxurious as this.

"This is it," replied Dirk.

They went up along the silver-gleaming side, through the entry port which stood half ajar in the moonlight and down a long carpeted corridor into a spacious control room. There, in the light from the vision screen set in one wall, glittered the simple standard controls which Alien engineering had adapted to all human ships and which everyone nowadays learned about in secondary school.

Mal sat gingerly down in the padded pilot's chair before the control board and touched the exciter key. No sound passed through the ship, but a little light sprang redly awake on the board. A few more touches on the controls and the yacht lifted lightly into the air, drifted across the mansion and dropped down to swallow the waiting atmosphere ship of Peep and Margie by the efficient medium of the yacht's wide cargo hatches.

"It can't be this easy," said Mal uneasily.

But it was.

The space yacht *Nancy Belle* rose gently like some silver torpedo from the soft turf. Gently upward, like a feather, she floated, flashed once in the moonlight—and was gone.

7.

New Dorado in the Venusian Midlands would have been a tent
city if tents had still been in use by the human race. As it was, it
was a city of ramshackle, hastily blown plastic bubbles,
crowded and jammed together as chance directed. The plateau
which was its base stood like some huge, upthrust island pushing out of the green jungle below; and every inch of its forty
square miles of area was jammed and crowded with miners—
prospectors, for the most part, individuals with a small stake, a
battered atmosphere flyer and a great deal of hope for the hard,
white organic deposits that went by the trade name of pellucite,
and which the Federation found so valuable for some unexplainable purpose.

But the large outfits were represented there also. In particular, Solar Metal, Pellucite, Inc., and Venus Metals, all sub-
sidiaries of the Company itself. These organizations were no
longer deeply involved in the terraforming process that had
begun on Venus—with Alien aid—seventy years ago; the spore-
seeded jungle was now maintaining itself while it transformed
the atmosphere and surface of the planet. The huge warehouses

needed early in that process were still useful, however, supply-
ing the plateau and provding quarters for what few small industries there were, such as the factory that turned out the bubble
plastic for the miners' shacks and structures, the hydroponics
layout, and a good share of the entertainment property of the
plateau.

The companies also prospected. That is, they sent gangs of
men out to comb the jungle below in search of pellucite pockets,
in the same fashion that the individual prospector followed. But
by and large their biggest business was in buying up claims once
they had been discovered by an independent, and then sending
in an ore-extractor crew to blast out the bucketfuls to a small
truckload of pellucite that was there. In fact, it was not practical
to work much otherwise. Pellucite finds occurred in such small
quantities and in such randomly scattered locations that it was
neither practical nor efficient to keep men on a payroll just to
prospect.

By far the largest percentage of the population of New
Dorado was made up, therefore, of the free-lance miners. These
either located the claim and sold it immediately or else grubbed
out the ore immediately themselves and brought it in for sale at a
slightly higher rate. And, as with most mining booms, all made
money, but very few kept it. What they did not keep went
directly or indirectly back to the Company through the gambling
devices and drugs that could temporarily take a man away from
the tangled, steamy wetness of the jungle below.

New Dorado had one landing field. That landing field was the
plateau itself. A ship approaching the town signaled its desire to
come in, and the control officer in the tower picked out some
few square yards of unoccupied space on the plateau's muddy
surface and directed the newcomer there. The fact that that
space might be the ordinary parking area of someone else who

was temporarily absent was no concern of the tower officer, and was treated as such.

Problems however, were still bound to occur. And a first-class one occurred when out of the pale whitish green of the Venusian sky there came unexpectedly, not a planetary flyer nor a square-shaped freighter, but two hundred and twenty feet of torpedo-shaped space yacht, with the incongruous name of *Betsy*, which requested permission to land.

The traffic officer cursed; and pounded the HOLD button.

On the freshly renamed *Betsy*, Mal snapped on the horizontal gyros, and the *Betsy* slid to a smooth stop in mid-air, as the delicate machining of her precision controls responded to the call of the gyros.

"What's up?" asked Dirk. They were all gathered in the control room.

"I don't know yet—" said Mal.

The communication screen in front of them lit up, cutting short his words. Framed on it was the traffic officer, a thin-faced, tired-looking individual in official gray.

"Identification," he growled.

"Space yacht *Betsy*, owner Wilhelm van Tromp, out of New Bermuda."

The traffic officer grunted. If he was impressed by the *Betsy's* obvious expensiveness and the millionaire's resort playground from which she ostensibly hailed, he gave no sign of it.

"Hold on gyros," he said. "I'll see if there's any room for you." And the screen on the ship went blank.

They waited in bored idleness for an hour and a half. Finally the screen flashed on again and the traffic officer directed them down into a little space of churned-up mud near the north edge of the plateau. Mal, who was no experienced pilot, sweated blood in the process of getting them down without a collision with the other craft surrounding the parking space. But the *Betsy* was equipped almost to think for herself; and they finally settled into the muck without even a scratch on her gleaming hull.

"Well, here we are," said Margie somewhat inadequately. They were clustered around the screen which showed the scene outside their airlock. As if by common consent, they all began to move toward the airlock.

"Wait a minute," said Mal, halting suddenly in the doorway. "We can't all go out."

"Why not?" demanded Dirk over his shoulder. His long legs had already carried him half the way down the corridor toward the airlock. Now at Mal's words, he reluctantly hesitated. Peep and Margie also halted and looked back at him.

"Because somebody has to stay with the ship," said Mal.

"That's fine," said Dirk. "You stay." He looked at Peep and Margie for approval, but failed to find it.

There was a long, hesitant pause. As with most people unused to space travel, the three humans were definitely land hungry, even after the short three-day period which had comprised the total time of their trip from Earth. Peep, and it was a tribute to his philosophy, was the first to break the silence.

"Young friends," he said. "why don't we draw lots?" Mal looked at him rather ruefully.

"You know, Peep," he said slowly, "I just happened to think of it. You won't be able to go out, anyway. This plateau is nothing but mud on top. With the weight you've got for your size, you'd sink out of sight and we'd never find you."

"I? Sink?" Puffing with a touch of anger, he trotted down the corridor, activated the mechanism that operated both airlock doors, walked down to the foot of the landing ladder and touched one small foot gingerly to the surface of the ground—in the manner of a swimmer testing the temperature of the water he is about to dive into.

The foot went out of sight.

"Skevamp!" snorted Peep, drawing back. The others had followed him to the airlock.

"Tough luck, Peep," said Mal consolingly.

"Kar e visk!" muttered Peep in a huff. Without a further word, he turned around and marched back into the ship, fuming to himself. Margie looked back over her shoulder at the corridor up which he had disappeared.

"You two go ahead," she said. "I think I'll stay here with Peep."

"He'll be all right," aid Mal.

"Well, I think I'll stay, anyway," said Margie. And before any further protests could be voiced, she turned on one foot and disappeared back into the interior herself.

Mal and Dirk looked at each other, shrugged and started out. The mud, which had parted like so much thick soup under Peep's concentrated mass, merely squished and sucked around their insteps.

"Fah!" said Dirk fastidiously, standing on one leg like an offended crane and trying to shake the ball of mud off his right boot.

"Might as well get used to it," said Mal. He expanded on the subject. "You eat, breathe, and roll in it here—according to the news services."

Dirk grunted ungraciously. He was not one of those people to whom dirt provided a natural environment.

8.

A visit to the New Dorado black market, however, resulted in disappointment. The local dealer in transportation units—a fat, piratical-looking gentleman by the name of Bobby whose voice squeaked and grated on their ears like a rusty hacksaw blade— informed them that there was no market for anything the size of the *Betsy*—but if they needed transportation and had the money to buy—

They had not. Twenty discouraging minutes later, after plowing back through the muck and losing their way twice, Mal and Dirk emerged once more from between two ancient atmosphere flyers onto the little open space that surrounded the *Betsy*. This last thirty yards or so should have been clear going. Instead, they found the way blocked by a considerable crowd, from the center of which the angry thunderings of a not unfamiliar voice reached their ears in tones of violent denunciation.

"What—?" ejaculated Dirk, bewildered.

"Why, there's Margie," said Mal. And, indeed, just at that moment, Margie spotted them and came squeezing her way through the press of bodies.

"What is it?" asked Mal, as soon as she reached them.

"It's Peep!" said Margie grimly. "Listen!" From the center of the crowd, and from out of sight, came Peep's voice.

"Brrr e yssk ta min pypp—arcomanyavak! Nark! Ta pkk yar! Spludinvesk! Burrr yi yi TTTTTT!"

"Man, can he cuss!" said one bewhiskered miner. And this appeared to capsulize the opinion of all.

"What'll we do?" Margie queried. "He's got himself stuck in the mud!"

"How in God's name—?" began Mal.

"Oh, he started brooding right after you left," answered Margie. "There was an old hatch cover with a handle on it. He got the idea that if he stood on it, he could hitch himself along, somehow. I tried to talk him out of it, but he just tucked the hatch cover under one arm and went off muttering to himself."

"Well, what went wrong?" asked Mal.

"He—he put the hatch cover down," said Margie, "on the mud. And he stepped on it. It held him. But when he tried to hitch himself forward, he slipped. There was a sort of splash—"

"Then what?" demanded Mal impatiently.

"Well, after the mud cleared out of the air, there was Peep, still holding on to the hatch cover by the handle, with just his nose out."

"But I thought he was right beside the airlock," protested Dirk. "How'd he get way over there?"

"That's the worst part of it," said Margie. "I tried to get him to keep quiet until I could get a rope to him. But he wouldn't listen. He kept going *kkk!* And *spssst!* And things like that. And then he started swimming through the mud—in the wrong direction!"

Mal glanced at the airlock of the *Betsy,* a good thirty feet away.

"All that way?" he said incredulously. "He couldn't have."

"It was awful!" said Margie. "He wouldn't let go of the hatch cover and he wouldn't stop swimming until he wore himself out. And now look at him."

Mal grunted and shouldered his way through the crowd. In the small area at its center, two eyes, a muddy nose and muddy whiskers stiff with indignation stared up at him. The rest of Peep, with the exception of his hands, was out of sight.

"Cha e rak!" said Peep.

"What're you doing down there?" demanded Mal angrily. "You ought to have more sense."

"Buk ul chagoukay R!" responded Peep furiously. The mud surged and boiled about him; and the hatch cover in the grasp of his muddy fingers bent back and forth like a piece of tinfoil.

"What a stupid thing to do," said Dirk, who had just shouldered his way through the crowd and now stood by Mal.

The effect of this final criticism was too much. Peep went speechless with rage.

"What are we going to do?" asked Margie from behind the two men. Mal scratched his head.

"I got a winch," spoke up an unexpected voice in the crowd. "If we bored a hole in that plate he's holding and got the hook end of a chain through it, maybe we could drag him out."

Peep said something more in Atakit, which clearly conveyed the idea that no blankety-blank winch was going to haul him out of anything. He would walk. The mud went into a tidal wave around him and he progressed a good six inches further away from the *Betsy*.

Mal turned and looked at the miner who had offered the use of his winch. He was a wiry little man of indeterminate age, with green, competent-looking eyes set wide apart in a leathery face.

"Thanks," said Mal.

"Back in a minute," promised the little man. He ducked away into the crowd and was back shortly with the end of a chain and a hook in one hand, and towing a winch with its power pack holding it some two meters aloft in the heavy Venusian atmosphere like some clumsy kite.

"Stand back!" ordered the little man.

Several other men in the crowd seemed to take his cue, pushing back the clustering observers until a sort of channel through the packed bodies was effected up to the entrance of the *Betsy*. Fastening the hook into the hatch cover through a hole which he made with a belt drill, the little man backed away, letting out chain as he did so, until he reached the airlock.

"I'm going to anchor her inside," he shouted to Mal, and disappeared inside the *Betsy*. There was a moment's wait, then a clinking noise came from within the yacht and the chain suddenly tightened.

"Ready out there?" came the little man's voice from the interior of *Betsy*.

"Ready!" called back Mal, looking anxiously down at Peep.

The clinking noise came again, this time in a steady rhythm; and the chain began to shorten. Peep rose slowly and impressively from the mire on a long slant back toward the space yacht, like a submarine emerging from the ocean depths. Completely coated and encrusted, he rose like a ball of black dirt with only paws, nose and eyes and whiskers visible; but with those eyes and whiskers expressing furious disdain of the mechanical contrivance that was rescuing him. Amid cheers he rose back toward the *Betsy* and disappeared through the airlock. Mal, Margie and Dirk bolted in behind him and closed the lock.

Peep, finding solid metal under his feet again, slammed down the hatch cover and stalked off in the direction of the showers.

Mal turned toward the little man. "I don't know how to thank you,'' he said. ''If there was some way we could pay—''

    ''Don't bother,'' said the little man. From somewhere inside his tunic he had produced a very heavy and efficient-looking blaster; and he held this pointed impartially at the three of them. ''Just get this can up in the air and follow the route I give you.''

9.

If the rest of New Dorado was at all surprised to see the *Betsy* take off without letting the little miner off first, there was no evidence of it. The traffic officer in the tower merely yawned when Mal requested clearance and waved them out. The *Betsy* rose and left the plateau, heading south and west out over the green tangle of the Venusian lowlands two thousand feet below.

They stayed on this course until the plateau dropped below the horizon behind them. Then, after some more or less aimless zigging and zagging about, they finally settled down into the jungle, literally diving from sight, beneath the sea of rampant greenery.

The vegetation here in the lowlands was generally of the giant fern type. Here and there, huge squat trees with spongy trunks, half buried by creepers and vines, interspersed themselves with the overgrown ferns. None of these, however, offered any real barrier to the eight hundred tons of Venus-weight *Betsy* and her yacht-weight hull. She went through them on ordinary drive and they bent, swayed apart and closed behind as she passed, while quick sap bubbled forth from the crushed and broken sections of limb and vine, and the damage began to heal visibly before the yacht had even landed.

Once down beneath the false sky of overarching green, the *Betsy* came at last to rest, sinking several feet deep into the spongy, moss-covered ground. She had slid into a small area where the ground was unaccountably clear of smaller vegetation, even of the white fungoid forms which could almost live without that sunlight which the larger plant forms screen off for themselves, and she lay on a moss like an emerald carpet.

"Open the lock, grab the keys and come on," said the little miner, gesturing with his weapon. Herded by him, Mal, Margie, and Dirk were forced to move ahead, out of the control room, down the main corridor and out through the lock on to the moss. It gave like sponge rubber under their feet so that walking on it was a little like walking on an unending stretch of inner-spring mattress.

"Your Alien friend won't follow us on this," said the little man with satisfaction. "Straight ahead now, and no tricks—" He broke off suddenly, eying Dirk with suspicion. "What's wrong with you?"

"It's not hot!" replied Dirk bewilderedly. And, in fact, the air was cool on their faces—even cooler than the plateau had been.

The little man chuckled.

"Don't go fifty yards off from here or you'll change your mind about that," he said. "This is a funnel area—something the meteorology boys are still talking about back on Earth. We've got a shaft of cool air coming down on us here almost directly from the sub-stratosphere. And don't ask me how, because I don't know. Every so often you run into something like this, down in the weeds here." He gestured with his gun. "Straight ahead, now."

They started walking. For twenty yards they went straight ahead over the yielding moss toward one of the huge, spongy-barked trees. They reached its enormous base and halted, looking back at the little miner.

He, in his turn, halted and looked at the tree.

"Sorrel?" he said.

"Right the first time, Jim," answered the tree.

There was a sudden, almost soundless whirring, a momentary vibration that set the teeth of the three younger people on edge; and the tree trunk between the ground and about ten feet up faded slowly into transparency, revealing a large circular room conforming to the dimensions of the tree trunk and apparently supporting most of the living tree above it while cutting it off completely from its roots. A tall, thin man in his middle forties with a scarred but cheerful face looked out at them from his seat at a bank of controls.

"Will you walk into my parlor?" he said with a grin.

Befuddled, Margie, Dirk and Mal stepped gingerly forward and found themselves in the room. The man called Sorrel did complicated things with the bank of controls, and blank walls reformed around them.

Margie cast an apprehensive glance upward toward the ceiling, where by rights, the tonnage of the Venusian tree should be pressing down on them. Sorrel noticed her anxiety and grinned even wider.

"Relax," he said. "Vanity, vanity, all is vanity—this whole area including the tree is illusion. If you knew anything about funnel spots, you'd realize they're always bare of vegetation because of the temperature, which is too low for most of the imported Alien weeds."

"Oh," said Margie.

"But now that you're here," went on Sorrel, waving them to

seats near his console of dials and switches, "sit down and chat." As they seated themselves, he turned his attention to the little miner. "What's the story, Jim?"

"I think this is what we're looking for," the latter said; and he rehearsed the account of Peep's rescue from the mud.

"Fair enough," said Sorrel, when the other was done. "Then they're the ones. There couldn't be two groups like that."

"Look," said Mal, breaking into the conversation. "What's going on here? What's the idea of dragging us off here? And just who are you, and your friend here, anyway? We're Earth citizens and—"

Sorrel laughed. "The way I hear it," he said, "you're all a prize package for anyone's picking up. Do you know what the Company's willing to pay for you—unofficially, of course?"

"What do you mean?" challenged Mal.

"Oh, don't worry," smiled Sorrel. "We're not going to turn you over to the Company, hopper. We want you for ourselves. Guess why?"

Mal looked at him.

"I don't know what you're talking about," he said in level tones.

"Well, I'll brief you, hopper," said Sorrel, leaning back and looking at him quizzically. "One Malcolm K. Fletcher—that's you—comes up with a special drive for interstellar ships. What happens? He disappears, the Worlds Council President disappears—"

"The President!" ejaculated Mal.

"You didn't know that?" said Sorrel, curiously regarding him. "Worlds President Waring disappeared three days ago Earth time—just before you three pulled your own act. He vanishes. So do you, and the heir apparent to the Company's biggest block of stock, and *his* personal secretary, and—to top it all—an Alien. Now do you know what I'm talking about, hopper?''

Mal thought for a minute. "Who told you I was the man on the drive?" he asked.

Sorrel sat up abruptly, his bantering air dropping from him.

"That's better," he said. "Now, let's get down to brass tacks. Fletcher, what you're looking at right now is part of something called the Underground—which is what's left of all the old human spirit of independence. And we need that drive of yours.''

Mal shook his head stubbornly. "I never heard of you," he said. "What is this Underground of yours?"

"I'm about to tell you," said Sorrel.

And so he did.

"Hopper," said Sorrel, "you've heard how when the Quarantine was slapped on us humans that things sort of blew high wide and handsome for a while. Practically everybody had a different idea about what ought to be done about the Aliens penning us up in our own back yard. Right about then somebody either back on Earth or out on the stars somewhere must have sat down and put in some heavy thinking on how to lightning-rod all those emotional reactions so that they didn't tear human society apart. Well, whoever did it, or maybe it was even more than one mind, came up with two fine let-off-steam-type organizations, being as you know the Archaist movement and the Neo-Taylorites. And things settled down. You either thought the Aliens were a good deal and thought along Neo-Taylorite lines; or you figured they weren't and bought yourself a suit of armor and went Archaist.

"All fine and dandy for the first half century.

"Then, by God, whoever had done the original thinking

began to notice that he'd overlooked something. The Archies and the Neos were all fine and good for ninety some per cent of the race, but there was a bit of a headache in the group remaining. Now, why was that, you ask.

"Well, I'll tell you. In that last group were all the people who in normal times would be bumping their noses up against some kind of risky business. They would have been starting revolutions, exploring frontiers, going up in balloons, down in bathyscapes, or out in ships, losing themselves on mountain tops or away in jungles. They weren't crackpots, you understand, like some of the Archies and the Neos, they just liked excitement and action in doing something that hadn't been done before. They were the physical-first-and-mental-afterward boys; and there was no spot for them in the new setup. So what did you have?"

He paused and waited, evidently for Mal to say something. Stubbornly, Mal let him wait.

"You had trouble, of course," Sorrel said, finally. "Now it wasn't that there weren't plenty of things to be done on Earth and the planets that hadn't been done there; or that there wasn't plenty of unexplored territory out in the solar system to go take a look at. But for the type of mind I'm talking about, all that had been spoiled by the Aliens. Our kind got their kick out of doing what nobody else had done or could do. And while there was no direct evidence to the fact that the Aliens had explored our own system long ago, everybody knew they sure as heck could do it if they wanted to—and where was a poor, ordinary human to get any credit out of a situation like that?

"So we had the Gang Period—if you'll remember your history of some years back—and general hell-raising by this minority I'm talking about; until, lo and behold, the first pellucite strike was made here on Venus.

"Then, what do you know? Three particular points became

apparent almost at once. One—pellucite was valuable as hell to
half a dozen worlds way down in the center of the Galaxy or
some place equally remote. Two—it was so scattered that large
company mining was impractical. Three—and top surprise—
humans were the only ones who could handle it in the raw state
with impunity. *Well, kiss my Aunt Susie!* said this particular
little section of the population I've been talking about, *but
here's something those Aliens can't do! Me for Venus!* And off it
went.

"Result—New Dorado, the roughest, toughest, sweetest little old hell-raising hole in the Galaxy, by God. The same people
that had been kicking around Earth getting into general trouble,
came up here, sweated themselves white in the lowlands, drank
themselves dizzy on the plateau and strutted around with their
chests stuck out, looking each other in the eye and telling each
other that, at last, by all that's precious, they were *somebody!*"

Sorrel broke off and looked at his audience quizzically.

"Well—?" prompted Mal.

"Well, now, what do you think?" drawled Sorrel. Mal
frowned at him.

It looks to me like you're building up to the accusation that the
Aliens deliberately organized pellucite mining to keep one section of the human race busy."

Sorrel said nothing, merely looked back at him with glittering
eyes, an icy, savage humor flickering in their depths.

"But what—why would they want to do something like
that?" said Mal.

"Maybe somebody asked them, you think?" replied Sorrel.

"Somebody?" echoed Mal. "But who—oh, I see." He
looked squarely at the other man. "You think the Company got
it done."

"Well, you sure are sharp," said Sorrel, throwing a glance at the little miner. "Now, who would have thought he'd see through it that fast. Took us nearly twenty years ourselves, didn't it, Jim?"

"But why would the Aliens do that for the Company?"

"They do business together, don't they?" demanded Sorrel. "You scratch my back, I'll scratch yours. Sure, a favor. Why not?"

Mal looked doubtful.

"There's no proof—" he began hesitantly.

"Look, how much of a coincidence can you take?" broke in Sorrel. "There was only one trouble spot and it got taken care of, didn't it? And not in any ordinary way."

"Perhaps," said Mal. "But there's a difference between coincidences when they're looked at from a small point of view or a large. Looked at from the point of view of Earth or from your own point of view as a member of a relatively small group or class, the odds against a pellucite discovery at that particular time and place were so astronomically big as to make the affair look fishy. Now, wait—" went on Mal, holding up his hand as Sorrel showed symptoms of interrupting—"I'll even bring up something you haven't, and that's this business of our not knowing what they use pellucite for. We believe that it's a petrified secretion—like amber—of some ages-extinct native Venusian vegetation—and that's all we know. But what I'm trying to point out is first, that its very suspiciousness gives it a clean bill of health. If the Company and the Aliens deliberately intended to deceive everyone, why would they be so obvious about it? Add to that the fact I'm driving at, which is that when you're dealing with the Federation, umpteen peoples and worlds, the law of averages makes this type of coincidence quite reasonable."

"Oh, hell!" said Sorrel, disgust heavy in his tones. "It's easy to sit there and carp. Do you want to hear the rest of this, or don't you?"

"All right," Mal shrugged. "Provisionally, I'll accept the fact. Go on. What's this got to do with your Underground?"

Sorrel told him.

The Company, instrumental in the spore-seeding that had begun to terraform Venus decades earlier, already had empty warehouses and a vacant base on the plateau when the pellucite boom began. Refurbished and staffed, these quickly became the supply center for the spate of eager prospectors, and no one gave that a second thought.

"Yeah, I was as itchy as anybody, back then—hell, I was only eighteen when I came out there on a work contract." Sorrel paused, his face abstract for a moment. Margie's face bore a sort of sad echo of Sorrel's distant look, Mal noticed, suddenly. Margie had told him something of her father. Already an older man when news of the boom came to Earth, he had been one of those unable any longer to suppress their adventurous leanings. For him the adventure had been disastrous.

Sorrel was going on with his story, telling them how the sharper observers among the miners—and some of the company men, too—had slowly begun to realize that they had been supplied with no more than a large playground, in which their spirit of adventure could make all the mudpies they wanted.

". . . The Company was subtle about it, sure, but once you put the pieces together its control could be seen easily. For one thing, the price the Company paid, as middleman, for pellucite was always rising or falling—in response to the Galactic market, they said. Meanwhile, though, the prices the Company was charging for supplies was *also* rising and falling; that was supposed to be in a ratio with something called the 'current operating cost index.'

"We began to get the idea of what was going on when we noticed that the two factors always managed to keep any one miner from making a really big fortune. Lots of guys made enough to let them go back to Earth for a life just below the luxury level. But no one, in almost three decades, ever managed to keep enough to put himself on a financial par with any of the group that control the Company. We decided to look into that—'' said Sorrel.

The type of people drawn to the plateau were inclined by nature for action—particularly of the dangerous sort. With a pool like this a sort of spy organization had been possible. Miners, ostensibly retiring to Earth, had infiltrated many facets of Earthside society. Among other things, they had kept their eyes open for similarly-included spirits, and gradually they built up an excellent network of men and women who watched all that happened in the System.

In fact, the miners had built something very like a cadre for a revolutionary movement, with men and women of the sort who enjoy that sort of danger. Strangely, they were not so much like the kind of people who dream up revolutions, as they were like those who fight in them; and so for a number of years now they had been an organization without a real head, without a goal. All they had in mind was to try to find the truth in a situation they knew to be contrived. They only did it because it was the sort of dangerous work their kind needed to feel really alive—yet, without any clearly defined purpose at all, they had actually gone a long way.

"We know most of how things stand," said Sorrel, earnestly speaking at last to Mal and Dirk and Margie, with the banter and half sneer of his earlier conversation forgotten. "Human society is sick—do you know that? Whatever the Company and the Aliens have been gaining from the Quarantine, the rest of us have been paying the price for. We just aren't built to stagnate. Not us. There's only two active outfits in the solar system today. One's the Company and the other's us. In the Company there's maybe twelve to twenty thousand people who are pretty sure they know what they want and are out after it. In the Underground we've got up to a hundred thousand men and women who are alive and want to work, but right now are just marking time. But the rest of the race is boring itself to death. You know what the average character does back on Earth? He gets up at around nine in the morning. He goes to some piddling little job that he keeps more to satisfy his need for self-respect than to ensure him an income, which, one way or another with all these allowances and aids, he'd get anyway. He puts in two, three hours, then knocks off. He goes home. Or he goes out and runs around outdoors playing some kind of sport. He has his big meal of the day. He goes out and takes in some entertainment. Then he goes home and sleeps—sleeps late until nine the next morning.

"Fine—isn't it? Ideal life for five years—maybe ten. Then what? Remember this is the average guy. He gets kind of tired of golf or tennis, or surf boarding—hell, you can't play games all the time. He gets tired of shows and night clubs. He needs an interest. He'd like to find it in his work, but his work isn't that important—or maybe it's a job he has a sneaking suspicion could be handled just as well mechanically or electronically if somebody a little higher up wasn't justifying his own job by keeping as many men under him as possible. So he gets bored. He gets deep bored. Too far for any kind of game or entertainment or play-work to pull him out of it. So he goes Archie or Neo—and becomes half a fanatic about it. Do you know the largest number of converts to either of those two outfits are men and women in their forties? It's true.

"And what is he, once he's put on either a tin suit or a yellow robe of peace?" demanded Sorrel. "I'll tell you: He'd dead! Dead and pickled and coffinned and buried. And anybody who kids himself differently is a fool and a liar."

A little space of silence put a period to Sorrel's words. For a moment it held the room; and then Dirk spoke up half belligerently.

"And what've you got to offer?" he said. "You say the Archaists are dead. What about your Underground? What do they do about the situation?"

Sorrel looked at him.

"Thank you, my friend," he said, sliding back into accents of lazy insult. "The gentleman from the audience—" he went on, turning to Mal and Margie—"has just inquired what the Underground plans to do about the situation. Now, I'll be honest with you honest folks. A year ago, I couldn't have answered that question. Really answered it, I mean, instead of mouthing a lot of pretty words Archie and Neo style.

"The Aliens chased us home to stay until we could build an interstellar drive. The Company started honestly to look for it, but when they saw how good it was without one, they started backing the Neos and sabotaging their own men—yes, we know about that, too," said Sorrel, grinning savagely at Mal. "You'd be surprised how many good men have been bought off, warned off, tricked off, or just plain gotten rid of."

"You still haven't answered me," insisted Dirk.

"Oh, yes—what we aim to do. I'll lay it on the line," said Sorrel. "We want that drive of yours for ourselves alone. We want to take it and keep it quiet. We want to build our own ships and put the drive in them and go sneak a look at this Federation.

And if we don't like what we see, then one day the Aliens are going to wake up to find an OFF-LIMITS sign posted by Pluto, and a fleet of armed ships standing just behind it to make sure they read it clean and plain."

He looked at them. He looked at Dirk, at Margie, at Mal. "Catch?" he said.

10.

For a long moment after Sorrel's last words, no one said anything. For a space of time, Mal sat, letting the implications of the Underground man's words sink in. When he roused himself, he became suddenly aware that all the others were looking at him. Margie, Dirk, Jim and Sorrel, they all sat silent, waiting for *his* response.

He exhaled a slow breath and turned to Sorrel. ''Let me sleep on it,'' he said.

Sorrel nodded, his swarthy face understanding. Then he rose and stepped over to the wall. He pressed a recessed stud, and a panel slid back revealing a force lift. He waited until the others had filed past him, then entered himself.

''If you want anything, just buzz,'' he said, waving at the console of controls. Then the panel slid shut again, and Mal was alone.

He pressed his buzzing head between the palms of his two hands and tried to resolve his mental chaos into some kind of order. But it would not resolve. Ideas, plans, concepts and beliefs—the minute he approached them, they went bounding off into meaninglessness, or changed appearance so radically that he did not recognize them.

And eventually his tired body won its battle, and he slept.

He dreamed that he was talking to Peep.

"This is a dream, you know," he kept reassuring the little Atakit.

"Of course, my young friend," replied Peep agreeably, sitting up and looking like a grandfatherly squirrel blown up to fairy-story dimensions.

"You're really in your room on the *Betsy*," continued Mal.

"So we are," said Peep. And so indeed they were, as Mal recognized when he looked around him. It was a little shadowy and indistinct, but there was the neatly made-up bed that Peep had never bothered to sleep in, the chairs, the other furniture and the wall screen turned wide open to show a view of the stars, which Peep liked to sit and watch while contemplating some question of his philosophy.

"Now, look here, Peep," said Mal. "You're the cause of all this."

"I?" replied Peep.

"Well, not you alone," said Mal, finding himself growing confused again. "But your kind."

"The Atakits, you mean?" offered Peep encouragingly.

"Not just the Atakits," said Mal desperately. "All Aliens. No—I mean—"

"You mean," said Peep firmly. "Everyone who isn't human."

"Well, I suppose I do," replied Mal defensively. "All right—suppose I do. Suppose I take you as a representative of every intelligence that isn't human; and I ask you, *'What are your intentions with regard to the human race?'* "

"I beg your pardon," answered Peep. "But do we have to have intentions?"

"Why—" said Mal, astounded. "Of course—don't you naturally?"

"Let me ask you something," said Peep. "Speaking to you as a representative of all intelligences that are human, suppose I ask you, *What are your intentions toward each individual race in what you humans call the Alien Federation?*"

"Aha!" snapped Mal triumphantly. "But you see I can't answer that because I don't know each individual race in the Alien Federation."

"True," conceded Peep. "Well, then, what about we Atakits?"

Mal found himself uncomfortably at a loss for words.

"Well?" asked Peep.

Mal fished frantically in his mind for the answer he was sure was there. But no words came. He was aware of Peep floating nearer, as the room in his dream appeared to stretch and grow.

"Well?" cried Peep.

The room had become a huge and echoing hall of justice. Peep, grown enormously, towered over him. Somehow he had become dressed in a tall cocked hat and a resplendent uniform. Medals glittered on his chest and his voice rang out like a trumpet.

"Well?" thundered Peep. He loomed far over Mal's head and his voice echoed up to the ceiling. *"As the right honorable and thoroughly accredited ambassador plenipotentiary from the ancient and established race of Atakits, I demand that you, Malcolm Fletcher, human, do now and for all time inform the universe of the intentions of the human race toward all other peoples now and henceforward until the end of physical time.*

And you shall speak the truth, the whole truth and nothing but the truth, so help you God amen!"

Mal woke up in a cold sweat. He had a hard time getting back to sleep.

11.

When he woke up again, it was morning and someone's hand on the bank of controls had turned the walls of the room back to transparency, so that he looked out over the smooth carpet of green moss to the *Betsy* and the jungle beyond. He blinked, stretched himself and sat up.

"Good morning, hopper," boomed Sorrel's voice cheerfully from some hidden loud-speaker. "The lift's right behind you. Grab it and come up and join us for breakfast."

Creakily, Mal rose from his chair, turned around, found the lift with its panel open and entered. Inside two buttons on the wall were marked, individually, UP and DOWN. He pressed the UP button and rose into a small interior garden, which, thanks to the same type of illusion that hid the funnel spot, contrived to give the impression of being out on a rocky hillside back on earth. A small spring bubbled out of a tiny cliff into a basin of natural rock, and through some flowing bushes, Mal saw his four companions seated around a table which apparently was placed on the edge of a cliff overlooking a waterfall.

"Shower and toothpaste to your right," said Jim; and Mal,

following the little man's pointing finger, stepped through some trailing vines into a very modern wash lounge.

When he returned to the hillside, he had not only showered and shaved but run his clothes and boots through the cleaner and he felt refreshed enough to realize the gnawing of a ravenous appetite. He came out on the ledge, found a seat at the table and fell to.

As he ate, he listened to the conversation going on around him. The rest had passed to the coffee stage and the talk was general; and, indeed, animated. It struck him that a great deal of getting acquainted had been going on since he last saw these people. Almost as if they had taken his decision for granted and had already gone about the process of settling down together. For a moment Mal felt slightly piqued that they should have taken his soul-wrestlings of the previous night so lightly. And then the thought reminded him of something else.

"Peep!" he said suddenly. "He's still in the *Betsy*. How about—"

"He's all right," spoke up Margie. "We talked to him over the ship-ground circuit. He can't come out because of the softness of the ground, but he's had a good night's sleep and a few pounds of food from his own supplies in his flitter in the hatch. He blessed us all and said he's going to spend the morning in deep contemplation of the Infinite."

"Oh—" said Mal. He went back to his breakfast.

When he had polished off the last sausage and piece of egg, he accepted a cup of coffee from the dispenser and leaned back. The others turned on him.

"Well?" demanded Sorrel. "What's the word, hopper?"

"I won't make any deals," said Mal. "I won't say I agree with your way of doing things. But if you'll help me, I'll build it."

"That's it!" yelped Sorrel. He jumped to his feet. "Excuse me, I got to do something right away."

He almost literally ran out of the room—followed by Jim. Margie looked at Mal curiously.

"Why?" she asked curiously.

"You mean, why did I decide that way?" said Mal.

"Margie!" growled Dirk, embarrassed. "That's *his* business."

"I don't mind telling you," answered Mal mildly. "I believe that the drive, whatever immediate uses it may be put to, is basically a good thing for the race to have. It's progress and we aren't ever going to gain anything by burying our heads in the sand; especially with the rest of the Galaxy so far ahead of us in other ways."

"You didn't come to any new decision, then," said Margie. "You practically said that same thing to me the last time—on the way to Venus here—remember?"

"Well, no," said Mal. "I guess there's nothing brand new about it."

"In other words," said Margie sharply, getting to her feet, "you didn't come to any real decision at all!"

"What?" said Mal, baffled. But Margie was already on her way out, her sharp heels beating an irritated tattoo on the stony illusion of the hillside. She vanished through what seemed to be a curtain of water and did not reappear.

"Now, what got into her?" demanded Mal, turning back to Dirk.

"You have done," said Dirk pontifically, "what I call disappointing a woman in her imagination."

Mal snorted. It was the best way he could think of expressing his feelings on the subject.

Sorrel returned, followed, as usual, by Jim.

"All set!" he said, in high glee, dropping into one of the

chairs at the table. "The Underground will back you to the limit, hopper. Now—what are you going to need to throw this gadget together? Twenty thousand? Thirty thousand?"

Mal glared at him.

"Five years, twenty million credit units, and a staff of fifty trained men, plus factory facilities, a testing ground and a fully equipped laboratory ship."

Sorrel stared at him as if Mal had just slammed him with a power wrench.

"That's all right," said Dirk reassuringly. "Give him about five minutes and ask him again. He's just been having a little argument with Margie."

But Mal was already pulling himself together.

"That's just what I need," he growled. "It doesn't mean that I can't get along without some parts of them."

"I hope to sweet blue heaven you can," breathed Sorrel. "What do you think we are—the Company?"

"All right," said Mal. With the prospect of his own kind of work before him, he was rapidly regaining his ordinary good spirits. "Let's go at it this way—what can the Underground give me in the way of equipment and space? If it comes down to that, I can do most of the actual work myself."

Sorrel winced.

"Well, I'll tell you," he said. "We don't dare try to get you off Venus and back to Earth. Undoubtedly by now the news of your Alien friend getting stuck in the mud has gone back to Company Headquarters and they've got scanner units blanketing the planet. That leaves this world which actually means your choice of two spots. Here or the plateau."

"How about out in the jungle, somewhere?" put in Dirk.

Both Jim and Sorrel shook their heads.

"Never do," said Jim, his wide eyes serious. "You've got no idea what it's like out there. You work with respirators and refrigeration units for a max of four hours a day when you're prospecting; and three days of that's the limit, even.''

"If we had the equipment for jungle building—but we don't,'' said Sorrel.

"Well, actually,'' said Mal, "The unit will, I believe, be small. You've got to remember I've never gone any farther with this than drawing up a report for the Company to accompany my request for experimental material. But I'm pretty sure the unit should, itself, be small and simple. However, I can still use all the space I can have; and it seems to me there'd be more of that here than on the plateau—right?''

"Right!'' replied Sorrel. "And there's your laboratory ship lying out in the front yard—'' he jerked a thumb in the general direction of the invisible *Betsy*—"but there's something else to think of. If you're going to need much in the way of equipment that'll have to come from the plateau, we're going to have to worry about drawing attention to the funnel spot here. The Company Police will be watching the plateau like hawks.''

"But look—'' said Dirk. "We took off in the *Betsy*. And, as far as they know, we never came back. Don't you think they'll assume we hit for some place farther out in the asteroid belt, or back to Earth?''

"Why, sure, Frank,'' said Jim, turning to Sorrel. "Why didn't we think of that? They'll figure these people have gone.''

"They might,'' said Sorrel, frowning. "But they'll still be watching the plateau, if only on general principles. That gives me a notion, though.''

"What?'' asked Mal.

Sorrel chewed on a thumbnail, his dark eyes abstracted. He turned to Jim.

"Jim,'' he said, "why the hell didn't I think of it? The Underground can pick up individual pieces of equipment and cache them in the jungle anywhere. Then we can go out overland and pick them up.''

"Why, sure," said Jim, his face lighting. "There's no problem to that. What else do we have to figure out now?''

Sorrel turned to Mal, questioningly.

"Well, let's see," said Mal. "There's just one more thing. If I'm going to use the *Betsy* to work in, we'll have to clean a lot of stuff out of her. For that I'll need some extra hands. In fact for work generally, I'll need some extra hands. How many men can you get me?''

Sorrel grimaced.

"Now, that's a sore point," he said. "I don't dare have people coming and going here steadily for fear of drawing attention to the place. They'd figure a big strike up on the plateau; and we'd have everybody and his Uncle John nosing around. On the other hand, I can't very well bring a bunch in and keep them here. There's no room and not enough supplies to feed them. This thing was set up as a one-man station for me. I'm the contact point between the Underground here and Earth.'' He hesitated. "Look—" he said suddenly. "There's me, there's Jim, there's Dirk here, and even your Margie. Can't we handle it?''

It was Mal's turn to look sour.

"Listen—" said Sorrel desperately. "I know it's tough. But when you've got to make do, you've got to make do. I could bring a crew of five hundred good men in here tomorrow, if I thought it would work. But you know how long the project would last then. Just long enough for the word to cross the plateau and the Company Police to get their flitters in the air. Look, I know I'm asking for a miracle—but can't you do it that way?''

Mal waggled his head in despair.

"I can try," he said heavily.

"That's it, then!" cried Sorrel, slapping him on the shoulder and jumping to his feet. "Let's go all have a drink on it, and then we'll hit the moss outside and get to work. How about it?"

"Oh, hell!" said Mal, with the beginnings of a grin, following Sorrel over to a large boulder which had just turned into a liquor cabinet. "What have I got to lose that I didn't stand to lose, anyway?"

12.

Josh Biggs would never have recognized his sleek yacht before the day was out. The recognizable items such as his luxury furnishings and some of the paneled partitions were no longer in the ship, but instead were flung in a disordered pile off in one far corner of the funnel spot; and the places they had occupied were stripped down to bare, gleaming metal.

This part of the work, indeed, progressed much more rapidly than had been expected because of an extra pair of hands which Sorrel had not taken into account. These were the slimfingered appendages of Peep. The Atakit met them at the entrance of the *Betsy* as they left the station ready to begin work, and was apprised of the plans over Sorrel's protest.

"Listen—" said the Underground man, dragging Mal off to one side after the beans had already been spilled. "What're you doing? He's an Alien!"

"Look!" said Mal shortly, pulling his arm loose from the other's grasp. "If it hadn't been for him, we'd have been in the Company's hands twenty times over." And he told Sorrel of how they had met Peep.

"Well—" Sorrel was saying doubtfully, when Peep trotted into the main lounge where they were standing.

"May I be of use, young friends?" he beamed.

"Why, thanks, Peep," said Mal, turning away from Sorrel. "You can. That partition back of the bar will have to come out."

Peep obligingly trotted over to the partition, grasped the edge of it firmly and pulled. There was a screech of tearing metal and a five-by-ten-foot section of tungsten alloy dyed and burled to resemble knotty pine, ripped loose in his hands.

"Just toss it outside, Peep," said Mal.

Sorrel turned white.

"St. Ignatius, be my friend—" he murmured and tottered out, making a large circle about Peep on his way to the door of the lounge.

The furnishings and the partitions came out. The rugs and the floor coverings were rolled up and set aside. Where the main lounge, the library, and the bar had been, now stretched one long room of bare metal walls and floor, with power leads spouting untidily here and there, like so many cable-headed clumps of mechanical bouquets.

"Fine," said Mal, beaming at the room. The overhead lights had been turned up to a maximum; and under them the room seemed to shimmer in a white bath of reflected light. "Lots of elbow room, that's what's necessary."

"What next?" inquired Sorrel, coming up behind him.

"Well," said Mal. "I'll want a work bench for the power tools there." He pointed to the forward corner of the room where the bar had formerly stood. "And a series of racks for power-pack lifters and hoists at the other end. Cutters should be spotted about the room. As for the other items—the auto lathe and the portable chucks should be ceiling anchored and the testing equipment can be on flotation packs. Of course we'll need a direct response meter-load generator, gallimeter, wave-impulse recordometer; and I don't quite know what we'll do with the tension box, but I'll find a place for it. The graviometer—''

"Hold it!" cried Sorrel. "Hold it!" He flung up his hands in despair. "Let's go back to the station and make out a list."

Mal gazed fondly about the room once more then followed the others out.

This time Peep came with them. The station had yielded power belts and with one of these strapped around his furry middle, Peep floated lightly over the moss and followed them up the lift and into a new level of the station, which was severely set out with a long table, filing cabinets and chairs, giving somewhat the appearance of a combination office and conference room.

They sat down to the task of figuring out what Mal would need in the way of supplies and equipment. It turned out that the station itself would be able to supply almost all of his needs, since it had been built to be almost completely self-sustaining. Most of the necessary materials could be smuggled out from the plateau by members of the Underground, after first being obtained by the black-market man named Bobby.

Bobby called on tight sub-channel wave length, agreed to undertake all commissions, except the one concerning the testing equipment—to wit, a tension box, a cold box, and a gallimeter.

"But I've got to have them," Mal protested.

In the communications vision screen Bobby shrugged.

"They're in the Company warehouses," he said in a rusty voice. "But they're priority items. How'm I going to get clearance papers on them from the weather station, the hospital, and the communication center? All those outfits got priority on that sort of stuff.''

"Okay, Bobby,'' said Sorrel, and cut contact. The screen faded and he turned back to the rest of them.

"Well, I've got to have that equipment,'' said Mal obstinately.

Sorrel passed a weary hand across his swarthy brow. "Let me think about it,'' he said desperately.

"Possibly,'' said Peep, lowering his upraised hand and combing his whiskers modestly. ''*I* could get your equipment for you.''

"You?'' exploded Dirk. "I thought you were neutral.''

Peep cast his eyes down toward the floor.

"That was my mistaken assumption,'' he sighed. "During this last night and day, however, I have been wrestling with myself—internally,'' he explained, "and I discovered to my sorrow that I am deeply in your debt.''

"In *our* debt?'' echoed Margie. "Peep, you know that if anything, it's the other way around.''

"No,'' Peep shook his head stubbornly. "Was it not you in the first place who opened my eyes to the falseness of Neo-Taylorism? I have been enamored of a concept of universal good achieved through contemplation while ignoring the good that may be achieved on an individual level by positive action. Your drive, Mal—'' he went on, turning to the young physicist ''—is a good thing because it will enable more of your kind to enter the great community of races now existing in the Galaxy. It will promote tolerance and friendship—and, in the end, I hope—love. So any small aid or assistance I can give you, I give willingly and with a whole heart.

Peep's speech had the effect of rendering everybody else in

the room tongue-tied for the space of about a minute. Then Margie and Mal began to thank him at once; and Sorrel's voice came battering in to interrupt.

"Hold it. Hold it!" he shouted. "Hang on a minute there. Before you start falling on each other's necks, remember I'm not sold yet on how far we ought to trust this Alien."

"You aren't?" snapped Mal, turning on him. "Well, I'll tell you—I am. And if you want me to go ahead and build the drive, we better get used right now to the fact that Peep's as trustworthy as any of the rest of us."

For a long moment, Sorrel stared, his hard dark face eye to eye with Mal's pale, smooth-skinned one. Then the tension went out of him. He sank back into his chair, shrugging his shoulders.

"What can I do, hopper?" he murmured. "You're writing the ticket."

"Just so we've got that one point settled," said Mal. He turned back to Peep. "What do you think you could do about getting those things out of the warehouse?"

Peep folded his hands together in front of him.

"How big, may I inquire," he said, "is this ventilation opening?"

Mal looked at Sorrel, who sat up.

"You could make it," said the Underground man, looking narrowly at the Atakit. "It's not too small for you. Of course there's a grill and some baffle plates in the way. . . ." he trailed off speculatively.

"If they're not made of too heavy metal—" said Peep almost shyly, "I imagine I could . . ."

"Judging by what I saw you do to that partition this morning," replied Sorrel, "you could and then some. But just how are you going to get up to the warehouse?"

"If you are referring to the softness of the plateau soil—"

"That's it," said Sorrel.

"As to that," said Peep, "I don't see why it shouldn't be possible to equip my feet with some sort of plates, which, by spreading my weight over a larger total amount of surface area, should enable me, if not to progress with my customary ease, to—"

"*Snowshoes!*" yelped Dirk unexpectedly.

Every eye in the place turned on him. The tall young Archaist glowed with self-satisfaction.

"Merely one of the little things we who interest ourselves in the past know about," he said. "A device used by the Western Indian of former times to enable him to cover ground buried under soft snow."

"What are they like?" asked Mal.

"Oh, there's nothing much to them," said Dirk. "Just some strips of polished hardwood bent around for frames and with a network of leather thongs made from deerhide lashed across them."

A heavy silence descended on the room.

"Nothing to them, eh?" said Sorrel gloomily.

"No," said Dirk, somewhat puzzled. "Simple, really."

"I imagine," went on Sorrel, "we should be able to whip some up without any trouble at all."

"I don't see why not—"

"And just where," inquired Sorrel, "are we going to get any hardwood on this planet of sponge plants? And where in hell—" his voice rose to an exasperated roar—"did you figure we would have some leather thongs made from deerhide stored away?"

Dirk's face fell. Margie bristled.

"You don't have to shout at him!" she snapped.

"It was a good suggestion, anyway."

"Oh, sure," said Sorrel, "brilliant."

"Now wait a minute," said Mal, before Margie could speak again. "We haven't the materials for orthodox gimmicks of that kind, of course, but we certainly should be able to throw together something on that order. Let me see . . ."

They adjourned to the basement of the station. Here, among odds and ends of replacement parts, was the inevitable pressure molder with a small pile of metal and plastic stock.

"The thing is," said Mal, as he frowned over the molder, "if Peep is going to use mudshoes—"

"Snowshoes," corrected Dirk.

"—They're going to have to be collapsible so that he can take them through the ventilator with him." Mal fingered some long strips of metal. "Now, if we had something that would fold or hinge in the middle . . ."

He went to work. The first try produced two boat-shaped objects consisting of flat wings attached to a central shoe. These promptly folded up around Peep's ankles when he put his weight on them. The next attempt was a sort of latticework of metal strips woven together, which Peep could unweave down the middle and separate. These were perfectly effective; but a trial run brought a general veto on the basis of time it took to unweave and reweave them when the job was done.

"If you could make something," suggested Margie, "in three or four pieces that just clicked together—"

"And what if one of the parts jammed?" inquired Mal. "No, too complicated."

"No, it isn't!" cried Margie. "You forget how strong Peep is. He could just force the parts together."

"I suppose—" began Mal doubtfully. Then suddenly, his face lit up. "Of course!" he cried. "There's nothing to it!"

Ignoring the excited questions of the others, Mal snatched up a quantity of tough elastic plastic, and began to feed it into the molder. What emerged was an elliptical sheet of plastic which graduated from a good four inches of thickness at the center to half an inch at the edges. He made another and attached foot fastenings.

"There," he said to Peep. "Take those outside and try them."

The whole party adjourned to the moss outside. Somewhat clumsily, Peep attached the shoes to his feet and stepped out on the moss. It yielded beneath the plastic; but did not break.

"Fine," said Mal in a tone of self-satisfaction. "Come on back, Peep."

Peep returned and removed the shoes.

"All right!" said Sorrel. "You've got him a pair of shoes. But how about the collapsible angle?"

"Oh, that," said Mal. "Peep, would you mind taking one of those shoes and rolling it up into a tube."

"Indeed," said Peep.

He gravely picked up the nearest mudshoe and rolled it across into a tube of about five feet in length and four inches in diameter. He did it with no more effort than a human being might have used in rolling up a piece of heavy paper.

"I don't know why it is," said Sorrel, turning a slight shade of green, "but it bothers me when you do things like that."

"Young friend," said Peep, turning his brilliant brown eyes on the Underground man, "strength is a curse."

"You think so?" asked Sorrel, somewhat relieved.

13.

Peep's expedition with the mudshoes and a power belt was made one dark night and turned out to be successful—although the little Atakit modestly refused to go into details about it. And with the gallimeter, the tension box, and the cold box all installed, Mal got down to work. Time began to hang heavy on the hands of all the others at the funnel spot—with the single exception of Sorrel, who had his own duties in the regular work of the station. They had been, and still were, partners in the crusade to get Mal's drive built. But the others had ceased to be working partners.

With the exception of a few small tasks now and then that required several hands at once, Mal had little for his three friends to do. As he himself said, this part of the job was "all theory and no practice." He spent long hours in the *Betsy*'s laboratory-workshop and emerged red-eyed and fatigued but with nothing more tangible to show for his effort than heaps of discarded paper covered with endless calculations. Occasionally, he would run some incomprehensible test, using the equipment he had ordered. But the results were not spectacular and obviously meant nothing to anyone besides himself.

His drive, of course, was no drive. The speed of light was the ultimate limiting factor where motion was concerned, and that was that. Mal's idea, however, like all the other serious ones which had been investigated since first contact with the Alien Federation, was concerned not with the problem of conquering distance, but of disregarding it. He was attacking the problem from the other end, posing instead of the question, "How can I get from *here* to *there?*" the question, "What factor or factors cause me to be *here* rather than *there?*" If he could isolate these factors, or this factor, then it might be possible to manipulate them at will, so that instead of being *here,* it was possible to be—instantaneously—*there.*

This much, Mal was willing to tell anyone. What he did not wish to disclose, and which he avoided disclosing by falling back on the perfectly true excuse that it could not be explained properly without a background comparable to his own in physics, mathematics, and spatial logics, was his theory of attack on the problem. Mal had become convinced that the key to the factors of positioning lay in a precise definition of the electron. By what amounted to a reverse process of reasoning he was starting with the Heisenberg Uncertainty Principle and backing up to the question.

All this, of course, was so much juggling with moonbeams. You built a ramp off into nothingness, walked off it and started climbing from nowhere to somewhere impossible; but an inner feeling of certainty kept Mal doggedly on the trail. It was scientific faith in its purest form; and while it enabled Mal to spend long hours in the laboratory it was not calculated to help him endure the well-meaning visits of his four companions, who, having little else to do, were often tempted to drop by the *Betsy,* "to see how he was coming along."

Dirk was the worst. Peep could take his boredom out in

philosophical contemplation; and Margie was perceptive enough to see that while her visiting relieved her ennui it also transferred the strain in a different form to Mal's shoulders. But Dirk was unappeasable—so much so, that, eventually to choose the lesser of two evils, Mal found him small tasks to do around the lab for a regular portion of the working day, rather than have him dropping in with jarring questions at unspecified moments.

To Mal's surprise, his action produced amazingly good results. Dirk brightened up, became a much more healthy companion to the rest of the company at the station; and with what must have been superhuman restraint, for him, refrained from bothering Mal during the time he was in the lab.

One day, while Dirk was running some quite meaningless and unnecessary tests on the cold box, Mal happened to reach the end of one long train of hopeful calculation, finishing, as usual, in a dead end. He slowly became conscious of Dirk, painfully and methodically running his checks on the box, running them again, and comparing the results for mean error. It struck him suddenly that Dirk nowadays had become different from the way he had been when Mal had first met him. Different in some way that could not at first be pinned down. Mal frowned, considering him. What exactly had been changed? Dirk was as tall as ever, as lean, as—of course!

"Hey, you've shaved off your mustache!" said Mal suddenly.

Dirk started, made an error in his calculations, and swore.

"Just a minute," he said irritably and went back to his work.

Mal waited, feeling a certain sense of humbleness that was wholly new to him where Dirk was concerned. He knew that the work Dirk was doing was completely worthless; but it was impossible to shake off a feeling that he had interrupted something important. This being on the other end of such an exchange, so to speak, was new and a little startling. Mal even found himself wondering if perhaps he had not been a little selfish in his curtness the past days where others in the station were concerned.

Finally Dirk finished. He brought the calculations over to Mal's desk and laid them down.

"What was it you said?" he asked.

"I just noticed you'd shaved off your mustache," answered Mal.

Dirk ran his fingers automatically over his smooth upper lip.

"Oh, yes," he said, not without a touch of embarrassment. "Stupid sort of a thing to wear, anyway."

"And," said Mal, noticing this, too, for the first time, "you're not wearing your Archaist costume any more."

"Oh, well, what we're doing right now really isn't Archaist business," said Dirk. He sat down on the edge of a bench.

"Changed your mind?" said Mal.

Dirk nodded.

"Not quite as suddenly as Peep changed his about Neo-Taylorism," he said. "But I finally got around to it."

"Good," said Mal.

There was a moment's awkward silence.

"How do you feel about things, then?" asked Mal.

Dirk paused, and then shrugged.

"To tell you the truth, I don't know," he answered. He looked at Mal and grinned a little. "I'm certainly in no hurry to hook up with any new trend of thought. I'd just as soon sit out the next ideological dance." He hesitated, "Mal—"

"Yes?"

"Tell me," said Dirk, looking at Mal seriously. "To be frank with you I've been doing more thinking about myself lately than I have about anything else—tell me, do you think I'd ever make a physicist?"

Mal rubbed his jaw in perplexity and some embarrassment.

"To be frank right back at you," he said finally, "no. It takes a sort of—well, almost a call to it, if you're really going to make a life's work out of it."

"I was kind of afraid you'd say something like that," Dirk said. "Well, I've got to do something, I know that. It never used to bother me before, but lately, I've started having nightmares that I might live my round of years and not do one damn thing in all that time that I considered was worth it. It's a funny feeling—sort of awful." He peered at Mal. "Did you ever have it?"

"Not exactly that way," replied Mal. "I've had it where I didn't know for sure if I was doing the right thing—with physics or whatever I was at at the time. It amounts to the same thing. I guess it hits everybody at some time or another."

"I suppose so," said Dirk. "Part of the standard trip toward maturity, maybe. You kick over the traces for a while and then you want to settle down. I suppose I've matured. Do you think so?"

"I think so," said Mal. "You're bound to as time goes on—if you've got anything to mature with. I've changed a lot lately, too. I don't know whether you'd call it maturing or not."

"You were always more mature than I was, I think," said Dirk.

"Oh well—" said Mal, somewhat embarrassed, but flattered. A new thought occurred to him. "You know, I wonder if the whole concept of maturing isn't twisted."

"How do you mean?"

"This idea of becoming mature in your thinking—as if it was something you did all at once at one particular point in your life and that before that time you weren't mature; and after it you are and don't have to worry about it any more. Take Peep for instance. Would you call him mature—or wouldn't you?''

"Well—" Dirk paused. "I don't know," he said. "After all, how can you tell? He's an Alien.''

"I know," said Mal. "That's my point. But try and answer it, anyway.''

"Well, I'll tell you," said Dirk. "I don't think he is so damn mature. Some of the things he does seem pretty childish. I'll tell you, I've certainly changed my ideas about Aliens since I've seen him. Of course, I've got to be fair about it, Sometimes, too, he does seem to be looking down on us from a long ways off.''

"All right, then," said Mal. "Now, here's my point. If maturing was something you passed, and only that—like a fixed point on the road of growth—then Peep should certainly have passed it long ago, considering he evidently lives several times as long as we do and because his race had already passed the entrance requirements for the Federation. But to you and me, he looks as if he's still trying to grow up in ways. Now, as you said, he's an Alien, and we've got no sure way of knowing, but suppose that maturing is something you go on doing all your life and all down the process of race development. Then you and I and Peep and everybody else fit right into our niches right on down the line.''

Mal stopped. Dirk looked thoughtful.

"You mean," he said at last, "Peep's immature in his own way, but that same immaturity is a couple of notches above our maturity?''

"That's it," said Mal. "More or less. You have to assume a terrific difference in background and education between him and us. We don't even know how the universe looks to him. For all we know, he may be in possession of some simple little facts that would completely upset our own picture of things. For instance, this struggle of his to love everything and everybody looks ridiculous to us. You would say and I would say that it just can't be done. Maybe, from Peep's point of view, it can be done. Maybe he knows some thinking beings that do. Maybe that's the way all life in the galaxy is heading. Of course, maybe he's just a crackpot, too.''

Dirk—surprisingly—took up Peep's defense.

''I wouldn't call him a crackpot,'' he said.

Mal shrugged.

''How can you tell?'' he asked.

''He shows too much common sense where practical matters are concerned,'' replied Dirk.

''Hmm.'' This aspect of the matter had not occurred to Mal before. For a moment he was tempted to make Dirk prove his point; and then he realized that to ask it would be carping. Peep's common sense had indeed displayed itself more than once.

''You know,'' said Dirk, ''you may have something with this relative-maturity-level notion. At any rate, it gives me an idea. Do you suppose you can spare me for a few days around here?''

''I think so,'' replied Mal, conscious of a sharp twinge of conscience at the thought of the deception he had been practicing to keep Dirk quiet. The old Dirk might have deserved it—this new Dirk quite obviously didn't. ''I'm just about at a stage where I'm going to have to work by myself, anyway. What do you have in mind, though?''

Dirk stood up.

''It strikes me,'' he said, ''that Peep might really have something to say. I'm going to look him up and see if I can get him to talk. Then I'll just listen.'' He looked at Mal. ''If you don't need me, I'll go looking for him now.''

''Go ahead,'' said Mal.

. ''Right!'' said Dirk. And with a friendly wave of his hand, he turned and disappeared through the door of the lab, his enormously tall figure erect and jaunty.

Mal continued to stare after him for a long moment. Then, a *ping* of expanding metal from the cold box, returning to normal room temperature, reminded him of his surroundings. Sighing deeply, he reached for his stylus and a fresh sheet of paper.

Wave phase differentiation 402, he wrote in small neat letters at the top of the page, *Venus, December 12, 13:45, Sheet Number 1*.

He began to calculate. After a little while the subject engrossed him. Dirk faded from his mind and he became lost in his task.

14.

"Look," said Sorrel, cornering him after dinner a few days later. "They've passed the special police powers bill for the Company and the Company Police are cracking down. We've several hundred of our people on Earth picked up already. It's only a matter of time now until they locate this spot. How close are you?"

"Sorrel," he said, "I've got a sort of mental jigsaw puzzle and I'm trying the loose pieces one by one. I may be one piece away from the one I want and I may be a thousand. I don't know. Look—if you want to duck, the rest of you go ahead. Leave me here to work on it and I'll take my chances."

"We can't," said Sorrel. "We can't take a chance of letting you get into the Company's hands."

"Why?" asked Mal. "I'll give you copies of my notes and an outline of my theory. Forget what I said in the beginning. Take them and find someone else with my sort of training and put him to work on it."

"We can't," said Sorrel. "We've got no time."

"What if it takes a few years longer?" Mal countered. "You'll get it eventually."

"No—" Sorrel's voice cracked. He lowered it to a whisper, glancing around to see if any of the others were within hearing. "I've got something I want you to hear. Meet me outside in twenty minutes."

Mal nodded, puzzled.

Twenty minutes later, he stepped out into the impenetrable gloom of the Venusian night and felt Sorrel's hand on his arm.

"This way," said the Underground man.

His hand drew Mal to the little flyer that was ordinarily kept around the funnel spot and pushed him in. Sorrel climbed in behind and took the controls.

"Where are we going?" demanded Mal.

"A special meeting spot," answered Sorrel. "Sit tight."

His fingers shifted on the controls and the flyer rocketed upward. For perhaps fifteen minutes they shot through the pitch blackness, flying blind. Then Mal felt the flyer settle and they dropped down suddenly into a globe of light that had not been there a moment before.

"We're under shielding," said Sorrel, answering Mal's surprised look. "Nobody can see the light from above."

He pushed open the door of the flyer and stepped out. A wave of damp, reeking air at blast-furnace temperature washed into the flyer and Mal gagged, feeling the perspiration spring from him in rivulets. Within seconds he was dripping wet.

"Welcome to the lowlands of Venus," said Sorrel sardonically from outside the flyer's door. "Come on, the boys are waiting."

Mal stumbled out, to find himself facing a table and chairs of bubble plastic, blown up upon the lush green of the moss. Around the table and seated in the chairs were six men—miners all, by the look of them. And standing at the far end was a little, thin man, whose dress showed him as probably being a city Earthman. It was to this man that Sorrel led Mal.

"Alden," said Sorrel to the little man, taking his hand for a quick shake and releasing it as abruptly.

"Sit down," Sorrel told Mal, waving him to a chair. "We haven't got much time." Still standing himself, he put a hand on the little man's shoulder and turned to address the rest of the group.

"None of you know Alden," he said. "But he's one of our Earth group; and for the last ten years he's been attached to the Presidential entourage in the government. Go ahead, Alden, tell them."

He sat down himself; and the little man turned to face them all. His face jumped nervously in the brilliant, artificial light.

"Men," he said, speaking in a rapid, high-pitched voice, "you've been hearing for some time that the President is missing, probably kidnapped. He's not missing; and he's not kidnapped. He's on Arcturus."

"I learned this three days ago, by going through some notes that President Waring thought he'd destroyed. They were notes for a speech pleading the case of the human race before a meeting of representatives of the Federation—the Alien Federation. Apparently, there's a meeting going on on one of the planets of the Arcturan solar system right now—whether it's just so Waring can talk to them or not, nobody seems to know."

"How—" began one of the other men.

"Hold it," said Sorrel. "Wait for Alden to tell us the whole thing."

"The point is, Waring's there because the Federation's about to consider this Quarantine that keeps us penned up under our own sun. It turns out the Federation's been in touch with the chief human authority from the beginning of our contact with it.

I've got a copy of Waring's notes here, anyway, and you can look at them for yourselves if you want to. However, to save time, let me run through the highlights now.''

He pulled an electronic notebook out of his pocket and began to read.

''The human race wasn't informed on contact, but it posed a special problem for the Federation. That problem lay in what had attracted the attention of people long before the first orbital flight beyond Earth's atmosphere—the question of the adjustment of the race to the fact that it was merely one of many. It seems that the record—our own past history—was against us in regard to such integration being successfully accomplished. To balance this fact, however, we had one point in our favor. It seems that the human race, in comparison with the norm of galactic races of the same type as our own, showed an extremely high index of adaptability. The question was whether this adaptability could produce enough of a revolution in human thought and emotion—without at the same time destroying the basic human character—to render the race psychologically and sociologically acceptable to the Federation.

''The Federation was not thinking of itself in its consideration of this problem. Its territory is incomprehensibly vast, the numbers of its associated intelligent races incredibly great and much more able than we will be for thousands of years to come. The Federation was concerned with us—whether it would damage us irreparably to have full contact. In essence, the problem it faced is the same as the problem of any great and civilized people who come into contact with a small and primitive people—will the sudden superimposition of civilized ways of life destroy ancient and effective habits of living; and so destroy the basic and valuable independence of character of the primitive race?

''Because of humanity's precocity in the field of adapability, an unusual compromise was adopted. Within the limits of our own solar system, we were to be allowed a limited acquaintance with the products of other technologies—for a limited time. At the end of that time, a decision would be made whether to accept humanity, or seal it off in its little corner of space until the necessary thousands of years passed to bring it—by itself—to equality with the galactic norm."

The little man paused and put the notebook back in his pocket. And odd, bright gleam of triumph lit up his tired face.

"Gentlemen—" he said—and the archaic word rang with a peculiar impressiveness—"it is the belief of President Waring that we've passed that part of the test. Our native culture's been violently upset with bubble plastics, force fields, power packs, greatly simplified methods of manufacture and Alien imports; but there have been no wars, no hysterias, and no panics. Nor are there any signs of true moral disintegration in this new world of ours where leisure and luxury have become commonplace. We are still struggling to adjust, but the crisis point has passed."

A low rumble of glad reaction ran around the table. The little man held up his hand.

"But," he said and paused, "what every President has known under strict steal of Federation secrecy was that not only this part of the test, but the other, was essential as well. It is not enough for the human race to show that it can adapt and imitate. It must also show its ability to progress. I refer to what everyone in the solar system knows about. The faster-than-light drive."

The eyes of those seated around the table moved to Mal.

"Everyone knows we've been trying for that," he said. "What no one knew except the current Chief Executive—and, somehow, in these last few years, the higher-ups of the Company—was that there was a definite time limit set in which we had to come up with this drive. That time has now expired. Waring has left in an Alien ship for Arcturus to exercise his right

of pleading for an extension on the basis that Company in-
terference has delayed this discovery or development from
taking place. But his opinion, expressed in his own notes, is that
the Federation will not accept this excuse on the grounds that a
race is judged on its achievements as a race, and not as a
melange of conflicting groups. If the Federation insists on this
attitude, and its judgment goes against the human race, the
imports of all Alien products will be stopped, all contact will be
cut off and we will be sealed inside the solar system until we
develop to a point where there is no longer any doubt of our
acceptability. I need not point out the results of such an action.
Our economy will collapse, the Company will take over by right
of might, and we will be dealt a psychological blow from which
it will take centuries to recover. It means, in short, a new Dark
Ages.''

The little man sat down suddenly.

Sorrel rose slowly to his feet; but they were looking at Mal
and without waiting for any preamble, he rose and spoke to them
all.

''I've been doing all I thought I could,'' he said. ''But in the
next few days I'll do more. I think I'm close. I don't know. But
if work can bring in the results I'm looking for in time to reach
Arcturus before the Federation decides against us—I promise
you I'll put the work out.'' He paused, looking at them, and sat
down abruptly.

They looked back at him without words.

When they returned to the funnel spot, Mal went directly to
the lab, and to work. In the station, Sorrel passed the news on to
the other three, who reacted each in their individual fashion.
Peep folded his hands and nodded wisely. Margie looked strick-
en; and Dirk sat rubbing his jaw thoughtfully. After a while, the
tall young exarchist got up and went over to the lab.

He found Mal bent over his calculations.

"Anything I can do?" he asked.

"Afraid not—" answered Mal, looking up at him.

Dirk whistled a little tune through his teeth.

"Well, if you want me for anything," he said, turning on his heel, "just call."

He left the room.

Some time later, Peep showed up.

"Young friend—" he said.

Mal looked up once more from what he was doing.

"Young friend," he began again, "in the anomalous position that such a one as I finds himself at such a time as this, a certain hampering of expression due to interior and early training and in duty imposed by harsh fact unfortunately inhibits what would otherwise be given with a good grace and a whole heart."

Mal puzzled over this tangle of words for a minute before he managed to sort them out.

"Oh, that's all right, Peep," he answered. "I wouldn't expect you to help me with this."

"This," said Peep, "however, should not be allowed to appear as a matter of will alone in opposition to what otherwise might perhaps be construed as the disagreement of the unqualified with those who stand by necessity in a position of which a requirement is the rendering often of painful and difficult decisions affecting the lives and happiness of many."

"You think the Federation is doing the right thing, then?" asked Mal.

"In the determination of the infinite and multifarious factors capable of determining and in fact determining, over long periods of time the mental, the physical, the group development of peoples—in itself the result of long test and trial and not without a history of occasional error hinging on sad experience over a great, though not inconceivable span of time—a mean, or in sort a compromise action, has appeared through a process of natural evolution. By the very ordinary and inherent standards obvious, and at once apparent, to a point of view in normal consequence nurtured, and I may without prejudice say cultured in an awareness of the magnitude, relatively speaking, of the overall problem, the question of unfairness, either through intent or oversight, becomes a impossible one, since it could proceed only from the assumption that the case in point was in some relevent essentials unique, or entirely without precedent, which assumption, because of the inconceivably vast time and the unimaginably vast number of previous cases occuring in this time, becomes one of incredibly small probability, since a due and proper search of records will produce cases of such similarity that it often requires a trained mind to determine the actual points of individual difference which set off the past example from the present. Nevertheless, in consequence of the unalterable belief that each living being and by definition, therefore, any race of living being, is and are unique, it is regarded as a duty to seize upon and develop any hope of variation, no matter how slight, from the past pattern. Unfortunately so slight is the variation in all cases during the last great period of time that the probability of development has in all cases been more a theoretical than a practical hope and the result has been failure."

Mal nodded.

"So that was it," he said. "The Federation played an impossibly long shot on us." He looked at Peep. "Don't you think it would've been kinder just to leave us alone to putter along at our normal rate?"

"Would *you* have preferred it?" replied Peep, with a bluntness that was amazing coming from him.

"I guess not." Mal grinned up at Peep and extended his hand. "Thanks for coming and telling me about it."

Peep took the proffered hand carefully in his own, as a human might grasp a very delicate piece of chinaware. To Mal it was like holding heavy steel covered with hard leather. They shook, and Peep brightened.

"And now," he said, folding his hands together, "I will return to the station to await news of your success." And he turned and left the room.

Sighing, but warmed a little by the glow of Peep's acknowledged friendship and concern, Mal buckled down to his work again. But he was to have one more visitor that evening—and that was Margie.

She came in very quietly and stood watching him—so quietly, indeed, that it must have been some minutes before he recognized the fact that she was there. It was only in lifting his head, as he reached across the table before him for a fresh sheet of paper, that he saw her.

"Margie!" he said, checking his hand halfway, "where did you come from?"

"I didn't mean to bother you," she said. "I just dropped by to look at you. I'll go now." She turned toward the door.

"No—wait," said Mal on sudden impulse. "As long as you're here—sit down for a while."

She turned at the door and came back.

"I'm interrupting you, aren't I?" she said.

"It might help," answered Mal. "I don't have time now to keep on going through the possibilities here one by one. So I'm hopping around at random, as hunch dictates."

"How about some coffee?"

"Coffee? That sounds kind of good," said Mal.

She jumped to her feet and went across the room to the food unit still in the *Betsy's* wall. Sitting at his desk, Mal watched her, small and deft of movement in the gray tunic and skirt, a half-cape rippling from her shoulders.

"Not too strong," he said.

"It won't be." With a comfortable, bubbling sound, the coffee cascaded into the two cups she held, and she brought them back to his table and sat down with him.

"Do you know what Dirk's doing?" she said.

"What?" he asked.

"He's writing down an account of everything that's happened to us—ever since we first met at the Ten Drocke estate. He's been working on it for some time without mentioning it to any of us. He's got his own account of Archaism and I guess he's been getting the details on Neo-Taylorism from Peep. Tonight he asked Sorrel for information on the Underground. Sorrel flared up right away—you know how he is—and then all of a sudden he stopped and sort of shrugged. 'Why not?' he said. And now they are over there working together and getting it all down."

"Yes—" said Mal. "Well, that's fine."

"You don't sound very pleased," she said.

"Oh, I am—I am," said Mal. "So Dirk's going to be a writer."

"Of course not," she said. "He's going back to the Company as soon as all this is over."

"The Company?"

"Of course. Dirk says that there'll be a use for the Company—a new kind of Company, when the Quarantine is lifted. He says that nothing man constructs is ever by itself good or bad, it's the handling of it that makes it that way. And Dirk is going to put the Company to good use."

Mal smiled wistfully. "And he will, too; he's got what it takes, now." He paused.

"So you and Dirk will be going back to the Company."

Intended as a statement, it came out as a question, one that his voice grated over.

"Dirk will, yes. I haven't decided."

"Ah . . ." Mal paused again, his mind struggling vainly to sort out a jumble of sudden thoughts. "Well, what are your plans?"

Margie did not answer immediately, but Mal lost this fact in the sudden awareness that he had more to say.

"Listen, Margie—you don't have to worry about that—I mean, you can stay here with me—"

He stumbled to a halt. Margie still said nothing. She was not looking at him. He made himself go on.

"Well, listen," he said, "you know, we—you and I—we've been in this thing together for some time now—I mean, we've gotten to know each other." He would down.

She looked at him then.

"Yes, I'll stay," she said.

In the following silence they moved together; and thereafter when they did begin to speak again, their whisperings could not have been heard by anyone more than a few feet away.

15.

Mal lost track of the time. Dark turned to daylight and back again and the hours slid by without meaning. Vaguely, he began to become aware of Sorrel or Dirk or Margie telling him that he must stop and rest.

"But I've almost got it," he answered and forgot them. The fever of his work held him. The room around him became the whole world—became the limits of the universe. Nothing not in it was real. Outside, time and space ceased to have meaning; the planets halted and the constellations stopped their movement, waiting for Malcolm Fletcher to catch the will-o'-the-wisp that danced before him.

"I think I've got it," he said finally to the Sorrel-Dirk-Margie face that kept coming back to him.

"You ought to rest now, then—" it said.

"No," said Mal. "There's more to do. There's just a little bit more to do. I've got to finish it."

And that was the last he remembered.

He opened his eyes finally to find himself lying in a bedroom in the station. He had come slowly out of sleep and now he lay wide awake, but with a strange, washed-out feeling, as if all the strength had been sucked out of him. He thought to himself that he would lie there a little while longer, and then he would take another little nap.

But his mind would not let him slide back so easily into oblivion. For a time his body protested drowsily against his reawakening memory and curiosity and then gave in. He sat up finally, and swung his legs over the edge of the bed. For a second he sat there, feeling somewhat dizzy. Then the dizziness passed and he got to his feet and set about dressing.

When he was dressed, he wandered out of the bedroom and into the second-floor combination eating room and lounge, with its imitation rock ledge and illusory waterfall. Sorrel and Margie were seated at one of the tables playing double solitaire. They looked up as he weaved in.

"Mal!" said Margie, then both demanded simultaneously: "How do you feel?"

"I think I'll sit down," he answered, dropping somewhat heavily into an empty chair at their table. "I feel weak," he explained.

"A little food wouldn't do you any harm," said Margie, with a touch of sharpness. "It's been three days since you ate."

"Oh?" said Mal. He considered the lack of sensation from his stomach. "I don't feel hungry."

He did not really expect to do more than play with the food Margie prepared. But the more he swallowed, the more his apetite seemed to revive, until by the time Dirk and Peep came strolling in, he was eating—there was no other word for it— ferociously.

"Good afternoon, young friend," said Peep, plumping himself down in a sitting position.

"Feeling better, eh?" put in Dirk.

"Mrmf!" said Mal with a full mouth, and waved a hand with a fork in it at them all. Then, having taken care of the amenities, he settled down to ignoring them until his eating was done.

Finally he sat back and sighed deliciously over a full cup of coffee. "That was fine," he said expansively. He looked at all of them and beamed. "What's news?"

"My God!" exploded Sorrel. "How about you telling us?"

"Telling you?"

"The last thing you told us before keeling over was that you'd got it. But we didn't see anything around the ship," snapped the Underground man. "Well? Well? Well?"

"I didn't actually build it," explained Mal. "I just ran enough principle tests to know it'll work. But there's nothing to it. I told you the actual device would be simple. It's simply a matter of using force fields to set up a uniform resonance of wave patterns in whatever's to be moved. Then, to move, you simply de-emphasize your resonance in direct ratio to the distance you want to move. In other words, it's a matter of making your present position in space so improbable that you move to the next most probable position. Of course it isn't really a matter of movement at all. I'll explain it a little more simply. You see in a strict sense, the position you believe yourself to be occupying isn't really the position you are actually occupying. In reality, you're really everywhere at once with a most probable position which can be defined by vectors of probability moving along a time coordinate. Now, imagine a three-dimensional graph enclosed in an n-dimensional universe of which one dimension at a time is extra-relative and time itself is represented in the graph by a—" Mal broke off suddenly, becoming aware of the stunned expressions on the three human faces before him.

"Maybe I'm confusing you a bit," he said. "Look, it's really very simple. What it all boils down to is that for purposes of theory you assume a positionless time, which by conversion allows you to postulate such a thing as timeless position. With Time considered as irrelevant and therefore disregarded—''

"Sure," broke in Sorrel. "Absolutely. You're one hundred per cent right. I see it now. Now, what kind of materials are you going to need to build this gizmo?"

"But you aren't letting me explain," protested Mal. "Now, you all understand the Heisenberg Uncertainty Principle—'' But his explanation dwindled away in the face of a dead silence.

"If you just—" began Mal feebly.

"Young friend," interrupted Peep, with a cough, "certain flights of knowledge are unfortunately restricted to those who already possess wings. And wings, I need hardly point out, are scarcely grown in a minute—under ordinary conditions, that is," he added conscientiously.

"Oh," said Mal. "Well—" he was struggling with the quite human and normal urge to tell somebody about what he had just accomplished. "Oh, well," he sighed.

"Now that that's settled," said Sorrel "I repeat—what sort of stuff are you going to need to build it?"

"Why, we can adapt the ship out there with what we've already got," said Mal. "I knew what we'd need all along. That's why I ordered what I did."

"You did? If you knew all along, why'd you spend so much time figuring—no, no, don't explain," said Sorrel hastily, as Mal opened his mouth. "I'll take it for granted you had a good reason. Well—there's no reason why we can't get started right away at fixing her up, is there?"

"What time is it?" Mal asked Sorrel.

"Afternoon," the latter replied. "About four hours of daylight left."

"Well, we can work by inside lights tonight," said Mal. "I

think I will stretch out on a lounge chair here and take an hour's nap. Feel weak and loggy from the food. . . . If someone will just give me a hand—''

Dirk stretched out a long arm and levered him up. Mal tottered across to a long, slope-backed lounge chair and literally fell into it.

"Oof!" It was a sigh.

"Of course," he went on, "I'll call you the minute I come to. It won't be long, just a half hour or so, I think—call you zzoon, and maybe ug zuggle mph then zzzzz . . ." His voice wandered off to a snore and inside of a few seconds he was deeply asleep.

Hard hands on his arms jerked Mal back into sudden consciousness. Two men he had never seen before stood on either side of him, holding him upright and he was imprisoned between them. He blinked at the lounge about him and saw it aswarm with men who were holding Dirk and Margie and Sorrel equally helpless. Among them were uniforms of the Company Police; and, as this fact penetrated, Mal made one furious, convulsive attempt to throw off the men who pinioned him; but his sleep-slowed muscles betrayed him. There was a stir in the crowd and a man with a familiar face pushed his way through to come up and stand before Mal.

"Thayer!" said Mal.

"That's right," said Ron Thayer. The spurious ex-cyberneticist was wearing the uniform of a colonel in the Company Police and his narrow face under the black hair above it was lean and drawn with fatigue. "Where's your Alien friend?"

Mal thought of five good answers to this at once—all of them impolite and most of them improbable—and ended by saying nothing.

"All right," said Thayer, turning away. "We'll get that information out of you later. Move them off, men."

Mal felt himself jerked forward by the two men that held him. The crowd closed in and out of the corners of his eyes he saw Sorrel, Dirk and Margie being shoved along in a like manner. The crowd boiled toward the entrance of the station and spilled out into the clearing where a large Company atmosphere transport stood waiting. Sick with disappointment and savage with rage against the man who had finally succeeded in destroying his hopes when they were all but realized, without a word, Mal let himself be shoved along, and locked up with his friends in the dark, metal-plated and thoroughly escape-proof pit of the transport's hold.

16.

"But what did happen to Peep?" asked Mal, after a careful check of the room that held them had failed to uncover any signs of a peek-scanner or a microphone. They had been moved to the Company Headquarters building at New Dorado—an edifice with an outer shell of bubble plastic, but with uncompromising metal walls and doors on the inside. The room had all the appearance of a lounge on one of the better space liners—and presented almost as much of a problem as far as the chances of breaking out went, particularly to people reduced to teeth and fingernails for tools.

"How should I know?" growled Sorrel. He was examining a black eye in a mirror on the wall of the room opposite the only door. He had put up a fight and was suffering the usual delusion of a hot-blooded hangover—to wit, that if only everybody else had thrown themselves as willingly into the fray as he had, the day would have been won.

"He went out somewhere—didn't he, Margie?" said Dirk.

"He went out for a walk."

"A *walk?*" said Mal.

"Yes," replied Margie. "You've been so busy working you didn't know, but Peep often went for walks."

"But how would he go for a walk?" insisted the perplexed Mal. "Where would he go for a walk? Why would he go for a walk—that's the thing. I can see him going power-belt flying—"

"He went walking on his mudshoes, out in the jungle," said Margie. "And he used to do it because he needed exercise. You don't know how hard it was on Peep to sit still the way he's been doing."

"Oh," said Mal. "Yes, that makes sense. Different metabolism, I suppose. That explains why they didn't find him. A human would never try to go any distance through the lowlands on foot, and it never occurred to them that Peep would either."

"So he got away!" Sorrel spun around from the mirror. "We didn't. Now, what're we going to do?"

"I don't know. I don't think we can do anything as long as they've got us locked up here," answered Mal honestly.

"If you hadn't been sleeping like—"

"Frank!" blazed Margie, taking fire like dry grass in an autumn wind. "After he wore himself out working the way he did you talk to him like that?"

Sorrel growled uneasily and retreated. Turning, he caught sight of Dirk lounging bonelessly in a chair.

"Goddamn useless long drink of water!" he snarled.

"Hey!" cried Dirk, shooting upright in resentment, which was to some extent justified. A good half dozen of the enemy had thrown themselves simultaneously upon him, apparently under the impression—which in spite of his apparent thinness was probably correct—that he was far and away the most physically formidable of the group.

"Calm down, Sorrel," said Mal, stepping into the breach. "Chewing over what's already happened won't help."

"I'd like to know how they found out where we were, that's all," muttered Sorrel.

"Maybe they spotted a radiation leak from some of the equipment," said Mal. "Maybe they saw someone coming or going. Maybe they found meteorological evidence of the funnel spot and wondered why there was vegetation underneath it on the ground. Does it matter? The thing is they've got us."

"Yes," said Sorrel. Reluctantly he brought his attention to a consideration of their present situation. "There ought to be some way to break out of here."

"Without tools, I can't see how," said Mal.

"Son of a gun!" said Sorrel. "Here we are in the middle of New Dorado. If we could just get word out to Bobby or some of the boys, they'd have this place apart and us out of it in five minutes."

"Sure," said Dirk. "But how?"

"Maybe somebody saw us brought in," brooded Sorrel.

"I doubt it," said Mal. "They waited until night to bring us in and you know how much attention anybody pays to what's going on around here after dark."

"Blasted mud-suckers!" snapped Sorrel.

"Yes," said Mal.

An unhappy silence fell over the four people in the room, everyone hoping rather hopelessly for a sudden inspiration which would unlock their present prison. They were still engaged in this when Dirk suddenly raised his head.

"Listen," he said. "Do you hear something?"

They all listened. For a moment there was undeniable silence; and then, distantly, from somewhere overhead, there came a faint, metallic scratching.

"Probably nothing to do with us," said Sorrel.

Nobody bothered to reply. They were all too busy listening. Slowly the scratching noise approached until it was directly beside the ventilator grill in the ceiling overhead.

"There's something up there—" breathed Margie.

Dirk reached out noiselessly and picked up a chair, which he hefted over his shoulder in swinging position.

Abruptly, the ventilator bulged outward with a small screech, tore loose and dropped with a muffled thud to the carpeted floor below. A sharp, bewhiskered face pushed through the resultant opening; and a familiar voice filled the room.

"Ah—young friends," said Peep.

Four people let out simultaneous sighs of relief; and Dirk set down the chair he had picked up.

"Peep!" cried Mal.

"Yes," said Peep. "Are you all well?"

"We're fine," said Mal. "How are you?"

"I, also," replied Peep from the hole in the ceiling, "am in excellent health and spirits."

"Oh, *Peep*!" cried Margie. "How did you manage to find us?"

"When I returned," replied Peep, "and found you all gone, I deduced from the appearance of the station what had happened. I located a power belt among the wreckage—"

"Wreckage!" cried Sorrel in sharp agony. The station had been his baby.

"—and came on to New Dorado. This building seemed the most likely place to find you, so I entered through the ventilating system, utilizing the methods that had met with success in the case of the warehouse robberies."

"Lucky break for us you weren't at the station when they surprised us," said Dirk.

"Lucky indeed," replied Peep. "The temptation to give way to the excitement of the situation might well have proved irresistible. I often ask myself," he continued chattily, leaning a little further through the ventilator opening, "whether a cosmic sense of justice is indeed preferable to a unique or individual one. It may well be that the broader view, apparently by far the preferable of the two, in actual practice, allows the fine perception of rights and wrongs in particular cases to become obscure or confused—"

"Sweet Susan!" cried Sorrel, jittering around like a man on a hot stove. "Are you going to talk all night?"

"True," said Peep. "Forgive me." He peered down into the room. "Do you suppose the floor is a sturdy one?" he asked a trifle anxiously.

"I think so," said Mal. "Why?"

"I was thinking of letting myself drop," explained Peep.

"Oh," said Mal, "I see." He stamped experimentally on the carpet, which seemed to be covering no more than the ordinary thickness of plastic flooring. "I don't think you better do that. Suppose we pile up some furniture. Then you can climb down."

"A much sounder course of action," agreed Peep.

Hastily, the three men gathered together the furniture of the room and piled lounge chairs into a sort of shaky pyramid, with its peak just below the ventilator opening. Then, when it was fully erected, they stood about it, bracing it with their bodies while Peep cautiously crept out of the ventilator, negotiated a difficult complete turnabout while clinging to the opening with toe and fingernails, and began his descent. The structure creaked alarmingly under his weight, but held; and to the tune of "Look out, Peep" and "Put your foot here now," he slowly descended to more solid footing.

"Ah," he said finally, with satisfaction, finding himself on solid floor. "And now?"

"Now we break out of here," said Sorrel.

"Wait a minute," interrupted Mal. "Let's plan it out a little first. Peep can probably open the door for us, but where do we go from there? Do you know how this building is laid out, Sorrel?''

The other man looked embarrassed.

''Well—'' he said. ''As a matter of fact—well, no, I don't.''

''Then we can't just shove off at random,'' said Mal. ''In fact, I think the safest thing would be to try to get out the way we came in. You remember how that was.''

''I wish we could just get out the way Peep got in,'' said Margie.

Mal looked at her.

''You might make it,'' he said. ''The rest of us are too big. It's an idea, though. If you want to try it alone—''

''Oh, no!'' said Margie quickly. ''I want to stick with the rest of you.''

''I think you'll probably be better off,'' said Mal. He turned back to the others. ''Now, as I remember it, the transport was set down in the Company yard between two buildings and we went into the right-hand one.''

''There was some sort of office at first,'' contributed Dirk.

''That's right,'' said Mal. ''We went through that and down a flight of stairs and along a corridor, one turn right and one left.''

''Weren't there two turns right and then one turn left?'' put in Sorrel. ''Seems to me I remember two turns.''

''One turn, I'm positive,'' said Mal. ''What do the rest of you remember?''

''One turn,'' said Dirk, and Margie agreed.

''All right, then,'' said Mal. ''To get out of here we go back down the corridor outside, turn right and then left, up the stairs and out. Right?''

The others nodded agreement.

''We'll go as quietly as possible,'' Mal went on. ''If we have the bad luck to run into anybody—rush them fast. All right,

Peep. Now, let's see what you can do with the door."

Peep, who had been sitting on his haunches during most of this discussion, got up and walked over to the door. It was a heavy, rectangular sheet of metal with a single button for the latch—now, of course, locked. Peep looked it over, put his hands against it, and pushed.

Nothing happened.

He paused and looked it over again, vainly, for a corner by which he might get a grasp on it. There was none.

"Skevamp!" he muttered, irritated.

He put his weight against the door again. It creaked, but held firm.

"Kck-kck-kck-kck!" he chittered on a rising note of irritation. He threw his weight against it. No result.

"Polsk? Nak yr!"

He hit it. Something snapped, but the door held.

"Burgyr! Vik ynn!"

His voice and temper were both rising.

"Not so loud, Peep—" cautioned Mal nervously.

"Bagr y chagpz U ! Snok a Polsk! Myg? Myg? Taez a yak—a yak—a yak—Yarrroooouch!"

With each *yak* he had slammed the door a little harder; and the final *Yarrroooouch!* came out as a sort of culminating, blood-curdling war whoop, accompanied by a smash against the door that tore it bodily from its hinges, and he tumbled out into the corridor in a fury.

"That does it!" groaned Sorrel. "The whole building will be awake now!" And they all held their breaths expecting to hear, at any second, a rising clamor of aroused voices from other parts of the structure.

But nothing happened. They looked at each other in amazement.

"Some kind of soundproofing?" said Mal.

"Must be," answered Sorrel. "We're down one level. It may be all the floors are soundproofed off from each other."

Peep got to his feet, looking repentant.

"How can you ever forgive me?" he said.

"Don't give it another thought, Peep," Mal answered. "If it wasn't for you we'd still be locked up inside. Remember?"

"There is nothing," said Peep earnestly, *"nothing* so annoying as a stubborn inanimate object."

"Of course," said Margie.

Peep looked grateful.

"However," he said, "that is no excuse. If I have brought disaster on you by my intemperance, the responsibility will be mine. I will lead the way, therefore; and be the first to encounter any trouble along the way."

He turned and marched off down the corridor. The others hurried after him but found remonstrance to be useless. Peep had made up his mind and, since he could not bodily be shoved to the rear, the rest were forced to put up with his decision.

The passage down which they traveled was paneled in imitation wood and floored by a heavy green carpet. The only sound, except that made by their own passage, was the gentle susurrus of air from the overhead ventilators spaced along the corridor at distances of about every two meters. The few doors along the length of the passage were closed and the five friends felt no desire to disturb whoever slept—if anyone did—behind them.

They made their right and then their left turn according to schedule and without incident and arrived at the foot of the stairs. And here their good luck ran out. As they reached the foot of the stairs there was no one in sight. But hardly had Peep, in the lead, put one small black foot on the first step, before a door opened unexpectedly in the corridor above; and a man in Company Police uniform came out of it and started to descend.

He actually came down half a dozen steps before it registered on his unsuspecting mind that the people approaching were not ordinary inhabitants of the Headquarters building. Then he checked, stared, and—the fact of their presence finally registering—turned with a wild yell of alarm to run back up the stairs.

"Stop him!" shouted Mal; and Dirk, snatching up an ornamental vase from a small table at the foot of the stairs, sent it flying through the air. It missed the guard but, smashing on the wall before him, distracted him momentarily so that he stumbled, and in that moment gained, Mal had bolted past Peep and was upon him. Mal caught the guard turning and lashed out with his fist. There was a jar which traveled the full length of his arm; and—somewhat to Mal's surprise—the guard dropped.

Sorrel snatched the hand gun from the fallen man's holster and fired, all in one swift motion. Twelve feet down the upper hall, a door which was opening slammed shut again as the wall beside it went white with frost and shattered into brittle pieces under the forces of its own internal tensions.

"In here," cried Mal, slamming open a door and all but throwing Margie through it.

"Look for another gun!" roared Dirk and dived through after her. Sorrel fired again and the Company man Mal had knocked down opened his eyes and tried to sit up. Peep bent over him solicitously.

"I sincerely hope you have sustained no permanent injury," he murmured.

The policeman turned white, closed his eyes and fell back again. From the end of the corridor another gun returned Sorrel's fire. Mal, Sorrel, and Peep scurried through the open door and locked it behind them.

They found themselves in a sort of storeroom. Crates of various sizes stood about. Mal tried to move one and grunted, unsuccessful.

"Help me block the door!" he shouted. And the others leaped to give him a hand at shoving the heavy crates against it. The metal of which it was composed was already beginning to turn white with frost and crack under the charges of the warp guns concentrating upon it. It was not until several feet of barrier walled them off from the corridor that they relaxed.

"Take it easy," panted Sorrel. "They can't get close to that wall themselves until it warms up some." He leaned against a crate and sweated.

"Not a blasted other gun in the place," said Dirk, in ferocious disappointment, casting his eyes about the dusty room. He finally gave up and returned to the group. "Well, what do we do now?"

"Exit," replied Sorrel briefly.

"Yes," said Mal. "But how?" And indeed it was a good question. The room in which they had just barricaded themselves was without any other exit or window.

"Through the wall," said Sorrel. "How about it, Peep?"

"Of course. Allow me," replied the little Atakit. He backed off and charged one of the metal side walls. It bulged fantastically with the sound of something like an enormous drum being struck and split down the middle. Peep's paws grasped the edges of the split and ripped it wide.

"Come on," said Mal. And they all tumbled through.

This new room was fitted up like an office. It contained a desk, other furniture, and—blissful miracle—a large dissolving window.

They leaped for it. Mal set the controls to negative and they dived through to land some half a meter below on the smooth concrete of the courtyard which the Company Headquarters' building surrounded. Just before them was the transport that had brought them from the funnel spot.

"Get inside!" shouted Sorrel, indicating it. "And hur—"

He broke off, choking suddenly, as there was a sudden explosion on the concrete before him, and a thick yellow gas began to float upward into his face. He wavered a moment, then dropped.

"Hold your breath and run," called Mal, setting an example. But even as he started for the transport on legs suddenly gone rubbery, he realized the advice had come too late. Dirk was down and Margie was falling. And as he himself reeled toward the entry port of the vessel, he saw Peep—Peep the mighty, Peep the indestructible—stagger and fall.

For a moment longer Mal continued to try to fight his way alone. Then the concrete floor of the courtyard seemed to swell up about him and he drifted off into darkness.

17.

Mal's first sensation was that he was lying on something cold. Then he became aware of a ringing, aching head and a sensation of emptiness about him. He opened his eyes and looked up into the high, distant yellow glimmer of an overhead light in a large storage building.

"He's finally waking," said Margie's voice beside him.

He turned his head slightly and saw her kneeling beside him. Behind her Sorrel stood, and behind him a host of rough, unfamiliar faces.

"What—" he began, with a thick tongue.

"Don't try to talk yet," said Margie.

"I'm all right," he said. "Where's Peep?"

"We don't know," said Margie. She took a cloth from his forehead moistened with some cold, soothing liquid. "Nobody's seen him since they gassed us. Maybe he got away."

"No," answered Mal, "I saw him go down." He looked beyond at the unfamiliar faces. "What—who—?"

"The boys," said Sorrel. And, looking at them, Mal was suddenly able to pick out the fat, expressionless features of

Bobby and of the small man, Jim, who had kidnaped the three of them in the first place for the Underground. "Thayer got them too. Martial law, just like we figured. And there must have been a leak somewhere, because they didn't miss one of us." He cursed. "And now they've got us locked up in one of the warehouses where a regiment of Atakits couldn't break us out."

"I see," said Mal slowly. He sat up. Dirk came pushing through the crowd.

"Look what I found," he said, handing Mal a couple of small white tablets. "Enerine."

Gratefully, Mal accepted and swallowed them. Peace came suddenly to his aching head.

"So that's where we are," he said. "In one of the warehouses." He looked around at the others. "How is it I took so long to wake up?"

"That was scopromane," said Sorrel. "The more you exert yourself when you breathe it, the harder it hits you. The last one to go out is usually the last one to wake. You say Peep was knocked out, too?"

"He went down," said Mal.

"Dammit!" said Sorrel bitterly. "I was hoping . . ."

Mal got to his feet, assuring Margie that he felt all right now that the enerine was in him. He looked around at the vaulted dimness and vastness of the warehouse.

"You say there's no way to break out of this?" he said.

"What do you think?" asked Sorrel. "Solid concrete all around."

"How about the entrance?"

"A two-foot-thick fire door with a cold storage seal around it at the edges," answered Sorrel. "Anything else you want to know, hopper?"

"Frank!" flashed Margie.

"Oh, I'm sorry, I'm sorry!" snapped Sorrel. "Don't let *me* hurt your feelings, for cripes' sake." And he stalked off to sit down on a crate and brood by himself.

Mal looked uncomfortably at the faces surrounding him. Hopelessly, they looked back at him.

A few hours later, the communicator between warehouse and warehouse office cleared its throat and requested that Malcolm Fletcher come alone to the fire door. Mal rose from where he had been sitting on a crate of tools, still furiously cudgeling his brain for an answer to their present problem, and went.

The heavy, thick door was closed. When he rapped upon it, however, it slid aside to show an opening, just barely wide enough to admit the passage of his body sideways and he slipped through. It rolled shut again behind him.

Mal found himself in a long, windowed section that was really more an addition to the warehouse structure than part of its integral design. It was, in fact, a sort of plastic addition built around the fire-door entrance; and its inner wall was the bare, blank cement of the warehouse itself. There were two young men in the uniform of Company Police waiting for him among the empty desks and stolid filing cabinets—fresh-faced beefy youngsters, the type so often seen in the Company Police during the last few years, perhaps somewhat short on brains and long on energy—but decent enough. They told Mal he would have to wait and offered to get him something for the after effects of the gassing he had taken. Mal refused but decided to say nothing of the enerine Dirk had found for him—on general principles.

After about twenty minutes, the outer door of the warehouse office slipped aside and Ron Thayer entered.

"Hello, Fletch," he said pleasantly. Mal looked at him without answering; and the dark, slim man turned to the guards.

"Outside," he said.

They went. Ron perched on a desk in front of Mal, one foot on the floor, the other in its slim, black police boot swinging casually in the air.

"Well, Fletch," he said. "I thought I'd have a talk with you."

"I'm listening," said Mal. "Get to the point."

"It's nothing important," said Ron. "I just thought I'd ask you what you knew about your friend's physical makeup."

"Peep?" Mal felt a sudden, small spasm of anxiety clutch at his chest with sharp fingernails.

"If that's what you call him," answered Ron. "He's down on the Neo-Taylorite rolls with a name as long as he's tall."

"What about him?" demanded Mal.

"He's a little slow coming out of the gas," said Ron. "We thought you might know something about him that would help us bring him around quicker."

"You mean he's still under?"

"What do you think I mean?"

"What's the matter with him?" snapped Mal sharply.

"We thought you might be able to tell us."

"Why, you damn fools!" said Mal savagely. "He hasn't got the insides of a human being. You may have poisoned him."

"All right, Fletcher," he said. "Just watch yourself now. If you want a chance to help that overgrown squirrel, keep your voice down and talk politely."

"Oh?" said Mal. His eyes were boring into the other man. "You wouldn't be a bit worried yourself, would you? If something's happened to Peep, you're the man responsible; and I wonder what the Federation will say about one of their full-class citizens being murdered by a human."

"Don't worry about me," Ron answered. "Worry about yourself. And the Alien."

He straightened suddenly and took a step toward Mal.

"I'll be honest with you, Fletcher," he said, looking Mal squarely in the face. "I don't give a damn for you or this Peep; and I don't give a damn for the Underground. But I give considerable for myself."

He turned and walked across to the outer door of the warehouse office, opened it and shouted outside.

"Bring it in!"

There was a moment's wait; and then he stood back from the entrance and the same two young Company policemen who had earlier been keeping an eye on Mal came through the entrance, guiding a heavy plastic sling or hammock suspended from two laboring individual power packs. In the sling lay Peep.

"All right, leave it there," Ron told the two policemen. "And wait outside."

They went. Ron put out a hand to arrest the sling's drift toward the far wall and came back to Mal.

"All right," he said, shoving his face close. "There he is, And now it's up to you."

"Up to me?" echoed Mal.

"You heard me." Ron's face was within a few inches of Mal's; and Mal found himself watching with fascination the visible white around the dark pupils of the other man's eyes and the light sheen of perspiration on the deeply tanned skin. "I worked a long time for what I've got, Fletch. Every dirty job old Vanderloon cooked up, he handed to me. I helped build the Neo-Taylorites into a tool for him. And I took the Company Police and made them over from a bunch of fancy-dress personal bodyguards into an army. I've got myself to the point finally where I'm irreplaceable. I'm their link with the machinery that's due to take over things. I can write my own ticket." He dropped his voice abruptly. "And I can use you, too, Fletcher. On my own side. I can save your life and see you get anything you want. I'm not like the old group that'd just as soon cut all progress off for good and all. Your kind of work is going to be needed, still. So I tell you—get that thing in the sling back on its feet and in a good humor and you can write your own ticket.''

''You're psychotic,'' Mal said disgustedly. ''You crazy fool. Peep there is my friend. Can you understand that? Anything I can do for him, I'll do for him—but for his own sake, not for yours.''

''I don't care why you do it, just do it,'' replied Ron. ''But I'll tell you this. I'm not going to be the fall guy for trouble with the Federation. I'll give you and him twenty-four hours. If you haven't got him on his feet by that time, not one of you is going to be alive to testify about what happened to any Alien. I don't care whether your ideas for a drive die with you or not. The Company can do without it, if I have to do without you.''

He turned and walked toward the outer entrance of the office.

''It's all yours,'' he said, turning in. ''Do anything you want with him. But just don't try to leave the building. I've got men outside with orders to cut you down if you try it.''

And then he was gone.

For a moment Mal stood staring after him. Then, almost absentmindedly, he turned and walked over to the sling. He looked down at Peep.

Peep lay still. Mal walked over to the wall, and pressed the control button that set the big fire door of the warehouse proper to rolling back into the wall. Ponderously but noiselessly, it slid away from before him. He returned to the sling and pulled on it. Heavily it resisted with the inertia of Peep's weight. Then, slowly and clumsily, it yielded and began to swim after him through the air.

He went into the warehouse, towing it behind him.

"I don't know what we can do," said Margie unhappily.

They had rigged up a series of power lights and under the white illumination of them, Peep lay still in his sling. His eyes were closed as he lay on his back, with no motion of his body to show whether he breathed or his heart beat. His feet were curled, and his small hands closed into tight black fists with the miniature thumbs on the outside.

"Sure," said Sorrel bitterly, looking at all of them across the silent Atakit. "You don't suppose Thayer brought him to us without trying every doctor and hospital on the plateau first?"

"The trouble is," said Mal slowly, "that we don't know a thing about Peep. There's even no way of telling what it was in the gas that knocked him out. It may not be what bothered us at all."

"What he needs," said Dirk, "is medical help from his own people."

"And the nearest of those," said Mal, "is on Arcturus."

He looked down at Peep. Under the still black nose, the sharp whiskers stood out, stiff and unconquerable.

"All right," said Mal. "Then we'll take him to Arcturus."

18.

Even after Mal had explained what he meant, the rest of them
still looked at him with unbelieving eyes.

"You're crazy!" said Sorrel bluntly.

"No," Mal shook his head. "I just know what this drive of
mine can do. There's no reason under the sun why we can't do
it."

"This isn't under the sun," said one of the Underground
men, a lean, faded individual with tired eyes. "This is out
between the stars. This is Arcturus."

"It's all the same," said Mal. "Arcturus or halfway across
the universe."

"You're nuts, I say! You're nuts!" insisted Sorrel.

"What're the odds?" retorted Mal. "What's the alternative?
I told you what Thayer told me. We've only got twenty-four
hours to live anyway."

"I tell you—" Sorrel was insisting when the creaky voice of
Bobby cut across his words and the fat man shoved himself to
the front of the group.

"Lemme hear this," he said. "I want to hear you lay it all

out. And if it works, we'll buy." He turned to the dark man beside him. "Now, you keep your mouth shut, Sorrel."

Sorrel subsided. The rest of the Underground was silent. Mal took a deep breath and started in again.

"Look," he said. "My drive is not a drive. It doesn't actually move anything. It just suddenly changes it from one spot to another." A slight, confused murmur whispered through the crowd. "All right, all right, I know it sounds like a paradox, but just take my word for it, please. The point is that with something that just stops being in one place and then comes into existence in another, it doesn't have to be built like a ship. It can be anything. It can even be this warehouse we're in right now."

A snort of outraged disbelief came from the rear of the crowd. Bobby looked over his shoulder once and there was silence again.

"Now, this warehouse, like every other one on the plateau, has all the necessary materials to build the drive; and, if we work hard enough, we can set it up in a few hours."

"Yeah?" said a voice. "How do we know you got a time limit from Thayer, anyhow?"

"Okay, Harmon," said Bobby, without turning. "You can go back and sit down now. What else's Thayer got to do but what Fletcher says he said he'd do? He's not going to risk being responsible before the Federation for this." And he pointed to Peep.

Harmon, or whatever his name was, shut up.

"Well, how about it?" asked Mal. "We leave here and show up on Arcturus. The Aliens will look after us and we can get Peep to a doctor. One of his own kind."

"All right," said Bobby. "So far. Now tell me. Can you hit Arcturus right on the nose with this thing?"

"Why—" Mal felt his enthusiasm suddenly falter. "Well—I can. I mean it's possible, but—"

"But what?"

"Well," said Mal, "you're right. The trouble is, I'd have to know first where it is in relation to where we are right now."

"Figured as much," said Bobby. "In short, boy, you need a navigator just the same as if you were flying an ordinary ship."

"Yes," said Mal dully, "you're right. I didn't think . . ." His voice trailed off in disappointment.

"Well, don't look so beefy," said Bobby. "We can get us a navigator."

"What?"

"Sure," replied Bobby. "We got our own spaceship terminal off in the swamps. There'll be two or three navigators sitting around out there."

"That's a great help," put in Sorrel.

"Now, you hush," creaked Bobby. "Mal, you can take us straight up about a thousand feet with just what you know now, can't you?"

"Of course," answered Mal. "Why, sure! As far as the plateau was concerned, at night like this, we'd just vanish."

"That's it," nodded Bobby. "And from there on, we go where we want. Well?"

"Well, what?" asked Mal.

"Well, what do we do first?" said Bobby.

It was a jury rig to end all jury rigs, put together by the untrained hands of men who had not the slightest notion of what they were doing. Luckily, in Bobby Mal found a man with a genius for organizing and distributing the work to be done; and Sorrel, once he came out of his black mood—which he did with amazing speed now that there was prospect of action of some sort—came up with a surprising number of ver practical suggestions, which had never crossed Mal's mind at all.

For example, while Mal had foreseen the necessity of a separate power source for the rig, it was Sorrel who pointed out that with the warehouse cut off from community power, the lights inside it would be off, and the heavy outer door would have to be worked by hand. And it was Sorrel who took the necessary steps to set up emergency power to take care of these things. Also it was Sorrel who foresaw the need for a vision screen rigged outside the warehouse walls, so that they would not find themselves flying blind once they got up and away from the plateau.

It was Mal, however, who discovered the problem of making the warehouse hover in mid-air. It was all very well to suddenly appear a thousand feet above the plateau; but what was to support them after they appeared? The answer, luckily, was found to be a simple matter of setting the controls so that the warehouse would be continually returned to the spot at which it was to appear, whenever it began to fall from it.

Dirk was amazed and somewhat concerned over the smallness of the power source Mal claimed he required for the rig. They had from the stock in the warehouse in almost unlimited supply of individual power packs. But Mal had only taken five.

"You don't understand," said Mal, raising his voice a little over the soft buzzing noise of several dozen men boring holes in the concrete walls for sychronizer lead-in rods. "The distance we have to move has nothing to do with it. All I need is power enough to control and match the resonances of all particles in our area."

"Well—I suppose so," answered Dirk dubiously. "But don't you think it'd be a good idea to have some extra ones in case of emergency?"

"What emergency?"

"Oh, something might come up," said Dirk vaguely but

stubbornly. And, in the end, because Mal saw others mirroring Dirk's attitude, he added another half-dozen, quite unnecessary power packs. He could not really blame them for their attitude. When a man has been brought up to believe that one individual power pack lifts five hundred pounds and no more, it is a little hard for him to accept the notion of five such power packs lifting a couple of hundred thousand tons of warehouse, supplies and people.

The resonance unit, Mal himself put together; and, when the rods were in place, he attached their lead-ins to his main cable. Then for a minute they all stood around and looked at each other: a little knot of tense people in the very middle of an enormous warehouse, with something that looked like a boy's homemade vision set on the floor at their feet and cable leads snaking away toward dusty, obscure corners of the building.

"All right," said Mal, "here goes—"

And he threw his switch.

Everybody looked from the equipment at his feet to the receiving screen of the viewing unit Sorrel had rigged, which sat on a packing case to one side of the equipment. Where a picture of the furniture in the empty warehouse office had shown only a second before, it was now still and black, with the faint exception of a tiny glow at the bottom edge of the black square. Sorrel played with the controls. The angle of vision tilted and the plateau stood out sharp and clear in its own illumination far below them.

"There it is," said Sorrel.

For a moment the bunch of people hung in silence, watching the screen, uneasily aware of the unfamiliar magic that held them suspended in nothingness. Then Mal forced himself to break the silence.

"Now," he said to Bobby, "which way?"

"Straight north," creaked the fat man. "About twenty-three hundred kilometers."

The direction was simple and the calculations also, since the new direction was still relative to the base position of the plateau. Still, it required a few minutes with the calculators clicking before Mal closed the switch on the rig again.

"There!" said Sorrel, peering at the screen. "About half a mile to the right and straight down. You going to land this thing?"

Mal hesitated. "I think I'd better not," he said. "Even if we knew the exact distance to the ground—"

"Which we don't and it isn't worth rigging an altimeter for," said Bobby. "We can go down by belt. You okay to wait here, Mal?"

"I'll wait," aid Mal.

And so it was settled.

The Underground went down by power belts into the night jungle—all of them; and, in the interval, which stretched out into a couple of hours, Mal and Dirk and Margie sat under the emergency rigged lights around the sling that still held the motionless Peep, just sitting and not saying much to each other.

After two hours there was the sound of feet landing on the sill of the warehouse entrance from which the big door had been slid back, thanks to Sorrel's auxiliary power units; and Sorrel and Bobby came into the bright circle of light around Peep's sling.

Mal looked at them.

"Where's the navigator?" he asked.

"None of them'd come," answered Sorrel. "Nobody wants to go. I'd go, or Bobby here'd risk it, but we're not navigators. And they're going to need the two of us back on Earth. Vanderloon's moving to take over already. We'll be fighting Company

Police in the street before this's over.''

"Then how are we going to get to Arcturus?" demanded Dirk. "We can't—"

"Bobby—" said Sorrel. And Bobby reached into his baggy pants and produced a sheaf of papers covered with calculations.

"The boys figured it out for you," the fat man said. "Here's all you got to know for the period of the next twelve hours. It ain't much, but it's enough, if you know how to use it."

Mal took the papers silently.

"Sorry, hopper," said Sorrel uncomfortably. "You can't blame them."

"No," answered Mal slowly. "No, I suppose not."

"Well, so long, then. Good luck!"

The two Underground men shook hands all around, Bobby with his white, moonface completely expressionless. Then they turned and walked away and off the lip of the warehouse entrance, framed for a second against the thin paleness in the distant sky that was the approaching dawn, before they dropped from sight. Mal walked over and pressed the button that closed the door behind them.

He came back to the other two where they stood by the sling and they regarded each other soberly. Three little people, a building never intended to be moved five inches from the place where it had been built, and a haywire rig that was more theory than practice—and one hundred and twenty long, achingly empty light-years to Arcturus.

Mal thumbed the switch that sealed the building's ventilators. With this act they were now sealed off in their own small, concrete world. Slowly he returned to the rig and sat down beside it. He spread the sheets of paper out before him and began to run his figures on the calculator they had unearthed from the pile of crated ones in the warehouse stacks. For a while there no sound other than the busy clicking of its keys under his fingers. Then he stopped and shut the machine off.

"Finished?" said Dirk; and he looked up to find the eyes of both Dirk and Margie upon him.

He nodded, stretching the kinks of out of his back.

"It's only approximate," he said. "I don't dare go too close on the first jump. We don't know where the planets of the system are—if any. And we don't want to land on the sun itself." And he smiled at them, a little tired.

Margie smiled back, a smile that warmed him, even through his fatigue.

"What are we waiting for, then?" asked Dirk.

Mal glanced at the chronometer attached to the rig.

"Just a few seconds more," he said. "It'll trip automatically when the departure moment hits. We're almost on it—hold on now—*now!*"

There was the slight *tick* of a closing circuit from the rig. As on the two previous occasions, there was no sensation to mark the fact of their transportation. Only the dim jungle scene in the screen was abruptly replaced by a field of stars.

For a moment they stood in silence, awe-struck by the immensity of their achievement. Then Dirk found his voice.

"But where—" he said, "where's Arcturus?"

Mal stared.

"We must have our backs to it," he said and he bent to the televisor controls.

For a moment the field of stars remained the same. Then they swam grandly off to the left of the screen and a blazing sun marched in on the right.

"Oh—*Mal!*" breathed Margie.

"Big, isn't it?" said Mal, dizzy.

They stood staring at Arcturus, floating in all his golden glory in the black ocean of his surrounding space. Then Mal had turned the warehouse past the blinding vision; and they were all blinking their eyes and trying to readjust to the normal picture of star-filled space.

"See anything with a noticeable disk that might be a planet?" Mal asked the others. They shook their heads. Mal turned the warehouse to a fresh section of the space around them; and they were just about to continue their search when the interruption came.

Behind them all, without warning, the wide warehouse door suddenly whipped back into its recess; and a tall figure stood framed in the opening, with the stars for a backdrop. Turning, they stared at him, too shocked by the unexpectedness of his appearance to wonder at the relatively minor miracle that was keeping their air from exploding all at once, out through the wide opening, sucking them with it into the vacuum of space.

The stranger was humanoid in appearance; and ever afterward they referred to him as The Golden Man, although none of them was ever able to remember later whether the glittering color encasing him was of his own natural skin or clothing of some sort. He stood a little taller than Mal, but not so tall as Dirk; and he walked as if his joints were oiled.

He walked toward them now and spoke to them in their own language.

"So you've finally made the jump," he said.

Mal nodded. There was nothing he could think of in that moment to say. Instead, he turned and indicated the sling behind them where Peep lay still.

"If you don't mind," he said, "we've got a friend here who needs looking after—"

The Golden Man looked and put his hand on Mal's shoulder reassuringly.

"We'll take care of him," he said.

19.

The Aliens on Arcturus Planet had been kind. They had been very kind. But they had also been firm. The plain truth of the matter was that it was not physically safe for the three humans to go wondering around the planet, or indeed to go outside a very narrow, circumscribed area. They had, in fact, been out once or twice with a guide to look after them; but the things they saw proved for the most part to be incomprehensible. There was a tall pillar, for example, in the center of what appeared to be a broad street, that flickered through a ceaseless succession of colors; and when they asked their guide about it the best he could do by way of explanation was to describe it as an orientation device. He was a fat, stubby little man, their guide—very human looking; and they all suspected him of being a robot made up specially to put them at their ease, but none of them had the nerve to ask him outright if this was so.

"What kind of orientation?" asked Mal.

"Physical," answered the guide.

Mal considered this. Like so many things connected with this world and the Federation, it always seemed just on the verge of making sense, without quite succeeding.

"For example?" he said, plowing ahead stubbornly.

"Well—for one type of example," said the guide, "haven't you ever wondered precisely in what direction and how far away some particular place might be from where you stand at this moment? A sudden nostalgic feeling takes you, say, for the place you call home on your native Earth. This—" he waved at the flickering pillar—"would answer your questions and strengthen the image in your mind, if you were educated to the use of it."

"Oh?" said Mal. He looked at the pillar. "Is it that important—I mean, is it necessary to some of these people to have something like that?" And he nodded to the various shapes and sizes of beings of differing races moving about them on the street.

"Oh, not necessary, of course," said the guide with a smile. "But rather nice to have, don't you think?"

Mal gave up.

There was also an empty space in a rather crowded street that the throngs of hurrying Aliens all carefully skirted for no obvious reason. As far as the three humans could see, it was just a bare stretch of thoroughfare, no different from the rest of which it was a part.

"Is that dangerous for some reason?" asked Dirk, stopping to look at it.

"Oh, no," said the guide.

"Then, why does everybody walk around it?" asked Margie.

The guide thought. "I don't believe I can explain this to you in any meaningful terms," he said at last.

"Try," said Mal, scowling. It irritated him beyond measure to be told anything was unexplainable to him.

"You'd need a thorough grounding in emotional science—"

"What?" demanded Mal.

"The science of emotion—you see?" said the guide. "The

very term sounds like nonsense to you.''

"Go ahead anyhow," said Mal doggedly.

"Very well," said the little man. "Perhaps the most simple way of putting it would be to say that the avoidance of that area is a voluntary expression of mutual good will and affection. It's symbolic. Perhaps a few minutes before we came along that area was just another part of the pavement, walked over like all the rest of it. Then some passer-by went a little out of his way to let another pass him. Another passer-by a short distance behind him saw and repeated the small detour as a gesture of courtesy and affection when he came to the same spot. And the gesture is still being taken up by those who come by, a little intangible tribute to kindness. It may last only a few more minutes, it may last an hour or two, if everyone coming along repeats it. Eventually it will disappear. Such repetitions—and I warned you in the beginning this would not make sense to you—are part of our empathic culture.''

"Empathic culure?" asked Mal.

"Why don't you just give up?" put in Dirk.

"I want to know," said Mal.

"The whole field of emotions," said the guide, "is something that your civilization has not yet begun to deal with on a conscious scientific basis. It is a baffling field in which there is no exactness and every element is a variable. I cannot possibly explain it to you.''

"Grmp!" said Mal.

Later—when the trip was over and they were back in their quarters, after the guide had left them—Mal appealed to the other two.

"What is it?" he demanded. "Is it me? Am I acting like a spoiled kid, or something?"

Dirk shook his head.

"No," said the tall young man slowly. "No, I don't think so. There's nothing spoiled about resenting an implication that you're backward or inferior. Do you think so, Margie?"

"Of course there isn't" said Margie.

Mal got up from the couch where he was sitting and strolled across the room to look out through an apparently paneless and force-fieldless window at walks and lawns stretching away into the distance under the light of a stranger sun. Was the short earthlike grass of the lawns real or illusory? Or had it been specially planted to make them feel at home?

"No," he said, with his back to them. "I am spoiled. Peep spoiled me. I got so used to Peep that I forgot that he was just one of many types of Alien that must make up this Federation—if it really is a Federation the way we understand the word and not something completely different. And most of the others naturally would be more advanced and more alien than he was."

"I wish somebody would come and tell us what happened to him," said Margie.

"So do I," agreed Dirk.

Mal nodded, turning back to face them; and for a minute they all brooded in silence. Their guide either could not or would not give them any information about Peep, or indeed anything at all connected with Earth's place in the Federation and how their presence here or the existence of Mal's drive might be affecting the situation. In the several weeks they had been cooped up here, they had been told nothing—not even what disposition had been made of their flying warehouse after the Golden Man had, by some magic of an unknown science, transferred it instantly from deep space to a field on the planet here, from which they had been brought to their present location.

"It could be official secrecy—the business of not saying anything until the whole thing's settled," Mal said. "But that's the sort of thing we'd do. Somehow, if Peep's a representative of one of their least, you'd expect them to do better than that.''

"We'll just have to wait, that's all," said Dirk.

"I suppose so," replied Mal. He grimaced. "Wait and put in the time. Chess anyone? Ballroom dancing? Or a fourteen-course dinner.

Margie came across to him and put her arms around him.

"Hush," she said. "Don't be bitter, Mal."

After that, they gave up going out. The low, roomy building that housed them was plentifully supplied with things to occupy the time—although these were without exception all of human invention. There was no tone film, tape, book or picture dealing with anything non-human or anything outside the limits of present human knowledge. Mal deduced an implication that anything else would be over the heads of the three visitors and resented it. Still, out of what was available, they all ended by finding means to fill their time; Mal with some technical texts of force-field mechanics he had always meant to get around to reading and never had. Dirk with his account of all that had happened to them which he was starting all over again—and Margie with a study in linguistics, which, somewhat to the surprise of the two men, turned out to have been her major in school.

The human animal is adjustable. They were all but settled down and resigned to their situation when their former guide showed up unexpectedly one morning with another man beside him. The guide's face was broadened with a smile. He knocked at the door and came in, surprising them scattered around the big room that was the main lounge of the building they inhabited, all busy at their various occupations.

"Hello," he said. "I've got a visitor for you." And he indicated the man at his side.

They all stared at the newcomer. He was a tall, slim man in

his mid-sixties, perhaps, with surprisingly dark hair, but with a face deep-cut by lines around a firm mouth. A disciplined erectness held him straightly upright; but his gray eyes were relaxed and cheerful.

"Don't even you recognize me, Dirk?"

For a second Dirk continued to look puzzled. Then recognition flooded his thin face.

"Why, sure!" he cried, jumping to his feet. "It's the President, Mal—Margie—this is World Council President Waring." He went striding forward to take the Chief Executive's hand. "He used to visit with us when I was a boy."

Margie and Mal also came forward. Now, of course, that Dirk had made the identification, they recognized the other's face immediately from the many pictures of it they had seen. It was just the unexpectedness of Waring's appearance that had taken them all unawares.

"Call for me when you want me," said the guide and, turning, slipped out.

The four humans shook hands all around and then adjourned to a small cluster of seats by one of the big open windows.

"Did they finally tell you we were here?" asked Dirk, when the early amenities of the conversation had been taken care of.

"I've known it for a long time," Waring smiled. "I've just been too busy to come."

"What brings you now, then?" asked Mal.

Waring turned to look at him.

"I've come to break the good news to you."

"Good news . . . ?"

"The Quarantine's been lifted," said Waring slowly. "The solar system's wide open from now on, with no restrictions on the human race. And you three are responsible."

"Us?" said Mal.

Ursula K. Le Guin

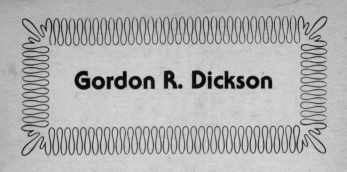

Gordon R. Dickson

☐ 16015	Dorsai!	1.95
☐ 34256	Home From The Shore	2.25
☐ 56010	Naked To The Stars	1.95
☐ 63160	On The Run	1.95
☐ 68023	Pro	1.95
☐ 77417	Soldier, Ask Not	1.95
☐ 77765	The Space Swimmers	1.95
☐ 77749	Spacial Deliver	1.95
☐ 77803	The Spirit Of Dorsai	2.50

Available wherever paperbacks are sold or use this coupon.

▲ ACE SCIENCE FICTION
P.O. Box 400, Kirkwood, N.Y. 13795

Please send me the titles checked above. I enclose _____.
Include 75¢ for postage and handling if one book is ordered; 50¢ per book for two to five. If six or more are ordered, postage is free. California, Illinois, New York and Tennessee residents please add sales tax.

NAME_____

ADDRESS_____

CITY_____STATE_____ZIP_____

FRITZ LEIBER

FAFHRD AND THE GRAY MOUSER SAGA

☐ 79176	**SWORDS AND DEVILTRY**	**$2.25**
☐ 79156	**SWORDS AGAINST DEATH**	**$2.25**
☐ 79185	**SWORDS IN THE MIST**	**$2.25**
☐ 79165	**SWORDS AGAINST WIZARDRY**	**$2.25**
☐ 79223	**THE SWORDS OF LANKHMAR**	**$1.95**
☐ 79169	**SWORDS AND ICE MAGIC**	**$2.25**

"That's right." Waring said.

"But—" said Dirk. "What happened?"

"Well," Waring's face sobered, "you may have heard that our original Quarantine had a time limit on it."

"Er—yes," said Mal, not sure about whether he should mention the Underground or not.

"I learned about it myself less than a year ago," the Chief Executive went on. "At the time—last September on Earth, it was—the Federation warned me that I should hold myself ready to make the trip here for the hearing that would be held locally—" he smiled again at the word—"locally here on Arcturus Planet. You see, the Chief Executive has been on the end of a direct communication system with the Federation ever since first contact. Nearly two months ago Earth time they picked me up and brought me here.

"They set me up in practically a duplicate of the quarters you have here; and for a few days I did nothing but meet the various members of the deciding group—board, or committee, or whatever you might call it. There were half a dozen members, all of the same race. It seems that they're a type that are particularly good at making judgments. At first I thought I was supposed to lobby them, or some such similar action; but it turned out they were just being polite, to convince me we were about to get a fair shake."

"Were you convinced?" asked Mal.

Waring nodded.

"They even gave me a chance to make any objections or challenges I wanted. I couldn't find serious grounds upon which to make any," he went on. "Well, to put it shortly, they went into a two-day huddle and came out with the answer that we had failed to show satisfactory progress and that a long-term isola-tion program would have to be put into effect. And I'm positive

they spun the business of deciding out, just so I wouldn't feel
that the decision was a hasty one.''

"You mean they ruled against us?" said Mal. "I thought you
just finished saying they hadn't?''

"I'm not through yet," Waring said. "The decision was
handed out and I was just about to pack my bags when you
people showed up. Of course they informed me about it, but
they wouldn't let me see you because the order of isolation had
already gone through. Of course, I immediately asked the deciding group to reconsider their decision. They told me, however,
that since the matter was already passed on, they had no authority to reopen it.''

"How in—" began Mal, and then closed his mouth.

"I don't really understand it myself," confessed Waring.
"These people all conform to some cosmic set of rules that
doesn't make sense to one of us at all. At any rate—one of the
rules was barring the way to a new hearing for us, unless it could
be authorized by someone with authority. It was then your
friend spoke up for us and saved the day by authorizing a
rehearing for us on his own hook.''

"Who?" said Dirk.

"What friend?" demanded Mal.

"That little fellow who looks like a squirrel.''

"Peep!" cried all three of the young people simultaneously.

"Is that his name?" asked the President with a frown. "I
thought it was Panja—Something long.''

"Peep's all right, then?" cried Margie.

"Why, yes," answered Waring. "He was a little weak at
first. I guess a touch of poisoning or something—''

"But wait a minute," put in Mal. "You don't mean to tell us
Peep is some sort of Federation official?''

"Well—yes and no," replied Waring slowly. "It's a little

hard to know when one of these people in the Federation is an official or not. No clear line drawn between—well, no real government, you see. It seems there're no true officials, as we know the term.'' He smiled at their puzzlement and his own. ''What seems to happen is that an individual will become accepted as a responsible person, and a person of authority in a particular field; and after that, if he chooses to act officially in that field, everybody else in the Federation accepts what he does as official. Do I make myself at least partially clear?''

''Peep? A responsible person?'' echoed Mal, unable to make up his mind whether to laugh or just be astonished.

''Why not?'' asked Waring, puzzled.

''But—'' said Dirk. ''It seems so unlikely—with Peep as we know him.''

''I don't understand,'' said Waring.

''Look here,'' said Mal. ''I'll try to explain it. When we ran into Peep, he was a member of the Neo-Taylorist group—and you know what nuts they are. He came away with us and for the next month he—he—'' Words failed Mal. ''Well, all I can say is, he must be the greatest actor in the universe. I know he's an Alien. He's got a heart of gold and we all like him a lot. But in all the time we knew him, he acted exactly like the most unwordly and impractical screwball that ever was. Now, if that was an act—you tell me.''

Waring shook his boldly sculptured head. ''I don't see how you could have come to that conclusion,'' he said. ''What exactly did he do to give you such an impression?''

''Why, the very first words he said—'' replied Mal, and plunged into an account of Peep's various adventures and misadventures. After he had finished, Waring sat silent for a long moment.

''Well,'' he said at last, ''I think you wrong this Atakit in

thinking he was acting while he was with you," he said. "I haven't known him and can't say, but it's possible he was acting entirely naturally."

"Then . . . ?" prompted Mal.

"I think," Waring went on, "that it's your fault, not his, that you got such a—low opinion of him. And that you're surprised to hear of his standing among his own people."

"I don't understand," said Mal.

"I'm fumbling at an explanation," replied Waring. "You see, in the Federation they've got something like a science of the emotions. And it's very highly regarded. In fact they seem to believe that emotional capability and not intelligence is the common bond between differing races, and the measure of their worth. It's in this field that Peep has his authority; and it was his opinion of our race's emotional sensitivity that allowed them to reopen the hearing and give us a second chance. An opinion based upon his experiences with you three, by the way."

"Did you hear him?" asked Margie.

Waring smiled at her. "No." He shook his head. "They deal among themselves in a sort of direct mind-to-mind contact we humans will have to be learning for ourselves now. I don't mean the individual races don't speak their own language at home. This is a device used when several members of different races come together."

"Ah," said Dirk thoughtfully.

"But Peep—" said Mal, bringing them stubbornly back to the original subject. "Why, his own emotions were—darn near childish from what we saw of them. And you say that in this field of emotional science he's an expert—"

"Practically *the* expert from what I've picked up." said Waring with a faint smile.

"Well, it just doesn't make sense," said Mal.

"Look here," put in Waring. "Let me give you an example of what I think led you to the wrong conclusion where your friend is concerned. Suppose—just suppose—that there was still an unexplored little section of our own world and that someone stumbled across it and found living there a hitherto unknown race or tribe of humans. The news gets out and a well-known anthropologist goes to live with these people and study their ways. He finds them taboo-bound, custom-ridden, lacking any vestige of the sciences and—in a word—primitive, but not completely without promise of future merit. This is a picture of the people of the tribe as *he* sees them."

He paused and looked at them.

"But what's the picture the people of the tribe, from their own limited viewpoint, get of him? Here's a man of unusual intelligence and a world-renowned authority in his field. But the primitives know nothing and care less about that. What impresses them is the fact that he can't walk around barefoot without hurting his feet, that he can't talk their language much better than a four-year-old child, that his nose is perfectly useless for hunting—in short, that he's a full-grown idiot that has to be watched continually so that he doesn't fall into a tiger pit or get poisoned by the first dangerous snake he runs across. This is the way they see him."

Waring stopped again for a moment to let his words sink in.

"Understand," he said. "I'm not saying it was this way with you and the Atakit: but in the time I've been here I've been able to acquire a healthy respect for all these Aliens; and I'm suggesting that what I described might be a distinct possibility.

Dirk was frowning, and Margie looked upset. "I just like Peep so well the way I thought he was!" she said.

"It's never pleasant to discover a supposed inferior was really a superior," said Waring, perhaps a trifle sententiously.

Mal sighed and pulled himself together. The conclusion following on Waring's suppositions hurt; but, Mal told himself,
there was no point in not facing it.

"So that's the reason he's never been around to see us," said
Mal.

"Oh, he hasn't forgotten you," answered Waring hastily.
"He's just been swarmed under by business connected with the
hearing. But he asked me to bring you to him after our meeting
today. If you'll just put in a call for the guide—"

20.

At the entrance of a low white building, Waring and the guide left them.

"Go right in," said the Chief Executive. "I'm afraid my schedule won't let me spare the time to join you."

"Couldn't you take—" Dirk was beginning, when Waring cut him short.

"I'm afraid not." He smiled. "I'm even a little overdue now. Now that the solar system's going to be out of Quarantine, the Federation will be moving in what amounts to a reclamation project." He grimaced humorously. "I'll have to work with it and—to tell you the truth—right now they're sending me to school so I'll know enough to cooperate properly. But enjoy your visit!"

He waved to them, turned with the guide, and was gone.

The three who were left looked at each other and at the entrance before them.

"Well," said Mal, "come on," and he led the way inside.

They went down a small corridor and through a further entrance into a long, wide, low-ceilinged room spotted with

cushions, hassocks and low tables. Peep was seated at one of the low tables, peering into the eyepiece of some machine, his whiskers a-quiver with concentration.

He did not look up immediately on their entrance; and they came to the table before stopping. Finally he looked up and saw them.

"Young friends!" he cried happily.

"Hello—" they answered.

Peep's whiskers wilted visibly.

"Is something the matter?" he inquired anxiously.

They looked at each other in some embarrassment. Finally Mal cleared his throat, scowled darkly, and spoke.

"We've had our eyes opened, that's all," he said. "We know what you really are now."

"You do?" said Peep in astonishment. "What am I?"

This left Mal somewhat at a loss. Luckily, before he could answer, Margie ran headlong into the breach.

"Oh. Peep!" she cried. "You could at least have let us know."

"Know what?"

"We thought you were dead!"

"Dead? Oh, dear! Oh, no!" Peep beat the air with his paws in an agony of contrition. "No wonder! Of course! Naturally, you would assume—but I wasn't. All these days—where is my perception?" And with one black fist he dealt his forehead a blow that would have dented armor plate.

"How impolite—how careless of me" he said. "Of course you would jump to the natural conclusion. Forgive me. Of course it was only a temporary paralysis due to a toxic element in the gas affecting my motor centers. How can I ever apologize for causing you this needless distress."

"Oh, Peep! Don't worry about us," said Margie. "It was you we were worried about—"

"All right, Margie," growled Mal. "You don't have to go into emotional spasms over it."

Margie stared at him. Peep stared at all of them.

"Young friends," he said firmly, "something is evidently bothering you. Something connected with myself. Would you do me the courtesy of telling me what it is?"

"I'll tell you," said Dirk suddenly. "We've just learned a short while ago how important you are—"

"It's not just a matter of importance," broke in Mal, stiffly. "I feel I owe Peep an apology."

"An apology?" echoed Margie. Now they were all staring at Mal.

"Of course. Having you around all the time, Peep, I forgot how advanced you Aliens are over a primitive race like our own. Forgetting this, I often must have imposed—"

"Oh, Mal, don't be stupid!" cried Margie.

"If you'll let me get a word in edgewise—imposed upon your natural kindness and good nature."

"Young friend," said Peep precisely, "you baffle me."

"It's President Waring," explained Dirk. "He's been explaining what you were really like."

"And what am I like?"

Margie told him.

"Ah," said Peep.

He glanced a little slyly at Mal, who was still standing sternly, almost at attention, his face showing his disapproval of Dirk and Margie. Something about the situation seemed to amuse Peep.

"I," said Peep, "belong to a race that has a known history of sixty-eight thousand years."

"Oh?" said Mal, seeing the remark was directed at him.

"We have played a part in the Federation for fifty thousand years," continued Peep. "I translate, of course, into terms of

your earthly calendar. Generation has succeeded generation, sons rising in knowledge above their fathers, until—in culmination you might say—roughly two hundred and thirty of your Earth years ago, I was born.''

Mal looked at him suspiciously. Peep moved closer.

''From my earliest years,'' he murmured, ''I showed great promise. Compared to my schoolmates on Jusileminopratipup, I showed startling brilliance—and of course you realize how the least of these would compare to a primitive human like yourself.''

Mal was openingly scowling now. If the idea had not been completely ridiculous—in a class with lashing out at a brick wall—those watching might have thought that he was on the verge of taking a punch at Peep.

''I put in fifty years of study in the field of the general sciences,'' Peep was continuing. ''Following this, I elected to specialize in the emotional sciences. After a hundred and twelve more years, I found myself a researcher and an accepted authority in my field.''

Mal snorted slightly. Just why was not clear.

''And then,'' went on Peep, ''I went in for field studies. I left my confreres far behind as I plunged into new and unexplored areas of research. For thirty years I blazed a trail in the development of a method of emotional investigation. Following this, I scouted far afield over the galaxy. I made countless studies. And finally—'' Peep had drawn right up to Mal's ear and was barely whispering now—''I was ready to come forth with my conclusion—my complete and substantiated Theory of Emotion, which would explain the common end toward which all races, all beings, were striving. I concluded, I checked. I double-checked. And finally I was sure. I had found it.''

They were all listening intently now. Peep's tense whisper and his dramatic recital were hypnotizing them.

"I leaped to my feet with joy and hurried outside my tree house—I was on Jusileminopratipup at the time, my home world. I whipped around to its other entrance and caught the Atakit who lived there just coming out. He was Lajikoromatitupiyot, a great friend of mine, and like myself, an earnest researcher in the field of emotion. Joyfully, I poured forth my theory to him—"

Abruptly, Peep stopped. The three humans waited tensely for him to continue, but when he merely went on sitting there, combing his whiskers with the fingers of one hand, it became clear that someone was going to have to prompt him.

"Well?" demanded Mal ungraciously. "What happened them?"

"Oh, I told you that," said Peep in his normal voice. "Remember?"

"Remember?" echoed Mal, astonished. And the three humans stared at the little Atakit in bewilderment.

"Why, certainly," replied Peep. "I remember telling you all about it shortly after we met for the first time. Poor Lajikoromatitupiyot was slightly skeptical of my process of reasoning in arriving at my theory. In a shameful rage at his purblindness, I picked him up and beat him against the tree trunk. Not—" put in Peep in parentheses—"that I make a habit of such reactions. As I told you, it is an unfortunate racial characteristic of us Atakits. Even Laj himself—who has a very calm and analytical mind ordinarily—has so forgotten himself as to break a table or some such over my head in the heat of discussion on several occasions. However—as I told you, the same thing happened with another of my fellow workers, with whom I attempted to discuss my theory shortly afterward. I ended by throwing him over a waterfall. Eventually I was forced to recognize the futility of such violent methods of discussing a Theory of Non-Violence. It was at that time I heard of your

Earth and the Neo-Taylorites and fled to them as to a refuge."

He looked at them all. For a moment they stared back dumfounded.

"Non-Violence—?" breathed Mal.

"Exactly," said Peep. "All emotional beings uniformly tend toward a future in which all possible violence to their emotions will be eliminated. Since my return to Arcturus, I have discovered that my theory, after all, has met with a great deal of approval after being checked by other workers in the field. This is very satisfactory, since it partially answers the long-standing question of what the eventual goal of civilization must be. I feel fairly safe in predicting that our professional group may jointly announce Non-Violence as a goal to be striven for. Of course—" and here he repeated his sly look at Mal—"I couldn't possibly expect a primitive like you to do any striving for about sixty thousand years or so—even though Neo-Taylorism and the practical application of your own work tie in so nicely with my theory."

"What?" said Mal and became conscious that all the rest were smiling at him. "But—but now, look, Peep. Waring had a point. The disparity between us—"

"Ah, yes," said Peep. "The anthropologist and the native. Now, assuming that that is a valid interpretation of our respective roles, tell me, Mal—after a primitive society becomes exposed to an advanced civilization, how long does it take to produce a member of that primitive society who fits into the civilization?"

"Why—" said Mal, "you could take a child of the next generation and if you brought it up in civilization—"

"Exactly," replied Peep. "And there is the solution to your problem. If a human is willing to grow up in the Federation as a full citizen of it, he can participate as well as any other member of it."

"That's all right for the next generation, then," said Mal sadly, seeing the beautiful stores of knowledge tucked away in the Federation dwindling into the distance. "But not for me."

"I can't agree," answered Peep. "Correct me if I err, but I have just finished telling you that I myself am somewhat over two hundred and thirty of your Earth years in age, and only at the beginning of a long and useful lifetime, we in the Federation having in some sense found a solution to the problem of aging. This solution will, of course, be available now to your people; and since you, I believe, are only in your twenties—mere children yet with your growing up still before you—" He let the sentence trail off slyly.

He beamed at them.

"And in fact," he said, "that is what you are, you know, in spirit and in knowledge and experience—all of you—children. And you will forgive me, I know, if I am therefore tempted to steal a phrase."

Peep's eyes were sparkling and whiskers fairly curled upward at the ends in satisfaction as he gazed at them.

"I would say," he said, raising one hand in the air, "in memory of our past companionship and in expectation of our companionship to come—I speak not merely of you three and myself, but of your kind and mine, and in the name of Non-Violence and true affection—"

Once more he paused, and his beam included them all.

"I would say—bless you all, my children."

And a tear of pure, shy happiness ran down from one eye and sparkled on the end of his black and shining nose.

About Gordon R. Dickson

by

Sandra Miesel

In Gordon R. Dickson's action-filled universe, grim fighting men and Buddha-faced mystics jostle teddy bears in spacesuits; dolphins leap and dragons prowl; indomitable heroes reshape heaven and earth by force of will or take bumpy rides in mailbags, construct analog models of the cosmos or befriend the Loch Ness Monster.

After nearly 40 novels and 175 shorter works spread over three decades, this motley band of character-types has brought Dickson from a subsistence diet of stale bread and peanut butter to the acclaim of his public and the esteem of his peers. He won the Hugo Award for "Soldier, Ask Not" (1965) and the Nebula Award for "Call Him Lord" (1966). From 1969 to 1971 he served as President of the Science Fiction Writers' Association and is a legendary mainstay of sf fan gatherings.

Dickson wanted to be a writer from his earliest years. He entered the University of Minnesota in 1939 at age 15 to study creative writing. After time out for military service during World War II, he completed his Bachelor of Arts degree in

1948. He withdrew from graduate school to become a full-time writer in 1950 and has been at it ever since. He is one of the few sf authors to have made writing his sole occupation.

Both training and natural inclination have made Dickson unusually attentive to matters of literary craftsmanship, not only in his own work, but in the sf field as a whole. He works tirelessly to upgrade performance standards through lectures, convention appearances, and even private conversations. His dedication to deliberate craft and philosophical argument combines what he calls the "consciously thematic novel"—the adventure story with a moral. As the author himself explains: "The action of the thematic novel is in no way loaded . . . with a bias towards proving the author's point. . . . The aim is to make the theme such an integral part of the novel that it can be effective on the reader without ever having to be stated explicitly."

Dickson has a compelling interest in the theory as well as the practice of artistic creativity. He studies—and writes about—issues like creative overdrive, performance under stress, interactions between different skills, and the social impact of gifted individuals. This stems from his conviction that man's proper destiny is to grow ever more creative. He sees unlimited potential for achievement in man and all other intelligent beings.

The highest and clearest expression of Dickson's views is found in his Childe Cycle. When complete, the Cycle will dramatize humanity's coming of age from the fourteenth century to the twenty-fourth in a series of twelve novels—three historical, three contemporary, and three science fictional. *Dorsai!* (1959), *Necromancer* (1962), "Warrior" (1965), *Soldier, Ask Not* (1968), *Tactics of Mistake* (1971), and "Brothers" (1973) have appeared so far. The last pair of sf novels, *The Final*

Encyclopedia and *Childe,* are currently in preparation. The author expects to spend the rest of his working life completing and polishing the Cycle.

The Cycle is a grand synthesis of Dickson's favorite themes and motifs. (However, a few germs of these can even be found in early novels like *Time to Teleport,* 1955 and *Mankind on the Run,* 1956.) The Cycle treats the human race like a single organism in which the condition of each individual cell affects the health of the whole. The progressive and conservative tendencies of this human organism, symbolized as estranged Twin Brothers, must be reconciled if the organism is to continue growing. Specialized, sometimes tightly organized, groups work to ease the problem but it can only be solved by the combined efforts of the Three Prime Characters—the Men of Faith, Philosophy, and War. When fully mature, humanity will exercise creative and responsible control over its own evolution.

But although the Cycle is Dickson's masterpiece, not all his fiction is that serious. (In fact, *Delusion World,* 1961 parodies the Cycle.) One showcase for his broad, bouncy sense of humor is the popular Hoka series written in collaboration with his close friend Poul Anderson. (Comedy is the only area in which these two dissimilar authors' attitudes and writing styles coincide.) As related in *Earthman's Burden* (1955) and *Star Prince Charlie* (1975), the Hokas are cuddly, bright-eyed aliens resembling teddy bears who have a mad flair for mimicry. They love to play at being cowboys or Foreign Legionnaires or other human adventure heroes to the endless frustration of the human diplomat stationed on their planet. These stories, like most of Dickson's humorous work, are based on the plight of a rational being in a preposterously irrational situation.

Whether he is writing seriously or humorously, Dickson makes thrifty use of his own experiences and interests as fictional raw material. Because he was born in Canada and has

spent most of his adult life in Minneapolis, he often uses Canadian and Midwestern settings to good effect. The quest for authenticity works both ways. For instance, it has led him to order a complete suit of fourteenth century armor as a research tool for writing medieval novels. Likewise, Dickson's fondness for literature, history, art, music, martial arts, and physical fitness is clearly evident in his work. Since he himself quotes Kipling, sings, composes songs, paints, and works out, so do many of his characters. Needless to say, artistically gifted action heroes are a novelty in sf.

The wolves, dolphins, whales, great cats, and other beasts populating Dickson's stories reflect his fascination with animals and animal behavior. ((Appropriately, his heraldic badge in the Society for Creative Anachronism is an otter.) This carries over into his treatment of intelligent extraterrestrials. Beings like the Atakit in *Alien from Arcturus* (1956) are directly modeled on familiar animals.

In conclusion, Dickson's work is the product of a keen, inquisitive mind purposefully shaping ideas into art. His stories are deliberately constructed, not casually improvised. He weaves structural and symbolic patterns into his fictional fabric to express philosophical convictions. At its serious best, his style is efficient, austere, almost relentless, like swift-running streams of icy water or beams of wintry northern light. C.S. Lewis's description of Norse myth applies equally well to Dickson's writing: "cold, spacious, severe, pale, and remote."

Current and Recent
Ace Science Fiction Releases
of Special Interest, As Selected
by the Editor of <u>Destinies</u>

POUL ANDERSON

78657	**A Stone in Heaven**	$2.50
20724	**Ensign Flandry**	$1.95
48923	**The Long Way Home**	$1.95
51904	**The Man Who Counts**	$1.95
57451	**The Night Face**	$1.95
65954	**The Peregrine**	$1.95
91706	**World Without Stars**	$1.50